I0687488

PUTTING DOWN

ROOTS

FALL OF THE CITIES – BOOK II

BY
VANCE HUXLEY

© 2016 Vance Huxley

Published by Entrada Publishing.

Printed in the United States of America.

TABLE OF CONTENTS

DEDICATION

To my Noeline and to the Joy of my life

Acknowledgements

Thank you to my editor Sharon Umbaugh,
for turning my words into a book worth reading.

My thanks to Rachel at Entrada
for all her hard work and encouragement.

Chapter 1:
From the Ashes

Deep in the mostly abandoned English city, a sports stadium towered over the mainly derelict housing nearby. A group of young men and youths armed with makeshift clubs and a few machetes and firearms moved down a street lined with looted and wrecked shops, many burned out. A tall muscular black man pointed at the stadium ahead. "See, I told you. Nobody touched it because there's sod all in there."

"Not even that fucking great mob of lunatics were interested." The overweight man in his mid-twenties frowned. "So why do we want it, Snoop?"

"Because it's a fucking fortress. All the entrances are steel plated to stop fans getting in without paying, or dossers getting in there when there are no games playing." Snoop ran forward. "If they've left all the kit you'll be a happy boy, Bull."

"I'll be a happy boy if they've left the hot dogs." Laughter rang out from the group around Bull as they followed Snoop. That turned to cries of alarm and then glee as a man ran from a ruined shop ahead, clutching a shopping bag. The group set off after him, quickly running the fugitive down and then beating him to the ground. They stripped off his shirt, jeans and shoes while one handed Bull the bag.

"Do we kill him, Bull?"

"No need, he's no danger." Bull laughed. "Bring the twat with us. He's local so he'll know where all the boozers are." The big man opened the bag. "Where the grub is as well. There's beans and a couple of cans of stew in here." He kicked the man. "Get up. You're our native guide now. If you run I'll let these fuckers kill you. One of stay near him. If he tries, cripple the twat so we can all have some fun." Bull looked up towards the stadium. "Now let's have a look at that place."

Shortly afterwards the gang boosted a youth up to prise away the wire mesh above a gate and an alarm sounded. The youth wriggled through the gap, ignoring the alarm, and dropped down inside to break the padlock and open the gate. A score of whooping, yelling young men ran through the empty corridors and one found the alarm, silencing the impotent warble with a club. The gang cheered when Snoop appeared wearing a helmet with a grill across the front and wielding an aluminium baseball bat.

"The electric is on but there's no hot dogs here." A youth shrugged. "Sorry Bull, there's a shitload of fizzy pop and tea and coffee, but no food."

"That don't matter, because Snoop is right. It's a fucking fortress. How many more of those bats and helmets are there, Snoop?" Bull held out a hand and Snoop handed the baseball bat over.

"There's lockers full of kit for baseball and that American version of football." Snoop rapped his knuckles on his head. "These have gotta be as good as crash helmets and there's knee guards and shoulder things."

"Magic. Give me that helmet then take this lot and get them kitted out." Bull turned to a young man with a healing cut down his cheek. "Scabs, you keep half the blokes and check this place out. If there's anyone here, strip 'em and throw 'em out."

"Scabs?"

"Yeah, all right, we'll find you a proper hard gang name when that's healed. Me and Snoop are taking five fighters each and going shopping." Bull grinned. "We'll spread out through the houses nearby and collect up food." He looked around. "We can drag more freezers in here if we have to."

"There are people in some of those houses, Bull." The youth who spoke looked embarrassed and then shrugged. "Those Army bastards were blowing the fuck out of anyone who'd been robbing and killing."

Bull laughed. "Not everyone. They missed us and probably hundreds more. The Army won't be back now so take the food or better still get anyone living near to bring their food. We'll need somebody to do the shit jobs, and carry in whatever else you find." Bull shook the aluminium baseball bat and checked his handgun. "But food comes first."

"Then booze and women, there's got to be some women among them."

"Another good call, Snoop." Bull hit the limping captive on the arm with the baseball bat, none too gently. "You hear that, native guide? We want a boozer and then find some women."

"I don't know any women."

"Fucking loser. Better think real hard about that." Bull slapped him across the back of the head. "I'll want to kill someone if I don't get a fuck soon."

"If I've had enough booze, I might not care you're not a woman." Snoop grinned. "Look on the bright side, Bull will kill you after so you'll not get pregnant." The horrified man stared at the gang as several offered to help with the rape or killing, before following a laughing Snoop to get kitted out. Soon half the gang, wearing a motley selection of American sportswear, headed for the nearby streets with Bull taking his unwilling guide. The rest began to really inspect the stadium as a potential new home.

*   *   *

Just under five miles northeast, miles of mostly abandoned, derelict or ruined houses, a red-headed man looked at the golf club in his hand and frowned at the bent shaft. "I say chaps, I think I might have under-clubbed. Perhaps a driver next time?"

The big man with close-cropped blond hair kicked a still figure with blood leaking from his head. "No, a nine iron did the job nicely. Maybe the problem is your grip or action, you didn't follow through properly?" He brandished a four foot sword. "You need one of these."

"But I wasn't the sort of freak who kept a real sword in his closet, and I'm unlikely to find one now. Did we get them all?" The redhead looked out of the door. "Yo, Kabir, did we get them?"

"Yeah, there were four, and a couple of women we've locked in a room full of beds. There's even an honest to God library over that end even if it's been trashed. This has to be good enough to fort up in." He grinned. "Are we using the gang names then or what?"

"We've got ours already. Carrot-top always signs on as Vulcan, and I've always been Gof." The big man laughed. "Luck with finding yours. We could poke out an eye and you can go with Cyclops?"

"Piss off." The man called Kabir looked up at an upstairs window as it opened. "Hey, what God are you then?"

"Are we really using that shit? In that case I'm Wayland. I need a horse and cart, soonest." The swarthy, very heavily muscled man laughed. "I'll need something to fetch my smithy here and a shitload of coke and charcoal."

The redhead looked along the line of upstairs windows with pretty net curtains. "What's up there?"

"There's bedrooms, some with one bed and some with three or four. I reckon this was a boarding school." Wayland threw something down. "You should get in uniform, Gof."

The man with the sword picked up the garment and waved it at the rest. "Sorry, I stopped wearing gymslips after my chest hair grew."

"Gymslips?" A bespectacled youth carrying a handgun came through the gates into the central courtyard and glanced back. "Come on girls, we've got you a change of clothes." The eight apprehensive young women who followed him didn't look overjoyed at the prospect.

Except one near the back. She grinned and held out a hand. "I can work with that. What do I have to do to be teacher's pet?" The petite dark haired young woman stuck out her chest and blew Gof a kiss. "I can be a very bad girl?"

*   *   *

Six miles northwest a small group of adults wearing suits or smart dresses under robes gathered in a wrecked and pillaged canteen and none were smiling. "We can't stay here."

"But where do we go, professor? There are armed gangs out there, preying on everyone in sight. Some have already raided the student dormitories." The harassed looking man in his forties looked out of the window. "We've nothing to stop them with."

"There's the University Archery Club, and some of the students practice Kendo and other martial arts." The older man frowned. "Did the fencing club survive the last round of cuts?"

"But the students who ran them will have already gone. We're left with the ones the government didn't want and who have nowhere to run." The woman in a long flowing dress wrung her hands. "Sorry prof, I just can't see what we can do." She tittered, on the edge of hysteria. "My students aren't going to fight anyone off with dance steps and face paint."

The older man put a hand on her shoulder. "You might be surprised what comes in handy, Celeste." He looked around the group. "First we leave here. Even if the government stripped the place those gangs will assume the University is full of loot of some sort. Gather up everyone, student or staff, who wants to come with us. Strip out anything in the facility or clubs that we can use and load up any motor with petrol or diesel. Anything really portable I mean, and think of survival rather than luxury. Even if nobody can use the kendo weapons and armour or the bows we can learn."

"But where do we go?" A middle-aged man with a goatee frowned. "Food is going to be a problem, even if the electricity holds out."

"We'll pick a place with electricity and water near a stretch of parkland, and fortify. Then the biology faculty, what's left of it, can start a farm. We'll need any seeds and cuttings from the greenhouses or the labs." The elderly man grinned. "We are supposedly intelligent men and women, as are our students. Let's see how dumb brawn fares against a bit of brain and a lot of knowledge." Around him backs straightened, shoulders braced, and a few faces even smiled.

"My students are dancers, but dancers are strong, and supple." The woman hugged the professor briefly. "Thanks prof." She turned and smiled at the rest. "We are going to have war paint to die for."

The man in his forties laughed, then rubbed his hands together. "Books. Books are knowledge, and knowledge is power. I've got an estate car that'll make a terrific library." He set off with a determined look about him, and the rest soon followed.

*   *   *

Three miles south a young man walked into an abandoned office and burst out laughing. "Christ, with those dark glasses and suits you look like that guy in the film, Men in Black."

One of the young men waiting inside reached down below the desk and brought out an Army rifle and a shorter police H&K G36 automatic rifle. "We're armed like those fuckers as well."

"Fuck, Jonesy, where did you get those?"

"City Centre. I worked out that at night all those rats and cats and dogs must swamp the infrared, and sure enough the helicopters didn't see me." He smirked. "Two of these poufs barfed and wouldn't come any further after the first really rotten maggoty type." He shrugged. "It really is gross, but there are still weapons and ammo out there. If we're quick we can have an armoury."

"Then what, join a gang?" None looked keen on that idea.

A tall, slim man in his mid-twenties came in from a side room. "Piss off. They won't reckon city boys like us. They'll have us all making tea and coffee, and I've served my time doing that for corporate types." He pointed at the guns. "We were all in training as market traders, business leaders, wheeler-dealers, all that obsolete rubbish. What were you told if the subject organisation shows weakness?"

"Hostile takeover?" The others were smirking and chuckling at that.

"Oh yes. Though first we'll be spending some time crawling around in the dark and barfing." He narrowed his eyes. "Then the Men in Black will look over the nearby enclaves to find a weak one with good assets."

"Does that make you managing director? In that case I'd better get in the Cappuccinos and suck up to you a bit, sir." They all fell about laughing, then moved in to inspect the firearms.

"Oh no, I want my sucking done by a secretary, one like my manager's guardian." The youth grinned. "Only this one won't be refusing to let me in without an appointment."

The older man picked up a weapon. "Maybe we'd better learn to shoot these first."

*   *   *

Seven miles to the west, the other side of a wide motorway, gunfire echoed among the empty buildings. Grim men carrying Glock handguns, shotguns or G36 rifles moved forward, covering each other in a smooth, practiced manoeuver and giving terse instructions or reports into headsets. The youths ahead retreated into a night club, firing wildly, as more fell. A sharp explosion echoed in the entrance and four men burst in, gunning down the last defenders before they recovered from the flash-bang. The squad moved deeper, and there were two more short bursts of gunfire.

Outside one of the men straightened, and put his fists into the small of his back. "All clear men. I'm too old for this."

"Not yet, sarge. Admit it, this is better than driving a desk into retirement." The speaker, a younger man also in police uniform, looked towards the club where four officers were escorting several civilians into the daylight. "Mostly young women again." He sighed. "How many more sarge?"

"Another three then we've cleared the local area of nasty little arses. Oops, hush my mouth. Misunderstood citizens with antisocial tendencies." The older man spat. "The powers that be didn't seem to think we were worth saving any more than them."

"They offered us passes, any surviving police officer." This officer, another older one, curled his lip in disgust. "But none for the families of the men who died on the streets or in that effing farce with the Mayor."

One of the four who had gone into the club came across the street. "The usual sarge, a few guns and some knives and makeshift swords. There's hard booze and drugs, but once we've taken anything useful one will burn the other very nicely."

"Keep some of the booze for disinfecting wounds and the beer, cider and pop. Right lads, back to Precinct Nineteen."

"Where?" Several men were looking puzzled while a couple laughed.

"My cousin saw an old film about some American coppers who had to fort up and beat off groups of gangsters. Our family have been calling the estate that for a couple of days. Though maybe we should relocate everyone to somewhere a bit easier to defend." The police sergeant shrugged. "We'll have to come up with some name for wherever we live before we can sign on the dotted line in that bloody bus."

"Precinct Nineteen will do for me."

"Me too."

"Precinct Nineteen it is. Hang on, did they win?"

"Of course." The small group of heavily armed ex-police officers set into searching and then destroying another potential gang headquarters that had been too near their families and friends. They'd decided to stamp the lice out now, before any of them grew to be a problem.

*   *   *

Just under a hundred miles northeast sat ten well-groomed, well-fed people. All belonged to the conspiracy responsible for triggering the current global devastation. A conspiracy that had arranged the destruction of many major refineries and several governments, then encouraged the chaos to spread. The group sat around a large circular polished wood table, watching the devastation on a wall-screen in a quiet, plain room. Their bunker lay a long way beneath an innocent stretch of English countryside, far from that devastation. In the background air conditioning murmured, and lights flickered on the other side of a sheet of glass along one wall. Through the one-way glass efficient, uniformed personnel could be seen monitoring screens and equipment and issuing orders and instructions in a ballet of unhurried efficiency. Also in silence as far as this room was concerned, due to the soundproofing.

Despite the cold December chill across the UK, the occupants of the bunker were warm and dry and wore satisfied smiles as they watched the scenes of destruction on the wall-screen. Short clips showed city after city exploding in violence, then in one city after another the armour and troops rolled in to crush any resistance. Occasionally someone would exclaim or nod in approval as some particular centre of resistance crumpled, or frantic hordes tried to overwhelm the assault with inadequate weaponry.

One of their number rapped on the table with a small auctioneer's gavel. The other nine people settled back into their comfortable seats and turned to face a distinguished looking man with dark hair showing white streaks at each side of his head. "Phase one is complete, and relatively successful here in the United Kingdom. Successful enough that we can all gather and meet face to face for the first time. The remaining Members of Parliament, Lords, and the Royals are safely tucked away for their own protection, and in case we need a familiar face to blame for something unfortunate. That leaves us the de facto government."

"I still worry about the Armed Forces, Owen." The slim grey haired woman in a light grey trouser suit smiled at the look on a younger man's face. "Yes Gerard, I used his name. I think that is safe here or our entire operation is hopelessly compromised. I am Grace, and for my sins I have been given the task of dealing with the work camps, both the prisoners and the refugee versions."

"True, Grace. Though as a nod to security we will use first names, and perhaps we can cut out titles? Otherwise the meetings will take twice as long." Everyone smiled or nodded.

"In that case I am Vanna, dealing with civilian contractors such as the mart guards, and I run the special facilities dealing with the aged, the seriously ill and other similar groups." The slim Asian woman looked over at the three men in uniform. "Will we be using military ranks?"

A spare balding man in an Army uniform chuckled. "Not really Vanna. The Armed Forces understand that we are the people liaising with the government during the State of Emergency, but we haven't the rank for commanding them. We all wear the uniform of the branch we deal with, so just call me either Joshua or Army."

"Victor, or Navy."

The third uniformed man laughed. "Royal Air Force is a bit of a mouthful, so Faraz."

Owen, the chairman, gestured towards a large black man. "Nate deals with information retrieval and dissemination, much easier now the last city is bottled up and the jamming is in place. He is responsible for the fake broadcasts replacing each city's radio chatter as we took them offline."

"Does that also mean propaganda?" The portly dark-haired man with the bushy beard waved a hand at the rest. "Henry, and I'm your farmer, both for the mechanised ones and those utilising Grace's people."

The black man smiled quietly. "Propaganda, censorship, TV, radio, news, music, weather reports, assessing the pictures from planes and reports from the Armed Forces, keeping in touch with our colleagues in other countries, and establishing an espionage network inside the cities. The last will take a while." He looked towards a stout middle-aged red-headed woman. "You must be Ivy."

The woman bowed her head briefly in acknowledgement. "Yes, responsible for preparation and distribution of supplies to both the captive and useful populations. Unfortunately my other task is mollycoddling the retail firms who financed us in return for running the marts as a total monopoly."

"As Grace already said, my name is Gerard, and I will hopefully deal with your transport requirements." The only person under forty smiled. "That includes bringing supplies from Europe if they are in danger of being overrun, and hopefully bringing food from further abroad eventually."

"Keris is en route for the Falklands to organise that, so she can't be with us. She will deal with any problems down there and liaise with the Argentinian cabal." Owen smiled. "Our last member is genuinely still doing his job since he was the Foreign Secretary." He gestured towards a portly man wearing an affable smile. "You all know Boris of course, if only from the TV?"

"I should give you my report now, just to get it over with, what?" Boris chuckled. "The initial strikes against governments and refineries went well. The response when local nutcases took up the cause, even without knowing what it was, rather took us all by surprise. Europe is more or less out of control. America will come right, because as planned most of the Army were abroad and the National Guard units have been encouraged to defend their home states. Once the general crackpots and armed militias have used up their ammunition the local cabals can start to take some control." He smirked. "That novelist who used an airliner to try and take out a Joint Session and the U.S. President might want royalties though the slightly amended version worked better than his.

Joshua scowled. "The Middle East and India didn't go to any plan, nobody planned on nuclear war. Worse, we lost men and a lot of heavy equipment and weaponry in Kuwait and in the Ukraine."

Boris waved a hand. "Nobody had a chance of controlling the irregulars in either the Ukraine or Middle East, and the Pakistanis and Indians have been dying to throw nukes at each other and really get stuck in for decades. The consensus among cabals was to leave the populations of both regions to kill each other and then mop up survivors. South America went well, as did the Western Pacific rim except for China itself. The cabals there tried keeping the cities intact and evacuating them to preserve their manufacturing, and the results are mixed. The suborned Army commanders there and in Russia went rogue as instructed and have broken any central control. Some have occupied major air bases and other strategic facilities. Our compatriots will have time to re-position."

Owen leant back, relaxed. "We agreed to let Africa descend into chaos and sort that out later as well. Did we have any real failures apart from Europe?"

"Only local ones, though China is still problematic. The cabal there only has tenuous control of the tactical nukes." Boris shrugged. "Tactical means limited yield so there'll be no global radiation effects, and one of the main objects of the exercise is to cut the world population by at least two-thirds. A few millions incinerated or poisoned by radiation instead of starved won't affect the overall picture."

"Cutting the population is really important here in the UK. There are, or were, seventy million hungry mouths, and after Blue Tongue Plus hit the sheep and the Ug109 wheat rust fungus devastated our harvests, we are importing

just over sixty percent of our food." Henry smiled, "Once the surplus population is dealt with we'll be self-sufficient."

"That is the whole idea so we must concentrate on Europe, and in our case
on the UK, to achieve a viable balance. For the immediate future our task is to
maintain the status quo since all the surplus populations are now contained or
in Vanna's facilities. We will concentrate on settling in the rest, those we need
to run the country, and maintaining the enclosures." Owen closed the file in
front of him and turned off the screen. "Each of us must ensure we have full
control of our aspect of the operation, and tighten that control where necessary. We will reconvene when the cities have settled into enclaves, and we have
a better idea of just how many survived."

*   *   *

In Orchard Close, one of those enclaves, Harold 'Soldier Boy' Miller looked
over the fifteen people carrying an assortment of packs and shopping bags, all
muffled up to one extent or another against the frosty, predawn December
chill. "I'm sorry to sound paranoid, but has everybody got rid of anything
remotely like a weapon?" He smiled. "Before we set off and you have to run
back here with it?"

"Yes Harold and I turned off the stove." The tall woman carrying a big
empty backpack grinned. "I haven't got a machine gun in my bra. Now can we
go shopping, please?"

"Too true Liz. I haven't had retail therapy for over six months." A shadow
passed across the face of Emmy, the big Jamaican woman, making her look
momentarily much older than her twenty years. "That was with Davy." She
hunched deeper into her big jacket, remembering her dead partner. She wasn't
the only one who looked momentarily subdued at the reminder.

Too many residents of Orchard Close, their fortified enclave on the edges
of the ruined city, had lost someone dear to them. They had been killed in the
desperate flight from the rioting and looting in the city centre or defending
the walls as the mobs roamed the ruins, lashing out at any survivors. Several
glanced up at the raised road, the line of the ring road that ran past close by.
The old bypass, now a ring of steel manned by the Army and penning everyone
in here in with the chaos and destruction.

"But not just guns and machetes, Liz. Knives, baseball bats, or over-large
nail scissors as well. We've all got used to carrying them, and the Army won't
be amused." Harold waved the list of things they couldn't take and couldn't do
on the road to the shops. A list provided by the Army, who would enforce it.

"Yes mummy. Can we go now?" Holly, another member of the girl club, as the unattached women called themselves, waved her backpack. "Or I'll make you help me pick out my new undies."

A smallish man at the back grinned. "We'll have to anyway, since he's insisting on us all staying in a group."

The large woman next to him raised a hand. "If I catch you helping anyone else with undies, Conn, you'll get a Berrying."

He grinned at her. "Hard luck Lillian, Berry isn't coming."

Lillian cuffed him gently at the back of the head, what was now known as Berrying after the girl who started it. "No, but I am and I've been practicing."

"Clear off you lot, so I can get back to bed. Seven o'clock is too early for me." The tallest person present, a bald man muscled like a bodybuilder, didn't have a pack but did carry a machete since he wouldn't be coming shopping. He tried to bury his smile in a scowl.

"Your bed will be cold now Casper so you can stay up and watch out for anyone trying to steal the silver." Harold turned to leave, and the car blocking the hole in the barricade across the road reversed out.

"Your bed is always cold. We'll see if we can spot a boyfriend for you, Casper." Emmy blew him a kiss.

"Not a blacksmith, or Liz will try and steal him. A lumberjack would be nice?" Casper watched them leave, laughing as a chorus of the Monty Python lumberjack song rose from the file of shoppers.

"I'm a lumberjack and I'm OK."

He turned and made his way into the nearby house, but Casper wouldn't be going back to bed. He had been left in charge of security for the remaining forty-three residents, including Harold's five-year-old niece and two-year-old nephew. Before dawn Casper would check on each sentry along the un-mortared brick wall that connected the outer houses of the enclave.

*   *   *

The laughter and singing died away as the group approached the bottom of the access road up to the bypass. Until now, anyone stepping onto that access had been shot. Harold stopped at the warning sign, the one marking the beginning of the three hundred yard exclusion zone. A spotlight lit them up and Harold put up a hand to cut down the glare. "Hello up there. Army? Shopping party to go to the Mart. Can we come up?"

A bullhorn answered after a short delay. "Take out your identification pass and keep it in your left hand. Single file and everyone has both their hands in clear view. You will walk between two soldiers with detection equipment. Anyone carrying a weapon will be arrested and sent to a camp. Do you understand?"

"Yes, we understand." Everyone understood because the TV and the leaflets had hammered it home. The clerks in the armoured bus that issued the passes and the coupons that had replaced money also recited the rules.

"Come ahead. Walk." The big light moved to one side and two smaller lights came on, illuminating a gap in the sandbags and the waiting soldiers.

Harold walked at the front, relieved to see the usual sergeant, one who seemed at least a little bit sympathetic though all the soldiers were very tense. One soldier each side of the narrow gap waved a wand down him and stepped back. "ID, Soldier Boy." The sergeant held out his hand.

"Harold Miller."

"That's not what your little army call you, not when there's trouble." The sergeant glanced at the pass. "This says 'soldier boy' as well."

"Ex-soldier, sarge. I left to look after my sister." Harold let the ghost of a smile show. "Now I've got to do her shopping."

The sergeant didn't smile, but there was a trace of humour in his voice. "No good deed goes unpunished." The humour went again as he continued. "Stay on this carriageway. If you cross the central divide, you will be shot. That's reserved for official vehicles now." Sarge lifted his hand and pointed. "Your turnoff is five miles that way."

Harold thought he'd ask, though the rules said no vehicles. "Any chance of using a pushbike another time, sarge?"

"Not even a wheelbarrow. It'll get the fat off all that lot." He looked past Harold. "Next."

Harold walked forward without replying. A lack of food in the period between the breakdown of law and order and now, when shops were available again, had left most people lean rather than fat. Just over fifteen minutes later Emmy came through, the last of them. "Ready to go, Harold."

"Five miles, everyone, so nice and steady. The Mart opens at 8:30 so we'll be there in time." Harold started walking. Behind him the chattering fell away as the group trudged through the gloom, unable to see much more than a few clumps of lights in the city. According to the TV the view the other side of the carriageway would consist of empty houses and deserted fields. The lack of any lights suggested that this time the TV might be telling the truth.

Along the central barrier between the traffic lanes stood a final reminder that there was no escape. The squaddies stood every couple of hundred yards, the other side of the central barrier, dim figures wearing night goggles and watching suspiciously with their rifles ready for use. Too many soldiers had been killed by the civilians and vice versa over the last months of chaos for there to be much trust left.

An hour later dawn struggled through the overcast. "I've been looking forward to some daylight, and now I wish I'd kept my eyes shut." Matthew pointed out into the open countryside. "I don't know which depresses me more, the bloody great strip of bulldozed buildings or all those fields that should have been ploughed or planted or have cows and sheep wandering about in them. I'd hoped the lack of lights was just because everyone was asleep."

"Maybe they are?" Emmy looked the same way. "I suppose the fields can't be ploughed because of the fuel shortage."

"If anyone was living there, there'd be evidence of farming." Matthew shook his head. "It doesn't take fuel to stick a few cows in a field."

"Maybe those roaming bands the TV rants on about have turned all the cows into steak?" Liz looked upwards. "Oh cripes, who put that word in my mouth? Fresh, barely singed steak dripping blood as my teeth sink into it. I swear, if there's steak I don't care if it costs me every coupon. I'll eat grass until we shop again."

"The TV pictures showed a depressing lack of fresh meat or fish in the marts." Harold frowned. "We're surrounded by sea, or the country is. There's got to be fish."

"My dad used to drag us out to sea in a little dingy sail whatsit with three of his mates. Then we had to watch them drown maggots for hours." Susan frowned. "I always refused to help but they always caught lots of fish, big fat things. Though he kept trying to show me how to clean them. Yeuk." She sighed. "I never complained about the home-made fish and chips afterwards."

"If you can find fish, I'll learn to do the yukky part if it means fish and chips." Seth grinned and indicated his sling. "One handed. If we hear of a chip shop Harold can go and make them an offer they can't refuse."

"Good luck with that." Lilian pointed the other way. "There aren't many lights out there, in the city." She sighed. "I'd hoped for more once daylight arrived."

The group all turned to look out over the city to the west, at the dimly seen roofs and streets stretching away, silent and dark. Here and there strings of street lights or clumps of lighted windows broke the gloom. Far in the distance something large glowed as it burned unchecked.

"Harold didn't want our place lit up in case we attracted any strays from the rioters so I disconnected the street lighting. Maybe others feel the same way." Finn looked towards the city centre. "I'm surprised we can't see the lights on a tower block. They should have lights in the stairwells, and on the top for aircraft." The group walked in silence for a while, though several exchanged glances.

Eventually Liz sighed. "I'll say it. Maybe because the whole city really is like this?" A sweep of her arm encompassed the scene as the growing light gave a clearer view over the nearest housing estate. A three hundred yard wide bull-dozed strip separated the housing from the raised roadway, the Army exclusion zone. Beyond that the houses were dark and silent, and from the frost on the roofs deserted. Many had broken windows, a good number missing or broken roof tiles, and in two large areas the houses were burned out shells.

"There are more clusters of lights coming on, here and there." Susan tried to sound cheerful, but there weren't many. The headlights of a convoy of vehicles a couple of miles away emphasised the total lack of traffic in most places. The conversation died away as the group walked, everyone busy with their own thoughts or murmuring quietly to a companion. Even the appearance of a few small groups of people among the houses inside the ring road didn't bring much comment because there were very few.

*   *   *

Three quarters of an hour after dawn the group had their first real view of a new shopping mart. Their only shopping mart now. "Somehow that looks more brutal than the pictures on the TV." Harold agreed with Liz. The huge windowless warehouse style building, surrounded by cleared land, had been enclosed by a high fence. The access road off the bypass ran past the front where razor wire topped an eight foot mesh fence. The watch towers at the corners and either side of the entrance gates each contained two men, men carrying shotguns.

"I hope they've remembered non-lethal?" Alfie might only be fifteen but a well-muscled fifteen and working hard to build more. He was determined to be strong enough to use the compound bow the residents had found in a burned out shop. Bows and crossbows, machetes, clubs and knives of any size were legal self-defence weapons for civilians, anywhere but on the bypass. Any sort of firearm or air weapon meant being shot at by the Army.

"The TV promised non-lethal unless we wave guns. I doubt that will happen with anyone coming off the bypass, not after the scan." Harold started down, watched by soldiers inside another sandbagged strongpoint. "Come on, before anyone else gets here." The walk had taken a little longer than he'd expected. All the group were reasonably fit these days, but weren't used to such a long, steady walk. The sixteen from Orchard Close followed another group through the gate in the mesh and across a wide, flat yard to the actual store entrance. Above the door a sign announced 'TesdaMart – the authorised retailer for all your needs.'

"That's got to be Tesco and Asda combined." Seth nursed his injured arm and frowned. "Are they all that's left, or have the others opened stores?"

"Who knows, maybe they've just used the names because they're familiar? Like Harold said, we're all mushrooms now. Bloody hell, how many guards do they need for shoppers?" Jon, one of the later arrivals at Orchard Close, pointed at the men behind sandbags on the store roof. "They're a bit like overkill considering the armoured car?"

"Not overkill." Liz looked carefully at the armoured car. "Not any sort of kill I hope. Is that a water cannon or the other sort, Harold?" Everyone in Orchard Close was nervous about the weapons on armoured vehicles after seeing them used.

"Water cannon, Liz. There's a big bowser for water on the back if you look." Harold called out to the man at the rear of the group ahead. "Where are you lot from?"

"We're from Cadillac's territory. Who's your boss?" The man glanced nervously towards the front of his group as he spoke but slowed.

"Boss? We're from Orchard Close, along the bypass about five miles. So where do you people live?" Harold frowned as he spoke, because a boss sounded like one of the enclaves where a gang had taken charge. The Army had supposedly cleared them all out.

"We live about three miles that way." The man pointed northwest, deeper into the city but also closer to Orchard Close. "You must be on the north boundary."

"The Army told us about boundaries. How big is your area?"

"Oy, you. I told you no gobbing off to strangers. Now get your arse in here." The man Harold had been speaking to shrugged apologetically and scuttled off towards the rest of his group, now at the store entrance.

The swarthy muscular young man who had spoken swaggered over, gently swinging a baseball bat. "Who are you lot?"

"Orchard Close. You lot?" Harold knew the type after turning a few away, a self-appointed guardian who protected and controlled a group of people. A guardian who would keep them safe from others, but at a price.

"The Hot Rods. Where is Orchard Close?" The man looked over the group and sneered. "You came along the bypass? That means you're unarmed and that's dumb." He laughed. "Someone might rob you."

Harold sighed. "We also outnumber you sixteen to one and if you've got a gun, someone up there on the roof will blow your head off. Where do the Hot Rods live?" Harold knew where the other man had said but was curious how this one had brought a baseball bat.

"Our territory starts just over there, past the line of houses along the road outside. TesdaMart claim that first strip." He waved his baseball bat. "So we don't have to worry about going on the bypass." He thought a moment. "Where did you say your mob are from?"

"Your northern border, I think."

"Right. In that case Cadillac will be over to see you at some time. He's the boss." Behind him the last of his party were going inside.

"Your friends are leaving you."

"Not really." The man pulled his coat aside to show two machetes. "I'm keeping these safe while the rest shop."

Harold hoped that meant no weapons inside. "I'm Harold. We're going in now, so see you later?"

"I'm Cooper. We'll probably be gone but I'll let Cadillac know about you."

"Thanks." Harold led the rest past. He was unsure if letting Cadillac, whoever that was, know about Orchard Close was good or bad.

*   *   *

Once through the rotating steel doors Harold took a few paces and stopped to wait for the rest. Emmy came up beside him. "Just like the pictures on the TV. Do we shop for undies or food first? You might not care about food after we've asked your opinion about frillies."

Harold smiled because this was standard teasing from the girl club. "Food because we don't know what the coupons will buy yet. Then we innocent males can avert our eyes while you lot squander the rest."

"You won't say squander if you ever get to see any of them. Now where is the meat because I'm fed up of salvaged burgers and rabbit?" Patricia, a trainee nurse of twenty-eight and one of the oldest on this trip, had ended up their only medic. "I'll need a look at what medications are on sale but don't hold out much hope."

"No, not after the ambulances taking away everyone like Mum, everyone needing regular medicine to live." Finn, their electrician, hadn't liked that much but with no medication available his Mum, Mary, had little option. Finn had been told she wouldn't be allowed to contact Orchard Close, which worried him.

Harold looked round, and his group had all come through the doors. "We need a list of prices, of everything." Harold smiled at the complaints. "Use the little recorders and then we'll get Hilda to write them up and collate them." The groans turned to smiles because the scavenged battery powered pocket recorders both saved paper and were easy to use. Hilda, in her early forties and an ex-clerical worker, really did like making and collating lists. She said that put the world in order. "We'll aim for food first, and then work down the list." He led off to where a big sign, hung from the roof far overhead, claimed the vegetables were.

Shortly afterwards a silent group looked at the offerings. "Anybody know what any of those are?" Holly peered at one heap of limp greenery. "That looks as if someone grabbed a handful of weeds."

"That's kale. It isn't popular, but it's edible. Sort of like cabbage but not in a nice neat ball?" Patricia looked at the rest. "Potatoes and swede of course and cabbage and Brussels sprouts. Leeks, onions, parsnips, beetroot, and I suppose these are some sort of winter greens."

"The leafy stuff is winter lettuce? How come lettuce is growing now, in winter?" Emmy was curious as well as decidedly unimpressed. "If there's no fuel to import them, where are they being grown?"

"That's not real lettuce. Those are squash." Bess pointed.

Seth lifted a grill and peered at the veg behind it. "I don't like salad on a good day, but these look a bit wilted."

"Those are different sorts of beets." Heads turned towards Patricia and she waved a booklet. "There's a list of what's here and how to cook it." She scowled. "The rotten sods are charging a coupon for the booklet."

Harold looked over the pricings. "More to the point, how many coupons will the veg cost?" Concentrated working out followed to see just how much a coupon would buy.

"Don't get excited, Harold. We won't be raiding the pantie store if the rest of the food is these prices." Emmy looked glum.

"Maybe that's even more exciting?" Seth was grinning.

"I'll tell Berry you said that." Liz's smile widened. "I'll tell her Dad, Nigel."

"Christ, don't do that." Seth looked truly worried. "He'll never let me get Berry on her own, even if Berry agrees." The teasing continued as a selection of vegetables were put into packs, spread out to keep the individual weights down. The smiling and occasional laughter died down as they came around a corner to the meat shelves.

"That's far enough." The young man looked them over. "We'll be cleaning this lot out." He smiled. "We'll sell you some?"

"How come? After all we'll have to pay as we leave." Harold could see half a dozen people filling big packs with tubes and packets. "Where's the meat?"

"That's it. Pastes and dried and a few cans. You give me some coupons and then you take your food through and pay for it on the way out." The young man smiled. "Sort of a tax."

"Nope. We outnumber you two to one so I guess we'll just shop for ourselves." Harold started forward again. He assumed the bloke was just trying it on but the man's face hardened. His hand dipped inside his jacket and brought out a small knife. "Wrong. This evens it up."

Harold sighed. He was in a good mood, and really didn't want to spoil it. The lull after the fighting for Orchard Close died down had been lovely, even if he still had dreams about it sometimes. "Everyone else go and get what we need. I'll stand here and talk to this bloke." The knife wielder looked startled and Harold glared straight at him. "We don't want trouble. They'll get the food and you'll threaten me with the knife. If you turn to go after one of them I'll kick you."

The others started going either side, and the man glanced at them, unsure. Emmy flipped her hood back as she did, and smiled as his eyes widened. He opened his mouth to object to being bypassed but only managed to splutter "you're a... that's, er, different." The yob stared at her hair, which was in long thin beaded plaits at one side of her head and cropped close at the other.

Emmy laughed. "You were right, Soldier Boy. Signature hairdo and bit of scarring really do appeal to the bad boys." She patted the startled man on the cheek. "Sorry fella, you'll have to get in line."

Seth scowled and pushed forward but the young man had turned back to Harold. "Soldier Boy? Are you that soldier type up north of here? Got your own place?"

"Orchard Close is north, and I used to be a soldier." Harold tensed a bit and cursed the habit some residents had of using Soldier Boy as a nickname, especially when Harold refused entry to some bunch of undesirables.

"Right. Sorry mate." The knife promptly went away! "I didn't realise you were another gang. We heard about you." He stood back and waved Harold forward. "The boss told me to scare anyone without protection so he could move in."

"You were lucky he's in a good mood." Liz came past, smirking. "Usually when someone threatens him with a weapon he offers to shove it up their ass." Harold didn't, usually, but neither did he tend to back down. Liz now called it his macho bastard technique.

The bloke grinned. "Yeah, we heard. Some asshole said his mate waved a gun at you and you told him that. Then you beat three of them to death, and later on you shot someone else through the eye."

Holly turned from putting tubes of meat paste into her pack. "A lot more than three now, on both lists. I think Casper is keeping count."

The young knifeman laughed. "I'll let the boss know it was true. We took the piss out of the pussy and he kept running. Are you really SAS?"

Harold grinned. "I'm not allowed to say. Official Secrets Act." He wasn't SAS, by a very long way, but the yobs and assholes he'd had to deal with seemed to be deterred by the very idea so he wasn't denying it.

"That means you are or you'd lie and say yes." The twisted logic suited Harold so he just shrugged. "Did you meet Cooper, outside?"

"Yes, he offered to rob us." Harold laughed. "I said no."

"Wait until I tell him. He'll be pleased he didn't try."

"So are you a Hot Rod? Who is Cadillac?" Since this one seemed chatty, Harold tried for some real information.

"I don't know what Cadillac's name used to be. There's him, Cooper, Bugatti and Charger, all named after cars. Then there's Big Mack after the trucks, because of how big he is. I'm working on getting a real Hot Rod name so I'm still Kev." Kev frowned. "Cadillac is a mean bastard but he looks after us, the Hot Rods."

"So where does he live, then maybe I can drop by?" Harold wouldn't but a location would be helpful for avoiding this gang.

"Don't do that. They'll shoot you on sight unless you turn up unarmed and you don't look that stupid." Kev thought for a moment. "If you lot are just off the bypass like pussy-boy said that'll be three or four miles from the Mansion, maybe less. We control a couple of small blocks of housing nearer to you than that. You know, poor innocents who need protection." He grinned. "From us, for starters. Where are you exactly?"

Harold debated briefly but Orchard Close couldn't be hidden. If they'd got a road map the road names would be marked on there. "We live at the next junction up and we've got a mile this way."

One of the men loading bags came up behind Kev. "We've got what you said, Kev. What next?"

Kev sneered at him. "Here. Find the games consoles, because Cadillac needs a couple of new games." Kev handed the man a list. "Any two of these for now." He turned back to Harold. "See you, Soldier Boy. Gotta keep an eye on this lot." Kev swaggered off.

Emmy came back from raiding shelves. "That gang seem well organised and it's happened very quickly. We asked some of the people filling bags and they pay these Hot Rods for protection, out of their coupon ration."

"Crap. It didn't take the yobs long to adapt, though the Army should have smashed any gang enclave according to what the TV said." Harold frowned because the TV was a long way from the whole truth, but he'd hoped that part was true.

"Not an enclave, Harold. The shoppers live in four streets that were just lucky and didn't get wrecked or lose their water or electricity." Her lip lifted in disgust. "These Hot Rods have a stronghold, and just come out to collect rent because they claim the houses are in their area."

"Ah. The officer asked about our area and put down a mile each way. Apparently some people were more ambitious." Harold stared after Kev. "Let's hope they're not too ambitious."

Emmy looked the same way and her voice echoed Harold's concern. "I really hope not." She perked up. "Ooh, corned beef." Moments later Emmy waved a can at Harold. "What's spam? How do you cook it?"

"Spam? My grandad told us about spam and it wasn't a happy memory." Susan, the thirty-year-old divorcee, took the can. "He reckoned fried or in sandwiches, and chopped up in mashed potato. Corned Beef for people without taste buds."

Seth came back from the aisle waving a packet. "These look like dog chews. Dried meat it says." He looked round. "We'll take for ever like this, so why don't we split up? I need an ink pad for thumb marking coupons and that doesn't need sixteen shoppers. Does anyone want any pencils and pads while I'm there?" Seth turned.

"No, we all go everywhere in a group because if there's another Kev you don't want to be alone." Harold ignored the half-hearted complaints, because he meant it. That yob with a knife had shaken him a bit because even the shops weren't safe, despite the guards with guns. "There'll be nobody nipping off to the shops on their own."

"What about if we need the loo?" Alfie shrugged at the stares. "Just saying. After all getting mugged in a public toilet wasn't exactly unknown before all this trouble started."

"Good point." Emmy smiled. "Though we'll probably scare the crap out of anyone in there, going in mob handed."

Bess sniggered. "Good, they'll be finished sooner." The entire group headed towards the stationery.

"You can look if you like, Harold." Harold would have thought Holly was teasing, except for the disgust in her voice. He turned. "You're not going to get excited even if I do cartwheels in these."

"She is joking, isn't she?" Seth's quiet voice from behind Harold echoed his own thoughts. The pants and bra were plain but Harold was very sure that Holly or any of the girl club dressed in them, cartwheeling or not, would definitely be exciting.

"We'd all get excited if you cartwheeled in a set of thermals, Holly." Harold grinned. "Are you adding cartwheels to the morning exercises for the girl club? I'll warn all the blokes."

"It's a thought." Emmy held up a similar pair of plain panties. "We could put some pink on them. All the men seemed to like Holly in pink." Holly blushed because that had been a pink tutu worn as a Halloween 'angel' costume and yes, the single men liked it. "I could draw something festive on these for the Christmas party."

"You could draw holly on them?" Sal sniggered. "Holly could just put Holly inside hers."

"Party?" Bess spoke up. "Um, when we were shopping, did anyone see any mistletoe?"

The women reverted to teasing Bess, and asking if she still needed mistletoe to kiss her new boyfriend. Nobody thought so, since a fiery, very forward Bess had laid claim to Matthew rather than the other way round. Like a score of others, Matthew hadn't come along because he hadn't recovered from a wound received while defending Orchard Close.

Harold took the opportunity to look at the rest of the clothing. Plain styles and plain colours more or less covered it for males, females and children. Nothing designer, and in fact all the labels he could see said TesdaMart on them. Then Harold looked at the prices and judging by the number of coupons each person received to live on, new jeans were going to be a major expense.

After they checked the prices, the women decided to skip underwear or any other clothes this time round. Harold's forays with his small scavenging party before the big mob attack had included women. As they worked through abandoned housing gathering food and other essentials the women raided wardrobes and drawers as well as makeup boxes and toiletries. Even Bess, who had arrived with nothing but what she wore, had plenty of clothes for now.

*   *   *

"Any more last minute shopping?" Harold looked round and everyone shook their heads. "Then I'll go first in case someone ambitious is waiting outside and I want you, Alfie, in that aisle." Harold pointed to the side. "Everyone else gets into the same two queues so there's no break, with Seth, Conn and Jon to watch the back."

Lillian nudged Conn. "I'll guard you." At more or less twice his weight, that might be true.

The group stood across the two aisles until the last person disappeared in through the door at the end and then filed in, eight into each one. The aisles were narrow corridors, separated from each other by a tall metal wall. The door light turned green and it opened a little, so Harold pushed and went in.

He entered a square, plain room, empty except for a table at one side in front of a blank glass panel. As the TV had instructed, Harold put all his bags on the table then stood on a red square to be scanned. Every item had been in a tight mesh bag with a bar code, or had a bar code stamped directly onto it. The beets and swedes had actually been individually stamped. This whole setup spoke of real planning, not a hurried stopgap and Harold hoped that included the bar codes being non-toxic.

Moments later a bored voice told him how many coupons were needed, and warned him that smudged or damaged coupons would be impounded and if he offered forged coupons he would be arrested. Harold put the completed coupons into the slot and used the ink pad to put his thumbprint on enough of the rest to pay. The woman or tape didn't confirm that the coupons were acceptable. The door in the wall opposite the entrance clicked open, which seemed a big enough hint to Harold. Beyond that door he found a smaller room. As soon as he entered the door behind Harold clicked shut, the one in front opened and he went outside.

The man by the door eyed Harold's size and hefted a baseball bat, hesitating. Harold spoke first. "Are you waiting for someone?" Before the man could answer another door clicked open and Harold looked past him. "Hi, Alfie."

"Hi, Harold. Is there a problem?" Alfie spoke from behind the man, who suddenly looked very nervous.

"No, this bloke is waiting for someone." Harold looked back at the man. "The next seven out of each of these doors are with us, mate, so you're at the wrong door."

"Seven? Ah, right. I'll just, er, wait over there?" The ragged man moved off and leant on the wall away from the line of doors.

Alfie grinned and came over, then the two of them stood away from the exit doors and waited. It took a while, but eventually the whole party had paid and they headed for the bypass.

"Single file and hand over your ID. Hands in plain view."

Harold went first. "We've just been shopping. We did all this to get here."

"Just checking for personal weapons. Orders." Harold had opened his mouth to point out the wand wouldn't work because there were metal items in the packs, and shut it. Orders meant no argument would work. A wand passed over Harold but not the pack and his ID went over a scanner. "Yeah. Came from Orchard Close this morning. All clear."

"What if I hadn't come along the bypass this morning?"

"Strip search and empty the packs so you can't smuggle weaponry."

"Fair enough. The next fifteen are with me."

"Still got to check. Next." The squaddie sounded bored, but the ones with rifles were alert.

*   *   *

The walk back didn't seem as long, even loaded down, since everyone spent the time discussing the visit. The level of paranoia shown by the mart, the weapons in the yard and inside the Mart, and the lack of variety in the goods for sale were the main subjects. Any attempts to talk to a group and several singles and couples walking towards the mart were met with silence. Nobody else wanted to talk to a large group of strangers. As Harold's shoppers came towards the access road down to Orchard Close another large group was heading towards them, away from the checkpoint.

"Which enclave are they from?"

"I'm not psychic, Liz. Perhaps we should wait until we get a chance to talk to that bloke by those cars wearing a machete?" Harold wasn't too happy, because wearing a machete openly like that probably meant another guardian. "First we'll find out just how long it'll take to pass through this checkpoint."

"Hello Soldier Boy. Head straight on down." Sarge gave Harold a little smile. "Unless you found an arms dealer on the bypass?"

Harold smiled back, since the soldiers were still lining the route. "No, but we could do with one at the other end. Some of the shoppers who don't come along here are carrying knives in the shop."

Sarge curled a lip. "Self-defence weapons are allowed there as long as they aren't missile weapons, or so I am told. Just don't bring them onto here." Harold flinched slightly because that meant the gangs near the marts would eventually be shopping with machetes. "Single file, and go straight through the gap. If you arrive another time when we're passing someone through, stay well back."

"Will do. Are you here tonight?"

"Yes, for my sins. Though the mart will be shut then." Harold hadn't meant that, as Sarge well knew. Though neither were going to mention the dish of hot chips that would be coming up the access road later because fraternisation was banned. Sarge beckoned Harold a little further from the rest. "You'll get a visit soon, to tell you to stay quiet and not interfere while the Army deal with the bodies in the ruins. In my opinion you should keep all your women out of sight."

"Why? You Army types seem to appreciate a smile and a wave from the girl club." Harold grinned and Sarge smiled a little because that was true.

"It isn't the soldiers. They'll be bringing work gangs to do the dirty jobs and you don't want them seeing your women. We're talking rapists, murderers, pedophiles, all the scum from the jails and any picked up since. Personally I'd have shot most of them but the government is using them for clearing bodies and crappy jobs like that." Sarge kept his voice down. "If you see a bloke dressed in orange coming towards your place, stick an arrow in him."

"What, even if he's unarmed?"

"The Army will be trying to shoot him so don't let the bastard use your people as cover. We've been told it'll be for a few days and then you can go into the ruins." Orchard Close residents had been banned from the ruins for the last fortnight. Sarge shrugged. "Not that there'll be much to scavenge now, though you might find some cans and sealed jars."

Harold was sure his people could find something useful in there. The Army instructions to keep out had been frustrating despite all the bodies laid about. Everyone knew that useful food and clothes were rotting since the houses were broken open, and rodents and birds would get in as well. Sarge seemed in a good mood, so Harold stayed watching the rest file through. "Who are that lot, the ones who just came through?"

"I can't tell you who your neighbours are two and a half miles that way." Sarge pointed straight over Orchard Close into the city. "Maybe that bloke down there can tell you more?"

"Cheers. See you." Harold followed Emmy through the sandbags, smiling quietly. Sarge had just told him where the other enclave was, even if the man waiting with Casper turned out bashful.

* * *

"Hi Harold. These are the neighbours." Casper had come out to meet Harold, wearing a machete but smiling. "That lot just leaving belong to him, and brought those." There were three more cars behind the first. "What was shopping like?"

"Not very exciting, except the mart lets people take knives inside." He turned to the man. "I hope a couple of your lot can handle themselves or they'll get robbed."

"There's three men along who won't take any crap, though I don't like the idea of knives." He frowned. "Are they robbing everyone?"

"Not if they belong to a gang. Are you a gang?" Harold assumed an enclave at least simply because of the big, almost new cars and the machete.

The man leaning against the big 4X4 looked embarrassed. "We are the Gods of Fire and Steel. It sounds stupid put like that, but someone suggested computer names as gang names. The ones we used for signing on to play games?" He shrugged. "Then we found a proper smith and since we'd already got a Vulcan and a Gofannon and they're old Gods, he's picked Wayland. All the other gangs are called weird names so we made one up. Otherwise they don't take you seriously."

"They take the Gods of Fire and Steel seriously?" Harold stared, unsure if this bloke was winding him up.

"Have you met the Hot Rods, the Geek Freeks, or the Barbie Girls yet? Anyway it's Gods of Fire and Steel so we can just say GOFS." The man sighed. "I've got to choose between Hephaestus and Brokkr, unless I can find another God of Smiths."

Casper looked him over. "You look Asian. How about Amatsumara? There's a T in the spelling and it's supposed to be three words, but he's the Japanese God of smiths?" He smiled. "Don't look like that. I was interested in how those swords were made at one time. Nobody here will know how to spell it anyway."

"Amatsumara, that'll get turned into Karma Sutra. Anyway, my grandad was Indian, not Japanese. There again it might be better than the others because I'll get a lot of piss-taking with Hephaestus, it sounds like disease." He put out a hand. "I'm Kabir at the moment, and pleased to meet a civilised bloke."

"Casper." Casper shook and sniggered. "Civilised and bloke are both up for discussion. Have your gang got a problem with gays?"

"No, but I don't think we've got any. There's a lot of gays, the blokes, who've formed a gang somewhere in the city, and a lot of the Barbie Girls are dykes. I don't care either way, but some do." Kabir curled a lip. "Have you met Cadillac yet?"

Harold frowned and shook his head. "No, but I'm supposed to have a visit according to someone called Cooper."

"Short for Mini Cooper, which makes a name like Brokkr a lot less weird.

Your people were lucky to find so many decent houses to live in after that mob came through." Kabir looked back at the charred ruins bordering Orchard Close. "Hang on, you were on TV. You were here when they arrived?"

"Maybe we should go in there and have a cuppa." Harold pointed back to the Orchard Close access road. "As long as nobody nicks your car?"

"Really? I can come inside?" He hesitated. "What are the rules in there?"

Casper smiled happily. "There aren't many. Be polite, no foul language, don't handle anyone who doesn't volunteer, and don't steal." He paused. "You'd better leave that at the door." Casper pointed at the machete.

"No swearing or groping, are you lot religious? Never mind, I'll lock up the motors and follow?" At Harold's nod, Kabir took out a set of car keys and Casper followed Harold round the corner and up to the gates.

"Are you sure we should let him in, Harold?"

"No, but we'll only take him into one of the houses near the entrance, then we'll pump him for information since he seems chatty. What was the bit about the machete? Someone will stick a crossbow bolt in him if he starts." Harold led the way through the gap in the barricade, already opened for the rest of the shoppers.

"That was just to make a point really. Not only that but now the danger is past we haven't got many who will do that, you know, shoot someone deliberately." Casper sighed. "Some of the girls, and blokes for that matter, are having a bad time remembering what happened and what they did."

That startled Harold, then he realised he should have known it would happen. Killing people really wasn't normal, even if some maniac is closing in with murder in mind. "Who can we rely on? Just a best guess."

"Emmy because she really won't let anyone take a second shot at her. Holly because of Brodie and Gabriela, I reckon, and Suzie because of her sister being killed. Possibly Gayle because she was nearly caught once, and Bess of course." Casper frowned. "I'll do it, but not too many of the men are up for a fight either though you can count on Alfie after Toby died. Rob won't unless Susan is threatened because that wound really shook him up. Finn will shoot though he's still wounded and Seth I reckon. Jon and Billy both seem solid in spite of only being eighteen and seventeen. Bernie maybe?" Casper shrugged. "A lot just want to forget the whole thing if possible."

Harold winced because Alfie was only fifteen, yet he really was angry over Toby dying. "A lot are still wounded, men and women, so they still might firm up. We'll talk about who to rely on later, but right now let's get a pint down this bloke and be his best friends ever. Nip and get your shotgun, and bring me a pistol, and get either Holly or Emmy to bring a crossbow and a pistol. Just to make a point." Harold thought quickly. "Make sure you don't mention where the beer came from." The price of beer in the mart had been a nasty surprise, and would make Berry and her Dad prime targets for kidnapping.

"I'll prime the women and get the weapons while you meet and greet. Use number three. There's nobody living there but we put a blow heater in the front room to warm it up if the guards needed to thaw out later in the winter." Casper held out a hand. "Give me that pack and I'll send it up to your house."

"Take it to Matthew's house, please. The rest will be there to sort out what we've brought but don't get excited." Harold turned to greet Kabir. "Come in, then we can close the gate." As soon as the man came inside the old car drove across the gap, and the driver took out the keys. Kabir frowned at the car and Harold shrugged. "We're working on it."

"Where do I leave this?" Kabir indicated his machete. "What about my knife?" The man tensed a bit at that. He probably didn't fancy being completely unarmed.

"Keep your knife but don't do anything stupid." Harry pointed up at the house nearby, where Bernie stood at the open window with a crossbow. "You'll be searched because we worry about guns." Harold had only just thought about that when he remembered Bernie had a handgun tucked out of sight as a backup.

"All right, though I left mine in the motor. I suppose we'll get rules organised once we get more visitors." Kabir stood and held his hands up while Harold searched him well enough to find any gun without getting personal. That was easy since under his thick jacket the man only wore a tee and jeans.

After a beer, and being introduced to Emmy, Kabir relaxed enough to let them know roughly where the boundaries with his neighbours ran. Though he wouldn't say just where the GOFS themselves lived. The boundaries were rough because they didn't actually meet, so there were unclaimed sections. The GOFS were doing what Harold had been told the Hot Rods did. They offered protection to isolated clumps of people living in their area, and those people supplied coupons or goods.

After the naming thing came up again, Emmy sniggered. "My brother was into that, Gods and all that stuff, when he was looking for his roots. He looked into becoming Rastafari but that's no good for you, though maybe Ogou, the Haitian spirit of ironworking, would work?"

"Right, thanks, maybe. Are all the women armed like you or are you different? Special?" Kabir seemed puzzled by Emmy having weapons. The looks at Harold and Emmy made clear what different and special meant and Emmy laughed.

"In his dreams." She sobered and gave Harold a critical once-over. "Maybe, but I'm still not ready for any of that nonsense. A lot of women aren't ready after what happened and who we lost. We carry machetes in case some oik won't wait until we are ready." Emmy delivered the last part with a scowl.

Kabir flinched at her tone, and looked over Emmy's weaponry again. "Bloody hell, that lot should do it. You'd fit in well with the Barbie Girls, except you seem to like blokes."

"I like polite blokes, what about your women?" Kabir looked decidedly uncomfortable about that, and moved the subject onto beer and general state of the city. Chatty though he seemed, Kabir seemed cagey about the GOFS women and Harold didn't think they were armed.

At least three times Emmy bit off saying Soldier Boy so she'd had her instructions. That was while describing the battle between the mobs and the Army, and how near Orchard Close came to being swamped. Kabir confirmed that everywhere else he'd heard about where the mobs had gone had ended up wrecked and picked clean, so Orchard Close really were lucky.

The GOFS hadn't been really well organised at that time, and were just lucky the juggernaut missed the place they'd forted up. They'd found a better place since, but he still didn't think it would have held out. Kabir worried about disease rather than violence at the moment because the GOFS were finding a lot of corpses. The mobs left plenty of evidence of their passing, bodies as well as destruction, and the GOFS were having to look through them to find any weapons. At least the houses nearest to Orchard Close had burned fiercely enough to cremate anyone in there.

Bernie came in just over four hours later to report Kabir's group coming back and everyone escorted Kabir to the gate, still talking. "You really haven't got a gang name?" He'd asked at least five times. "Some of them will think you aren't a proper gang and they'll take liberties." He grinned at Emmy. "Until they meet you. I'll tell the others you're Orchard Close and they can buy some really good beer. We'd prefer to trade if possible rather than use coupons?"

"We'll think about it. Call in for a beer the next time, in a fortnight." Harold shook Kabir's hand, as did Casper and Emmy. Then Casper escorted Kabir out of the gate.

*   *   *

A gloomy group sorted out the groceries, because they'd been told about prices and now they were assessing the quality. They weren't pleased to learn about the gangs surrounding Orchard Close either because the TV claimed to have smashed them. At least the prospect of scavenging again after the bodies were gone cheered a few up. A weary Harold trudged up the road to home and a small whirlwind engulfed him as the door opened.

"Coco Pops! Uncle-Harry has brought Coco Pops!" Five year old Daisy did her best to open Harold's pack as he tried to get inside and take his coat off.

"Not until tomorrow, for breakfast. Scoot." Her Mum, Harold's sister Sharyn, scooted Daisy away. "Let me get these unpacked and let Uncle-Harold have a cuppa."

"Drawing first. You owe me big-time for no drawing this morning."

Harold mouthed "big-time" over Daisy's head as she tried to tug him away towards her crayons and colouring books. Sharyn mouthed "Hazel," the four-teen-year old orphan living with them. Then he allowed Daisy to drag him away for a colouring session. At least this one didn't include drawing, which wasn't Harold's strong point.

Eventually Harold made up for missing his morning duty and escaped to go and work on strengthening the wall around the enclave until bedtime, when he read to Daisy because tonight was Uncle-Harold story night. By then Sharyn had found out there were no Coco Pops in the shopping so she'd keep using drinking chocolate to make Daisy's breakfast cereal turn brown.

*   *   *

"Cripes, it's a pity we didn't have that lot when the mob came." Liz frowned and looked at the weapons and ammunition in the garage. "I've already fixed two crossbows but some of these might be past that." The tall, wiry metal-worker looked at the damaged crossbows properly. "Four just need TLC and maybe another three or four might repair, if Sandy helps with some creative woodwork?"

"Good, that will make us up to a dozen full size, two pistol bows and the three child versions. How did you get on with machetes?" Harold smiled because arrows for bows were relatively easy to make, unlike bullets.

"Not too bad. I've straightened eight, but that and making arrowheads is using up my charcoal." Liz pointed. "We collected lots of knives though. If there are enough broom handles I can make a lot of spears with knife blades, really cheap."

"Eight is enough machetes since we aren't allowed outside the walls yet so nobody needs to be heavily armed. Take the rest of the heavy metal gear off to your lair, while we sort out the firearms."

"Cripes yes, I don't want that ammunition near my hot forge." Liz looked around. "Come on, let's see some muscles and get these shifted."

"Not too many muscles or you'll be after my fair body." Casper, six foot three with the physique of a bodybuilder, grinned. "You're not my type."

"She's the wrong sex for you which is a bigger problem." Finn, a spare man in his forties and their electrician, frowned. "I'll carry something but only one-handed until my arm heals. Any firearms will be better for defence than the poncy air pistol."

"Can we have some extra guns now, Harold? For the guardhouses." Matthew grinned. "Then Bess can go crazy with both hands."

"You can have some for the guardhouses but get her to slow up. With shooting at least." Everyone laughed because Bess had definitely set her cap for the red-haired ex-traffic warden. Harold looked over the firearms. "You can have six handguns, and two shotguns which will double the firepower but there's still not much ammo. I can reload the brass, but I've not got the propellant to load a lot."

"What about the rest? There are another half dozen handguns, and those two shotguns." Casper bent over and picked up one of the pistols. "They're all different sizes."

"Only five calibres and most are nine millimetre, which is lucky because the recovered ammo is mostly that. I'll clean and check the rest, then swap them out for what's being used. Just remember, do not let the Army get a hint of even an air pistol or they'll shoot." Harold put weapons into his pockets. "Come on, I'll lock these in the study at home." He grinned, "Then I've got an excuse to lock myself in there away from Daisy."

"Cripes, luck with that," Sal, one of the original residents, smirked. "I thank your all and any Gods I was never tempted into rugrats. Daisy at five is enough to make me swear off them for life."

"More to the point is what you can be tempted into?" Jon ducked a feigned slap.

Bernie grinned. "Are you a chocolates or flowers girl?"

"Unless those marts sell chocolate, a small bar of Cadbury's Dairy Milk could be the equivalent of a pint of Spanish Fly by Easter." Sal smirked. "Though if anyone's got chocolate he'll never hold out until then, not with the entire girl club working on him."

"All of them?" Jon looked upwards with a rapt expression. "A man can dream."

"Man? A pimply youth."

"I've heard about men's dreams."

"Holly is a man's dream."

"Any blonde is."

"Matthew prefers brunettes – or else."

Harold smiled at the joking, but he worried as they took the weapons up to his new home. Extra firearms would help but all the ammunition, including arrows, had been used up in a few frantic minutes as the mob closed and had barely slowed them. Without the Army the lunatics would have run right over the place. Most of the firearms came from dead lunatics either before or after the big attack, but none of them carried much ammunition. Harold could make up a few more rounds, but there still wouldn't be enough for another emergency.

*   *   *

"Harold, Harold!" Harold smiled because Hazel seemed incapable of saying his name once when anything exciting happened. "There's a soldier at the gate. He wants to talk to you."

"Five minutes Hazel. Nip down there and ask someone to tell him please." Harold smiled again as he heard her race off down the stairs because Hazel also seemed incapable of walking anywhere.

About five minutes later he stood on a box to look over the barricade at an armoured car with an officer looking back out of the turret hatch. "You wanted me?"

This one wasn't chatty. "We will be marching a party of prisoners through here to clear away the bodies. If any escape, do not give them shelter. We will come in to get them."

"Don't worry, I've got the message and all the women are hidden. Any problem if we stick an arrow in any who try?" Harold tried not to smile as surprise wiped out the officer's stern, official expression.

"What? Ah. You've heard." The officer shrugged. "That might be a good idea but make very sure no missile comes near any of our men. They will construe that as an attack."

"No problem." Behind the armoured car the first of the prisoners marched past and they were all dressed in the orange suits made infamous by video clips of Guantanamo Bay. Not military marching but definitely in time and closely watched by soldiers in an open lorry holding their weapons ready. The armoured car reversed and the turret swung to cover the orange-clad ranks.

"There'll be guns out there among the bodies." Casper had come out of the nearby house to talk quietly.

"I know. It's why they won't let us scavenge and I'll bet those blokes with rifles will be watching the prisoners really closely." Harold raised his eyes and looked towards the west. "At least the bodies will be gone before that lot finish with the city centre." A thick cloud of birds still hung over the thousands of corpses where the rioters made their last stand, two weeks ago. "I didn't fancy those descending on us."

"I didn't fancy the smell if they didn't, or the rats." Despite the cold weather a definite whiff of corruption came from the wide swathe of housing that had been shelled to stop the rioters. There were also rats and carrion birds in there, but not in huge numbers. "Bess and Holly are in number six with full sized crossbows because we can trust both of them to open fire, especially now they know who the prisoners are. I reckon Jon will as well."

"As long as the women stay hidden. You took all the guns away from the guards?" Harold glanced up at the house nearby, used to guard the gate, because normally a two-two rifle and at least two handguns lived in there.

"Yes, there'll be no mistakes. I'll stay here with a crossbow and two of those smaller ones, the kid's version. Emmy is the other side of the gate in number two, with a big crossbow. Does that repaired one work?" Casper pointed at the heavy crossbow in Harold's hand.

"Yes, it was only the stock and Sandy made something that works. Liz is working on the other damaged ones." Harold turned. "I'll be at the far end." He held up his small cheap walkie-talkie. "I'll keep in touch."

Harold stayed on duty all day, until Casper confirmed that the orange-clad convicts had marched back up onto the bypass. Six times Army rifles fired short bursts deep in the ruins but nobody came out towards Orchard Close.

*　　*　　*

On the second day two JCBs followed the prisoners so the bodies were presumably being buried. Just after midday Harold heard shouting and when he looked out of the side window he saw an orange clad body. The corpse, with two crossbow bolts sticking up out of his chest, lay halfway between the ruins and Orchard Close. Bess and Holly had let him get close enough to be sure of a kill. "Alfie, Billy, keep a close look the other way because I'm watching the gap towards Bess."

"I've got it Harold." Alfie had a full size crossbow and a pistol bow poised to shoot; despite his age he was capable and willing to pull the trigger, even at the age of fifteen. The death of his friend Toby at the same tender age had removed any qualms Alfie had about self-defence.

Harold clicked the radio. "Bess? Jon? Holly?"

"Bess. Holly is talking to the soldiers instead of Jon because," Bess sniggered, "she looks harmless." Harold smiled because despite being an innocent looking seventeen-year-old blonde, Holly was implacable where rioters or gangsters were concerned.

"What do they want?" Harold spoke again before Bess could answer. "Don't let the prisoners see Holly."

"Holly only let the soldiers have a quick look to show how sweet and innocent she is then ducked back inside to talk. The soldiers want to make sure we aren't going to fire on the men who come for the body. Though it's a temptation." Harold could see what tempted Bess because four more orange clad men had left the ruins. These four were accompanied by two squaddies with rifles. "She's asked the soldiers if we can have our arrows back, please."

Harold watched as a soldier pointed at the body and two of the prisoners pulled the bolts out, though one had to brace himself and use two hands. The prisoner passed the bolts to a soldier, who inspected them before throwing the shafts towards Orchard Close. The radio crackled. "The Army is impressed by Liz's latest arrowhead." Liz had sworn to make a head that couldn't be extracted without it costing a limb. The four prisoners took the body away closely watched by the soldiers, though one squaddie waved as the group went back into the ruins.

*   *   *

By the end of the fifth day there had been five more orange-clad bodies in the cleared strip between Orchard Close and the blackened ruins. Two prisoners had been shot by soldiers as they ran, and three were killed by crossbow bolts from inside Orchard Close when they came too near. The radio brought Harold back to the gate and the armoured car waiting outside. "Are you done?" Behind the vehicle the prisoners were marching up onto the bypass.

"Yes, and a note has been made of your helpful attitude. Please do not stray over there until tomorrow because we are still filling in the graves. If you find any firearms missed by the searchers, please hand them in to the soldiers on the checkpoint." Harold didn't smile even though the officer's voice held a hint of humour. "Send them up with that innocent looking lass, but without her crossbow."

Both Harold and the officer knew bloody well any weapons would be kept, but it all had to be said for the record. "No problem. I'd be more worried about one of that lot keeping something nasty."

This time there was definite humour in the officer's voice. "They strip completely and walk through a scanner before loading up. They all know by now that any sort of a weapon means we bring them back and put them in the hole."

"Er, good." That startled Harold. Summary executions weren't normal even these days, or he'd thought not. "Have you left us anything?"

"We don't allow the prisoners to loot, though the place is a bit banged up. Remember, not until tomorrow." The armoured vehicle, a modern one rather than the older version at the mart, reversed to follow the prisoners.

Harold turned to the waiting crowd. "You heard, we only have to stay in here until the day after tomorrow." Harold laughed at the cheer, because he knew exactly how relieved they all felt.

Chapter 2:
Setting Boundaries
Mk II

Harold looked into the proffered tin. "Is that it?"

"Yup. I've been using drinking chocolate to turn ordinary cereal into chocolate cereal for weeks now. Not exactly Coco Pops but near enough, apparently," Sharyn smiled. "Either find some or explain to Daisy why her supply has stopped."

"Cripes, not likely."

"Are you coming or not?" It hadn't taken long for Liz to get fed up of waiting and she had come inside to roust Harold. "Casper has already taken his group out, and Emmy will be gone any time now." She scowled. "You were the one who said this is urgent, that we'll need all the food we can get to save coupons. If you didn't insist on coming Holly would have already left with our lot." The residents of Orchard Close, or over a third of them, were really keen to get out there and find out what the Army had left.

"Coming." Harold hung the two-two rifle over his shoulder on a long strap, stuck a nine mill pistol in the back of his belt, and put on his long leather coat to cover them. Then he hugged Sharyn and Daisy, and joined the eight others in the street.

"Straight that way, towards the GOFS." Harold pointed towards the city centre where the birds still circled. He led the way into the centre house on that side and out of the door onto the cleared area, waiting until he heard the bars and bolts slam shut before moving away.

The first fifty yards of ruins were fire-blackened and nobody even bothered to look in any remaining structures. Very few walls were above head height, and even the trees were charred stumps. "All that charcoal, gone to waste. I need it all for metalworking."

"Sorry Liz, but there wasn't time. Mark every remotely salvageable tree you see on the map and we'll get them later, unless they're fruit trees." Harold waved the rough map he carried, copied from a road atlas. "Everyone spread out in a long line and keep an eye open for chocolate powder."

"Fat chance. You don't honestly think the men are going to get anywhere near chocolate, do you?" Holly grinned and headed for the left flank.

"It's for Daisy, because otherwise there will be serious trouble. Big-time trouble, I'm told." The line spread out, with about thirty feet between the searchers, and started forward.

"A lot depends on what he's trading for the chocolate."

"I want hugs."

"I might want those slow hands I've heard about."

"I'd settle for a slow dance."

"I've got mistletoe." The banter died away quickly as the true state of the housing became clear. Worse, the prisoners might have cleared most of the complete bodies but they hadn't got everything or even everyone.

"I don't fancy searching the bodies, Harold." Until now every dead rioter or gangster had been strip searched for any useful items but Robert, one of the latest arrivals, had a good point. These bodies were definitely ripe.

"Leave them, and mark them on your map." Harold thought quickly. "Black cross, a plus sign like a church cross. I'll sort out a few people with strong stomachs to shift them." The searchers carried a selection of coloured pens and crayons salvaged before the riots, but those working out the coding had expected the bodies to be gone.

The line moved forward slowly, marking down possible fruit tree and bushes, and patches of vegetables that hadn't been ploughed up by explosions or the Army diggers. These houses weren't burned but nobody went inside because many were badly damaged. Another quarter of a mile into the housing that changed, dramatically.

*   *   *

"How come those aren't damaged, Harold? Well they are, but you know what I mean." Liz pointed across the wide road running across in front of the searchers. The houses on the far side had broken roof tiles and windows, but in most cases the brickwork seemed intact. Harold looked them over carefully.

"That's shrapnel, the bits of metal that were whizzing about when the Army shelled the houses near us. They've used air bursts, more or less anyway though a few shells landed." Harold pointed. "Look at the old bloodstains and clothing. Shrapnel kills people instead of chewing up the real estate. These are the ones that ran away so everyone was in the open."

"The bastards could have done that nearer to us rather than smash up all that food." Tim's scowl probably came from the pain of his wound as well as the damage to housing. At least everyone's wounds were healing now even if some would never recover the proper use of limbs or hands. The damage inflicted by baseball bats still incapacitated some, even where arms and fingers weren't broken. If the fight hadn't happened in winter with everyone muffled up in thick clothing, the injuries would have been even worse.

"The Army wanted to frighten away the closest rioters, and houses blowing up and burning does a great job." Harold had no idea of the real reason, but that sounded right. "From now on we'll be going slower because we go into houses. Double up folks, one outside the house on lookout, one to search. Put any bigger containers, especially plastic petrol cans and the like, out near the road. We'll make a run with the pickup to get them."

"Are we collecting weapons today Harold, because there's a machete and a lot of arrows here?" Holly waved the lightly rusted machete. "Though it was in this grass so not easy to see, and we'll miss some spread like this." She looked around the overgrown lawn. "There's empty bullet cases as well, and a wooden baseball bat."

"Fill your pockets with empty brass, and pick up any machetes. If we've room for the rest on the way back we'll take it." Harold headed out onto the road and stopped.

"Hold it right there. This is our place." The voice came from the houses ahead.

"Fair enough, we'll just move back a bit." Harold looked left and right. "Back into the ruins of the houses behind us, everyone, then move in closer."

A few minutes later the group gathered together. "I thought we had a mile each way from Orchard Close, Harold?" Holly glared across towards where the voice came from.

"We do, and we need it with all the close stuff being smashed. But first we find out who this is." Harold raised his voice. "What are you lot called?"

"What? Called? Who are you?"

"Orchard Close, and according to the map the Army has, this is ours."

"Army? Are you one of those gangs?" The man sounded a mix of cautious and puzzled now. "In that case, why haven't we seen you before?"

"You have, on the TV, but the Army had to move all the bodies and wouldn't let us out. You must have seen the Army?" Harold sighed. "Look, why don't you and I meet in the middle and talk instead of shouting?"

"Ooh, macho stuff. Talk loud enough so I hear," Liz grinned.

She was interrupted by the voice again. "All right. Nobody shoots, Ok?"

Harold answered the mystery man rather than Liz. "No problem because I'll be out there as well." Harold lowered his voice to answer the worried looks. "It'll be a miracle if they hit me from there with a handgun, and I'll be watching for the first hint of a rifle barrel. I want to find out how many there are." He glanced left and right at those still carrying injuries. "We're not up to a big fight, not without some reinforcements." Harold stood up and raised his voice. "Meet me in the middle of the road. Let's see you."

The man who came out of a house door wore a motorbike jacket and jeans, and carried a handgun. Harold took the gun out of the back of his belt and held it openly because they were safe here, with ruins blocking the view from the bypass even if the Army had a real sniper up there. Harold limped out as an excuse for taking his stick and as they came closer to each other the man looked at the gun, and past Harold at the ruins. "How many?"

Harold grinned. "Nine here but I can bring the rest. In fact if I pull the trigger you'd better have a lot of backup in there." He shrugged. "Anything up to sixty."

"Yeah, but at least half this lot are women, and some are wounded."

"Wounded means they all fight if necessary." Harold smirked and raised his voice, "Holly, this bloke thinks the women don't count for the macho stuff."

"We've got lamp posts if he wants a boundary line to show him different?" Holly paused. "Be really careful what you say next, mister."

"Christ, she's armed to the teeth!" The man relaxed. "Bet she's your woman, right? That's why she's got that lot."

Harold raised his voice again. "Everyone start waving weaponry because he thinks Holly is my girl."

"In your dreams. Unless that's a serious offer?" A couple of other women echoed Holly's snigger. Harold wasn't sure what people waved behind him but could see the fight go out of this bloke.

"We just want someplace to stay, right?" He looked past Harold again. "Fuck it, if we can have a woman between us we'll join up?"

"If you say that louder, these women will tie you to a lamp post and execute you." Harold smiled, "If you use crude language again it'll cost you the gun, or possibly your nuts. If you don't fancy those rules, just back off to the boundary."

"Where is the boundary?"

Harold called back and arranged for a sketch map after all the marks were transferred to another. "Now you keep a really civil tongue in your head because the last man to give Holly crap really did lose his nuts, and was alive to feel it. I also want to see all of your lot. Just outside the doors will do, so I know who to shoot if you come back. Don't do anything stupid." Harold opened his coat to show the rifle.

"Ooh, flashing your weapon, Harold?" Holly must have looked past Harold at the man and his four friends, now stepping into view, because Harold could hear the sneer without seeing it. "You'll never see the big rifle or hear the bullet coming."

"Hush Holly, that's supposed to come as a surprise."

The man shrugged. "Give us five minutes, all right, and we'll f…, be clear. We just want someplace to live."

"Then join up someplace because eventually all the enclaves will meet, and there'll be no clear space left." The man nodded acknowledgement and backed away, watching Holly rather than Harold. When Harold turned he realised why. Holly had put a real Liz special in her crossbow, with a head covered in little spines to make the bolt harder to pull out.

When the pair of them re-joined the rest, Liz gave Harold a little tap on the chest. "Not up to the usual standard." Then she turned to Holly. "I can't thump you on the chest, and anyway it isn't macho from you." Liz sniggered. "The offer certainly wasn't." Then she sobered and ignored the blushing Holly. "We should mark the boundary, without heads."

"True, we'll do it with spray paint. Everyone watch out for cans though we won't get to the border today. Today we search the next few streets properly to get a real idea of what might be left. If the electricity is on, check out the freezers." Harold sat down. "Right now we have a drink and give them chance to get clear."

*   *   *

Sometime later a distinctive burst of sound cut short the searching. "That sounds like pistols and then a shotgun, and Casper went that way. All non-fighters head back home sharpish with what we've got. Shooters come with me." A distant crack that sounded like a two-two rifle punctuated Harold's words.

"Will the others be safe without an escort?" Holly glanced at Liz while trying not to be obvious. Liz simply couldn't hit people even in self-defence.

Harold pointed. "We go back together as far as that wide road, then it's a straight run through the ruined part for them and an easy route for us towards Casper." The searchers were already gathering, coming out of houses and garages, and quickly split into two groups. "Straight back, Liz."

"I'm a mouse, and so is Hazel. We'll run." Liz shuffled the pack on her back. "All right stagger, since you've lumbered us with the loot."

"Not all of it, just enough so we can move quickly." Harold looked round. "Are you sure you'll be all right Tim?"

Tim waved his sound arm and the handgun. "The best place for defending is out here, not right on our doorstep. I'll shoot because I'm not letting anyone that close to Toyah again." While Toyah gave Tim his thank you and said goodbye Harold looked over the others. "Holly, no macho crap, and the same from you." Billy, unscathed but for small cuts and bruises, nodded and brandished his two-two rifle. "Come on, at a good fast walk." Harold set off at his best pace, and his leg wound actually made him the slowest.

*   *   *

"At least they're talking." Holly spoke quietly although the voices were still some distance, as were the occasional shots.

"Better still, shouting, so those other shots weren't our people being captured." Harold had slowed to a walk, moving along the fronts of the houses while using them and the front garden hedges and fences as cover. "Keep in tight and your heads down."

A few minutes later the shouting became clearly audible. "Just back off. You're inside our boundary." That voice definitely belonged to Casper.

A stranger's voice answered. "It ain't marked, and if you can't stop us it's not a proper boundary anyway. Give us that shotgun and you can go home."

"Not a chance. Last chance to leave or it costs you your guns."

The stranger laughed. "Fuck off. Come and get them."

"I warned you about the language. Now it'll cost you the machetes as well." Casper sounded utterly confident.

"Casper has got the macho bit right." Holly barely murmured that as she crept up close behind Harold.

"No, he's keeping them occupied until we arrive." Harold sniggered. "And he's got the macho bit right. Liz won't be happy she missed it."

"What do we do, Harold?" Holly glanced back. "What if there's too many?"

"First we find out. We'll go through here and up the backs of these houses, nice and slow because they're not attacking Casper so he's safe for now." The four of them moved up until they were level with the voices and occasional gunshots, then crept into a house and upstairs to get a decent look. Seven men, most with handguns and all carrying machetes, were in a half circle around this side of a small supermarket's car park. Movement, and then shouting from inside, explained how Casper had been caught out.

Casper was still keeping the men occupied, though that couldn't last forever. "Time's nearly up. What's your name so we can put it on the marker?" Even as Casper spoke a man halfway round the arc fired at the supermarket, while one at the end nearest to Harold moved in a bit closer. Sooner or later the gangsters would be close enough to rush and Casper might not have enough fighters to stop seven. A voice from further across spoke but Harold couldn't see who. "Just keep yapping. I'm gonna really enjoy explaining our rules to you if you survive."

Harold put his lips close to Holly's ear. "Can you hit the second one along, in front of next door?"

Holly tapped her crossbow. "Yes, with this."

"Find a good spot here or next door and wait. When you hear my rifle, nail him. Then if the bloke this end doesn't surrender when asked, do your best with the pistol but only use six." Harold thought that the incoming would keep the bloke's head down even if Holly didn't hit him with half a clip.

"I'll want lessons after this, with a handgun." Holly flashed a quick smile.

"Done. Now keep your head down and get in place. Nice and quiet." Harold beckoned Tim and Billy close and spoke to them. The three of them left and one at a time crept into a house.

Harold played fair because he still didn't like shooting people in the back without warning. He had a clear view of the speaker now, a medium height, slim built man with short light brown hair and dressed in a pair of overalls. Someone had written Bugatti across the back in thick black marker. "Oy, Bugatti. Stay very still."

Bugatti didn't, he dropped, rolled and tried to bring his pistol up and round but the roll took him into a doorway. Harold cursed silently and shot the next man along in the neck as he tried to aim at where the voice came from. Moments later there was a short scream from back towards Holly, the crack of another two-two rifle, and a half dozen shots from a handgun. Then two more handguns as Holly and Billy joined in and there was more screaming. Harold shot at the man on the far end as he reared up trying to find a target with his shotgun.

"Cease fire." Harold bellowed and his people did, though one of those below carried on so Harold shot him through the wrist he had sticking out of cover. The gunman dropped his weapon and started rolling about and clutching his wound. "Surrender or we kill the rest."

"You'll do it anyway." Harold could see movement in the shadows, but not a target. "At least if you come to get us we'll make you bleed."

"No Bugatti, but at least two will bleed out if you don't give it up soon."

"Shoot them Soldier Boy, right through the eyes. They shot two of ours without warning." Casper sounded mad as hell.

"Soldier Boy? Hang on. What happens if we give in?" Bugatti suddenly sounded a lot less belligerent.

Harold shrugged mentally. That name was starting to be an actual asset. "Casper? How are our people?" If they were dead Harold would take his time and kill this lot. A voice at the back of his head pointed out it wasn't necessary but right now Harold didn't care, if he'd lost more people.

"Not good, but they should be all right if we get them both home. The bleeding has been stopped. That lot opened up without warning."

"Are you willing to let them go? We've killed some of them and wounded most of the others." Harold had calmed down a bit, and wounded survivors might be a better message.

"The survivors pay a fine for foul language. Especially him, the one you're talking to." Casper laughed and Harold could hear that some was sheer relief. "Have you got Holly with you?"

"Hi Casper." The wounded man on the end looked towards her voice but made no move towards a weapon. He concentrated on cutting open the bloodstained sleeve of his jacket.

"Enough chat. You heard them Bugatti, and now you know you're surrounded. Surrender and pay the fine and you can go home. Otherwise I work my way round while this lot keep you pinned and shoot you all dead, one at a time." Harold tried to see how many were left alive.

The one he'd shot first stopped kicking and gurgling. Both the wrist shot man and the man on the far side, the man with a shotgun, had dropped their weapons and were nursing hands. The one with a crossbow bolt in his back wasn't moving while the second of Holly's targets concentrated on trying to staunch his wound rather than shooting. Tim had either hit his man or scared him half to death since the man crouched with his hands on his head. Billy had definitely hit his man, leaving the bloke doubled up round a gut wound.

Harold laughed, though it came out a bit forced. "You're the only one not wounded, Bugatti. I won't even have to shoot most of the rest if you leave it a bit."

"Give it up Bugatti, for fuck's sake. I'm bleeding to death!" The youth in front of Holly looked up towards where Holly's voice had come from. "The bitch is going to nail me with a crossbow."

"That's another fine for foul language." Holly sounded absolutely serious. "Shall I finish this one, Soldier Boy?"

"F…bloody hell, no! I surrender." His handgun clattered on the tarmac and then the young man in front of Tim threw a machete out into the road. The shotgun at the other end flew through the air followed by another machete.

"Fucking pussies!" A few moments silence followed. "All right, we surrender, but Cadillac is going to carve your lot a new one."

"Cadillac? You must be Hot Rods and so you know about Orchard Close and our boundary. Step out with your hands on your head. The rest of you, get rid of any other weapons now." Bugatti looked furious when he did step out of the doorway, but he stood very still until Tim had searched him.

Holly came downstairs to keep an eye on her second victim, while Billy kept him covered and advised him to keep very still. She hacked off a branch and threw it to the white-faced youth so he could tighten the cloth around his arm. "Here. I don't want you to bleed out until you've paid the fine." She kept her crossbow on him while he tightened the impromptu bandage and got to his feet.

Harold and Billy came down to join the rest after Casper and Alfie came out and pointed weapons at the Hot Rod survivors. Eventually five Hot Rods stood, disarmed, in the middle of the supermarket car park with the gut-shot man on the ground nearby. Bugatti gestured to him. "What about Razzle?"

"He can go to the Army? They might fix him." Casper grinned and waved his machete. "Or I can put him out of his misery." Casper had definitely cheered up a bit at the sight of the opposition, especially the corpses.

"You've got bandages." Bugatti gestured to Casper's wounded, who were both bandaged up and one could even walk. Zach would need a ride home because he'd been shot in the leg.

"Yes, we've got bandages. We found them in our supermarket, in our territory. You can use bandages from Hot Rod territory." Alfie sounded determined. A ninth Hot Rod out in the ruins had Alfie's two-two bullets in him, and one reason Harold's second victim had quit fighting after a hand wound might be the bullet already in his shoulder. Alfie pointed his two-two at the gut-shot man. "I can stop him moaning if it annoys you?"

"Shit no! Where do we give him to the Army?" Bugatti looked at the firearms. "How do we get near the Army?"

"Just over half a mile that way." Harold pointed. "We'll have plenty of crossbows to keep you honest, and even more behind the wall. Now pick him up and let's go." Bugatti and Tim's target, who had been unhurt but terrified by the bullets from behind, picked Razzle up. He screamed once and then mercifully passed out. When a pickup arrived carrying Orchard Close reinforcements because of the shooting, Razzle went in the back.

*   *   *

"Hey there, Army!"

"Do not step into the exclusion zone."

Harold cupped his hands and yelled back. "Tell the sergeant we found a wounded man and we don't want him."

After a short pause the bullhorn bellowed. "Who is he?"

"A stray, sergeant. We found him out in the ruins." Harold tried to sound serious. "He's been shot somehow."

"Nothing to do with that little fire fight we heard a bit back?" Sarge did sound amused.

"No idea. The TV said anyone who was seriously injured could be taken for treatment, but wouldn't come back." Harold did wonder, after the comment about the orange-clad prisoners, if Razzle would be shot out of hand.

"Yes, if he recovers he'll work on the farms to pay for the treatment. Will he do that?"

"That or die, Sarge, he's got a gut injury."

"Send him up and make sure whoever comes is very well behaved and clearly unarmed."

"No problem." Harold turned to Bugatti and the other uninjured man. "Strip to your boxers and carry him up." Bugatti stood hesitating for long moments, but stripped eventually. The pair left Razzle laid on the road outside the sandbags and came back with their hands on their heads.

"You can get dressed and go home now." Harold pointed south. "If I find you within a mile of here again, I'll kill you."

"Cadillac will burn this place." Bugatti still seemed confident.

"Tell him to come and talk first; it'll save him serious losses." Harold stood and watched the four leave, and hoped this Cadillac would actually agree to talk before shooting.

*   *   *

A familiar voice shouted "Harold, Harold!"

Harold put down the gun he was cleaning, stretched wearily and stood up. "Yes Hazel."

"There's a posh car at the entrance and a man wants to talk to the Soldier Boy. He's got a crossbow and a machete and a great big man with him." Harold put a handgun into the back of his belt, under his jacket, and opened the door to leave his little gun room. Then smiled because Hazel stood right in front of him, more or less hopping from foot to foot.

"Just let me lock the study up." Harold set off down the street with Hazel still hopping about impatiently. "Ask Casper and Emmy to join me please, Hazel. Then you keep clear in case there's trouble." Hazel ran off at top speed and Harold shook his head and smiled.

At the gate Alfie came out of the guardhouse, number one. "He's got those overalls on, and the bloke with him would make a perfect boyfriend for Liz, or Casper."

"Thanks Alfie. Keep an eye open for any others while I talk, all right?" Alfie went back indoors and Harold stood on his box to look over the barricade. Hazel was right, a big posh car with a white cloth tied to the aerial sat at the end of the access road and there were four men round it. Cooper pointed at Harold and spoke to the short, squat man in the middle, a young man, maybe in his mid-twenties with a bald head. When he moved Harold got the impression that his girth wasn't flab. Behind him stood a man who couldn't be far short of seven feet and built like the proverbial outhouse.

"Are you Soldier Boy?"

"If necessary. You must be Cadillac. How can I help you?"

"I am Cadillac and you can give me back my property. What you took from the men who were trespassing." Cadillac stood relaxed, as if he'd made a perfectly reasonable request.

"Your men opened fire without warning. When they were told the rules and where the border is, they continued to use foul language and shoot at my people." Harold kept his own voice calm and reasonable as well, because this wasn't a hopped-up nutter demanding this and that.

"Foul language?" Apparently shooting wasn't significant.

"Yes. Please be warned. We do not tolerate foul language and you will be fined." Harold looked up at the houses on each side to show how he intended enforcing his rules.

"Yes, we have rules as well. May I come closer?" Cadillac paused. "Without breaking any rules?"

"You can come inside, if you disarm." Negotiating would be a lot easier without the Army listening.

"I would want a hostage out here, just in case there is an accident. The big bald man or the black woman with the startling hairstyle." Cadillac sounded as if hostages were expected and he'd got some real information about who lived here, and who was senior in a way. "I will bring my bodyguard, but he will disarm as well?"

"I'll go." Casper had come up behind Harold. "One of that lot would say the wrong thing to Emmy and she'd kill them all."

"I'd leave the biggest one for you in case he's gay." Emmy had arrived as well.

Harold ignored her and called to Cadillac. "You get Casper and he meets you halfway." Harold saw the man turn and speak to the others before answering.

"My men will be polite, and no foul language." With that he started up the approach.

"Cripes, where are the car keys?" Harold looked each way because they were kept in one of the houses.

"I'll sort it. Do I have to disarm?" Emmy had come loaded for bear, or Cadillacs.

"No, because this is our home. I want Alfie in the room with your shotgun, Casper, because that big bloke would take some stopping." By the time Jon came out to drive the 'door' out of the way Emmy had collected Alfie, and Casper had handed over the shotgun without the Army seeing it. "Keep your machete Casper." The door opened and Casper set off. He looked up and spoke briefly to the big man and carried on down while Cadillac and his man came in.

The polite greeting included handshakes for Emmy as well but Cadillac's eyes were everywhere, weighing and assessing. Harold took the two men into number three as he had with Kabir. Cadillac didn't seem startled by Emmy being armed or perturbed by Alfie standing in one corner with a shotgun though he did double-take when Holly turned up with the beer, also armed to the teeth.

"I've heard about you. The survivors are torn between being in love and being terrified."

"She has that effect on most men, although those who get to know her aren't terrified." Harold glanced at the big man. "I would have thought your bodyguard is more terrifying."

"Big Mack? He's a pussy-cat once you know him. Aren't you?" Cadillac smiled at the big man, who hadn't spoken up to now.

"Unless you mess with Cadillac. Then I 'ave to 'it yer."

Harold smiled. "I'd best not mess with Cadillac then. Now, you wanted to discuss the fracas between your people and mine." Harold wanted to swear because the suave bastard had got him doing it, treating this as some sort of almost amicable meeting. Though maybe it would be if the bloke didn't push too hard.

"Yes. I might have got a garbled version. You say that the weapons were taken as a fine for trespass, foul language and opening fire without warning." Cadillac smiled but not with his eyes. "Bugatti didn't realise he was trespassing. You haven't put up any markers." He looked round the smiling faces. "What did I say?"

"The only time we put up a marker we used three bodies tied to lamp posts and nine heads." Harold shrugged. "Since we fought off the mob the Army haven't allowed us out because of the weapons in the ruins. Today they let us out again and we found two parties of trespassers."

"Two?"

"The others accepted their warning and the rules and left without trouble." Harold smiled. "I'm sure you wouldn't have wanted Bugatti as a marker?"

"That would have led to a different sort of visit, with rather more men." Cadillac sat in silence for a few moments. "I can accept a fine but the amount seems excessive. Can we run through what happened from your point of view?"

Harold, with some help from Alfie, got it all straight. When they'd finished Cadillac took a drink of his beer and thought for a few minutes. "So you warned Bugatti before you fired, and he fired without warning. I must have a chat about him being truthful and wasting ammunition even if it causes, um, unpleasantness." Cadillac glanced at the women with a little smile as he avoided his first choice of words. "Very well, I can understand why you need some recompense. All of the firearms is excessive, especially since you took all the ammunition and machetes. After all, you killed four of mine."

"Three. Razzle was alive when last seen." Harold found himself in a genuine negotiation over the relative values of a fine for shooting without warning, trespass and foul language. Cadillac definitely rated dead men well below getting his firearms back and didn't mind spending time haggling. He even bought beer for his other two men and Casper since the negotiation took so long. Cadillac seemed smooth, but Harold watched his eyes and the hot spark of anger that came and went. The gang leader tried to appear urbane but violence lurked, and not all that far behind the façade.

Eventually Harold kept three handguns, a crossbow, and the machetes and ammunition from the dead and Razzle. Holly's wounded victim paid a fine, his ammunition, for shooting at Casper's party, and his machete for foul language. Bugatti paid the same fine. All the knives were personal weapons and everyone lost those, "for being so bloody stupid and getting captured or killed." Cadillac really did consider all the rest his personal property and assured Harold the men in question would repay the losses, though he seemed quite relaxed about ammunition. A worried Harold had to assume the Hot Rods had plenty.

Once Cadillac had his machete again the gang boss paused at the gate. "With you being Army and such a good shot, how come you wounded those two instead of killing them?" From the way the gang leader's interest sharpened, that wasn't a casual remark.

Harold thought for a moment about how to reply, about what Cadillac might be trying to find out. "I killed the first one because he was aiming at me and too close. I took a snapshot at the man with a shotgun to stop him firing and knew I'd get either his face or hand. The other man was aiming at someone else but I could see his hand and wrist." Harold put absolute sincerity in his voice. "If they pull that stunt again, I will shoot them dead."

"You really can shoot then. I'll tell Samuel he is lucky you were in a hurry, and a finger is better than an eye. I intended coming to see you anyway after hearing from Kev and Cooper, because we need a proper meeting soon. One between you and I and all the neighbours this side just to make sure we understand each other's rules. It will be cheaper." Cadillac looked up at the bypass. "Away from nosy people with big guns." He held out a hand. "Not exactly a pleasure, but the beer is a pleasant surprise." Big Mack carried a crate under one arm, paid for with coupons already bearing the second thumbprint.

Casper set off as soon as the Hot Rod pair cleared the gate and they crossed halfway. When he arrived back Casper wanted a serious word, right now. "They trade women, I mean they swap them with other gangs. Those are seriously nasty people Harold." Then Casper sniggered. "I thought they'd choke when I asked about the big bloke, if he was straight or gay. I doubt there are any gays in their lot at all from the answer, though neither actually insulted me straight out."

Harold held out the coupons Cadillac paid with. "He had a pocket full of these, coupons with the second print already on and several different names. Protection money. He acts really smooth but that bloke is a nasty piece of work." Harold scowled. "Worse, he seems to have lots of ammo. What he gave up just now didn't bother him, but was a significant increase for us. We don't want a war with that lot."

"Yes, and I did think he might do that, start a real fight, when he found out Holly really did kill one of his men. He's got a lot of control but I reckon the Cad has a hell of a temper. The nasty, vicious type and he really doesn't like women who fight." Emmy looked towards the gate, towards the sound of the car turning and driving away. "That Bugatti bloke is in a lot of trouble, because he'll take it out on him." She smiled. "Couldn't happen to a better bloke according to Holly."

"We will have to take some precautions before the meeting. Just in case he decides on some payback." The rest agreed with Harold, and also about not wanting to stand around any longer nattering in the cold.

*   *   *

The next morning both pickups and the minibus came round onto the road because the boundaries needed marking as soon as possible, even if that cost scarce petrol and diesel. By then Orchard Close had a logo. After tea the previous evening an intense discussion started over different logos, from an apple and pear through to a skull with one eye and a rifle. Daisy wanted to know what all the drawings were for, since she wasn't asked to join in. "A picture to show that we are Orchard Close."

"That's easy." Daisy picked up a marker, drew two parallel lines with a cloud at the top, and a few circles in the cloud. "There, an apple tree. Draw lots and it's an orchard." She looked puzzled when the five adults burst into laughter.

Over the following days, all along the border, walls and houses sported a spray-painted tree with Orchard Close one side and Keep Out the other. While doing that the small community began to get an idea of what they had claimed, or been given. The spray painters were also realising that Orchard Close itself was the only part that still had both electricity and water, so there were no other inhabitants.

No permanent ones anyway. Three men and a woman, all loners, ran away when they saw a group from Orchard Close. From the state of their houses, those people were living rough and scavenging what they could. After the first loner ran away the Orchard Close team investigated and found warm ashes in the grate. After that the guards looked out for the occasional thin lines of smoke that could be seen first thing in the morning, showing where more loners had lit fires. The marking and mapping groups checked any such smoke immediately.

Harold had stopped going on the salvage and mapping runs to concentrate on sorting through and where possible, reloading the amount of used brass being found. The much less frequent live rounds were even more welcome. A radio call from Emmy disturbed him from the work. She had checked on reported smoke while heading out on yet another mapping expedition and needed Harold and his rifle.

Harold used his pickup so it was only minutes before Emmy flagged him down. She pointed at a pair of semi-detached houses. "Someone is still in there. Whoever it is started to leave through the back, realised the scavenger line could see him, and ducked back inside. Did you bring it?" Emmy looked as Harold opened the rear cab door enough to show his big rifle and smiled. All the groups now called Harold at any sign of trouble. There would be no more relying on seeing a throat or other soft spot.

"Do you know if there's more than one?" Harold tried to see himself, but the houses appeared to be deserted. "Which one are they in?"

"The one with a decent roof." That meant only a few broken tiles, whereas the other house had a large patch of tiling smashed and the felt beneath ripped open. "Do you want me to call out? A woman might be better." Emmy scowled. "And if they're the other sort they might come after me, and then you can just shoot them." News of the offer to join up for a woman, and then Casper's assessment of how Hot Rods treated women, made a few of the Orchard Close females almost eager to shoot someone.

"Send Suzie out. You'll just scare them, or they'll stagger out love-struck and we'll get no sense." Harold settled down with the rifle where he could see the front and side. "Who is round the back?"

"Alfie and Billy with a little rifle and pistols." Emmy set off and a few minutes later Suzie walked out into the front garden across the street from the strangers.

"Hello there. We know you are in there. Please explain who you are and why you are hiding."

A man's voice answered. "Go away."

"Come out and talk to me please." Suzie stood poised, ready to duck, even though there had been no sign of a weapon or even movement.

Or not until the door cracked open. "Then will you go?"

"No, we live here. Our people are looking for food so we can't leave strangers here without knowing who you are." Suzie flipped her hood back and opened her coat. "See, no weapons." That also emphasised Suzie's sex, if her skirt and voice hadn't got the message across.

A grey haired and bearded head came around the door and looked up and down the street. "Who else is there?" He looked more carefully at Suzie. "Can you show me your upper arms, please?"

"Really? All right. I'm not a druggy." Suzie took off her coat. "Be quick because its cold." She pulled the sleeves of her jumper up for a long moment, then pulled them back down before putting her coat back on. "What was that for?"

The man came out a little bit further which showed that he held an axe, one of the big fire-fighting types. "Bruising. How are the women treated where you come from?"

"Well Harold doesn't allow foul language, or abuse, if that's what you mean." Suzie sounded unsure. "We can carry a weapon if we want to? What do you mean?"

Harold knew what the man's problem was now. He clicked his radio. "Emmy, show him how well armed the women are. He's got someone he cares about in there, a girl or woman." Harold knew when Emmy showed herself by the expression on the man's face, at first wary and then a small smile.

He relaxed and came onto the doorstep. "Who are you people, and who is in charge?" He frowned. "What will it cost to get a woman one of those crossbows?"

Harold stood, leaving the rifle where it was. "Nothing. Any of them can carry one if they will use it. May we come in and meet your family?" He smiled. "I'll send a crossbow in first if you like."

The man looked at Harold for a long time, weighing that up. "No need, though I'd like those two ladies to come in first please. Just so my, um, family understand." Emmy and Suzie walked across the street and he showed them in, then a few minutes later Emmy waved Harold over.

The man stopped Harold in the hallway, though he could hear Emmy and Suzie talking to someone in the nearby rooms. "Hello, I'm Barry, and my granddaughters are through there. We've been running for three days. Some men called Geek Freeks came to our houses and said we had to pay protection. They also told us they'd want some women." Barry gripped his axe tighter and Harold gave him time to come up with what bothered him. "One of them came back and tried to take Matracia, Matti. He grabbed her and then threatened her with a machete when she pulled free." Barry sighed and looked down at the axe. "I had to stop him."

"Did you kill him?"

"No! Or at least I think he'll live. I don't know."

"That's a pity because sooner or later that one might see her and try for payback. You'll have to stay out of sight until your daughters either grow or cut their hair and dye it to look different." Harold smiled. "You could shave off the beard and then dye your hair. How come you had that handy?" Harold nodded towards the axe.

"Oh, well, I'm a fireman. Was a fireman, and on the way out of the city the lads at the station left me some presents. Matti has its baby brother through there, and Dolly, Doll, has the man's machete." He gave a big wracking sigh. "I doubt either of them could use the things, but they feel a bit better that way. With all that, I'd appreciate you being sort of careful through there. Matti is a mess because he, he handled her and she thought I'd run off."

"No need for me to go in. Grab your gear and come back with us, and Emmy will explain on the way. She's the one with the signature haircut." Harold clapped Barry on the shoulder and went back out. He stayed with the mapping group while Barry and his family came out with their bags and headed back to Orchard Close. Doll, the one with the machete and a cowboy hat, had already started an intense discussion with Emmy.

*   *   *

Doll, Matti and Barry were perfectly happy to adjust their appearance so they could slip into the life of Orchard Close anonymously. The two women proved to be enthusiastic about Christmas, and keen on gathering up any coloured lights discovered on scavenger runs. The streets of Orchard Close started to take on a festive air as residents put up a string of coloured glows either inside their houses or on the outside walls and fences.

That ended suddenly and brutally.

"Thank all and every God for that." A bullet or bullets had broken the window, but not hurt anyone. "Have you any idea why?"

"None." Suzie looked understandably shaken. "I'd just finished spraying Merry Christmas on the window with a can of snow and there were bangs and the whole window came in. There were more bangs, shots, and I think I heard a window break down the street."

"Keep your curtains shut and the light out and I'll get it boarded up straight away." Harold looked down at the glass on the carpet. "Do you want help with this before Sukie gets near it?"

"No thanks. She's fast asleep in spite of this." Suzie paused. "The light wasn't on, just the Christmas lights around the window. It's more festive like that."

The second and third broken windows also had Christmas lights around them, and Harold sent messages to everyone else who had done the same. The flashing and coloured lights that had been brightening Orchard Close went off one by one, leaving the estate dark again. "Do you think it was the Geeks? Because of Barry and his lasses?" Casper held the hammer he used to fasten up plywood as if hefting his machete.

"I doubt it. We'll look in the morning but I don't fancy going out there just now." Harold looked at the other two groups hammering away. "It might be Geeks, or Cadillac because we fined him, or just nastiness. Damn! People were just cheering up a bit."

"They can still put lights up indoors, and we can find extra curtains so nothing shows?" Casper turned to the boarding again. "Though I really would like to find who it was."

The morning showed a scattering of 9 mm brass casings where someone with a handgun had sprayed shots at the windows. They'd even used clumps of rotting curtain to make a rest. Harold made sure the sentries with two-two rifles knew that next time they didn't wait for a proper target, just shot towards the muzzle flashes. Harold had lectured everyone about wasting ammo so Billy had held his fire, hoping for a decent target.

* * *

The intense young woman with straight black hair, Gayle, Harold thought, looked apprehensive and ready to burst into tears. "I really am sorry. It's my fault but I'm not really trained so I never thought about it until all the wounded were screaming and crying and there was nothing to stop the pain." She took a breath. "Now, with the shooting, I just realised it could happen again."

"Slow up and calm down. Have a cuppa first if you like. Gayle, isn't it?"

"Yes. I came in with Conn just before the big fight. I saw your wounded all patched up and thought that Patricia had all that sorted out." Gayle sighed and sat down on the armchair Harold was pointing at.

"Tea or coffee?" Sharyn, in the dining room with Daisy, had heard voices and come through for the hostess bit.

"Coffee? Please? Black with one sugar?" Gayle sighed again. "I suppose the rest of us will have to learn to manage without coffee soon."

"All of us will unless we scavenge or grow enough food. Though everyone should be able to buy a little if they consider coffee a priority." Harold smiled. "Some people will prefer chocolate or cigarettes."

"But will we be able to afford coffee? I suppose it depends on how much rent we pay to make sure you've got enough." Gayle seemed suddenly worried by what she'd said, or maybe the bitter tone it was delivered in. "Sorry, we don't mind because we're grateful."

"But you live rent free? We explained there's no arrangement like the Minutemen. Those who can will fight, those who cook or sew or garden do that. What did you do before the mob?" Already before the mob or before the crash were phrases to cover any sort of horror during the last half year or so.

"But." She paused. "Someone said that, you know, those fighting would have to be fit so they'd be well fed." Gayle shuffled in her chair, definitely uneasy.

"If that was a fighter I'll have a word because we aren't allowing that nonsense in here." Harold grinned. "Berry will slap them and Emmy will hold them while she does. Is that what worried you?"

"No. Yes, some of it. What happens, how will all the food be divided up if there's not enough grown? Will those who came last have to buy their own anyway?" Gayle looked up as Sharyn brought her a coffee. "Thank you."

"Good question little Bro. How do we sort that out?" Sharyn patted Harold on the back and looked at Gayle. "Sometimes we have to find out there's a problem before setting him on it."

"I never thought about it. Things have been a bit busy." Harold frowned. "I'd better find out if Hilda has proper lists of what we've got, and who we've got." He looked at Sharyn. "You told me I didn't have to do all this organising crap, Sharyn."

"You don't idiot. You just have to find the right people and delegate."

"Good, I delegate you to find the right people." Harold grinned at Gayle. "You and Gayle."

"What? No, nobody will listen to me. Lillian and Janine and Pippa will all be better at it." Gayle's worried face brightened. "I'll be too busy scavenging."

"Sharyn will need those names, and will no doubt find some more and then wash her hands of the whole thing." Harold's eyes narrowed. "Scavenging? I thought you were helping Patricia with the wounded."

Gayle went back to worried. "But you won't know if the drugs are the right ones, or the equipment, or if it's the right gas. Ah, right. That's what I came about." Gayle took a deep breath. "We need Midazolam or Diazepam so I can make people not care if they are hurt, sort of semi-asleep. Not right out because I'm not trained and might kill someone, but close enough to help their pain?" She glanced at Harold, her face tight. "I should have thought about it."

"Why, since you aren't a medic?" Harold knew because everyone was asked. Patricia, the trainee nurse, repeatedly complained about being well out of her depth when treating hacking and gunshot wounds.

"I'm a dental trainee. I helped with administering IVs and did some under supervision, and know the theory. If we can find the opiates as well I can take the pain away for the bad ones, if it happens again. I'm trained to use the dental equipment if we find some that works?" Gayle was back to nervous and apologetic. "I'm sorry, I never thought because my training isn't for medical, for gunshots?"

"You didn't think, I didn't think, nobody did? I've had treatment at a dentist and barely remember any discomfort, yet it never crossed my mind. Just another thing nobody put together." Harold's eyes sharpened. "Can you actually fix teeth?"

"Maybe. I can manage simple fillings or pull a tooth, but I'm not so sure about some of the other work. I was training, not qualified." Gayle smiled, just a little one. "Mr. Trentham at the college would go crazy."

"Mr. Trentham would be proud of you and grateful if he'd got toothache. You might not get any drugs because they'll be looted, Gayle, but the equipment would be a start." Harold grinned. "You've got out of food rationing and into midnight sneaking around because we'll probably end up in someone else's territory."

"Have you got something to open a safe, a proper built in one?" Gayle's smile became a bit more confident. "Even if the rioters stole the ready-use drugs, our dentist at least had a second safe for most of the serious drugs. Too many dentists were being robbed so the extra safe went in, new regulations. If someone broke in they tripped alarms, but also found a really obvious safe, the old one." She sighed. "If they got into that there wasn't much, and the police would be getting near. That's what I was told, anyway."

"Let's hope we can find some dentists nearby in yellow pages, and they haven't been burned. Then hope that brute force with a variety of implements will open the safe." Harold mentally berated himself again. Dentists and how to share crops, another two he'd missed; though as yet there weren't any crops. No toothache either, as far as he knew.

Gayle's smile brightened. "The new safes were fireproof. We might even find laughing gas if the looters missed the gas store, though we'll need an unburned dental surgery for equipment."

Harold smiled. "Now the Army are done and we can scavenge again, be prepared for long cold nights trudging through ruins." Harold would risk some trespass so he didn't have to hear Patricia setting bones and cleaning bullet wounds with only booze to dull the pain. Twice was enough for any lifetime.

So once again he crept through the ruins in the night, eyes and ears peeled, and crawled home just before dawn, shattered. Gayle turned out to be right, and he brought back both drugs and equipment. Carrying the dental equipment and gas bottles through the night while trying to be both quiet and stealthy reminded Harold of those games shows that used to be on TV, though he didn't fancy the penalties if he failed this game. Harold did get a good night's sleep eventually so he'd be awake for shopping.

*   *   *

The shopping trip to the mart ended up sort of deja vu. "Ten percent tax to use this aisle." This yob and his two friends had also chosen the meat aisle. He openly waved a machete and both his friends had sheath knives out.

Harold swung the almost empty Bergen off his back and held it in front of him, then pulled out Sandy's latest brainwave. "There's eight of us and we've all got these, so no tax."

"He'll stick it up your ass if you keep trying."

The youth ignored Emmy and stared at Harold's weapon. "What the hell is that?" He grinned. "It's wood so I'll chop clean through it."

"It's teak so you won't. Worse than that, you might not think much to the point but it will blind you, or mash your nuts." Harold grinned. "This is the same size truncheon that the British Bobby used for a hundred years and it'll lay you out cold." He wasn't sure about that but knew the original Bobby's truncheon wasn't all that big.

The length of teak taken from an old banister felt reassuringly heavy for its size. Only about forty centimetres long with an oval cross-section, the fat knife shape had a taped grip and the other end did have a sort of point. A wooden point that Sandy told them might not break the skin. The recipients, Harold among them, had been dubious. After everyone had smacked an innocent piece of padded timber and realised what sort of blow could be delivered, confidence soared. Being unarmed at the mart when the yobs had blades really had been worrying everyone from Orchard Close.

Jon gained a lot of credit for volunteering to test Sandy's theory. He put one of the weapons into each boot, under his jeans, and went through the Army checkpoint long before the rest. As Sandy had told them, the wand didn't pick up the wood and the weapon was thin enough not to show like a baseball bat would. Then other men carried more weapons through for the women as well, since if anyone had to go to a camp nobody wanted a woman there. Once off the bypass and out of sight of the Army, they'd shared.

The yob swung and Harold used the Bergen to fend off the machete, then kicked at his shins. Harold jabbed but missed his eye and while the yob ducked Billy and Alfie beat on his machete arm and he dropped the weapon. Harold put a foot on the blade and all three yobs backed off, one of the knifemen with blood trickling down his head. Then they whirled and fled. "Hey it worked. We just kept beating like you said and they backed off." Billy sounded surprised.

Harold turned to see what the steady repetition of cripes meant, and found Jon holding his arm where a knife had got him. "Cripes?" Sal smiled as she splashed watered disinfectant on the cut and started bandaging.

"If I say what I mean you'll slap me." Jon hissed as the disinfectant bit. "Cripes, cripes, cripes."

Sal finished and then kissed the bandage. "There you go."

"I'm sure he hit me in the face." Jon grinned.

"Fat chance." Sal grinned back. "You should buy mistletoe before getting in strife if you expect that sort of thing. Anyway, it's not that bad because your coat stopped a good bit of it. Harold's rucksack thing got cut worse."

"Only on top." Harold picked up the machete. "This should stop any more trouble while we shop. Let's get the meat."

"You mean the dog chews." The complaint was one they all had, the dried meat had to be sawed or snipped into bits and then used in stew to make it palatable. The meat paste had more taste, but the flavours on the tubes were more ambition than an accurate description. Spam turned out to be, remarkably, quite a treat compared to the others. At least Holly's traps were producing rabbits again, and cat and rat for Lucky the Labrador. Rascal, Hilda's ancient poodle, would soon run out of dog food and move onto rat.

After shopping Harold tried to give the machete to the store while paying for his purchases. After several attempts to get a non-standard response Harold decided the voice had to be a recording and gave up. He considered sticking the thing inside his Bergen since those weren't scanned on the way back, but daren't risk it. He called out to one of the soldiers on the bypass. "Hey, can we turn this in?"

"What do you mean?" The soldier raised his rifle. "You can't bring that on here."

"I don't want to. I found it and want to give the damn thing to the Army." Harold held the machete out to the side in plain view.

"Why?"

"So the bloke I took it off doesn't have another go?"

"Hang on." Hang on meant wait until the soldier shouted to the side and a sergeant came out. After a bit of muttering the sergeant came three steps down the ramp.

"Are you serious? Chuck it into the ruins." He pointed at the row of houses on the opposite side of the road to the Mart. "If you step on the access with it we'll shoot you."

"I'll take it." At the interruption Harold looked back and up at a mart guard on the nearest the tower. "Poke it through the mesh and prop it against the bottom of the tower. It'll make a good souvenir." The man chuckled. "I'll chuck you a couple of fags?" Harold shrugged and handed the weapon over since he really didn't want the previous owner getting the damn thing back. The cigarettes really had value since tobacco commanded a high price in the mart. The few smokers in Orchard Close were deep into withdrawal as they gave up. At least the difference between the mart guard and the Army's reaction was a better subject on the way back than either Jon's wound or the depressing lack of Christmas treats for sale. There weren't even any Christmas crackers or trimmings!

*   *   *

When Harold's shoppers arrived home, Kabir had already had a beer and bought a crate with coupons though he left soon after as his group had set off earlier this time. The GOFS 'soldier' already knew about machetes inside the mart. "We've been wondering about running a convoy along the border between the Hot Rods and the Murphy's, a group we've come across nearer the city centre. There's a decent road that's their border so really doesn't belong to either. Then we could go armed."

"Will the two gangs allow it?" Harold though about what he'd seen of Cadillac and didn't believe the gang boss would like armed convoys on his borders.

"They aren't exactly friends with each other so it'll only be one that shoots, and the other might back us up then. We'll let both know we come in peace." He grinned. "But shoot to kill." Kabir had seen the paintwork on the minibus. "If I'm not here next time, that's what we've done. If I'm back the time after that, we got shot up and won't be trying again."

"Maybe you can arrange something at the big meeting with Cadillac?" Harold wondered if that had been a Caddi windup, or if the Hot Rod boss really wanted a meeting.

"Yeah. He says you'll be there."

"That depends on where there is." Harold scowled. "I'm not keen on anywhere Cadillac picks because we had some strife. He might want payback."

"Everyone's had strife with Cadillac but Gofannon reckons the Hot Rods don't want a war with any of us. Not until Cadillac is sure the rest won't join in to slap him down, so some sort of proper treaty would be handy. How about that traffic island up the road for a meeting place? It's a straight run to there for any of us including the Geek Freeks if you give them safe passage along your road." Kabir shrugged. "It's also near enough the Army so nobody will start a war, and far enough so a couple of shots and carrying guns will be no problem."

"A couple of shots?"

Kabir grinned. "Didn't you know? Cadillac reckons he wants to see you shoot, because he can't decide if you wounded his blokes on purpose or missed." He sat forward a bit. "Can you shoot?"

Harold laughed. "Make sure you come to the party, and stick to the dress code."

"Oh yes." Kabir touched his knife hilt. "With Caddi there, I'll probably go over the top to be on the safe side."

*   *   *

"We wish you a Merry Christmas." The Orchard Close Christmas Eve carol singers were definitely dedicated because despite the cold the women were only wearing tight jumpers, jeans and trainers as well as tinsel and a selection of greenery. The clothing worked and after giving the soldiers a twirl the six of them were allowed to take hot chips and beer up without a search, though the contraband had to be confiscated by a grinning pair of privates. The sergeant made sure the squaddies refused the waved mistletoe but didn't mind a bit of repartee. When the six retreated, hi-fiving, sarge relaxed enough to allow all the soldiers to wave.

The dance that evening included Christmas music from the TV though the picture faced the wall, and someone turned the sound off whenever a statement tried to tell them all how lucky they were. After a monotonous onslaught of assurances followed by examples of violent suppression of riots, nobody trusted the TV any more. MP4 players filled in the gaps as everyone found either festive or dance numbers in their stored music. The first few were fast, but soon the mood quietened, with more slow numbers.

The girl club had put on their party frocks, but that wild edge from Halloween and Guy Fawkes had gone. "We're all a bit down." Liz claimed her wimp dance early, allegedly before the rush. "Not me of course because I'm a callous bitch, but the rest are. This is the first Christmas for those who lost someone in the crash so it's still hurting, and tomorrow will be rough. We've banned serious drinking because soused and sobbing revellers doesn't help the mood. One or two have gone the other way and decided that now might be the time to move on." She sniggered. "As you might find out."

"I'm not following waving anything into dark places."

"I'll tell them to pull out all the light bulbs so it's all dark. Most have dressed down to lull you blokes into a sense of security, because this is their chance. We won't know if someone stays out all night." Liz grinned at the puzzlement on Harold's face. "We shuffled everyone around so one girl house is sprout free tomorrow. Casper is a nice type but he has some gross habits, and Brussel sprouts on his Christmas dinner is one. I've thrown him and a few more out. The sprout perverts next door have made room for them and we've let fellow sufferers come to stay until Boxing Day." Liz beamed. "That means if someone doesn't come home?" She wiggled her eyebrows.

Harold looked around the dancers and under the bits of tinsel most were dressed relatively soberly, relative to Halloween anyway. Though Sal wore something red, plunging and backless, while Suzie had found a traditional little black dress. Emmy had gone for white again, but a longish flared skirt that she twirled now and then just to tease the blokes. Holly wore a modest pleated skirt, pink of course, and a simple white blouse with a big Kiss Me Slow badge so they weren't very well disguised. Harold's eyes stopped at Celine, in her long white evening gown again, because Celine stood alone. "Where's Alicia?"

"She can't face it, the dance and pretending to smile. Celine really wants to push past the rape and move on so she's here, but Alicia is just sinking deeper into depression." Liz sighed. "We can't even diagnose her, let alone treat whatever the problem is. Well, we think we know the problem, and its fear. She keeps thinking the bastards are coming over the wall or through the doors again. Her Mum died in the estate car." The car had been riddled with bullets trying to escape as a mob overran their block of flats.

"Are you sure she'll be all right?" Harold considered going to find out because several blokes in the Army had got depressed and one ate a bullet.

"Alicia is getting by, but she'd be better if we could move a bloke in as a guard. A bloke because she doesn't rate women guards regardless of the evidence." Liz banged on Harold's chest with a fist, gently. "We can't put someone like you in there because Celine would have a breakdown. Casper offered but Celine nearly passed out at the thought and he's gay." Liz stepped back as the music ended. "Hard luck, your dance is over and you missed your chance again."

Harold never got the chance to reply. "Goody. My turn." Emmy put her mouth near Harold's ear. "Have you worked out who donated the stocking yet, or do you want to do the Prince Charming thing? Bring it round to the girl's club and you can try it on us all one at a time." They swung away into a waltz, near enough. "Though it'll have to be one a night, because if you're fitting a stocking I'm not letting you get away until morning."

"Naughty. Remember I'm a bad boy and might take you up on that." Harold did his best with a twirl and didn't step on Emmy's feet. "I haven't got the stocking with me."

"Hey, that's real smooth. Though I was hoping for a slow dance." She put her lips next to his ear. "Or the last one. That could turn into stocking trying, because half a hint and someone will find one."

Harold chuckled. "I'm running away to hide before the last dance."

"Ooh, where are you hiding?"

Harold laughed. "Hiding means I don't tell you, idiot."

"You could tell just one of us and find out if she turns up. Liz says you've got a favourite but she's not telling." Emmy pursed her lips. "So we're all going to keep testing until we find out who."

"She won't tell me who it is either, which makes it a bit awkward." The music stopped and Emmy moved off to be quickly claimed by Curtis. Harold smiled because the gardener could manage a slow dance with his home-made crutch, or he could the way Emmy kept in one place. In the next room Seth did his best to monopolise Berry but she kept dancing with other blokes now and then. Though when she came for her Harold dance, Berry confessed she just wanted to wind Seth up. Then she gave Seth a Berrying for dancing with Liz.

"Hey, you were dancing with Harold."

"Are you arguing?" Berry raised a hand again.

"No, but now the first one needs kissing better, and my arm?" Seth smiled hopefully and pointed at the arm hit by a crossbow bolt only a month ago.

"Oy, are you playing fast and loose with my daughter?" Nigel, Berry's Dad, stood right behind Seth so the wounded man couldn't see the big smile. The rest of those nearby were soon smiling as well until Berry rescued a spluttering Seth and took him off to dance.

Harold had a lovely evening, despite the succession of hints about the last dance and the expected results of Christmas kissing. The usual suspects had something planned and Suzie at least had joined them this time. Who the victim or victims would be wasn't clear and several single men were being wound up, though Harold's next partner had no plans for getting too near any man. "I'm going early Harold. I'm sorry, I can't do the last dance thing, any dance really." Celine shrugged.

"Don't apologise, Celine. Next time maybe. After all it would be a waste not to show that dress off a few times a year." Harold smiled. "Happy Christmas."

"And you Harold." Celine set off for the door, speaking to a couple of people on the way, while Sal seized Harold.

"My turn now or it will be once the tune starts. A slow dance regardless of the music." Sal giggled. "Now I'll find out what those hugs feel like on skin." She would, because the dress only had a back over her ass, and Harold wasn't holding that. Actually, if Sal wasn't so full-on, and it was a bit more private? The continuous close dancing definitely seemed to be having an effect on Harold. Sal had snuggled in and complained for about the fourth time that Harold hadn't got a proper grip, when the door flew open and a distraught Celine dashed in.

"It's Alicia! Patricia, quick, it's Alicia. She's tried to kill herself." Even as Harold headed for the door Barry moved past, catching up with Patricia as she went out of the door.

*   *   *

They found Alicia laid at the bottom of the stairs in a pool of vomit. Barry turned her and then Patricia quickly checked for injuries but if she'd fallen, Alicia hadn't obviously hurt herself. Harold gave Barry a hand to carry Alicia round to Patricia's house, the hospital in effect. Then the men were expelled while Patricia and a couple of other women set into trying to save the young woman. When the pair arrived back at Alicia's home four others were busy cleaning up the mess and spraying to cover the smell of vomit.

"If she hadn't taken the tablets and booze this would have worked. She passed out or tripped and fell before getting the noose on." Barry took down the rope tied to the upstairs banister and trailing over the edge and inspected the loop. "She's not made a proper noose but it would have tightened." Barry moved closer to Harold and lowered his voice. "That would have been a hard death, I've seen it happen. What was bothering her?"

"Being unprotected. She keeps expecting the worst." Harold explained as best he could, and about Celine.

"Why don't they split up?" Barry shrugged. "Alicia could move in with someone different, maybe a couple?"

"The pair of them have sort of bonded in a partners in misery sort of way. No, not misery, more like fear, they're both frightened of something." Harold shrugged as well. "Maybe we can get another woman to move in but that doesn't help Alicia."

"My lasses could move in, and I'll visit a lot? If I'm bothering Celine I'll go home, but the rest of the time I'll be here?" Barry laughed and indicated himself. "Despite the black hair and shaved chin everyone knows I'm here with my grandkids and past all that." Doll's blonde hair had been dyed light brown and Matti's dark red tresses were more like ginger now so the whole family were disguised.

"Bring your axe to reassure her." Harold looked at the rope. "But make sure Alicia doesn't get hold of it."

Harold went back to the hospital, and Patricia invited him in. "We were in time, Harold, and that Barry is brilliant. He had her into recovery position in seconds. Alicia must have taken too many too quickly, because she brought up whole tablets." Harold could smell vomit but Alicia looked clean and seemed to be sleeping peacefully. "I've been rationing her sleeping tablets, but I reckon she found some more while scavenging." Patricia gave a wan smile. "On the other hand, your long-range scavenging trips brought in the shot that saved her. Your midnight raiders brought a lot of things that didn't appeal to yobs but will save lives, I hope." The last remnants of her smile died. "I'm working half blind here, Harold."

"You're performing miracles. There's people walking around today who'd be dead without you." Harold tried for a confident smile. "Don't you start getting down. I swear your smile works better than the medicine."

"We're all getting down because it's sinking in. This is it. We survived, and the reward is to live in the zoo with the animals loose outside our cage." Patricia glanced at her phone. "I can't even get to the internet for advice now the phones have shut down, if the internet even exists anymore."

"We'll keep bringing in books. Hilda says she always fancied being a librarian so her house is the library now and Faith, Toby's mum, is moving in to help her. I'll ask them to let you know if any of what we bring is a medical book." Harold wasn't hopeful, unless one of the houses they were looting belonged to a doctor.

"Any help would be brilliant. Those men in the tanks saved up to ten people with the antibiotics and the other medical supplies, though some folk will never be right because I can't do the doctoring bit properly for the bones and tendons." Patricia produced another sad smile. "And we can't even pass a message to thank the soldiers or they'll be in trouble. How screwed up is that?"

They sat and talked about how screwed up things were while Alicia slept, proper sleep as near as Patricia could tell. By the time Harold came back past the house used for dancing, everyone had gone home leaving the place silent and dark. He trudged home with a few flakes of snow falling, which at any other time would have been a reason to celebrate. Snow at Christmas, the TV would have gone barmy about that any other year. Harold went in and took off his coat, opened the door into the lounge, and two arms went round him.

"Thank the gods you're back." Harold held onto a sobbing Sharyn. He knew there'd been offers to babysit, but Sharyn had refused and seemed content to stay home. "I've been sitting here thinking, what do I do tomorrow?" More tears poured out and Harold patted her back and made sympathetic noises. There was nothing he could actually say. "Daisy will ask about Daddy, I know she will."

"He's in the special place made of love." That was what Daisy had come up with, after a long talk about the first deaths here. "She drew a picture, we did, and it's on her bedroom wall with Gabriela's and the others."

"But it's Christmas. That's different."

"No, we'll just tell her Daddy needs tinsel in his picture." Harold couldn't do this stuff; this needed a few of the girl club but not this time. Sharyn didn't need to hear about Alicia just now.

"Oh, er, should I? Can I do anything?" Hazel came in behind Harold. She'd been at Betty's, playing computer games with Alfie and possibly Veronica, the other young teen.

"You'd better go to bed or Santa won't leave presents." Harold gave her a sort of smile over Sharyn's head, and Hazel rolled her eyes in reply and went upstairs.

"What about Hazel?" Sharyn looked up, tears still streaming. "She's…"

"Shush." Harold's finger went onto her lips and he spoke very quietly.

"Hazel doesn't need to hear you talking about her dad being dead or where her mum might be."

"Oh." Sharyn's face crumpled again. "I can't think straight." Her head went back on to Harold's shoulder. "I miss Freddy." Eventually the storm subsided and Sharyn went to bed, which left Harold to make up reloads and clean guns and generally knacker himself so he could sleep through his own dark thoughts.

*   *   *

Santa left Christmas presents on the doorstep, presents that were precious to those who parted with them. A selection of containers each held little portions of drinking chocolate or cocoa powder, each with a little message. Every one threatened that the giver would demand personal compensation from Soldier Boy, and although not one put a name on their present all the tracks in the light snow led back to the girl club houses.

Daisy asked about Daddy, and Harold took her up to her bedroom where they put tinsel on the picture of Daddy's special place so he could celebrate as well. Then they put a bit of tinsel on the other pictures of special places and moved them together so Gabriela and Toby and the rest could have a Christmas party. Though before that Daisy squealed and laughed and had a proper five year old Christmas with chocolate milk cereal. Harold had brought Christmas paper back on his forays, and wrapped an impressive array of colouring books and another plastic horse, a black one this time. Daisy didn't seem to mind some of the books being partly completed.

Wills played quietly, a serious almost-three year old who smiled but didn't squeal and run about. He spent most of the time on his hands and knees playing with a big plastic lorry, and ignored the other presents. About right for him, according to Sharyn. Wills would get to the rest once the novelty wore off. Sharyn feigned shock that Harold actually remembered her favourite perfume even if the bottle wasn't full and left the tears, because Freddy wouldn't smell it, until the kids were in bed.

Hazel looked pleased with a computer game, one that Alfie must have found and saved as a gift, and the clothes and presents from others. Pleased but not happy, and she spent much of the day quietly reading. Daisy dragged each of the adults, and Hazel, out of their thoughts so they could play or draw, and probably kept Christmas alive in one house at least. Christmas dragged by slowly and very quietly, with even the girl club subdued. The TV played old Christmas tunes and reran some very old Christmas films, mouthed platitudes, and there was no King's or Queen's speech.

Boxing Day brought more of the same, and Casper came to see Harold the following morning. "We've got to do something Harold." He sighed. "I'm as bad as the rest. We're all looking ahead and the view is crap."

"I'll take you on a raid into the city, to find that gay gang and a boyfriend?" Harold had half considered that, because he did feel that dragging Casper out to the edge of the city meant the bloke had no chance of finding anyone for his mistletoe.

"No you prat, though I did miss the parties. I meant something to give everyone a lift." Casper frowned. "A bit of a laugh."

"Like Halloween and Guy Fawkes?" Harold thought hard. "Snow Fawkes since we've got some?" The light snow on Christmas Eve had been followed by a proper covering.

"Make a New Year or Christmas Guy, snowman? Give prizes?" Casper's smile faded. "No, most people won't care about any prize we can come up with."

"We need Liz."

*　　　*　　　*

"Fat lot of good you are as a leader. I distinctly put blacksmith on my list and look, no blacksmith." Liz sniggered. "Though Jon got a Christmas stocking filler he didn't expect. That's if Sal wore stockings."

"Sal and Jon?"

"She said something about one hero being as good as another at Christmas, and she'd seen one that wouldn't run away." Liz sniggered again. "Jon didn't try. Two slow dances and most of his brain was mush before she dragged him out of the door." Then she frowned. "Most of the rest called off their plans after hearing about Alicia. We've got to find a way to help that lass because Patricia hasn't got many of those magic injections."

"Barry says if she'd skipped the tablets the rope might have worked. Ah. He had a suggestion. If Matti and Doll move in that won't upset Celine, and he'll visit a lot." Harold watched as Casper and Liz thought it through.

"That only works if Matti and Doll swear off blokes. If they bring one back, Celine will have heart failure." Casper frowned. "Matti won't take anyone home just now because whatever happened put her off men for a bit."

"From the finger marks on her arms it got a bit too close before grandad bashed the bastard on the head." Liz grinned. "Doll livened up a few of the eligible men though. She'd got you on her list, Harold, but nearer to the last dance. Wearing a denim miniskirt in this weather? That girl has dedication, possibly as much as Holly at Halloween. Though her boots are nice and I might borrow them if a blacksmith turns up. I reckon living with grandad might be cramping that one's style but they won't leave him living all alone."

"So you'll ask them about a move?" Harold smiled. "Barry suggested it so maybe he wants a bit of peace."

"That could work, and Louise is still on her own so I'll see if she'll move in. A sort of mini girl club. Cheering the rest up, including the girl club, will take a bit of doing. The women, or the girl club, will go for fancy dress if the prize is worth it?" Liz eyed up Harold.

"Not a chance. There's only one of me and anyway some of that lot weren't eyeing me up. You'll need more prizes." He grinned. "There'll be a good few blokes willing to offer their bodies in a good cause."

"Got it!" Casper grinned. "Two competitions and only couples are exempt. Everyone else has to take part."

"Except babysitters. What competitions?"

Chapter 3:
A Brave New Year

The suggestion livened everyone up, and the scavenging parties later that day were much more cheerful. They also smuggled a good few items out of houses with wagging fingers and promises of surprises. Four more days without anyone shooting at them, or anyone trying to do the job to themselves, raised spirits all round. The snow that fell for two of the days helped, smoothing the ragged edges of the ruins and covering up the marks of fire and explosives.

The snow reassured everyone as well, because the two pickups and the minibus carried the parties out to scavenge over virgin snow. Not a footprint or tyre mark marred the gardens and streets, just animal and bird tracks. Either the neighbours were respecting the boundaries, or they were staying at home to celebrate. Harold took the opportunity for a bit of unobserved target practice to get the rifles more accurate.

The scavengers stopped worrying about the boom of the big old rifle, or the sharper cracks as Harold got his two-two into as near perfect condition as he could. In between Harold loaded ammunition or stripped and inspected weapons. At least he had a hell of a lot of cleaning gear and primers, presses and all the rest. The booklets he'd picked up as he stripped each gun club or stockist helped.

Midday on the last day of the year the scavengers were home and every unattached male over sixteen lined up in the cleared section. "I shouldn't be here really. I'm a grandad." Barry looked downright embarrassed.

"Nor me. Look I can barely walk." Sandy hobbled a couple of steps.

Stewart Baumber still had dressings on his chest and shoulder wound, and a drawn and haunted look. "I'm not looking for a girlfriend, Harold."

"I know Stewart. This isn't about getting a girlfriend." Harold smiled as several shouts of 'speak for yourself' rose from the younger men. "This is about who you'll dance with at midnight. As long as you hold hands and move a bit, that's dancing, and there's no need to kiss if either of you don't want to."

"Can we trade?" Emmy grinned. "Can we swap our partner for someone else?"

"I hope so." Sharyn scowled. "If I've got to do this I'm not dancing with my little brother."

Harold mimed sticking fingers down his throat. "Yeuk, no thanks."

Doll waved to Barry. "Sorry gramps, but you aren't on my dance card."

"As long as you don't tell anyone who was rejected, except who you swap with. Some of us have got fragile egos." Harold smiled. "Though that means the men can swap as well. No wrestling over numbers, all right?"

"Only the very nicest sort, right after the kissing bit." Doll blew Harold a kiss, then blushed when Barry looked at her.

Suzie seemed to be keen as well. "Come on, or it'll be dark. I need time to get myself beautified."

"The best snowman gets number forty five and so on upwards. We've all got an hour."

"They all know. Three two one go!" Liz whooped as some men set off at a run to the middle of the open space. The rest walked out and started gathering snow.

*　　　*　　　*

"What is that?" Liz walked around Harold's attempt, followed by all the other women who would be competing for a number later. They were also the judges.

Harold looked at his sort of sculpted heap of snow and suddenly it didn't look as good. "A snow Dalek?"

"Oh, right, I thought the weapon was a bit high. Er, for a ray gun?" Holly blushed.

"I was surprised to see a weapon out in this snow." Liz grinned. "I thought the weapon um, barrels became brittle, Soldier Boy?"

"In the depths of a Siberian winter they can get a bit fragile, allegedly. This is nearly summer for the Army." Harold took another look at his creation. It didn't look any better. The women put their heads together and muttered, and numbers were written down. Then they trooped off to the next.

"It's a snowman fireman." Barry grinned. "It doesn't look great because I was going to put a helmet and my axe on it, but I'm not allowed."

"Bits of wood and stones only. We banned carrots because some of us are innocents." Liz led the women around Barry's effort and critiqued before they moved on. Eventually the women all stood in a huddle and worked out the score.

"I still think Casper should be in our group. No offence Casper, but I'm looking for a bit of action from whoever I get." Sal blew Casper a kiss. "See, it just bounces off."

"There were too many single women which is why all the single men have to take part but some women don't." Harold grinned. "Unless some of you want to double up?" Several women had been offered a pass and enough had accepted to even up. Neither Hilda the librarian nor Faith had wanted to take part, and Betty, the oldest woman, preferred to babysit the young teenagers. Sharyn had been pressganged after Harold mentioned her Christmas Eve soggy to Liz.

"Does Casper's count as a snowman? It's a what? Dog?" Jon had his head to one side, looking at Casper's creditable attempt at a sitting snow dog.

"It's a good job Lucky isn't on our team." Sal turned from the marking. "All right you lot, line up and hold out a hand." The women moved out and began to put numbers into hands. "Remember, put your paper number on when Kerry announces it, just before midnight."

"Don't we get to know who won?" Seth laughed. "Not me, but I'd like to know." He'd tried to get Berry to agree to being a couple and exempt from all this, but she'd said no.

"Nope, and you lot do the same with our numbers." Liz wagged a finger. "No cheating, you aren't good enough to escape my wrath and a bed ornament. Now I'm off to get into my fancy undress." The women marched off in a line towards the spectators, singing "hi-ho, hi-ho."

Casper came across to Harold. "Well that part went well. What number did you get?"

"Naughty. You'll tell the girl club."

Casper laughed. "They already know, idiot. The cheating will be intense and not just to get you fixed up." He looked over at his creation. "Maybe I should have made the antlers bigger?"

"You'll need antlers and a crash helmet if you don't get off the firing range. Come on, see if you can kill a Dalek." Everyone who could do so was picking up half-bricks to throw at the snowmen, a less pointed way of removing possible cover for attackers. Some of the spectators might not even realise why the snowmen were being pelted. Daisy waved a half-brick in each hand, one each for Uncle-Harry and Uncle-Casper, so Harold hurried before she accidentally clobbered someone. The heap of snowballs were for the kids and those without a decent throwing arm.

*   *   *

"Oh no sis. Get back up there and try again." Harold grinned. "Fancy dress, remember."

"I'm not getting tarted up."

"Not tarted up, but fancy dress. You could use the Womble costume?" Harold sniggered. "It would be a bit short, though with the head on nobody would know it's your legs?"

"Stop it!" Sharyn put her hands on her hips. "I am not in the mood for this."

"I wasn't in the mood to be Rambo then or now, but someone insisted." Harold sobered. "And I'm not in the mood to find you sobbing your socks off when I get back."

Sharyn stared. "Oh." She sighed. "I never thought of that, which isn't fair." She sighed again. "Womble, but not tarty? I can do this." She turned and went upstairs.

"Can I come in yet?" Hazel looked much too serious.

"It wasn't an argument, Hazel, and if it is then you can come and rescue me."

Hazel giggled. "Sorry, but Sharyn didn't sound happy."

"She won't be happy for a while, maybe years." Harold looked up the stairs. "But sitting in here brooding won't help her either."

"I know. That's why I'm going to Betty's to play computer games." Hazel looked sad for a moment, then smiled, just a little one. "Thank you Uncle-Harold." She hugged Harold and kissed him quickly on the cheek. Harold watched, gobsmacked, as the young orphan or probable orphan went out the door. Hazel seemed to be handling it so well, and then she came out with that? Harold touched his cheek, he was Uncle-Harold to her as well?

He turned at the sound of feet on the stairs to see what would be a very tarty Womble, if it wasn't for a pair of baggy shorts and thick tights or leg warmers covering her legs right down to Sharyn's boots. "The girl club sent these tights round so I'd better wear them." That explained the Holly and Mistletoe pattern all over her legs. "Though I thought Holly should have them." A muffled snigger followed from inside the pointed head. "She'll probably find something much more unsuitable."

"You won't have to worry about a New Year kiss under there, but you might get a bit thirsty." Harold smiled, because Sharyn did sound a lot happier. "You may as well take the head off until the babysitters arrive."

"Susan and Rob? When they volunteered my last excuse went, the rotten gits. Though it means they are a couple now, if only to avoid the last dance lottery." Sharyn smiled as her face reappeared. "At least they've finally made it official. We should throw rice over them."

"Rice is food, I'll look out for some confetti on the next scavenger runs. It's the nearest we'll get to marriage which will make divorce easier." Harold grinned. "We could make them jump over a broom?"

"Mean. Rob's not allowed to jump about at all yet though I reckon he'll get a dance and the midnight kiss." The doorbell rang. "They're keen enough."

"No, on time. Somebody took too long getting ready, or arguing about it anyway."

"Someone isn't ready. Where's the stocking?" Sharyn smiled happily. "Payback, little Bro."

Harold tried hard to come up with an excuse and couldn't. He'd worn these ruined jeans and a torn tee used for scavenging instead of the much briefer originals because the women had been adamant. The men had to wear fancy dress, and Harold had to be Rambo again. "You do know what some of them keep saying about the stocking?"

"No, and yeuk, I don't want to. Though I know you'll still have it, probably in your trophy box." Sharyn turned towards the stairs. "Shall I go and look?"

"No!" Harold surrendered, as usual. While he collected the stocking he could hear the laughter downstairs, though as he came down much of it was about who in the girl club might have worn Sharyn's costume without the shorts.

*   *   *

"Oh cripes." Harold muttered that quietly to Casper. "Whose bright idea was this? At least Celine has stuck to her usual white dress, even though she's got a tinsel hairpiece. I was surprised that Celine agreed because I offered her a pass."

"She really has decided it's time to move on. Now Celine reckons her brain has to tell the rest of her that it's all right to be near a man." Casper scowled. "In her own time. Anyone pushes it and it's chopper time."

"I'll hold him down. Both Alicia and Matti seem to be feeling better as well. Now we've got to decide who wins the fancy dress and that won't be easy." Harold looked at the crowd of women waiting. "What is Louise dressed as?" Louise wore a pair of tight jeans, a shirt and jacket, workmen's boots and a baseball cap. Harold blinked and forgot Louise. "Holly is actually overdressed, just."

"If stripy knitted stockings can be classed as clothes." Holly came properly into view and Harold could see they really were stockings or leg warmers, not tights. Casper sniggered. "Half the blokes won't look that far with that tutu on again. Louise has come as a bloke." Casper laughed. "Sal is wearing something different. Well, different from Halloween."

"That red dress really does suit Jessica Rabbit though. Her makeup is good, really good." Harold smiled. "We'll have to go scavenging for more lipstick and eye whatever that is, just to top Sal up."

"Yee-ha." Billy only murmured but the men near him nodded, though most glanced to see if Barry was near first. "If I'd known I'd have gone for cowboy instead of Robin Hood. I thought they ran in a hurry?"

"Priorities. Some people think a Stetson is essential." Bernie, in a white paper overall and holding a goldfish bowl as his spaceman helmet, grinned as he spoke. Doll wore her cowboy hat, and a little checked blouse and fringed top to go with her denim shorts and cowboy style boots. "No whip or lasso though."

"Come on you lot, stop drooling and start judging." Liz grinned "What?"

Harold grinned back. "The staring is because they're wondering what that is, apart from half the net curtains in Orchard Close."

"This is the ghost of Christmas hopeful. Take a good look because if you don't find me a blacksmith soon this could appear anywhere." Liz beckoned with a finger and headed off towards the contestants.

*　　　*　　　*

"So if number one dances with number forty five, who will you be lip-locking?" Liz sniggered. "Don't tell me you didn't check the numbers before handing them out?"

Harold managed a twirl without stepping on Liz's feet; his dancing was improving with all this practice. "Nope. Even if I did, I wouldn't cheat." Harold would end up dancing with Berry according to the numbers, but he'd bet coupons that it wouldn't be Berry. Seth had already asked to swap numbers and Harold told him no, not yet. He had visions of both Seth and Berry swapping and really getting it wrong. "At least her dad Nigel will be occupied so if Seth is lucky and can get the last dance with Berry, he'll have a clear run."

"He doesn't need luck." Seth and Berry were already dancing, while Nigel danced with Sharyn and tried to find out who hid under the Womble head. Sharyn seemed to be joining in now she was here, though so far staying in disguise. Not that half those present didn't already know or guess.

Three dances later Harold smiled as Sal moved in. "Hi there Roger. I'm trying to get a trade, since I've got all this lipstick to get rid of." She put her arms up around Harold's neck and glanced down. "I'm supposed to stick these out to keep in character."

"Yours or Jessica's?"

With all the lipstick Sal's pout looked magnificent if a bit alcoholic. "Come on Roger Rabbit, get a proper grip. You lost this argument at Christmas so let's have some hands on skin, or I'll start pattycake right now."

Harold got a grip as instructed. "I thought you were fixed up now?"

"Maybe I is and maybe I ain't. Maybe I'm just making sure he's keen?" Sal giggled. "Is he keen?"

"I'm not sure. His eyeballs are out on stalks and he's tripping over his tongue. Does that count?" Harold could see Jon, who definitely kept an eye on Sal even while he danced with Patricia the nurse.

"Perfect. Now it depends on who I can swap with. I could end up with anybody." Sal gave a little shimmy. "But do I want to worry all year about a knife in the back? One or two are getting very competitive about you, Soldier Boy."

"Liz keeps saying I've chosen someone."

Sal giggled. "But has she chosen you?"

"That would be a mess, wouldn't it? Maybe I should just let Liz arrange it all? Then I could let it come as a pleasant surprise."

"You trust Liz to do that, with her sense of humour?" Sal raised her eyebrows to go with her wicked smile. "She's likely to fix you up with Casper." Harold laughed, at least partly in relief because although Sal danced very close, she wasn't going overboard this time. Not only that, but Sal certainly had Jon's attention. He almost trotted over when the music stopped to claim the next dance.

"Me next, because I owe you this one." Emmy wore a huge grin. "Since I won't get a New Year kiss from you."

"Is it rigged then?"

"Mine is, and don't you dare say so." Emmy was very serious. "I was a bit tempted to burn my fingers at Christmas, but that probably wouldn't have happened." She quirked her lips in a half-smile. "If you lived in the next town then I reckon I could have rocked your world, just briefly Soldier Boy. But you don't, so I'm not risking it." Her big bright smile flashed. "Curtis is going to get his world well and truly rocked tonight when I walk him home."

"I thought he was supposed to walk you home?" Harold hugged and smiled, and he didn't need to force either because he really felt happy for Emmy. "Good luck. Though of course, given your stunning looks, signature hair and sparkling personality, luck won't come into it. Are you making it all official?"

"Sort of. I think I should go out with him for a week or two, all open and above board, before dragging him into bed permanently. What do you think?" Emmy laughed. "Since you've already given Curtis advice."

"Hey, I didn't know that was about you." Harold leaned forward a bit and kissed her on the nose. "Though I'm pleased it is. He really did fancy you way back, before the hair and all that."

"And he's been really sweet as well, not pushy, which seems to have worked." They danced until the song ended and Emmy's lips met Harold's briefly. "Thanks, Harold. Happy New Year." She laughed, and just as she turned away winked. "You've already been traded at least once." He had? Now Harold wondered who had been Seth's original partner, and had no idea.

*　　*　　*

The music paused at ten to twelve, and Kerry held up two sheets of paper. "The results are on here, or the original results are. You men go and get safety pins for your numbers so the poor girls can see their fate." Kerry tried for a threatening glare but her smile kept winning. "If there is an argument this list will settle it so trade numbers, don't steal them."

Harold pinned his number on and tried to see who had what, but a good few were keeping theirs covered while trying to make trades. Liam, one of the original residents from the flats, looked a bit like a rabbit in headlights as Suzie waved her number at him. Matti claimed a dance, a very modest one without hugging. "This is working, I'm already eyeing up the talent. Next time round I'll be giving that sister of mine some competition." She smiled. "How often do you lot have dances?"

"I don't know. Not often?" Harold smiled. "Are you moving in with Alicia and Celine?"

"And Louise, because that way gramps won't know just what we're up to all the time. He's lovely and I'm grateful, but?" Matti glanced around. "If we can get a bloke to guard Alicia and someone to live with gramps, both of us are moving into the girl club." Her eyes widened and she giggled. "We could fix gramps up with Alicia?"

"Talk to Liz, she seems to be plotter-in-chief." With a forty year gap Harold didn't think that would be happening, but who knew? They danced a bit more until the music ended and Harold answered the impish smile from his next partner.

"I tried but number nine won't swap." Holly pouted and then grinned. "But I have got the dance before." She put her arms round Harold. "None of that hand holding. I remember the huggy thing so come on, let's dance. Ooh, that's mean."

"No, this is a faster one because the midnight one is slow." Harold still couldn't see who had number nine. "Who did you end up with?"

"Sandy. I'll have to walk him home because he'll never get to the girl club and back to his place without falling over." Holly sighed. "I've never been walked home."

"Bet you can find volunteers."

"I'll remember you volunteered. After all, you owe me for chocolate." At the end of the dance Holly insisted on a second-rate drinking chocolate kiss, a chaste Holly version, because she couldn't have a proper New Year one. Harold looked around and noticed others smiling at Holly, so that had been another dare like Halloween. He was more interested in finding out who he was supposed to dance with, and saw a huge smile and a Stetson coming his way.

"This had better be worth it. I turned down several offers to swap, but I've heard rumours about hugs." Doll pointed at the number nine stuck to her little jacket. "Three were quite keen to swap though that might have been because of who they drew. Now, how does a slow dance go?" From the way Doll put her arms round him and snuggled in, Harold was bloody sure Doll knew all about slow dances.

"Gramps will be watching."

"Gramps will be busy wondering if he's been set up with Alicia, and anyway he's dancing in the dining room." The house for dancing had a large lounge and dining room, with wide sliding doors between them. Jon came past with Sal, and his brain was already history. He was closely followed by Billy who seemed bemused by finding he'd drawn Gayle, while Liz stuck her tongue out at Harold as Casper whirled her around.

"Quite a few people will be wondering who was set up." Harold sniggered. "My sister among them." A headless Womble, now clearly Sharyn, danced with Nigel. Not a particularly close dance because of the bulky costume, which probably suited Sharyn.

"Oops, I'll have to tilt my head up so I don't take your eye out with my hat." Doll's Stetson brim came to about nose level on Harold until she looked up.

"Yes, a few people wondered about your choice of escape clothing."

"I wore my hat and boots and the rest doesn't take up much room, but I had to leave the really good stuff behind." Doll sighed. "I had a full fancy dress for parties, chaps and a gun belt with a big plastic cap six-gun. That went down really well unless Matti nicked my shorts. Grandma had some old videos of a singer called Christina Aguilera and she wore a get-up like this. Some of her other gear would definitely be popular with the blokes here."

Harold frowned. "Matti nicked them? She seems to be feeling better but isn't dressed like a shorts sort of lass." Matti wore a mid-shin dress with her hair in plaits, bead necklaces, and a feather in a headband.

"If she ever finds the right dress to do her real Hiawatha, it'll burn out brain cells. Matti came to visit me at the University so we could go to a couple of dances together and chase blokes. I may as well warn you, we have competitions or will have once she's past that asshole. Then the Army sealed the place up and the University shut down. The food in the canteen ran low so we moved out and descended on gramps. Mum and Dad are still in Manchester, or were when everything went to hell and we were shut in." Doll sighed and hugged a bit tighter. "Gramps is a sweetie really. It was a hell of a shock when he came through the door and brained that asshole, but a welcome shock."

"There's been some of that about. Were all the students sealed in?" The mere idea horrified Harold, all the students being still trapped in the city during the violence.

Doll stopped even her sad smiling and this hug had nothing to do with dancing. "Buses turned up and took a hell of a lot of students away. They were supposed to come back for the rest, and never did. Then we realised that those taking Maths, Physics, Engineering, and all the other solid academic subjects went on those first buses. We got the message after a couple of people found that the labs had been stripped." Doll giggled. "Mmm, that works. I feel better already."

Harold realised that as Doll had been talking, and her voice had become more bitter, he had hugged her tighter and started stroking her back. "It's a talent, apparently."

"Keep it up just a bit longer, so I'm in the mood for midnight." Even as she spoke, voices started counting down. Harold ended up with a proper New Year kiss from a totally unexpected source. "Whew." Doll pouted. "After that, it's a pity that gramps will be waiting when you walk me home."

"You might have had a lucky escape. After all I'm a rough soldier, not like those smooth college types." Harold walked Doll over to collect their coats.

*   *   *

The walk to take Doll home seemed more like a well-behaved extension of the party since Alicia and gramps and Louise and Stewart Baumber were along, as well as Matti and Bernie who held hands but decorously. Celine walked determinedly close to Finn even if they weren't touching with Finn being really careful not to brush against her. It crossed Harold's mind that Celine wouldn't be in any danger of getting a hug anyway since although the sling had come off, Finn's arm wouldn't be up to that sort of treatment for some months.

Both Louise and Matti went for a quick hug and a kiss on the cheek, and Finn actually put his hand out to shake Celine's as a goodbye. She took hold of Finn's hand and murmured something and he hesitated, then bent over and kissed her knuckles very gently. It was probably an evens bet who had the reddest blush. Doll gave up trying to keep a straight face and turned towards Harold to giggle as gramps took that escape route, kissing Alicia's hand.

"Not in front of you, gramps." Doll sighed at the look she got in reply. "I'm only just out here and it's freezing, and we've both got long coats on. Crikey, Harold's is leather so he's not going to get all rough soldier." Barry looked a bit embarrassed and went inside with everyone but Bernie, who headed home trying not to laugh at Harold's face.

"All rough soldier?" Harold grinned.

"No time to talk, he'll have a stop watch." Doll treated Harold to a repeat of the midnight kiss, with added something. "There, now I'd better get inside before he comes out with that axe. He'll not leave until he's sure we're safely tucked up. Happy New Year, Soldier Boy."

"No wonder he's white-haired. Happy New Year, Doll." Harold left once the door closed behind her, smiling and shaking his head gently. At least four of the girl club seemed to be settling down, including Sal, but the new pair were going to make up for that. Walking home really felt peaceful with the snow and hardly anyone about, though his mouth twitched as Harold wondered if he should give Sharyn a bit longer. Not a serious thought after Christmas Eve, more so when Nigel, then Susan and Rob came past.

"Harold, have you seen my halo? I'm sure I didn't lose it out there but I can't see it in here either. I've found a Womble head?" Harold smiled and followed Holly's voice back into the dance house. Holly had the place to herself with only the dancing room lights still on, though the TV still sang carols to the wall. Sure enough the Womble head sat on a table among the wreckage of the buffet.

"Daisy would raise hell if this was missing." Harold looked round. "You'd lost your halo before dancing with me."

"Pity, I was hoping you'd, um, right. Then it will be here someplace." Harold smiled when Holly blushed as usual after speaking without thinking. She bent over and looked under the table. "There it is, and I'm sure I didn't lose it under there." Holly stood waving the wire and tinsel contraption triumphantly, then fitted it back on her head.

"I thought you'd be home by now."

"No, I took Sandy home and realised I'd forgotten this. I'll need it for the next dance." Holly looked round. "We'd better turn everything off." She headed for the TV and stopped, before turning with a big smile. "It would be a shame to cut the last tune short when there's a dancing partner." Holly had already unbuttoned her coat in the warm room, and now she smiled and pointed at Harold's. "Come on, undo that."

He laughed and did so, and Holly snuggled in close for all of about thirty seconds before White Christmas stopped. "Just long enough to qualify." Harold didn't ask what for as a soft kiss landed. Then Holly went to turn off the TV. "Will you get the other light please Harold, and the Womble?"

"Especially the Womble or Daisy will be asking what Mummy was up to." Harold did as asked and a few moments later they left and shut up the house.

They walked in companionable silence up to the end of Orchard Close and turned in, and Holly looked up the street towards the big house at the end. "Do you need to give Sharyn a few minutes, or get there quick to rescue her?"

"Neither, Sharyn was a mess over Christmas and nowhere near over Freddy, so Nigel had a very quick walk. Rob and Susan have already been evicted. She might already be in bed."

Holly's hand took hold of his. "Good, because you've got time to walk me home." She sighed. "I wasn't kidding, I've never been walked home."

"It's just here, idiot. You're already home." They were just coming up to the gate into the first girl club garden.

"I live in the next house, and I mean round to the door, proper like." She squeezed his hand. "Payment for chocolate?"

Harold didn't point out that she'd claimed a chocolate kiss earlier. "I'd expected a higher price. I'd walk you home anyway Holly, if it's that important."

"Very important. A rite of passage according to Liz. Every girl should be walked home at least once, even if she drags him inside afterwards."

Harold laughed because that sounded like Liz. There would be no dragging anywhere tonight since there were plenty of people about in both houses according to the lights and laughter. "Come on then, I'll risk it."

"Leave Womble on the gate post." Holly adjusted her halo. "Wouldn't want to lose this in the snow, I'd get frostbite." Round at the side door she hesitated, scuffing her toe and looking down. "What's the traditional ending for walking a girl home, Harold?"

"Naughty, you'll make the others jealous." Holly had definitely puzzled Harold because although she joined the teasing game in public, Holly still seemed upset about Brodie.

"But this will only be a little kiss. Firstly because that's the rule for the first time." Holly's face came up and she smiled. "Secondly because we're both all buttoned up in big coats, though I expect to feel the hug." Her smile widened and Holly raised her voice. "Lastly because Mummy Casper is listening from the other side of the door."

"I am not, I was just walking past." Casper's laugh could be heard through the door until Harold's and Holly's drowned it out.

"Right. A little kiss, silent and leave your halo intact. There." Harold thought even Barry couldn't object to that kiss. "Now you'd better get inside before I walk you down the path and up again to find out about the second time."

"I'll get instructions for then, Liz will know." Holly turned and went inside to be greeted by questions about what Sandy had got up to. Harold wandered down the path and picked up the Womble head, then made his way home. He remembered what Emmy had once said about stopping this whole competition business. Pick a girlfriend. That sounded like a pretty good idea after tonight. He just needed to find one up for a laugh without getting too serious, and one not traumatised by one thing or another.

Sharyn had gone to bed so Harold put the Womble head on the table and did the same. At least dancing seemed to have helped with the dreams.

*   *   *

The smiles and cheery greetings the next day, even from the established couples, were a real contrast with the previous week. Since everyone seemed so happy, Harold decided to keep them all together today. He knew one place that warranted a combined search, the partially wrecked supermarket where

Casper had been trapped. This time they took all five working vehicles to carry away everything useful in one go. The place wasn't really a full supermarket, more of an overgrown convenience store but after the initial looting nobody seemed to have bothered the place much.

"Cripes Harold. I hate skimmed milk but even so I wish this lot hadn't gone off." Liz carefully moved the swollen plastic containers aside with her foot. "Anyone pops one of those and I'll make them drink it."

"I'll help to force it down because the stink will make me barf." Casper glowered. "If anyone opens any freezer cabinet I'll make them sit in there for a while." The power had been off long enough for the frozen and chilled foods to have spoiled, and for some of the rest to collect mould. "Most of the packets on these shelves are damp."

"Don't worry about the outside boxes being damp or even a bit mouldy. Check inside and if there's a bag or liner the chances are its waterproof." Harold turned a corner. "There's a good few cans that aren't even rusted. Like these, canned milk. This place might have been intact right up to the last big riot, only six weeks ago. Liz, come here and load while you drool." Liz headed over with a huge smile.

"Some of the other cans have lost their labels. Mystery stew might include rhubarb or custard." Emmy, Berry and Seth pulled away a fallen set of metal shelving. "Ooh! Harold, what's the prize if one of the girl club finds real Coco Pops?"

"I thought you were off the list now Emmy?"

"I am, but I could trade. Better still, auction them?"

"You'll get some fierce bidding from Doll after last night." Bernie laughed. "She didn't look happy about the chaperones on the way home."

"Oy, Grandfather present." The banter died away into sniggering and Barry smiled at Harold and shrugged. "Wait until it's Hazel."

"Oh cripes." Because Harold already worried about the world Hazel might grow up into, and the sort of lads she'd meet.

"Shush you lot, there's a motor coming." Billy came in through the smashed window, pointing. "From towards the Hot Rods. We can hear it clearly from out there."

"One motor?" Harold ran for the pickup and his rifle, and waved the rest of the shoppers with crossbows or firearms to cross the car park and spread out into the houses near the road. "All right, I can hear it." Harold raised his voice. "Hold your fire because one isn't an attack."

The approaching car revved and, from the sounds, spun its wheels before they found some grip again. A low red soft-top sports car skidded around the last corner towards the store and the driver hit the brakes. The gleaming motor performed a complete twirl, almost came straight again, then bounced off the kerb and ended up slewed across the road. The engine fell silent and the car sat, motionless.

"Billy, Seth, Bernie, Casper, all stand up and point a weapon at the car. Don't shoot if the door opens." Harold stood as well and pointed his rifle. For long moments nothing happened, and then the driver's door swung open.

What nobody expected was a black high heeled shoe, followed by a slim leg and then another. A wriggle and shimmy, and a small slim woman with long straight blonde hair, wearing a little black dress, stood up. She put her hands on her hips to wriggle her dress straight and walked to the front of the car, before sitting on the bonnet and putting one foot on the bumper. The woman leant backwards, showing an elfin face with a big smile, and put her hands on the bonnet behind her to arch her back a little. "Do any of you men want a personal trophy blonde?"

Shocking enough, but the mismatch between bright smile, body language and the utter hopeless resignation in her voice jarred even more. Harold opened his mouth then paused, non-plussed, before finally answering. "Sorry. We don't do that in Orchard Close."

A heartfelt sigh answered. "Oh well, I suppose I'd better drive up there and ask the Army. Unless you just shoot me now?"

"The Army will shoot you if you drive up there." Harold couldn't get his head round what the hell was going on.

"But they won't expect me to service all the soldiers first. I'm too old for that now, and anyway I've used up all my tranks." She slid off the bonnet and turned back towards the driver's door. "Through the head would be good, so it's a surprise?"

"Wait up." The woman stopped and stiffened as Holly spoke, then she slowly turned.

"Ah, got a younger model already."

Another woman stood. "Not really." Louise wouldn't see thirty again and dressed in baggy jeans and a big thick jacket which definitely scotched any trophy blonde or younger model ideas. "We don't do that sort of thing. Harold doesn't allow anyone to mess with the women." For a moment Harold thought the woman would collapse as all the tension drained out of her. Her legs buckled, and she swayed and put a hand on the soft top of the car. Then Holly, Emmy and Louise were running forward.

"Leave them to it." Harold waved Casper and Billy back, away from the car. "Bernie and Casper, set off up the road to see where she came from. Let me know where she crossed the border, if she did. The rest of you get back to scavenging. Clean the place out sharpish because we might have visitors." Harold hoped nobody had followed that car, but if they did he preferred to leave nothing if he had to retreat.

The scavengers headed into the store, glancing back at where the woman was being held by Emmy with Holly and Louise close by. They set into scavenging with a will, quickly taking the goods out to heap in the pickups or vans. Harold had just spotted loose cans of baked beans under a fallen shelf when Casper came back in. "We followed the tyre tracks to the border and she came from the Hot Rods. There's no sign of anyone following her yet."

"Any idea who she is?"

"No, though Emmy and Holly have got her into the Minibus." Casper laughed. "I was told to sod off."

"Fair enough. Give me a hand with this shelving because look, right back there."

"Corned beef? Don't tell everyone or there'll be a fight." Casper took a firm hold of the steel. "Come on wimp."

*   *   *

"We have to get going." Harold stood clear of the minibus, or rather clear of the woman sobbing sporadically onto Emmy's shoulder even after nearly three hours. Holly came out.

"There's a problem. Three Hot Rods will be looking for her when they wake up. She fed them her complete supply of Valium, Rohypnol, and Temazepam for starters and the gods know what else, mixed with really good booze. By the time they'd finished their party with her, all three were stoned out of their skulls." Holly glared. "I'd really like to wait here for them, with half a dozen guns and no warning?"

"If they survived that, shooting them could be a mercy. My guess is the Hot Rods will come in mob handed but slow so they aren't trespassing, and then demand her back." Harold frowned. "I'll say no, but it's the next part that could get bloody and cost us people."

"They'll want her presents as well, two modern crossbows, about thirty bolts for them, a couple of boxes of ammunition and a lot of good booze. Tabitha daren't touch the guns and machetes the men were wearing and couldn't make herself shoot them with the crossbows, so she ran. After one dose of Hot Rod partying that woman really is ready to drive onto the bypass." Holly glared towards the south and the Hot Rods.

"Does Tabitha want to stay, and does she understand the rules?" Holly nodded. "Then tell her she has to cut and dye her hair and change her name, and never breath a word of today to anyone not present."

"What about that car?" Holly pointed at the bright red poser Porsche.

Harold grinned. "So sad. Get everyone loaded and gone, and take her presents with you except some of the booze." Harold turned and raised his voice. "Casper, I'll need one pickup and half a dozen men with serious weapons."

"I'll stay."

"No Holly, because just now you'd shoot someone for blinking out of turn." Harold turned her and pushed. "Get everyone home safe and get that lass disguised." He smiled. "Give her some chocolate to make her feel better."

"Ooh, I'll let everyone know you're paying."

*   *   *

An hour later Casper leant close. "You owe me, big-time."

"You like bagging up the trash. Now shush and look really annoyed but not at them." Harold straightened and held his rifle low but sort of pointed at the first of the three SUVs that were pulling into the car park. He waggled the barrel as a hint the cars should stop.

As the first car stopped a familiar face immediately got out of the passenger side. "Where is she?" Cooper wore mechanic style overalls and no doubt had his name across the back. Harold bit back a smile as two young men were helped from the second car. Both had to be held upright and were spattered in vomit.

"She? Was that a woman?" Harold gestured behind him at the store, firmly ablaze with the distinctive rear of the red Porsche sticking out of the flames. "If this is your fault I'll want paying for the food that burned. Not only that but when the ammo went up it nearly killed Alfie."

"Not a chance. She's a runner and any damage she did is your problem. Though we really hoped we'd find her alive because she killed one of ours." Cooper looked at the burning building and the car. "F...damn, that would have been a real poser motor for Porsche." Harold tried hard to keep the disgust from his face because Cooper didn't seem worried about the woman. Then the Hot Rod's eyes narrowed in suspicion. "Is she still in there?"

"Go and look. We tried to put out the fire because of the food in the shop, but all we got is three bottles of whisky. Decent stuff though." Harold shrugged and pointed at three bottles on the bonnet of the pickup. "Those must have fallen out when the car hit. It's a soft top and the rest went up like a torch." It certainly had with a couple of bottles of spirits, a hole in the petrol tank, and an assortment of flammable liquids from the store to help.

"Trev, bring those, er, crap-heads?" Cooper looked a question at Harold.

"Crap-heads is fine. We get more fussy about language around the women." Harold waved towards the car. "I hope you haven't eaten."

Although they were taken forward to look into the car as well as the flames would allow, the two men were never going to identify the driver. One of those supporting them turned and shouted "the bitch is dead" to Cooper. Harold daren't look at Casper or they would have laughed. The nameless head had been laid on the dash in front of the steering wheel of the Porsche, with an assortment of other bones and rotten clothes gleaned from the surrounding ruins on the driver's seat, in case someone got really nosy.

"Satisfied?" Harold let his annoyance show. "Because I'd prefer your lot on the way home before we go, since some of them are a bit light-fingered."

"Not now." Cooper scowled. "Not since the rules were explained, though the rules might be altered at the meeting. Cadillac will be letting you know where that is."

"At the island back there would be good? Nice and easy for all three of you to find, and near enough to the Army to make starting a war a bad idea." Harold shrugged. "Someone else pick a time and date. Bring a decent shooter if there's going to be a competition."

Cooper opened his mouth and then hesitated. "I'll pass the message, though Cadillac might want somewhere else."

"Send someone with the message and I'll speak to the GOFS." Harold watched the flicker in Cooper's eyes as he realised that Orchard Close were already in touch with other neighbours. Harold and his pickup full of armed men followed the Hot Rods to the border to make a point, and then went straight home. By the time they arrived, every scrap had been unloaded from the other vehicles and stashed away. Willing hands set into moving the boxes and bags in the pickup.

Sharyn greeted Harold with a smile but before she could speak a five year old hurricane descended chanting Coco Pops at the top of her voice. A triumphant Daisy waved a drawing of dogs and cats eating Coco Pops. Hazel, apparently on drawing duty, waved from the dining room and rolled her eyes at the chants.

"I know Coco Pops are important, but selling your body? Who found them?" Sharyn spoke quietly but Harold saw some real humour in her eyes.

"Selling my body?"

"There were strong hints of compensation and favours for those who found them."

Harold laughed. "Emmy found them and she's otherwise occupied."

"But she's not actually er, whatevered for another month, because that's when the house will be ready and Curtis's splint comes off." Sharyn frowned. "It wasn't Emmy who delivered them." A wicked smile spread over her face. "If you don't know who you owe, I'm keeping quiet."

"Emmy will be whatevered?" Harold went for the diversion rather than Coco Pop compensation.

"With confetti but we can't have weddings?" Sharyn shrugged. "Matthew has his sling off and he managed his first two handed hug so him and Bess are official now. Finn has his sling off but he hasn't been spoken for." She snickered. "The latest one might be more his style. Oh, right, did anyone mention the new woman? The scavengers brought her back."

"For Finn?" Harold thought of a groomed Tabitha and the balding forty odd year old electrician and that didn't add up.

"Holly says June is nearly forty and going a bit grey." Harold listened to the explanation of how June had been walking up the road and Daisy's complaints about school with a little smile, because that disguise for 'June' would be perfect if everyone kept quiet.

*   *   *

Within a week the TV did its best to destroy any good feeling after New Year. "Didn't we accept some of that lot, the refugees from Africa and Syria?" Sharyn looked rightly worried as a tide of humanity swamped the Army positions around a huge refugee camp, seized the weapons, and flooded across the countryside nearby.

"And Jordan, and Iraq, and Lebanon, and Gaza, but we never had the really big refugee camps because the government refused to take any more. Eventually the EU stopped letting the boats cross over the Med, but before that the richer countries paid the poorer ones to round refugees up instead of letting them through." Harold looked at the thousands of people heading anywhere but what had been their home, in some cases for the last decade or more. "Where the hell will they go?"

"These are the scenes as militant elements in the refugee camp on Sicily overwhelmed their guards. The escaped refugees are storming the outskirts of Palermo, though conflicting reports claim that the inhabitants are assisting or joining the uprising."

On the TV a warship fired into a harbour packed with shipping, continuing until nothing remained afloat. An overhead view showed a familiar river of smoke and fire spreading through what the caption said was Palermo, heading for the harbour. The scenes shifted to warships firing on a flotilla of small craft and a large freighter full of people, then into yet another harbour. This time the caption said Tenerife.

"The Spanish government has been forced to isolate the Canary Isles to prevent the occupants of the refugee camps there from escaping to the mainland. Since the refugees seized a ship bringing supplies, no more will be sent. All across Europe an obviously co-ordinated uprising is threatening the stability of the region. Refugees from two camps have combined to break through the Greek Army lines surrounding Corinth. Despite the valiant attempts of the Greek military, the insurgents have seized the crossings over the Corinth Canal and are advancing on Athens."

Onscreen a camera swept over what was, from the caption, Corinth. Little life showed in the devastation, though fires were raging here and there. "Crap, they've got hold of military kit." Onscreen a missile rose lazily into the sky and blotted out a helicopter. Harold glanced up. "Will you check on Daisy please, Hazel? You might as well stay up there and listen to some music you like rather than watch this miserable stuff."

Hazel stared at him. "Will it be bad again, Harold?"

"Possibly." Harold sighed. "Though a long way away. No need for you to have these pictures in your head."

Sharyn leaned closer as Hazel went upstairs. "You don't think so do you, about it being a long way away."

"No because although we didn't take many, the newspapers claimed the better part of half a million were on the Isle of Wight and in Northern Ireland." Harold frowned. "Though there was no mention of refugees during the reports of trouble in Northern Ireland so maybe they were moved. If that lot are now on the mainland Hazel will just get worried."

"Fortunately the British government acted quickly once the first breakouts occurred, and the Isle of Wight has been isolated. Unfortunately, the warnings were too late to save the remaining inhabitants of Cowes. There is evidence that those confined in Ryde and Newport conspired with the refugees to break out and join the assault."

This time a Royal Navy warship smashed ships in a small port, including a loaded ferry. As that went down struggling figures spread across the cold, grey January waters. An Army post disappeared under those attacking from the ruins of a town and more attackers streaming in across the fields behind them. The scenes shifted to more soldiers being overwhelmed by screaming hordes who then poured aboard a ferry. More overhead scenes showed mobs rampaging over farmland and through smaller communities, killing guards and freeing the orange-suited workers in the fields.

"The Isle of Wight was expected to provide early vegetables to ease the food situation. Now everyone is urged to tighten their belts and ration any food until the farms on the mainland start to produce."

"We'll concentrate on getting in the veggies, any that are still in the ground. That's if we can find them with this snow. We'll also strip the outer houses first to put off anyone sneaking over the borders." Harold reached for his radio, but left it until morning.

*   *   *

The same pictures were showing on the wall screen in the bunker. Owen, the chairman, cleared his throat to get the attention of the rest. "The southern European refugees should clear many of the local large population centres down there in search of food. They will strip the marts and then denude the entire area. After that it's just a matter of keeping the entire population in the same area a week or two as they starve. I'm disappointed with the result in southern France because that mob is out of control. We must hope those move south to join their comrades in Spain, or the French get their act together." Owen spoke in his quiet, public school voice but his tone showed annoyance. "The Isle of Wight didn't go well. Those refugees weren't supposed to get to the farms."

Joshua, the Army man, frowned. "But the big population centres are now empty and what's in the fields won't last the mobs long. Additional forces including armour are already clearing out any die-hards in the ruins and sealing the perimeters again so nobody can get back in. Scattered as they are now, the mobs can't break through soldiers. The rest of our operation worked out close enough, or it has done so far. Once the scattered groups die or come close enough to the Army to be shot, the entire Isle of Wight will be clear." Joshua gestured to the redheaded woman. "The invasion of farms should give Ivy a good excuse."

She inclined her head. "Yes, we intended reducing the amount of food supplied to marts sooner or later to reduce the population. Perhaps now is better before any of the captive populations start growing their own?"

"We want them to do that, so there is no need to send as much of the produce from our farms to the marts. Eventually we will inherit the cultivated land. Please arrange for someone to look at contingency plans, just in case we have to really cut sooner than expected." Owen turned to the youngest cabal member. "Gerard, how is the evacuation of supplies going from Calais and Zeebrugge?"

"Very well, they're nearly stripped. Hamburg, Rotterdam and Antwerp are all being difficult, or their controllers are. We'll start on Le Havre and Dunkirk next though Dunkirk has been badly damaged by rioting." The younger man shrugged. "Our colleagues in France arranged for the nuclear powered French warships to be posted to French Polynesia after escorting our share of the Israelis to Australia. There's not enough control left in France to order them back or stop us emptying any port."

Boris, the diplomat, sighed. "Which is a pity. France is supposed to be our breadbasket and the base for eventually pacifying the rest of Europe. What happened at Marseille and then Toulon is unfortunate, and a warning. If a mob looks like getting onto the naval ships in Brest or Cherbourg the Royal Navy must be ready." He shrugged. "I've tried persuasion and even bribery, but unfortunately the French Naval Command there will not abandon their bases even with transport for their stores and personnel and a safe haven this side of the channel." He relaxed a little and smiled at Gerard. "At least our other refugees are doing their job properly, the ones in Ireland."

"They are now the Loyalists have decided black Anglicans are preferable to white Irish Catholics. Some of them were quite stubborn about that, but now the weapons have been distributed and that evened up the numbers between north and south. Once both sides have used up all their ammunition and killed each other's hotheads Ireland is another breadbasket." The young man curled his lip. "Beef and potato basket, providing they don't eat the place bare first."

"They will though by then they'll have used up the SAMS and armour piercing. Those weren't planned for either. The old weapons from the troubles weren't as decommissioned as advertised." Owen made a dismissive gesture and shrugged. "Maybe half a dozen tanks and seven aircraft is a fair exchange if we finally solve the Irish problem. Any word from across the Atlantic?"

"Not any that makes sense. There were too many private armies in the USA, or there certainly are now. Using up all their ammunition could take a long while so our colleagues are keeping quiet." Nate glanced over at Boris. "We've been putting our heads together but there's little help we can offer. The American Navy and Air Force are still obeying orders and staying in their major bases, but I think our transatlantic cousins were a little bit optimistic in their other predictions."

Grace, now wearing a blue two-piece, thumbed through her file. "I'm more worried about China. That really isn't going according to any plan and we may lose control of the surveillance satellites. We should have moved some of ours, or the American ones, into different orbits."

"Some whistle-blower would have noticed and realised we had prior warning about the destruction of all the others, the civilian and minor nation hardware." The older man smiled. "We knew there would be a warlord scenario in many places, and even set some of them up. Providing our allies keep control of the satellites and have neutralised the strategic nuclear weaponry, China can play itself out." He shrugged. "We have four missile subs and five Hunter-Killers around the globe that are now crewed entirely by our own people, and will deal with any real problem."

"We hope. There's a lot of playing out to come yet, and already too much hasn't worked according to plan." Gerard frowned and clicked a control to put a map of Russia on the screen. "The pipelines from the Western Siberian oil and gas were supposed to be cut, but the actual production facilities should have been protected. We wanted those available for when refining came back online."

"Our colleagues in Russia must find a way around that. From our own point of view we now have refining capacity, or will have within a year." The older man changed the view to another map. "Keris reports that the Argentinian solution is working well, and our allies there have started moving workers and equipment out to the Falklands. With the Royal Navy almost intact we can ensure the safety of the undersea wells, the new refining facilities, and the tankers moving the finished product."

"We will still have enough warships to seal the channel?" The slim Asian, Vanna, frowned. "I don't trust the Belgians and Germans to stop those so-called refugees and I'm not sure anything in France can. Not now units of the French Army have broken or turned."

"I'll check the contingencies, and we can move units from Gibraltar if required. Otherwise the ships should stay there, bottling up the Med. Just in case the few warships taken from Toulon decide coming this way is more important than settling old disputes in the Middle East and North Africa." Owen used the remote to turn off the screen. "We'll reconvene for a full meeting in a month to review progress, but until then everyone will still be busy keeping our own projects in the UK somewhere close to the plan."

*   *   *

Everyone in Orchard Close understood the unspoken message in the news reports. The marts wouldn't have enough food, and the prices would go up. The teams visited every spot marked as a vegetable garden before the snow came and dug up the hardier crops like swedes, beets and carrots. Rabbits and surprisingly a deer had been at the Brussels sprouts and cabbages but partially nibbled veg tasted better than none.

Even so spirits remained high, not least because the cloud over the city centre finally lifted. The birds had been gradually diminishing, but now flocks of seagulls and rooks accompanied by buzzards, crows and other scavengers flew overhead daily, heading out into the countryside. That made no difference to daily life, but the birds had been a constant reminder of the sheer scale of the deaths and violence.

A Muntjac deer escaped because the startled scavengers missed their chance to shoot it before the equally startled animal bounded out of sight. The scavengers teased Emmy mercilessly about missing her chance, and a change of meat would have been welcome. So far Orchard Close hadn't run out of fresh meat since the snow covered up much of the grass. The rabbits went for any available food which made them easier to find and Finn's practice with the poncy air pistol converted into rabbit hunting. Meanwhile the tracks meant that Holly's trappers could pick the best places for their wire nooses, and any surplus rabbits were frozen.

The rats in the traps became either fresh dog food or frozen future dog food, and not just for Lucky. Rascal now ate mostly rat or cat, though the hunters did the gutting and skinning for a grateful Hilda and boiled the meat. Alicia worked on overcoming her squeamishness to prepare rat for her own new pet. Alicia, the girl club, Zach and Toyah had all tempted cats in from the wild. Berry and Nigel were after one as well, to keep the rats and mice away from their sacks of potential beer.

That might be easier soon since Robert had caught one to keep any rodents away from his wife Pippa's bakery supplies, and Stripes was pregnant. Stripes because of her markings, and as a reminder to six year old Joey not to get scratched again. Hunger or loneliness brought moggies into Orchard Close and spared Sandy from making cat traps, a blessing for him as the cold bit into his arthritic joints.

Harold remembered Veronica's comment about the little radios, and a couple of others about communications, and made casual enquiries. Not entirely casual, but his real target being wounded helped to make the whole approach look accidental. "Hi there Isiah, how's your leg and Kerry's arm?"

"Not too bad Harold. Kerry thinks she'll be able to embroider and sew properly soon. It may sound silly, but even if she holds the needle in her other hand her broken arm made it difficult." Isiah looked down at his leg. "Patricia doesn't think I'll limp any worse than before this injury happened."

"Maybe, but I still feel partly responsible about that. If I hadn't gone to see what was happening, we might have prevented your injuries or Sue being killed." Harold sighed and that wasn't faked. "If we'd had telephones I needn't have gone. Finn has looked at making some of the phones work but it isn't really his thing."

"A simple system doesn't take much. We could probably manage with a few car batteries and some of the parts from the old phones." Isiah stopped, and looked embarrassed. "I'm sorry, I should have come up with that, a phone system. I used to work for telecoms."

"Really?" Harold kept the smile from his face. "Could you rig up a few? Between the three guardhouses would be a great help."

"A lot depends on what kit there is or what could be found scavenging. I could probably manage to rig that up and more if you want. Would you rather have a switchboard type system to put your house on as well? It wouldn't be too much harder if we find enough jack plugs?" Isiah already looked much happier than Harold had ever seen him. "There'll be LEDs on broken electrical kit, and if not little Christmas lights would do it."

"A proper exchange? Can we use the phone lines?"

"It won't be a modern exchange, and I can't put everyone on it, or not yet. You'll need someone sat there all the time or near enough to hear a bell or buzzer." Isiah sat thinking for a few moments. "Ordinary phone wires work well but a lot of these places might have used buried cables." He brightened. "I can use any electrical wire really, as long as there's two cores at least."

"That would be fantastic. Would you mind? It'll be a big help."

"No problem. I might need someone to climb and crawl here and there?" Isiah pointed at his leg.

"I'll have a talk to a few people and work out if we want a telephone exchange and where it would go. Thanks a lot Isiah." Harold left with a big smile. Veronica had been dead right about her dad knowing about phones, and needing a challenge to cheer him up. Back in the house Isiah had already started dismantling the house phone to check on the components.

* * *

Matti drew a number from her sister's Stetson and waved it in triumph. "My turn, Soldier Boy." Behind her Sal concluded a really intense discussion with Holly and then tickets changed hands. Drawing numbers for last dance and walking home seemed to be established now, with Matti definitely up for some competition with her sister. Harold smiled and winked at Sharyn.

"I've got to walk the other way, so you've got plenty of time." Sharyn stuck her tongue out as Sandy claimed his dance. She'd probably be walking home alone since he would offer, but be only too pleased with a refusal. Sandy only danced three or four times because he's been pressganged into attending, to make up the numbers of men at the end. All these new rules had appeared along with a demand from the girl club, and most of the younger blokes, for a dance every fortnight.

Harold walked a giggling Matti home in a group with Alicia, Celine, Doll, Louise and Holly. Holly saw his puzzled look and laughed. "I'm walking Barry home because he's worried about Billy." He certainly should be, considering how Billy and Doll were sniggering together. Celine seemed relaxed about her escort this time since Stewart Baumber had no designs on anyone. The machete blow across his chest had knitted but not healed yet, leaving him in no fit state for even hugging. Liam ended up with a peck on the cheek from Louise, blushed and half ran up the street.

"If Finn walks me home again I'll start to worry about a fix." Alicia smiled as Finn spluttered his denials. Finn had become Alicia's shooting instructor, using an air pistol, because Alicia had decided that if the worst happened she wanted to shoot at least one. According to Emmy, Finn was an acceptable tutor because of being half armless, a reference to his injured arm. Finn had also developed into a good shot with an air pistol.

After Finn, and then Barry, had kissed hands and gone in and Stewart left to go home, Holly turned away and covered her eyes. "I'm much too young to see the next bit."

"She might be if gramps wasn't heading for the front room to peek round the curtain." Doll wrapped her arms around Billy and connected. Harold was going to reply but Matti wasn't wasting snogging time on talk.

"There." Matti looked definitely smug. "Now you can compare that with my sister's pathetic attempt." Harold had no intention of making any comment on that, but Matti's eyes sharpened and she turned to Holly. "Hey, no fair. Now you'll get him to walk you home. Worse, you haven't got a gramps."

"No but I've got Mummy Casper lurking behind the door. Anyway he isn't walking me home." Holly hooked her arm through Harold's. "We just happen to go up the same street and Billy is along as a chaperone. Harold will dump me at the gate." Her mournful tones didn't go with Holly's grin.

"The curtain just twitched." Doll unwound from a wide-eyed Billy. "Just remember where we got to if you draw my number again." The two sisters hi-fived each other and went in.

"I'm not likely to forget. Do you think she likes me?" Billy now wore a daft grin and smeared lipstick.

Harold sniggered. "If she drags you into the shadows for a repeat without drawing your number, yes. If not we are both being used by that pair to compete."

"I'm good with that." Billy hooked his arm through Holly's free one. "There you are, the safest girl in Orchard Close."

"Or the one in real trouble." Four doors down Billy made a half-hearted effort to claim a kiss for being walked home, and went into the house he shared with Jon and Liam. As Holly and Harold came around the end of the street Holly looked over with a little smile. "I've found out what happens the second time."

"Really? What?"

"Oh no, you have to walk me home first. Especially since you owe me for June's chocolate comfort drink." Holly gave Harold's arm a little hug.

"No I don't. Unless? Doll already claimed a chocolate prize after her dance." Harold smiled just a little bit because even if the sisters weren't in the girl club, they seemed to have the qualifications.

"Oooh, that was naughty. Now you'll have to pay twice."

"So who did actually provide chocolate?" Harold opened the gate and stood back to let Holly through.

"Oh no, it's not that easy. Anyway." Holly stepped in close and looked into Harold's eyes. "Tell me you don't want to walk me up this path and find out about the second time." The sheer mischief in her voice would have been enough but yes, Harold wasn't averse to that at all. Especially since Holly's kisses were very innocent and gentle. She wouldn't try to swallow his lips or play tongues, or try to give him a frontal massage.

"I'd love to walk you home and find out all about second time, Holly." He put his arm around her. "Safe enough with Casper poised to rescue me."

Coming away afterwards Harold wondered about innocent kisses. This one had lingered, though not quite as long as Halloween. Long enough to make Harold think some not innocent thoughts and hug very firmly. Now Harold wondered if Holly had decided to test the water as it were and find out if she'd moved past Brodie dying. Though if she did, Holly would end up with one of the younger blokes like Jon or Billy, someone more her own age.

Maybe Holly had been testing with Soldier Boy before going after the real target, just like Emmy did.

*   *   *

Harold cursed under his breath because the electric alarm clock in his bedroom had stopped. "Harold, Harold." That brought a smile to his face.

"Yes Hazel, that's me."

"My clock stopped, Harold, and my tablet won't work this morning." The scavengers had found several tablet computers and every house now had at least one or a laptop. Those were of limited use without wi-fi or the internet, but each one had some information. How useful that turned out depended on what the owner had been interested in. In addition they made excellent notebooks as paper became scarcer.

"Is the…?" Harold bit that off and tried the light switch. A chill that was nothing to do with weather ran through him because the bulb didn't come on. "Leave it with me, Hazel." He really didn't want to tell Hazel the electricity had gone off, not without checking the trip switch. As he dressed and hurried downstairs Harold worried that the cut wasn't the trip switch.

The big switch in the off position left Harold a bit weak-kneed for a moment and he realised just how worried he'd been. The slender wire lifeline bringing electricity kept Orchard Close going, and could be cut too easily for Harold's peace of mind. He turned the switch to "on" and went to the TV to check for a report, and the TV wouldn't come on. The standby lights were still out, as were the ones on the CD player, though the room light worked. "Damn." Harold spoke softly because no light on his phone charger as well meant a serious problem.

A quick walk around the house showed that the cooker had survived, and any equipment not plugged in, but some of the rest refused to work again. Harold's little battery walky talkie started buzzing and Casper reported similar problems in the girl club. Someone hammered on the door. "Come in."

"We've got problems Harold. Is your electricity on?" Betty's looked much older than her sixty years, her face pale and drawn with worry.

"Yes, but some of the equipment won't start up again. How about you?"

"Nothing, no electric at all and I looked at the trip thing and turned it on. There aren't any lights on down the main street, Harold." Betty sat down and rubbed her face with a hand. "I'm a mess, because I thought it had all gone. If yours is on, others will be, thank God."

"Casper has gone for Finn so we can work out what the problem is."

By the time Casper and Finn arrived Harold's lounge had filled up with distraught or puzzled residents. Even the demands for hugs were very half-hearted. Harold held up his hands as a storm of questions greeted the electrician. "Quiet! Please." He smiled. "Hello Finn, how are you Finn, and what happened?"

"Firstly we had a power cut. How many of you watched the storm last night?" The storm had been spectacular as it rolled over the city and away across the countryside to the west. Hands went up and Finn gave them a little smile. "The lightning you were all going ooh at must have struck a line or substation. That's not so bad because this morning the electricity is on again."

"But my MP4 doesn't work." Holly waved the little music player.

"I'll bet that you had it on charge?" Holly nodded and Finn sighed. "We had at least one power surge and my money is on two at least. One came down the power cables when those were hit, and then one that might have come down the old phone lines or TV and internet cables. Those are the same if the house is connected by cables underground." All eyes went to Harold's TV.

"That's dead along with Hazel's tablet and several clocks, a phone and two music players like Holly's." Harold looked around at the rest and heads were nodding in agreement. "Can we fix them?"

"Some of them, maybe, but not all. I can fix the electrical systems but probably not the devices." Finn looked around the room. "All of you, disconnect anything still attached to the old phone lines and cables. If a surge comes down the phone line and jumps to the electrical socket powering the phone, it's past the big trip switch." Many people still had their house phones plugged into the landlines, hoping that one day they'd work again, and most phones were also connected to the mains.

"What about my music?" Liz looked horror-struck.

"My pictures?"

"All my notes on treatments?" Patricia looked really worried. "I used my phone to record what worked best."

"Finn? Will everyone get their information back?" Harold wasn't happy because he'd got pictures of Cyn on there, in her waitress uniform in case the Army had got nosy.

"A lot depends on how you saved it. Some chips might survive, but anything in the phone memory will probably be gone. The CDs will be untouched if you find another player, and some problems might just be fuses in plugs." Finn grimaced. "I'm more worried about the number of fuses in the boxes and sockets that have blown. I'll have to look at all the houses, then we need every fuse or three pin plug we can get."

"Guess what the scavengers are doing today, and tomorrow, and possibly for a week? Finn, I'd appreciate it if you concentrate on making sure all the houses have electricity and heat first. Then we'll work on the rest." Harold forced a smile. "Personally I'll be charging up my stuff while I'm awake, and I'll unplug the lot at the first mutter of thunder."

"Do that anyway at night, the TV aerials as well. If the surge can't reach it, your kit is safe." Finn braced himself. "Right, who hasn't got the main power back on?"

"Me please." Betty stood up and three others went to join Finn. The rest filed out to get breakfast and come to terms with the new threat.

As the last one filed out, Sharyn whispered from behind Harold. "That smile was a bit forced, Harold. What didn't you say?"

"Not much, but if this happens a few more times we'll gradually run out of music players and phones, TVs and electric clocks. Maybe even fuses." Harold sighed. "I lost some memories on my phone, or maybe I did."

Sharyn looked distraught and turned to the table in the corner where a frame held a small screen. The slide show of pictures was blank. "Freddy."

"You've got other pictures. Weren't they copies, and anyway the chip might be OK?" Harold held out his arms because reassurance wasn't working. Nothing did for a few minutes until Daisy came downstairs and pointed out that Wills was shouting and couldn't she get a moment's peace in this place. Sharyn sniggered at that because the five-year-old delivered it in the exact tone and wording Sharyn used when Daisy was being particularly trying.

* * *

An impressive, in a depressing way, list of items no longer worked. Much of the music couldn't be replaced, nor could the information lost on one of the computers. Hilda, Veronica and Hazel set into copying every useful download onto DVDs in case another hard drive failed for any reason at all. They also copied all information from salvaged tablets and laptops, regardless of if it seemed useful, onto a few extra salvaged tablets and laptops because there weren't enough blank DVDS or CDs. A dedicated sweep of the empty housing in Orchard Close itself produced some replacements for TVs, microwaves, and clocks.

The following day the scavengers had a list from Finn, and some stern warnings about testing first. Surge protection and a selection of spares from fuses up to entire fuse boxes were ripped out of houses that had no electricity, and stored in Finn's garage. By the first evening the storage grew to include a whole house with replaced windows and a sound roof. Oil filled electric radiators kept damp at bay while Sandy, Stewart Baumber and anyone else with handyman aspirations put up shelves to stack a growing selection of electrical loot.

Orchard Close took the warnings from Finn to heart, with all electrical equipment turned off and unplugged when not in use. A necessary precaution because too much of the electrical equipment in the ruins turned out to be already damp and useless. Finn hoped some would work after drying out but even with the memories backed up someplace, replacement equipment couldn't be guaranteed. Mobile phones and music players went on the scavenging list, and any chargers were saved even without a phone.

Worse for some than any other problems, they lost all their personal music. Because so much music had been either streamed or downloaded prior to the internet dying, many lost songs couldn't be replaced. Over the ensuing days Harold thought he'd given more soggy-hugs, genuine ones, for music than for anything else. Almost obsolete CDs and even vinyl media and players suddenly went to the top of several personal lists, more so when Rob mentioned how restricted the BBC radio playlist had become. The protest and rock genres were extinct.

*   *   *

"I've been hoping to get you by yourself. Stand back." Barry swung his heavily insulated axe to 'disconnect' the mains from a house that seemed to have no electricity. There had been two frights and a bad burn when wires were still live, so now the scavengers took no chances.

"I'm not hard to find. You talked to me a few days ago about moving in with Finn." Harold smiled. "Some were betting on you moving in with Alicia after New Year."

Barry laughed. "Don't you start. It just seemed pointless heating two houses instead of one, especially with one or the other of us not being at home much of the time." He grinned at Harold. "I have to keep going round to see Alicia just so I don't find the local oiks climbing through my granddaughters' windows." Harold grinned back because the real plan had worked well. Celine could handle Barry downstairs watching TV and talking to his granddaughters, while Alicia felt better because she had a man in the house. Louise now lived there as well, and Finn sometimes joined Barry in helping Alicia feel safer. If all that failed, Matti and Doll could bring a smile to a statue.

"So what did you want to talk about?"

Barry hesitated, looking embarrassed. "I've heard you were in the SAS."

"I've never said that." Harold also didn't say he'd been a clerk because not only did Orchard Close find his alleged expertise reassuring, but it also backed off the yobs.

"No, but you never say you weren't and I've got a problem with that." Barry paused. "With the SAS part. Tell me to shut up and I will."

"Go on."

"When we set fire to that car, you didn't know which products to use. Well you did because most of you read labels and used the ones that said flammable." There was a question in Barry's voice and face, but Harold wanted to hear it all.

"Keep going."

"I knew exactly which ones would burn well, because of my training. I would expect an SAS man to know for an entirely different reason." He shrugged. "Since then Alicia, Louise and even Celine now and then talked about the attacks on the flats and Orchard Close. Because I wondered, I asked a couple of very casual questions. Why did you make petrol bombs at the flats?"

"To burn any vehicles attempting to force an entry."

"Why didn't you make pipe bombs, especially here when that mob was coming?" Barry had got to what bothered him and had tensed right up.

"I don't know how." Harold gave a short laugh. "I'll bet Stones would have known."

"What?"

Harold smiled. "Stones is, hopefully still is, really SAS. Unfortunately I'm not."

"What are you?" A very tense Barry still held his axe in what would be a white-knuckled grip if Harold could see under the gloves.

"An ex-soldier, honourable discharge, who came to rescue his sister and arrived too late. The residents assumed SAS and it made them feel better and the SAS bit frightens the yobs, so I let it ride." Harold tried to put every ounce of sincerity he could into his voice. "I promise I have never, ever claimed to be other than a soldier."

"Thank God for that." Barry sighed and relaxed. "I wondered about deserter, but the others told me the Army know who you are and that Sharyn really is your sister. The Army bit explains your shooting. I'll bet you had a big rifle with bloody great sights like those on the TV."

"No but if we still paid anyone I could keep the records in perfect order."

Harold grinned at Barry's baffled expression. "Come on, we'll take a break, drink this flask of tea, and I'll explain."

The tea had gone before Barry sat back with a big sigh. "Stupid as it sounds, I feel better. I assume you don't want everyone knowing?"

"I won't lie to them." Harold had long since decided that lying and being found out would be worse for morale than just being caught out not denying.

"I'll keep quiet. In that case, would you like to know how to make a pipe bomb?"

Harold stared at Barry's sad smile. "What? But your job is to stop things going bang, or burning anyway. Oh."

Barry nodded. "To do that we learn what shouldn't mix with what, and the type of thing that should never be heated or chilled, and what will go bang or burn and when. It's a hell of a hint on how to make them do just that." He sighed. "It goes against everything I've been taught, but a pipe bomb will stop a bunch of those Geeks if they get past your rifle."

"Will anyone realise why I put the ingredients on the scavenger list?" Harold still didn't fancy this idea, because there'd been plenty of warnings about people who tried to make bombs and ended up dead or crippled. In the Middle East a good few bomb makers among the nutters trying to kill soldiers were missing fingers.

"Come with me, into the kitchen." Barry stood up. "This is your average house, so here's your first lesson." Five minutes later, after a trip to the bathroom as well, Barry gestured at the table. "Cut off a length of pipe, even plastic downpipe from a gutter, and seal it really well. What's here will make the damn thing into a killer, or at least something to blind or cripple anyone near enough."

"Bloody hell." Harold stared at the collection. "Er, how hard is it? This lot won't just go bang else half the houses in England would be ruins." He looked round. "Oops, they are, but you know what I mean."

Barry finally smiled, a welcome relief after his expression since the offer. "True. No, they're all relatively safe like this or Health and Safety might have been involved, though you will be surprised how easy it is to alter that. Just heat and a fridge will do for some." He looked round. "Where do you want to learn all this, and make some of each?" He smiled again, just a little one. "Carefully, and not in huge quantities."

"Cripes yes." Harold looked at the collection. "Sugar might be a problem because a lot of it is damp or set in a lump."

"Sugar is harmless. We dry out the wet sugar and grind the solid into powder again, it doesn't even matter if there's a bit of muck in it. Then when some of these are doctored and mixed in with the sugar?" Barry shook his head. "I'd get drummed out of the Brigade if I'd still been in."

"If we can get one ready before I meet the neighbours, they might give you a life-saving medal."

*　　　*　　　*

By the time Cooper turned up to announce that the meeting would be at the traffic island, Orchard Close had grown by another three men, seven women and two more children. At least two of them had bad bruising, and some of the others were very close-lipped. As Cooper drove off, in a Mini Cooper of course, Alfie spoke quietly to Harold. "Whoever it is seemed very interested in that. They've moved up near enough to hear what was said."

"After three days maybe it's time to see who it is. Where are they?"

"Third house along away from the Army, this side of the road." Alfie chuckled. "Top left window, because Sal has got the binoculars on them. Though she still can't make out if it's a man or woman."

"Woman is my bet, they're more cautious." Harold cupped his hands and shouted. "You in the third house along, at the bedroom window, come out and talk." Harold pointed at the window and then cupped his hands again. "Come into the open and either a man or woman will come to talk to you. Your choice."

"Send a woman." Then after a short pause "Unarmed?"

"I'm pleased I didn't take the bet because that's either a young lad or a woman from the voice." Alfie made a small gesture towards the guardhouse. "Your rifle is upstairs in number two, Sal is keeping it warm. Are you sure you want to be upstairs with Sal?" Alfie had a definite snigger in his voice.

"She's been less manic since Christmas and New Year." Sal still lived in the girl club having told Jon she wanted a bloke for the holidays, not for life. He was still sulking. "Maybe I should send Sal out there anyway, she's fairly reassuring." Harold raised his voice. "Almost unarmed."

"All right. Where?"

"Come out of the back door when you see her, and when she gets closer, step clear of the house." Harold turned to go and get Sal.

"I'll go."

Harold stopped and smiled. "Good idea, June." June, at five foot five and genuinely almost forty, definitely classed as non-threatening. At the moment the mousey brown and grey hair cut into a bob was down to a careful dye job, but should be permanent once that grew out. According to Emmy and Liz, June had once been a trophy wife which explained her manicured appearance. When her industrialist husband left the city before the Army sealed all access he'd taken both teenaged children and, presumably, the young model he kept on the side.

"I have to find a new profession anyway. Mediator sounds about right." June patted her machete. "Though this probably isn't the accepted wear." These days her smiles were much more genuine than the first one Harold saw. "At least I can eat chocolate now, providing I can find any more."

"I'll ask the girl club for some if you can talk this one inside. I get nervous about strangers hanging about." Harold glanced up at number two. "Give me a chance to get upstairs so I've got a rifle covering your back."

"Get someone to tell me to slow up if you aren't ready." June turned and headed for the back wall.

"We should have a proper gate rather than the car. It's a pain walking round to save petrol."

"It's on the list, Alfie."

June took her time and Harold had the rifle ready before she walked across the overgrown back gardens. A muffled figure came to meet her, with a big scarf wrapped round most of her face and a woolly hat with a pompom. Three or four minutes of arm waving and pointing, and an inspection of June's machete that had Harold's sights settled firmly on the scarf, and the meeting ended. June stood and waited as the figure went back into the house, and came out carrying a backpack and several carrier bags.

Harold put the safety on and propped his rifle up in the corner. "You were well behaved today."

"I'm a good girl these days." Sal grinned. "Though if I'd known you were coming I might have put a hot water bottle in the bed."

"That's better. I thought you'd been exchanged for someone almost sober."

"Not really. Most of us have sobered up a bit since Christmas and I really needed to. I got a bit too far into the bottle for a while." Her smile flashed. "Jon helped. I sort of let off some steam, released some tension or whatever. I'm not usually a tart, or only after I get to know the bloke a bit and maybe have a few drinks. Liz says it's Darwin's fault."

"When did he move in?"

"No, idiot, the scientist bloke. Apparently an urge to breed, or practice breeding, is an automatic reaction after near disaster or a narrow escape from death. Wildlife populations boom after a forest fire, that sort of thing." Sal grinned. "Though since I have got to know you a bit, and I sometimes have a few too many drinks, don't relax."

"Does this mean the entire girl club will be backing off a bit?"

"Hmm." Sal actually gave that some thought. "You'll get teased, and some of us might not say no on a moonlit night, but the edge has gone off if you know what I mean. Though a few are definitely serious, so if you relax you'd better check if the bed has been warmed up first."

Harold put up fingers to count off. "Cold bed, no booze, no mood music, I'm off."

"Typical bloke, the girl has to do all the work." Sal picked up the binoculars and moved to her seat by the window. As Harold opened the door she sniggered. "Just remember that Doll and Matti haven't had chance to take the edge off yet." Her laugh followed Harold down the stairs.

*   *   *

"I want to see an armed woman in there before I come over this wall."

Harold smiled at the suspicious eyes peering between the hat and scarf. "How many and how well armed? They can't show firearms because the Army is just up there."

The figure gave a big sigh. "It's too late now anyway but you really meant what you said, didn't you? To the man in the car."

Harold thought a moment and was sure what she meant. "The bit about foul language?" Harold had reminded Cooper that the meeting would be on Orchard Close property, so there were rules.

"More the bit about it being a rule, even right up to that roundabout, especially since he agreed." She, definitely she when the scarf unwound, climbed over the wall. "Don't you have a door into this place?"

"Yes, but it costs petrol. We're working on it." Harold held out his hand. "Hello, I'm Harold."

"Harold Soldier Boy do what he says but he seems a nice enough bloke, according to June." Behind her June shrugged. "I'm Patty, which will do since unless your surname is Boy, one name is enough here." She inspected Harold, put out her hand and shook. "You need a scarf in this weather, and I'm just the right person."

"You are? Come on Patty, I'll take you to the girl club until you work out where you want to live. That's a home for single females." Harold waved a hand up the road. "Along here a bit and behind those scrawny trees."

"That's civilised. Do the men have a house as well?" Patty looked about as she walked up the road, and seemed totally relaxed now.

"No, they usually live in pairs so they have someone to drink with when the girls turn them down. Again." Harold turned up towards the girl club. "Those two houses there, on the right. I live in the end house."

"Convenient?" Suspicion crept into her voice again.

"Not really, I live with my big sister. Though Liz says it's reassuring having me parked at the end of the road." Harold raised his voice. "Anyone home?"

"Of course, especially if you're calling." The door opened and a signature hairstyle popped into view. "That's mean, bringing your own." Emmy grinned. "I'll just call up and tell them to forget the frilly stuff."

"Naughty. You're spoken for now." Harold waved towards Patty. "Emmy, this is Patty. Patty, this is Emmy and if you want to see a heavily armed woman this is the go-to girl."

"I hope there's another hairdresser." Patty stuck out a hand. "I'm told it's an all-woman house in here."

"Apart from the resident housemother." Emmy shouted back over her shoulder. "Casper!" Harold left them to it. Patty already sounded as if she'd fit right in. Then he remembered.

"Emmy? I promised June a bit of chocolate for going out to get this one. Any chance you could organise some? Just a little bit?" Harold smiled as innocently as he could manage.

"Oh I'm sure someone can find some, especially at the prices you'll pay. You still owe some of us for Christmas."

As he set off up the street Harold could hear Patty's first question. "I thought we were all supposed to do what he said?"

*   *   *

Patty fitted in with hardly a ripple, once she knew someone would teach her to use a crossbow. "Knives are messy. The next bastard trying that crap is going to get a steel tipped migraine" was a direct quote. Since the girl club were perfectly at ease with those sentiments, Patty moved on to her passion in life.

"Knitting?" Harold stared. "What, scarves and the like? Hats with pompoms?"

"No, real hand knitting. Cable, Fair Isle, Aran, Lace, bespoke, or do you fancy a scarf with Soldier Boy on it?" Patty looked back at the girl club. "They said you haven't got any wool or needles."

"I wouldn't know." Harold shrugged. "I don't know anyone who knits."

"Bloody mass production or designer labels have a lot to answer for.

What happens when your jumper gets a hole because I've heard the ones in the marts are expensive?" Patty had her hands on her hips now and looked decidedly indignant.

"And really thin. You've got a solution?" Harold could spot a losing argument these days.

"Yes, look up all the wool shops in yellow pages and empty them. Then when the other morons wake up and realise that they're cold and Santa won't be coming, we sell them woollens. Lovely new thick ones." Patty's gaze sharpened. "So I can buy my own crossbow."

"We've got crossbows." Harold had enough so anyone willing to use one could have that or a rifle, and a handgun as well. He was hoping Patty could actually do what she wanted, and stick a sharp something into another human, because shooters were scarcer than crossbows. The quote about knives being messy seemed promising.

"I want one of those posh ones that wind, the ones with lots of power so the bastard really feels it." There wasn't any give at all in those sentiments.

"Righto. So where do I get this wool? Most shops have been looted." Harold knew he was wrong from the big smile.

"No, the morons take all the ready knitted stuff, or some of it anyway. I've slept in two wool shops, tucked up nice and warm in a pile of skeins that have been ignored. I can tell you where the nearest is?" Patty looked around, apparently for a map to appear. Harold winced because as one of the morons he'd taken this jumper from a wrecked shop and left any skeins, whatever they were.

"It'll have to be quick because in four days that meeting will set out boundaries. After that we'll get shot." Harold grinned. "We might get shot at before that."

"So go at night, and use that sneaky stuff the Army taught you. Have you got a map?" Harold directed her to Hilda in the library, and went to see Sharyn and check out this knitting business. It made sense, sort of, but he needed a sanity check.

"Children grow out of clothes overnight. If she'll knit new clothes for Daisy and Wills I'll go out and sneak around myself." Harold got similar answers from Liz, Casper, and even Barry and Suzie, the opposite ends of the Orchard Close spectrum. Knitting would be very good especially since now they'd apparently got someone who knew how, to teach others. Harold braced himself and sorted out a raiding squad.

Chapter 4:
Rules for Kissing and Killing

Casper smiled sunnily. "Try not to yawn, they'll be insulted."

"Sod off. I was crawling around half the bloody city while you were getting your beauty sleep. The woman's a slave driver." Harold smirked. "Though I get the first jumper, a big thick winter job."

"Not a balaclava?" Casper gestured up the road. "That lot would be impressed."

"Enough. Just remember that if you make gay jokes, so can they." Harold would bet that Casper, Emmy, Alfie and Holly were all as nervous as he was. Just up the road fifteen gangsters, nutters or yobs waited to meet them, and they'd all be heavily armed. This was a recipe for disaster.

That feeling wasn't allayed as the minibus drew up because each group stood in front of their parked vehicles, each still on the approach road from their own enclave. The empty traffic island in the middle made that look more like a standoff than a meeting. "Holly, Emmy, have you unloaded your crossbows? They all have, just as promised." Casper pulled up just before the roundabout and the five of them lined up just as the others had. As they did the rest moved forward, and soon all four groups were closer, stood in the road around the central island about twelve feet apart.

"Hi there Kabir. Did the convoys work out?"

"I went with Ogou as a name and we'll be talking to Cadillac about the next convoys. Thanks for the name, Emmy." He turned to the tall well-muscled man next to him. "I told you about Emmy."

The man nodded and put his hand on the hilt of what looked a lot like a long heavy sword on his belt, a real one, opposite a pistol and a knife. "I'm Gofannon, and this is Vulcan." The smaller man, still well built, had short dark red hair and a small, neat pointed red beard. "The other two are soldiers." Two men with crossbows and machetes nodded. Both had small metal

Stop signs on one arm as a shield.

Harold turned to the Hot Rods. "Hi Cadillac. I know most of your lot already. Cooper, Kev, and I do believe that is Bugatti." Harold smiled. "Risky."

"I thought Bugatti could do to learn how much better it goes if he doesn't shoot first. The other one is Porsche and just a bit annoyed about the car fire." The fifth man had a machete, crossbow and a definite scowl. Only Kev didn't wear the mechanic style overalls. Cadillac nodded towards the fourth group. "Those are the Geek Freeks."

"I'm Hawkins." The thin youth wore what looked like a shop assistant's smock over a suit, and tapped a name badge as he spoke. Harold kept the smile off his face because the others were dressed the same so they also had a uniform. "Darwin, Marconi, Einstein and Tell. William Tell." The Geek indicated each one as he spoke and Tell carried one of the complicated bows with pulleys and cables.

"I thought William Tell was the crossbow type?" Kabir frowned. "Shouldn't he be Robin Hood?"

Hawkins laughed. "There's already too many Hoods." His wave indicated everyone there, then paused at Harold's group. "Though I don't know who your lot are. You are the Soldier Boy, but the rest?"

"Casper, Holly, Emmy and Alfie."

Einstein, a short fat man with thinning hair eyed Emmy. "I'll trade you a chink for that big black. We've got two chinks but no blacks yet. Christ, I'd break out a new mattress for her welcoming party."

Harold ignored Einstein for a moment, looking at Cadillac. "Did you explain about rules?"

"I told them that you expected everyone to be polite to women, and no foul language." Cadillac tensed because Emmy had started moving. "Though I didn't expect women at the meeting."

Emmy walked behind Alfie and the sound as her hands were momentarily hidden was distinctive. Emmy still used a child's crossbow because she had the strength to cock it without bracing, and she had fitted a bolt by the time the weapon reappeared. The point centred on a startled Einstein as Harold spoke. "Emmy?"

"He offered to buy and then rape me Harold. We haven't tested the latest points." Most eyes went to the point on the crossbow bolt and hands went to weapons all around the roundabout.

"I didn't say rape." Einstein had gone pale because at this range the intricate concoction of spines and barbs would fillet him. Darwin started to pull his pistol but stopped because Casper's shotgun swung to cover him.

"Everyone stay calm, because shooting would be a bad idea. I had intended this to be a demonstration later, but now might be good." Harold's rifle barrel wandered a little towards the Geeks. "Give me time to persuade you, because this will go through two and Emmy won't miss. Casper, watch the others."

"Staying calm sounds a good idea and I'd been hoping for a demonstration anyway." Cadillac definitely stood ready for anything, with his hand on his pistol butt. "Soldier Boy's demonstrations are usually instructive, Hawkins. Aren't they, Bugatti?" Bugatti didn't answer and Cadillac smiled.

"Everyone look back down the road behind me." Harold raised his voice. "Bernie!"

"Here."

"Demonstration, please."

Harold didn't look back, but fourteen of the fifteen men facing his way did and they were seeing Bernie come out of a house three doors down. Then they were seeing a puff of smoke, followed by something trailing smoke over the garden wall and in through the broken front window of the house four doors down. If it hadn't gone through the window Bernie would be legging it across the gardens and yelling for people to duck. The bang was louder than Harold expected, though Barry warned the confined space would increase the effect.

"Show them the real thing, Bernie, then get back in cover." All the men's faces showed varying degrees of shock and Darwin had moved his hand off his pistol.

"Real thing? What the f… What was the first one?" Gofannon glanced at Holly with a wry smile, then back at Harold.

"That was a pipe bomb, a demonstration since we don't want shrapnel whizzing about. The second one is wrapped in all sorts of nasty stuff. I don't want to be dodging that even if it hasn't actually landed next to me." Harold waited, watching faces to see if any of them would give a hint. Barry had been certain that gangster types and certain sorts of youths especially would know how to make bombs.

"They're a lot more impressive in real life than in a computer game." Cadillac had lost his urbane pose for a moment as the bomb went off, but came quickly back on balance. "There you are, Bugatti, you were actually very lucky. If he'd tossed one of those in wherever you were hiding, a fine wouldn't have really bothered you."

"We all got the message, but is she really going to kill Einstein? He didn't say rape." Hawkins' hand drifted towards his gun again. "I can't just let her kill him, not at what's supposed to be a peaceful meeting."

"Technically he didn't, though it was definitely implied." Vulcan smirked. "Is there a penalty short of death?" His voice and language were more cultured than expected, though Vulcan seemed amused rather than horrified at the possibility of Einstein being spiked.

"He offered to trade me for another woman, and then said he was going to put me on a mattress for a party. I didn't hear may I or please." Emmy's crossbow hadn't wavered, and Einstein hadn't looked towards the explosion. "That's slavery and rape." She sighed. "Not the words, but it's at least the same as asshole said to Holly."

"This gets more and more instructive. What did asshole say to Holly?" Cadillac chuckled. "More to the point, what did Holly do, because Einstein might prefer shooting."

"He said he'd come back and overrun Orchard Close, and told Holly he was claiming her." Harold's smile had no humour. "She tied him to a lamp post and gelded him. We had to kill his friends first, but we saved him specially."

"We didn't waste them, their heads made a great border marker." Alfie still covered the GOFS and Casper had let his shotgun drift back towards the Hot Rods.

"Three bodies and nine heads as a marker. I remember that bit." Cadillac actually looked happy about finding out the details.

"F...Hell, that was you!" Darwin glared at Einstein. "You stupid er, prat. Didn't it cross your tiny mind it might have been this lot?"

"No, nor mine so zip it." Hawkins spread his hands, palms up. He had a sort of smile though Harold could see that the Geek boss's eyes were furious. "We saw the bodies and heads after the birds and rats got to them, and the, er, big mess where his jeans were pulled down. That's why we never pushed this way but we thought whoever did that got run over by the riots." His gaze fixed on Cadillac. "The warnings of rules and penalties were a bit short on detail. There's got to be a way short of gelding if there's going to be peace between us all, because we couldn't let that ride. How about a fine? Cadillac mentioned fines."

"It'll be a hell of a fine to compensate her for a set of nuts." A big smile broke over Gofannon's face. "How about that chink, the one he offered?"

"It's a reasonable exchange for his nuts." Cooper chortled. "Maybe it is, we don't know how big his nuts are." He calmed down a bit. "Come on, what's one girl? There's plenty more and we've got more serious shit to sort out than that." His eyes narrowed. "I want to see the result of Cadillac's test."

"Yeah, though I think we've answered my question." Cadillac curled a lip and sneered at Einstein. "Come on, make your mind up. After all, if she sticks that thing in your guts or takes your nuts the chink is no good to you anyway."

Einstein looked at Hawkins, who nodded, then he turned back to Emmy. "All right, you get the chink. Just point that damn thing away from me."

Even as Emmy's crossbow drifted fractionally off-target, Cadillac spoke up. "Good. Now I want my question answered. How well can you really shoot, Soldier Boy?"

"How well can your man shoot, Cadillac? How far away can he shoot a man through the eyes, or through the head?" The gang boss opened his mouth to answer but Harold kept going. "Without a telescopic sight." Harold grinned as Cadillac frowned.

"He can kill a man at oh, three or four hundred yards? Can you?" Cadillac's little smile reappeared.

Harold's smile was completely genuine. "Alfie, take the targets out please. Twelve, three hundred and three fifty paces in that direction." Harold pointed directly downwind. The wind wasn't strong but it wasn't quite steady either and he wanted all the help he could get. If Cadillac was saying three to four hundred, the gang leader would be egging it a bit and meaning body shots which was a relief. The bastard hadn't found a decent shooter.

While Alfie fastened up the thin plywood panels with figures painted on them Harold collected his own two-two rifle from the minibus. He went into a nearby garden, to one of several stacks of bricks arranged so Harold could always shoot up or downwind. Harold needed that edge because he wasn't a hunter, an outdoor marksman. He could shoot, especially on a range, but hadn't the experience for dealing with varying wind conditions.

Harold laid a folded jacket on top of the bricks and waited until Alfie raised an arm and moved back into cover. There were doors already waiting in various directions, and timbers to prop them upright and now black man-shaped figures were clearly visible fastened to three of them.

Hawkins raised a pair of stubby binoculars to his eyes and a light blinked. "Eleven metres, two seventy five metres, and three twenty metres. Now let's see you hit them without sights."

Harold felt happy, and contented, because he was in his favourite place.

A rifle, a target, and his head shut out all the other nonsense. The wind would make him shoot a bit high, but as long as it didn't veer he could do this with iron sights. He heard someone speaking but that sounded sort of distant, and he waited as a gust settled and then let the shot go. He flipped the bolt and slid another little round in, then did the same.

"This next bit is what I want to see." Cadillac's voice seemed far away and not even a bit annoying. Harold tucked the big brass plate of the 303 into his shoulder and breathed gently and steadily. He concentrated on the old notch sights and carefully lined up the post on the front of the barrel. The sights settled, his elbows were nicely braced on the rest built into the bricks, and the rifle nestled into the folded jacket.

"One," he breathed as he let the shot go and worked the bolt, moving the sights onto the nearer target and firing with less hesitation. Four times Harold worked the bolt in a steady rhythm, then dropped the clip and slid another in, just in case. The world crashed back in and Harold looked at a mixture of curious and definitely impressed eyes and faces.

"If those hit anything like accurately, I'm a believer." Gofannon looked towards the targets as the centre one twisted and fell. "Well you hit that at least once."

Alfie came out of cover and walked back collecting the three sheets of thin ply. As he approached Alfie had a huge grin and Harold started to relax. "Prop them against the end of that garage, Alfie, so everyone can see." Harold did his best to sound off-hand, even if he might be more curious than anyone.

"I'm a believer." Gofannon turned with a smile. "Though I reckon that was just being flash, an eye shot at, what was it, three twenty metres?"

"You missed the eye though." Hawkins tried to sound unimpressed. "Why didn't you use a proper scope or those tube sight things?"

"Peep sights?" Harold had those on his two-two, and would have loved them for the 303. "We haven't time for Alfie to walk out to a half mile." Harold walked a bit closer because he was truly curious now. Then he breathed a silent thanks to the Gods of shooters, gamblers and possibly fools. The head shot at the far target had drifted, and gone through above the painted eye where an eyebrow would be instead of just under the nose.

Cadillac nodded at the nearer one. "I expected the eye shots on that, and possibly through the body on those." He smiled ruefully. "Not that fast though, and not through the far one's head. Fair enough, you're a real Soldier Boy and one item is off the agenda for this meeting."

"Which is?" Harold could see the gleam in Cadillac's eye and Hawkins had tensed.

"Whether we should combine to run over your place with crossbows and machetes, and divvi up the people and weapons." Cadillac nodded at the target with a hole above the eye. "Relax Soldier Boy. Orchard Close is too expensive, especially after your other little surprise." The Hot Rod boss smiled. "I'll have to buy my beer."

Harold hoped he kept the shock from his face. "Hell, closer in I've taught others to do that so you've made a really smart decision. Now let's get the borders and rules sorted."

"That's another thing settled, your rules stand on your territory." Gofannon didn't sound too bothered about that while Kabir tried not to outright laugh at the Geeks. "Now the posing is over let's get the maps out and talk properly. Which house, Soldier Boy?"

"Beer, table and chairs in there, as promised. Just us four."

"Yes, the rest can stay out here and be polite." Cadillac looked at Hawkins, definitely tweaking him. "Polite will be cheaper. Einstein can compare fines with Bugatti."

A bruising half hour of debate later Harold actually had a larger territory, because of how the roads ran. Each border now ran along a succession of roads, and the gaps between the territories were gone. Better yet, if any one gang attacked any of the others, the other two would join in and slap them down. Harold hoped self-interest would ensure that really happened.

The gangs would all have a clear run up to the bypass to allow their people to use it for shopping. Harold didn't think most of them would do that, but agreed to the actual roadway being neutral territory. Being near the road onto the bypass also meant that Orchard Close would get a steady trickle of refugees turning up, and now there would be rules about those. All four of them agreed they wouldn't accept refugees from the other three gangs. Runners, as they were referred to.

The neutral road also meant Orchard Close would have visitors from all three gangs to buy beer at least. After some more enquiries, Harold had the impression that skills outside of fighting were in short supply elsewhere. The four of them started discussing safeguards for plumber and electrician visits. "I'll want one of your top people as the hostage for a plumber."

"No, a top person as a hostage only if a gang boss visits. Tradesmen and ordinary soldiers just visit if they want to, but disarm." Gofannon grinned. "And keep to the rules or pay the penalties." Hawkins scowled because the other pair kept tweaking him about that.

"A plumber is the same as a gang boss. Be fair, if the toilets stop working, the rest might actually swap the boss for a plumber." Harold shrugged. "It's an incentive to keep the place running."

"I might swap Bugatti for a plumber, but I couldn't get him to visit Orchard Close anyway. I could do with that electrician if he's any good. A lot of our electrics blew and I don't trust some of the repairs."

"How good is your medic?" Hawkins frowned. "It's only a smashed tooth but I don't want the bloke bleeding out or getting infected when the bits are pulled out. Maybe it'll have to be cut out, there's not much showing except a couple of jagged bits." He shrugged. "Our bloke can sew up a bit but inside a mouth is a bit dodgy and we aren't sure a hot iron will work in there."

Harold winced at that, then smiled. "How much will you pay? We can go from a smack on the head and me with pliers right up to a dentist and pain relief so he barely feels it." Harold grinned. "He'd better not swear if he's nearly out and at our mercy."

"Serious dentist? Drilling and filling?" Gofannon winced. "Definitely with pain relief because I wouldn't wish that on anyone."

"I'd pay for you to drill out a couple of teeth for someone without any pain relief? Though we'd have to tie him down for you?" Caddi grinned. "Maybe not, I can use a Black and Decker for that."

"Stop pissing about, Cadillac, I'm serious. One of our managers got hit in the teeth during a bit of strife with the neighbours and he's been stoned for three days to stop him screaming." Hawkins shrugged. "I'd have put him down but he's smart and we need him."

"I'll have customers for your dentist depending on what can be done and the prices." Gofannon shrugged. "If we can pay in trade goods?"

"Not women."

"We can produce tempered steel weapons, or most things in steel? We can probably shoe a horse?" Everyone laughed and Gofannon began to list what he had available to trade to any of the others, which included some bottled gases and welding rods, and plenty of decorating supplies. The GOFS had surplus bolts of cloth to make into clothes and plenty of buttons, thread, zips and haberdashery. Gofannon offered to trade a couple of sewing machines and an overlocker if anyone wanted them. That was something to do with sewing so Harold made a note to ask Kerry.

The Geeks had steel plate and some steel tube, cement, putty, various sealants and hardware, mattresses and bedding, and some music players and radios, the two-way type as well as the others. Hawkins didn't know what the electrical bits were that had survived a fire and looting, but offered to trade some for the use of an electrician. He also had blank CDs and DVDs but only a few recorders and players, and very few original music CDs. Everyone wanted those after the power cuts.

Cadillac had charcoal, at two prices when Harold asked about purity, and some coke and coal. The Hot Rods had a selection of pipes, fittings and tools that might be of use to a plumber, and would trade them. He had some heavy metal tools that came from a rail workshop if a smith could use them. Cadillac seemed happier to pay in coupons than the other two so Harold thought he might have more tenants. Both Cadillac and Hawkins offered hard drugs, and they were interested in the source of the really good marijuana Gofannon offered. Eventually the meeting came to a halt with an agreement to keep the peace and trade rather than steal.

All four had taken the clips from their pistols and put the clips and weapons on the table as a sort of truce, and now all four reloaded their weapons. Cadillac's eyes sharpened. "Hey, that's one of the guns you took as a fine, the Glock. It's a poser job but didn't work properly so none of our top men wanted it." He looked closer. "It looks in a lot better nick than before but I recognise those marks. They're where it had to be bashed when the clip jammed but it doesn't stick any more."

"No, because HM doesn't like dirty or sticking weapons. It leads to hours spent polishing toilets." Harold couldn't be sure what had caught Cadillac's interest but the gang boss wasn't angry, or even trying to get a rise.

"Can you fix jams in the weapons themselves?"

Harold sat and thought hard while three pairs of eyes watched him with definite anticipation. Did he want to repair guns for this lot, even if he could? Harold knew he could clear a jam, sort out a sticking clip, and strip and clean even handguns after London. "I can clean them up and fix simple problems. It'll depend on the weapon." A vagrant thought brought a smile. "I'll charge double if some asshole has tried first, just to fix what they did."

"Nasty bastard. Now we've got to work out if it's worth having a go first." Though Gofannon smiled as he spoke. "How much?"

"Depends on the work. If I can't do it, I'll say so." Harold shrugged. "Bring the weapons, but be prepared to pay."

Hawkins had stopped scowling about the fine after dental work came up, and was now very interested in having weapons repaired. "What exactly, if it's for gun repairs?"

"I'll have a think but I'd want propellant if possible, powder for bullets." The last bit was to answer the puzzled looks when Harold said propellant.

"Crap, that's what you used for the pipe bomb!" Hawkins looked angry at being fooled. "Well hard luck if you're short of it now."

"No he didn't as you should be able to tell from the smell. I tried that and powder bombs use a lot and the result isn't the same." Cadillac grinned at Harold. "What did you use? We had two blokes who talked a lot about what would go bang and one blew the crap out of himself. Well, burned himself badly enough so I shot him but you get the drift. The other one can't make a bang like that, but he's going to try harder now."

Now Harold knew Cadillac had one of the types of people Barry had talked about. "Whatever it was, I've got plenty. But I do want propellant."

"If you can do the job, I reckon we can find what you want." Gofannon looked at the others and they nodded. "Are we about done for now?"

Once outside a disgruntled Einstein came across to talk to Hawkins, quietly. After a couple of exchanges Hawkins raised his voice. "I'm not f...messing up a proper dentist for Wellington just for one bloody woman. I'd rather shoot you than him so zip it." He turned to Harold. "We'll leave the fine at the border." Hawkins glanced at Einstein. "Big mouth can deliver her." He seemed more annoyed at Einstein and Cadillac than angry at Harold since gun repairs and dentistry had been agreed.

"I'll follow you home to collect the fine." Casper smiled but without humour. "Wouldn't want the goods damaged by careless handling on the way."

Einstein sneered. "So you get to her first?" He looked puzzled at the laughter from the Orchard Close group.

"No, but this means you won't be able to take it out of her." Emmy sneered at him. "Try to remember, if anything happens to Casper then Soldier Boy will be visiting." She pointed at the targets. "I'll ask him to shoot you someplace fatal, but slow and painful."

"That or maybe Holly here can practice her carving." Cadillac was loving this, so Harold broke it up before Hawkins or Einstein were pushed too far.

Though before the GOFS left, Ogou came across for a quiet word with Harold. "Have you seen a lot more rats lately?"

"Not really, no."

"Brace yourself. Watch out for bites as well because we reckon they've come from the city centre." Ogou shrugged. "Our first aid bloke reckons if they've been eating rotten bodies the bites will be septic, more septic than usual. We're using baseball bats, machetes and gauntlets to keep them out of buildings, and we've had to seal up the sewers."

"Thanks, we'll be ready. I owe you one."

Ogou grinned. "Two? Beers?" Harold nodded and he left.

"Let's get moving before the Army get curious about the shooting and boom." The groups loaded up and set off, except for Harold, Holly, Alfie and Emmy. Casper had followed the Geeks in the minibus so the other four walked back, collecting Bernie. On the way they made plans for a rat invasion.

*   *   *

The cheer as Casper climbed out of the minibus in his shirt and underpants died away as they saw why. The nervous oriental woman who followed wore Casper's jacket and trousers with the cuffs folded up, and was barefooted. Emmy and Holly quickly led her away.

"He threw her out of the gates buck naked, Harold. I wanted to gutshoot the bastard there and then." Casper glanced up the street where the woman was being taken to the girl club. "That lass thinks she's been sold and I don't think she believes me. Now I'm going to streak right through Orchard Close because I'm bloody freezing in my underwear."

Liz passed on the rest of the tale, along with the significance of the mattress comment from Einstein. The Geeks really had a bedding store and each of the girls gathered up for the men had her own mattress. Nobody outside the girl club saw the rescued girl for some time, and then only briefly as she came to terms with real freedom. Except when Umeko insisted on meeting Harold to ask, very formally, for sanctuary. Harold might push Einstein into a mistake if he ever caught the man without witnesses, and the girl club definitely would.

*   *   *

"At least the freezer will be full. We'll be able to feed the pets for a year on these." Holly wasn't smiling as she used a broom to move dead rats away from the door to the brewery storeroom. "The cats are stuffed and they've given up."

"We could sell some as mince or burgers?" Seth didn't smile either because one rat had bitten clean through his gauntlet even if the wound hadn't gone deep.

Harold looked at the bodies. Most of the rodents had gone straight through Orchard Close heading for the countryside, ignoring both people and houses, but the rest were really insistent. "Just remember to leave the bricks on all the manholes until we're sure they've gone from the drains. At least they've eased off today. I didn't think there were that many rats in the bloody city."

"It probably wasn't that many, though the size of a few really worried me." Nigel looked down at his multiple layers of clothing. "I really worried these might not be enough."

"Look on the bright side, everyone wanting crossbow practice got plenty and even those big ones couldn't handle their own person gift from Liz." Seth grimaced. "Is it a good idea to freeze these for animal food, with what they've been eating? Even cooking them might not be enough to kill whatever they've picked up."

"I don't think anyone has had time to gut and skin any, so maybe we'll just burn the lot. Then we can all sleep for a long, long time. The last few days and nights have been a bit fraught." Harold smiled. "Keeping Daisy penned in is a chore for an armoured division at least."

"Cripes. Is that why you volunteered for rat bashing?" Holly grinned. "Or was it so you can walk me home?"

Seth sniggered. "You'll never feel a hug through that lot."

"It's the principle that matters." Holly looked down at herself and at Harold. "Yeuk, on second thoughts there's limits." She looked down at the rats. "I really am tempted to sell a few to the Geeks in burgers."

"They'll be skint after paying Gayle and Patricia, so perhaps we'll skip that?"

*   *   *

Gayle didn't look at all happy about working on a Geek regardless of pay, after hearing about Umeko. Her latest objections came as the Geek convoy pulled up to deliver the patient, which meant too late really so Harold had to pacify her sharpish. "If you really can't fix him just say so. Though if you can we'll get paid really well in putty, cement and propellant for ammunition." Harold glanced towards the gate. "He's not Einstein and you can always use the excuse he's too bad to fix. Then Hawkins will shoot him."

Gayle winced at that, then scowled. "He's one of the same lot. I'll have a go but only if Patricia helps. First bloody word I don't like and he can go home and bleed to death."

"Fair enough. Here, a present from Patty." Gayle stared at the balaclava. "All the gangs were very interested in us having a dentist, so Patty knitted you this. Just in case one of them gets ambitious."

"This isn't helping." Gayle pulled on the balaclava. "Let me have a look at him."

Wellington had been helped through the gates by Hawkins and another Geek Freek, one without a suit. When the wad of padding over the side of his face came off everyone winced at his mashed and swollen lips and lower face. "Well?" Hawkins looked from his man to Patricia and Gayle, or two anonymous women since Patricia also opted for a balaclava.

Both of them moved closer. "Can we see inside his mouth?" Patricia stared at the scabs and swelling. "Christ, how long since he was hurt?"

"A while before the meeting. We've had rats since." Hawkins sounded defensive. "He can't feel anything." Hawkins and the other man took hold of the injured Geek and Hawkins used one hand to pull his split and swollen lip back. The brief thrashing and low moan gave the lie to Hawkins' assertion. "Well not much, he's stoned out of his skull."

"I can't do anything until he's properly out, and we'll have to get those drugs out of him or what I use might kill him." Gayle sounded less belligerent now. "Shock might kill him anyway."

"I might be able to get that swelling down, and if um, the dentist fixes him I can try to sew it up. He'll be here a while." Patricia glanced at Harold. "We'll need a talk about what can be done."

"Back in a minute Hawkins." Harold took the two women next door. "Well?"

"It'll cost us antibiotics Harold, and whatever Gayle uses." Patricia glanced towards the next house and the patient. "If we turn him away it's kinder to shoot him, because that'll infect if it hasn't already. Infection will kill him anyway and I wouldn't wish that death on anyone." She frowned. "We could be a while getting whatever he's taken out of him and something else in, and he'll hurt like hell, but he ought to stay." Patricia looked over at Gayle. "I'll try if Mz dentist will, but they've got to understand he might die anyhow."

Gayle sniggered. "Ok Mz doctor." She sobered. "From what you said we might have to cut the bloody thing out, and I don't fancy that one bit. Can we send him home after, to recover?"

"Yes. He can come back to be checked. If he doesn't all bets are off." Patricia looked at Harold. "Your call. We've got to use some valuable drugs to do this, valuable as in rare."

"Can you use hard drugs, cocaine or heroin, for pain relief? If so I bet I can get some in part payment. What about marijuana?" Harold shrugged. "For gangsters at least so you can save the good stuff?"

"I'd be happier with Morphine, the real thing from a doctor, or any of the others if its medicinal quality and not some street crap. Hell, even dihydro-codeine or something similar will help, though they're all addictive." Patricia shrugged. "Addicted instead of dead might be a good option, or he can break the habit since it'll not be for long?"

"You want to know what he's on, if they have clean drugs, and if he can stay over for maybe a few days? On top of that we can't guarantee he'll live. Does that cover it?" Harold looked from one to the other and they nodded. He discussed why street drugs were no good and more details about what would be done, then Harold left them there while he went to negotiate.

The Geek Freek boss didn't take long to decide he'd take the chance. "We've got a shitload of drugs but don't take them ourselves. It's a mugs game." Hawkins shrugged. "Just a bit of coke and pot at parties."

"Have you got drugs taken from a doctor or an ambulance, still pack-aged? If not whatever it is might kill him anyway because they've got to judge it right and there'll be no guarantee of strength or what's mixed with it." Har-old looked at Wellington. "He'll need antibiotics afterwards or it'll infect and kill him anyway. Those are bloody expensive because we can't replace them. They'll need to know what the hell you gave him and he'll have to stop over."

"I'll get someone to bring over a selection and exactly what was shoved down him. Who will be the hostage?" Hawkins frowned. "Either a woman or the pouf will be a problem."

"No hostage because this is medicinal. You've got to agree here and now he might die, and I'm not losing someone if that happens." Harold shrugged. "We'll try because you'll pay well for success and it'll take the edge off with your blokes about the fine."

Hawkins thought long and hard about that. "Ok, because if he's not fixed I might have to shoot him anyway. I'll send someone for the drugs, and you get those two to start on Wellington." Hawkins stopped suddenly. "Damn. If he's drugged like that Wellington might say something well outside your rules. No gelding, right?"

"Not if he's medicated. If one of your blokes visits and gets stoned or pissed, that's his stupid fault."

The Geek sent off for drugs burned rubber on the trip, and within half an hour he came back with the information and goods and Hawkins and the rest left. Then Casper and Harold held Wellington down while Gayle and Patricia tried to see what the problem really was. After a lot of discussion between them, and consulting books and packets, Gayle ensured that Wellington went off to a peaceful sleep.

Five days later he staggered down the street, still woozy and leaning on Harold but in a lot less pain, and left in a Geek Freek convoy. Gayle and Patricia privately confided that they hadn't been totally sure about the drugs, but had definitely got out the rest of his tooth and stitched the worst of his mouth and lip. Now either the antibiotics worked or they didn't. Both were quite proud of their work even if Wellington's face was still blown up like a balloon and he'd be scarred for life. They were even more pleased with the phials of morphine, tubs of dihydrocodeine and marijuana for Sandy's arthritis if necessary.

While they worked on healing Wellington, Harold worked on making as many residents as possibly capable of hurting Geeks or anyone else as he could manage. He still had more handguns than people he could rely on to shoot a human being, and actively looked for more. Especially since the extra income from Wellington's treatment meant he had enough extra propellant to burn off some in practice.

*   *   *

Doll sniggered and wiggled her bottom against Harold's front. "Mmm, assume the position."

Harold opened his arms and stepped back, his voice and face stern. "Time and place Doll. If you won't be serious there's plenty of volunteers." He pointed at the handgun. "That is loaded. It will kill you, me, gramps or a passing stranger at the twitch of a finger." It wasn't just the memory of someone else saying that, Harold really needed these people to get serious about how they handled firearms. They'd seen too much TV where guns only went off on purpose.

"Sorry Harold. I really want to learn, I do." Doll's voice suddenly sounded harder, harsher. "The next arse that comes for Matti won't get a headache." She scowled. "I wish I'd had my gunbelt, or rather I wish it had a real gun in it."

"You'll have the real gun part if that happens again." Harold just hoped enough would pull the trigger when the time came. The sudden flood of people seeking tuition came after the neighbours started coming for social visits. Shorter skirts, even knee length, had disappeared within days, at least on the main street where visiting gang members were allowed to go. The visitors had watched their language but the looks, whispers between them and the wolf whistles had been enough.

"Then we'll try again." Harold moved closer. "Both hands, bring the weapon up nice and steady. Remember, this will kick but that's all right. Just let your wrists absorb it. Elbows out a little bit more?" Harold stepped back and moved her head a little. "In the middle and don't hunch your shoulders. Relax them. Nice and smooth, now take up the trigger."

"Did I hit it? Ow, my wrist hurts." Doll took one hand off the weapon to shake her offending wrist.

"That is still loaded so don't mess about. You probably did hit the house, but if you hit the actual door first time it's a miracle." Harold frowned. "Are you skimping the exercises for your wrists?" He really didn't know much about shooting a pistol, just a couple of leaflets picked up from a gun club, so a lot of this was guesswork. Harold did know that the strength of his own wrists definitely meant he had less trouble than most when holding a pistol steady.

"No, but I don't want wrists like yours." Doll held up her own and put it against Harold's.

"These take dedication and long lonely hours with no fun at all. Come on, let's make certain you hit the house this time." Harold smiled because although Doll hadn't hit the door the bullet kept low enough to hit a person. What they all really needed was more live practice, but Harold daren't burn off enough ammunition.

*   *   *

While Wellington had his tooth fixed, Harold cleared jams in seven handguns for gangsters and then cleaned and oiled them. Three for Cadillac and two for each of the other gangs, and their condition puzzled Harold. Ogou admitted the pair from the GOFS were a test, just to see what sort of job they got for the money. Cadillac came personally to collect his three, and to have a decent beer he claimed.

"May I?" Cadillac put out his hand and Harold offered one of the re-paired guns. Cadillac slid the clip out and produced one of his insincere smiles. "This had ammunition in."

Harold returned the smile. "You get the ammo at the gate. You're hardly unarmed if I hand you a loaded weapon, are you?"

"Nor am I suicidal." Cadillac glanced at Alfie, in the room with a shotgun again. "This is a really good job. Expensive, but a good job. The thing is, if was a bit cheaper I might have more work."

Harold's smile widened, because he had started to realise that Cadillac enjoyed haggling. The gang boss also enjoyed violence and abusing women, but not here. "Why can't you fix them yourselves? I can't believe gangsters couldn't keep their illegal weapons working before the crash."

"They probably did, but most of them are dead." Cadillac smiled at Harold's puzzled expression. "You don't know? I'll tell you for a crate of beer?"

"Anything from one bottle up depending on how much is bull droppings." Harold really did want some explanation because the weapons from all three gangs showed a lack of simple cleaning and oiling. "Though I don't want some sort of windup."

"No need, because the reason is both simple and weird. More or less every significant armed gang, even street corner punks, went into the city centre to take over." Cadillac smiled whimsically. "I had a chop shop, and no delusions wild enough to get me in the middle of that lot. The BBC got it dead right, about there being a conspiracy."

"To take over the country? Bull. That was a fantasy by some government mouthpiece."

"No, just to take over the city. I don't know who started the notion but the idea spread, to set up like this, no cops. Though their version didn't include wrecking the place first. A group of the top gangs, all of them it seems, believed that with the police and mayor gone they could share the city out. They literally invited everyone with a gun to the party and weren't taking no as an answer. Or rather they made it clear anyone not there didn't get a piece of the pie." Cadillac shook his head. "That didn't work out too well. I reckon most of the gangs never survived the first night once those honest law-abiding citizens got moving. What do you know about the gangs, here or anywhere else?"

"Very little? Nothing? Movies and newspaper reports? Though the films were usually about America and I didn't get much news for a few years." Harold tried to connect gangs being dead to the current situation, and that didn't make sense.

"You really were an honest citizen? There had to be one. Gangs here, in England, don't call themselves the Pink Panthers, or the Barbie Girls, or the Gods of Fire and Steel for Christ's sake." Cadillac sniggered. "At least Hot Rods has a basis. All the motors we dealt with were definitely hot."

"You were a car thief?" Holly must have been trying to work from car thief to gang boss and her puzzlement showed. "I was as innocent as Harold, probably because the news never named any gangs. The TV just talked about criminals and named the ones who were prosecuted."

"As I just said we ran a little chop shop." Cadillac grinned at Holly. "Chopping up stolen motors for spares?" Holly nodded understanding and he continued. "I took one look at who was dying on the TV when all hell broke loose and called Cooper. We nipped down the street with a crowbar and an axe and smacked the only guard on the club belonging to the Tolbert twins, our local nasty boys. We took his gun and then stole everything that wasn't nailed down because I'd just seen most of their lot gunned down and the rest disappear under a mob. I persuaded one of the staff to show us where a few more weapons, a lot of ammo, money and drugs were kept, and broke the lockers and safes open." Cadillac's smile became feral. "Then we went round the area, shot a few local pimps, and commandeered the contents of the brothels and the street girls. By then I'd attracted some recruits."

"Christ. So how did you end up with the fortress, the Mansion?" Harold wasn't fooled. Cadillac wanted to tell someone this to show what a smart bloke he was, but Harold didn't care. He might be able to dismiss some of it as Cadillac flattering himself, but the bones sounded truthful. Harold remembered all those armed groups on TV, getting into fights or being swallowed by the mob.

"When those big mobs came this way we moved sideways, sharpish. On our travels we actually found a mansion. You'll have to visit sometime. Then we commandeered some labour and made a nice safe place for the fighters we were picking up, and our recreation. The um, young ladies were dead handy for attracting recruits. We got rid of the diseased ones, girls and blokes, and the real hop-heads have gone as well now." Cadillac tipped the neck of his beer bottle towards Harold. "You did it the opposite way and rescued the needy, all decent and moral, but you ended up the same place." He spread his hands. "Forted up with a bunch of young ladies and fighters."

Holly scowled. "Some of ours are both."

Harold headed off the argument. "Those Geek Freeks are really shop assistants? They look a bit manic for the usual lot who wished me a nice day."

"They were probably already nasty little sods on a weekend but yes. Opportunity knocked, or rather barged in the door and presented them with one golden chance to move up the leagues." Cadillac curled his lip in disdain. "They know less than we do about guns, but that Tell really can use that bow and they really think he can make a proper crossbow. Add in the goodies in that industrial estate and the bad lads they've attracted, and you've got a gang." He laughed. "With managers."

"The GOFS have a strongpoint, some weapons, and a real smith to make more." Harold spoke more or less to himself. "They don't seem quite as manic."

"One of them knew who or where to raid for handguns and ammunition, and enough of them are nasty sods. That's all it takes, as you know." Cadillac frowned. "That lot are smart enough to be trouble, so maybe having you here on their flank is handy." The gang boss grinned. "So where's my crate of beer?"

"Six bottles." Harold's reaction was automatic. Berry would give him hell anyway for giving away beer.

"Ten and I'll count the two I've supped here." Cadillac smirked. "Throw in one of those crossbow bolts? I'll use it to encourage my smith to try harder."

"No, because that's only an experiment. Our smith wants to make a head that can't be pulled out. The limb has to come as well." Holly smiled happily. "The last test went well."

"I'll mention that." Cadillac sighed. "I suppose I'd better go before my blokes think I've been seduced into staying." He tipped his empty beer bottle towards Holly. "Your fan club is alive and well. Just alive in one case and he'll be one-handed for a bit yet."

"I'll do better next time." Holly smiled which impressed Harold because she wasn't getting as annoyed as she usually did round Hot Rods. "Especially if you run off without paying."

"Good point." Cadillac nodded towards the crossbow point and grinned, then turned to Harold. "I'll call to the cars and someone will bring up the payment." He had arrived in two cars this time. "Did we settle on ten pints and one bolt?"

"Holly only delivers them one way, so just ten pints." Harold would live with that because the lack of people who were comfortable with firearms had really bugged him. In England nobody but criminals and police had handguns, so if both were dead the situation made sense. Sort of, though having vicious amateurs in charge instead hadn't working out very well so far.

Down at the gate, after the payment had been checked and the weapons had been returned, Cadillac paused. He looked at Holly and Emmy, guarding the gate, with his little smile. "Einstein is a little bit annoyed. He might try for some payback."

Emmy grinned. "Ooh, good, we can test some bolts." Holly tapped the one in her crossbow and smiled. Though she frowned after Cadillac had left through the gate, shaking his head and laughing.

"I want to kill him but I've decided I can ignore the winding up until I find him someplace private." She sighed. "Do you think Einstein will try?"

Harold shook his head. "He won't get backing to do it just now because of Wellington, though I doubt gratitude has a long shelf life. He won't try personally, just in case one of you gets him alive."

Emmy and Holly hi-fived each other. "Too true."

Chapter 5:
Hunting Techniques

"We may as well bring everything in including the floorboards, since rotting clothes now qualify." Bernie looked disgustedly at the wet, smelly mess that Patty put into a carrier bag. "We've been through these houses three times now when new ideas come up."

"Dirty and soggy, not rotting. Once it's washed and dry I'll pull this down." She grinned. "You'll be pleased next winter when I knit you a long thick scarf with the wool."

"Give it up, Bernie. I asked as well and you don't want the long version." Harold smiled as he moved along to the next room. "Curtains and bedding as well even if they're a bit tatty, because they'll be washed and dried and put away." Patty turned out to be a definite asset when scavenging because she didn't miss a thing. The demon knitter, as she claimed to be, had managed without coupons until reaching Orchard Close and signing on in the bus, so she wasted nothing. Worse for other scavengers, she had teamed up with Liz on a mission to strip everything potentially useful from the houses.

Liz and Casper worried about Patty because privately, back in the girl club, the brash newcomer suffered from survivor's guilt. The local gang threatened to take Patty, so her Dad insisted Patty ran. She'd spent the early winter in a small community and then a gang found them. Patty had run with two other women and both had died, one from illness and one shot while trying to steal food. All three had been looking for Orchard Close though not by name, just the rumour of a safe place.

After the first repeat, dances had been increased to one a week. Two dances later Harold grinned as Holly waved her number. "You mean I actually get to walk you home this time, instead of finding you lurking by the gate?"

"Lurking? There I am walking home nice and peaceable on my own when this bloke drags me up the path."

"To your own door."

"Hmm, yes, I must be doing something wrong. Never mind, I'll ask Liz."

Holly slipped her arms round Harold. "Ooh, hugs. Proper last dance ones." Which brought a fit of giggles but Harold didn't mind at all. He could hug Holly and dance without having a convenient patch of skin slid under his hand or her wriggling against him. At the end of the dance Holly gave him one of those sort-of innocent kisses, and whispered "Wait until you get me home."

This time Barry walked Sharyn home, because she'd insisted. As part of some master plan to get Doll and Matti walked home without gramps. This time the sisters had captured and unsuspecting Billy and Lemmy, a seventeen-year old recent refugee. Harold walked up towards the girl club chuckling with Holly about that, and Sal readjusting her sights onto Bernie, and other bits of gossip. "I want to see if the trees have started budding."

From any of the others that would have been a come-on but Holly really did inspect branches and twigs on bushes, as well as she could by moonlight. Finally she straightened and sighed. "No sign. We'll check again after the Valentine's d... Er, I mean, I'll check." Harold knew if the moon had been brighter he'd see a blush.

Harold chuckled. "If I was a betting man I'd put money on the first version."

"Really? Is that an offer?" Holly had that mischief in her voice again.

"If you happen to be walking home all alone? Of course. Now I'd better do that, walk you home, before Mummy Casper starts looking." Harold took hold of her hand. "Come on or you'll be late."

A few minutes later, outside the door, Holly kept that innocent kiss going way too long for Harold's peace of mind. If it wasn't an innocent kiss, lips together and just pushing on his mouth and moving a little bit, he'd be getting ideas. "Whew. So that's a level four? I'm getting interested in level five."

"Oh. I forgot. About the fourth, the next level, what to do." Holly had to be blushing again. "Now you'll have to kiss me again." Or maybe not since that sounded mischievous.

"I'm up for that, and even more intrigued." Harold went for the proper fourth level kiss and his arms tightened involuntarily. Harold's brain pointed out that Holly must have licked her lips and her usual innocent kiss but with wet lips felt way past innocent. Though maybe not from Holly's point of view. Harold held that thought and didn't kiss back how he really wanted to.

"Oh." Holly breathed heavily afterwards as well. "I, er, well, Liz said." Holly took a deep breath and managed a little giggle. "I wonder what level five is like?" Though right now she didn't seem sure about five being a good idea.

"We could go back to three or rerun level four just so you get the hang of it?" Harold didn't think Holly had expected that result so maybe she needed to back off a bit.

"Naughty." Holly sniggered. "Not right now because Mummy Casper is waiting. But all right, we'll try level four again before the next dance." Holly's smile shone bright and happy in the moonlight as she turned and opened the door. Harold stood for a few moments, nonplussed. He'd meant repeating the four after the Valentines dance! Harold wasn't sure he could keep up this innocent kissing business if Holly kept licking her lips and practicing in between. The idea of a girlfriend sounded better and better, then Holly could rock Billy's or Jon's world, someone more her own age. She definitely seemed to be getting over Brodie.

*   *   *

The survivors who were turning up at Orchard Close as the snows melted often had something to get over and knew where they were looking for. Rumours had spread about a place that treated everyone, especially women, decently. A place guarded by, depending on the rumour, the Army, a big black woman or a soldier. A good few of the arrivals suffered from the aftermath of what they had seen, been through, or run away and left behind. These survivors all had tragedies behind them and just wanted to slip into the community and live peaceful, anonymous lives.

Some like Trev just wouldn't talk about their past. The small, thin middle-aged man turned up in the middle of the night, badly beaten, and literally begged for entry. Trev set up a small workshop with scavenged tools and parts and began repairing TVs, radios and stereos. As a first job he tried to resurrect the music and pictures lost in the power surge and when he recovered some, Trev cemented his place in Orchard Close. Enough to have his name in the hat for walking home after last dances.

The Orchard Close territory included a small park, too far away for gardening but Liz had gleefully marked the trees down as potential charcoal. As the snow slowly released its grip charcoal moved up the list, along with body clearance. Harold and Casper didn't so much clear as heap up the driest roof timbers found nearby on any bodies, doused in enough flammables to make a big fire. Unfortunately the bodies or part bodies had to be searched, in self-defence at least when five or six rounds were ignited by one bonfire.

As the latest pyre crackled away, Harold and Casper sat upwind and drank strong coffee to kill the smell in their throats. "I've got a problem. I need a girlfriend."

"Not as badly as I need a boyfriend." Casper grinned, then looked closer and frowned. "That's a serious face. Bloody hell, you really are fussy."

"No idiot. I need a girlfriend that wants a laugh, nothing serious, just to slow up the rest. Holly has started this walk home thing and I've stopped thinking pure thoughts. I'm liable to give her the sort of hug she's a bit young and innocent for, so it has to stop." Harold scowled. "Bloody Liz is egging her on and well, and the last time was a mistake."

Casper looked puzzled. "Holly wasn't upset when she came in."

Harold smiled because that meant the daft lump really was Mummy Casper at the door. "No, but the result shook her up. I'm worried Liz is pushing Holly too fast because Liz finds all this funny."

"She wouldn't hurt Holly, not on purpose. She'll hurt you if you hurt Holly, that I believe." Casper sounded serious about that. "I'll find out." He grinned. "I might even tell you."

"You're twisted."

"No, fairies are pure and innocent. My mummy and daddy brought me up all proper before they cast me into the cold cruel world." Casper clapped Harold on the back. "Pick on both Matti and Doll, and tell them it's a competition. That's enough fun for a lifetime."

"Barry would kill me."

"Matti and Doll combined might? A short life, but oh how much fun you'd have. Now let's find more carrion."

*   *   *

An eternity of carrion clearing later Harold had two rusted handguns, three rusted machetes, six rusted knives and had lost his sense of taste and smell. At least the current pyre marked the last body, except for some smells from under rubble that might be ignored. "Back to training and lumberjacks tomorrow or the next day."

"Yeah." Casper grinned. "You'll find plenty of trainees, but I still haven't found a lumberjack."

Guns echoed periodically as the best of those with handguns practiced but currently without Harold. They were allowed a few shots each a day and Harold reloaded the brass each night when he'd done burning bodies. He still worried about how fast all the ammo had been used up during the big attack, and wanted the maximum ready at all times. "That's not practice." That was a single very loud shot followed by a short rattle of lighter cracks.

Before they could say any more both Harold's and Casper's radios crackled. "Lumberjack trouble. Load for bear." The voice sounded like Bernie but the radios weren't that great at over a mile.

Harold and Casper were flagged down short of the tree felling by Bernie. "Someone took a shot at Emmy."

"Did they hit her?"

"No, but he came close and with damn great bullet." Bernie looked grim. "The shot came from the Geeks, or from their territory." Another loud gunshot echoed and several handguns and a two-two replied. "Damn, he's having another go."

Billy met them looking angry but determined. "Sorry Harold, I missed him." He lifted the two-two. "I'm OK close up at something not moving, but not a running man."

"Did you see who it was?" If Billy recognised Einstein, Harold would to camp someplace near to the Geeks until the nasty sod put his head up in the wrong place. "Was he short and fat?"

"No, he wasn't tall but definitely not fat. He wasn't wearing those shop smock things the top Geeks wear." Billy pointed towards one of the nearby houses. "Emmy is in there with Robert, trying to stop the bleeding."

"Who got hit?"

"Pippa, Robert's wife. He got her in the arm and it's bad, Harold. I'll go and see if I can hit the bastard this time." Billy set off running and Harold did the same towards the house indicated.

"Come on my love, hang on. It's all right, I'm here." Despite her husband's words Pippa keened quietly to herself, hunched over as Emmy and Robert. Robert looked round. "It's her arm, Harold." Outside there were two pistol shots and the two-two cracked, then silence. No celebration so they still hadn't hit whoever.

Emmy looked up. "Get him Harold." Harold nodded, hard-faced because he'd just seen Pippa's arm. Even with a quick glance he could see her forearm had bent in the middle so the bullet had smashed the bone. Emmy used a machete in a sheath to tighten the bandage above the wound and stop the blood.

"The pickup is back there. Get her home. Bernie, which way?" Bernie pointed.

By the time he reached the group with weapons out Harold was too late. Doll pointed across the road between two houses. The next row stood in Geek territory. "I saw him run out from behind the garden fence." Doll spat into the grass and waved her handgun. "I tried but missed him. How's

Pippa?"

Harold reckoned the range at seventy or eighty yards, so no wonder Doll missed. "Not good but I reckon she'll live. They've more or less stopped the bleeding."

"But why would a Geek shoot at Pippa? I thought it was Emmy they had a problem with?" Doll glared towards the Geeks.

"Maybe he saw Pippa and thought it was Emmy?" Bernie grimaced. "Some people don't see past colour, especially if it was only a glance. To be honest she's probably lucky to be alive going by what just missed Emmy."

"Show me. Doll, ask three people to sit in bedroom windows as lookouts and the rest of you start woodcutting again." His lip lifted in a snarl. "He might come back. If he does, use the radio to tell me. Just say chop chop in case he's listening." That had been a nasty shock a few days ago when they'd heard Hot Rods talking to each other. The little radios could be overheard by anyone near enough with similar kit. Harold followed Bernie towards the park.

"Here Harold. That's a hell of a rifle." Bernie pointed to the hole in a tree trunk.

Harold looked closer. "I doubt it and that probably explains why he missed at this range. There might be a rifle that size someplace but I'd bet on a shotgun with solid shot." Probably close to twelve bore Harold thought. "If he comes back, he's got to get close. I'll hang about for the next week or so until we get the trees cut."

He headed back to see if Emmy had managed to get Pippa away, and the other pickup arrived with Holly, Patty and Jon. As he came to the house, Harold stood aside to let Emmy and Robert carry out an interior door with Pippa laid on it. Her coat arm hung out, soaked in blood, but Pippa's arm lay under the jackets piled over her. "Patricia said keep her warm. We'll put her on the back seat."

Within minutes Harold's pickup headed for Orchard Close with Patty driving, while Robert and Emmy watched over Pippa. Harold went upstairs and nursed the big 303, hoping the man with the shotgun came back.

At dusk he went back in the other pickup, loaded with timber for Liz to make charcoal with. Holly drove, since she'd been having lessons before the crash and wanted to finish learning. That became Harold's routine for three days, watching all day and then a lift home at night in one of the pickups carrying the day's timber. Holly practiced reversing which made her a bit late setting off the fourth evening. The minibus and other pickup were out of sight by the time they were heading through the deserted streets, nice and steady since Holly still drove cautiously.

*　　　*　　　*

"About here I think." Holly pulled over. The evening sun lit her face, but Harold didn't think the sunset explained how pink she was. "Time for practice, or it will be Valentine's."

"In a car, Holly? That's a bit more than walking you home." Harold smiled. "I'm supposed to drive and run out of petrol."

Holly giggled. "Idiot, the whole world has run out of petrol. This is because after the shooting I needed a hug but I waited so I can get a kiss as well. Snogging in the car is also a rite of passage, I'm told. This way I get my comfort hug, we try out a level four again and I also tick off a snog in a car." Her eyes dropped. "Though not the back seat. I'm not ready for that."

"Holly?" Her eyes came up, a little apprehensive. "There are no rites of passage. You do what you want in your own time, including goodnight levels two, three, four or five. Liz sometimes forgets the rest of the world hasn't her sense of humour."

"Oh no. Liz only, well, I wanted to try this and I trust you Harold." Holly sighed. "I want to do all the things that have gone away, Harold. Walking home and kissing in the car and holding hands, but that world has gone away."

"Well I was looking for a girlfriend and that covers those." Harold swore silently. His big mouth had gone and done it because Holly definitely blushed and her eyes were wide in surprise.

"But the girls said, when you choose, you know. That?" Holly looked definitely apprehensive. "It'll be knicker inspections?"

"They've got dirty minds." Harold was relieved when Holly giggled. "Never mind, if you don't fancy the job I reckon Billy or Jon will be front and centre with a bunch of flowers."

"Not a chance. You really mean it, none of the… You won't, wouldn't?" Holly tried hard to come up with something that covered what she expected Harold to want from a girl.

"No advanced techniques? No walking to the door level twenty-two?" Harold smiled happily because Holly would be a perfect girlfriend if all she wanted was a kiss and cuddle now and then. If she didn't want knicker inspections Holly certainly wouldn't be expecting rugrats. The more intense in the girl club would calm down since none of them would upset Holly, and Sharyn would behave as well.

"Oh Harold. Yes." Moments later Harold tried to remember no advanced techniques because Holly connected for her snog in a car. At least this was one of the dry lip ones. Holly snuggled in afterwards, and sighed happily. "That was really nice. Do I get one every time I drive you home?"

"Possibly. I told you, there are no rules except how you feel." Harold hugged her. "Girlfriend not whatever you thought the girl club had in mind."

"Oh God no." Holly sniggered, then stopped. "This wasn't why we stopped." Harold heard the mischief and remembered why.

"A fourth time doorstep kiss might be a bit intense in a car." Harold knew it would be because a three had been fairly potent.

"I'd better find out before Valentines, in case you drive me home." This time Harold saw Holly carefully lick her lips. She didn't do it sexily, well she did but not deliberately, but that didn't detract from the effect when Holly connected.

"Wow." Harold felt he had to say something and that sort of summed it up.

"Whew, yes. You were right about cars." Holly cuddled up. "It's a good job we're only practicing level four, because five apparently involves coat buttons and that could be a problem in here."

Harold grinned. "Are you winding me up?"

"A bit but that part is true. Though since you say we make our own rules, we can change them. Am I really a girlfriend now, Harold?" Harold turned his head as Holly raised hers from his shoulder, and looked into a pair of serious grey eyes.

"After a snog like that in a car? Too true." Harold smiled and kissed her gently. "There, a signing on bonus. Now you'd better get us home before a search party comes to look."

"Ooh yes." Holly laughed. "If we ever work up to advanced we'll have to find a better parking place." She set off with a big smile on her face, a smile echoed on Harold's. Though she looked a lot more apprehensive as they reached Orchard Close and Holly manoeuvred carefully around to the side nearest the Army.

"Are you worried, Holly?"

"Just a bit. Did you mean the girlfriend bit, like properly, all open and public?" Holly had her back to him, opening her door, so Harold couldn't see her face. "It wasn't just the snogging?"

That came after, Harold thought, but bit that off. "I meant it. I've wanted a girlfriend for a while and if you want the job, it's yours." It would also be disappointing if Holly changed her mind since he'd been thinking it over on the way back. Well, in between talking about the tree felling and Holly's pistol practice. The more Harold thought, the better he liked the idea.

"I just wondered." Holly got out and went up the steps onto the wall and Harold opened his door and went around to join her. Holly waited on top of the wall and both Bernie and Emmy were coming towards them, probably to ask about the delay. Holly turned and her hand caught hold of Harold's. She licked her lips, carefully making sure she got all of them.

"Holly?" Harold remembered thinking Holly only wanted a kiss and cuddle and would be a safe girlfriend, and could hear the crackle of bridges burning behind him.

"If I'm your girlfriend, then I want it really official. Not sneaking around."

"I'm all for that, but..." But died because Holly must have thought her lips were wet enough. By the time she pulled her head back anyone watching would have got the message.

A bit of mischief showed in her smile, and more danced in Holly's eyes. "Is that official enough?"

"Good enough for me." Harold smiled. "I was thinking of walking up the street holding hands but I'm not complaining."

"You were going to walk me home and try for the level five doorstep kiss? Was it the unbuttoning thing?" Harold could see the laughter in Holly's eyes so he joined in.

"That was quick work." Emmy grinned. "Classic though. Did you run out of petrol?" She looked at Harold.

"Hey, I wasn't driving. I was enjoying the sunset and pow, I've got a girl-friend."

"Nice moves Holly." Emmy shook her head. "I'll hide the booze and sleeping pills before the news spreads to the girl club." Several others arrived to hear the news, and Harold suffered the gibes and laughter. Then the rest told Holly to leave the timber unloading and parade her capture up and down the road for a while. Which meant that Harold did hold Holly's hand and walk up the road, and felt about sixteen again.

He felt a lot older when they visited Pippa, because the sheer scale of the damage worried Patricia. Patricia and Gayle had doped Pippa so she wasn't actually out, but wasn't in much pain, which left the trainee nurse in a quan-dary. Patricia was certain that Pippa's arm ought to come off, given the lack of any real facilities. The trainee nurse could handle broken bones but not smashed and splintered, and Patricia couldn't even tell how far up towards

Pippa's elbow the fracturing went. Worse, sealing the stump and sewing everything off went well beyond her capabilities. Or not unless she resorted to heat to seal the blood vessels, which Patricia really didn't want to do. The plus side of a girlfriend turned out to be that Harold needed a hug this time, and there was one on offer.

* * *

"Hi Sharyn."

"Wipe off your feet, and the smug smile. That poor girl." Sharyn sighed. "At least she's got the good sense to make sure you take her home first." Harold whirled and looked out of the open curtains and yes, he could see the side door of the girl club in plain view. Luckily Holly had decided on a two in daylight, thought Holly still thought level five might be on for Valentine's.

"Drawing a horse, drawing a horse. A blue horse with a cat. A striped cat." Daisy pouted. "I'm not allowed to touch Stripes but you can draw her and the kittens."

"Sorry Sharyn. I've got to draw, and then eat, and draw again, and bedtime story. You'll have to save whatever slander you've heard until then." Harold smiled at Sharyn's protruding tongue and relieved Hazel on drawing duties.

"Uncle-Harold, they won't let me draw at school." The school had finally started and apparently Daisy didn't think much to day four.

"But you need to learn lots of things as well as drawing. Is that a cat?"

"No, silly. That's a dog. I'll draw you a cat and then it's your turn."

* * *

"Uncle-Harold." A very serious five-year-old face looked up from the pillow. Just before Daisy supposedly went to sleep, so this could be an attempt at an extra story or a serious problem. Daisy occasionally sprung problems on Harold about now. Things like why do cats and dogs fight on TV and does that mean we can't have both? Or why is Mummy crying? Or why does Hazel have a bra when she's not grown up? Harold braced himself.

"Yes Daisy."

"Why do I have to go to school?"

"You have to learn to read and write, and do maths. We have no computers to do everything, so you have to learn from books." Harold felt quite proud of that for a few seconds.

"I can read now but it's better if you do. You make funny voices, and the cough when old Dragon has a fall of soot, and the splutter when the little dragon gets the smoke down the wrong pipe." Daisy giggled. "Though your little girl voice is silly."

Harold grinned. "I never got any practice at being a little girl, but I have been in a smoky place once or twice."

"Have you had a fall of soot?"

Harold recognised a definite attempt to spin out bedtime. "No, because I'm not a Dragon. Come on, sleepy time if you've had enough reading."

"Not until the little girl and the little Dragon are friends, and the love in his heart makes his fire hot enough." Daisy opened the book and pointed at the page. "We were here." Definitely an attempt at extras since Harold read this story two nights ago. Harold went with it because Sharyn waited downstairs with sister-questions. He read until the little Dragon breathed his flame and promised to be best friends forever.

"Time for sleep now."

A very wide awake cheeky smile looked up. "But you never answered. Why do I have to go to school? Writing is hard and computers are easy."

"I told you, we all have to learn to manage without computers now. You know that some of the computers stopped, and the others might. You and Joey and Georgina all have to learn like I did, from a book. Sukie will be starting soon. You like books." Daisy did, but if she was in a contentious mood she'd say no. Harold had his fingers crossed.

"I do like books but only the ones with bedtime stories. I can count as well so why do I need to learn more about numbers?"

Harold flinched because couldn't see much future use for higher maths. "For when you grow up. Then you can use the books and the numbers to learn how to do your job."

"I want to be a soldier. I want to be Emmy with a signature haircut. Can you put beads in my hair, Uncle-Harold?" Harold hated these discussions because Daisy changed the direction in a heartbeat.

Though this one wasn't so bad because he could invoke Mummy. "Tomorrow I'll ask Mummy, and if she says yes then I will. I'll get Emmy to help so they're right."

"Fan-tastic! So I don't have to go to school."

Harold blinked. That probably seemed a logical step to a five-year-old but just now Harold had trouble following it. "Yes you do. By the time you need a job, there won't be any need for girls to fight as soldiers.

"But they will let me because you'll ask. Everyone says you are our Soldier Boy so you can ask for me."

Harold quickly abandoned both trying to explain the military hierarchy, and cursing the habit of calling him Soldier Boy in front of his niece. "You'll need to be as big as Emmy, and learn lots of things from books and lots of maths."

"Why?" It had taken a while, but Daisy had finally used the W-word.

"There are tactics, and strategy, and history so you won't make the same mistake twice. Then you'll have to write reports, and you need geography so you can find your way around. You'll need maths if you aim a bow. You must know how far up to aim so the arrow will fall enough to hit the target, and that's geometry and will take years to learn properly." Harold really needed to talk to the teachers tomorrow before Daisy did.

"But that will take for ever and ever and ever. I'll be oooold. As old as Mummy."

"I'm nearly as old as Mummy and still not very good with a bow and arrow. You can learn other things as well, all about how to grow blackberries and peas?" Daisy liked both blackberry cordial and peas.

"Did Curtis go to school to learn? How long did it take?"

"Yes he did and it took ages." Harold saw Daisy's lip come out and waiting ages wasn't in her world view. "But if you are good at school he might teach you some things now." Now Harold needed to get to Curtis before Daisy did.

"What about soldiering? Can Emmy teach me or Holly? Can Liz teach me what Cripes means? They could all teach me instead of school?"

Emmy, Holly and Liz went on the list of people Harold had to talk to before Daisy got there. "School first because you need maths, and that means sleep. If you are tired you won't learn, and then the Army won't take you."

"When can I have a bow and arrow?"

"When your teacher says your maths is good enough. Now go to sleep, all right?" Harold definitely needed to talk to the teachers.

"Tucking in and goodnight kiss first. Nighty night Uncle-Harold."

"Nighty night Daisy."

*   *   *

Harold's head reeled and he had to talk to Sharyn about Holly next. But not yet because Hazel waited at the top of the stairs. He really hoped whatever she wanted to ask wasn't too complicated. "Harold, how long will I have to go to school?"

Harold laughed. "Daisy already started with that one. You need to keep learning just in case this mess ends."

Hazel's face fell. "It won't, or it will take my whole life, so why do we need to take all the lessons? There isn't even an exam at the end." A tear trickled down her cheek. "I don't care about the economic importance of Brazil because they probably have no economy now. All the books are out of date."

Hazel started moving and Harold opened his arms. This didn't happen very often because Hazel's sad tended to be quiet rather than weepy. Though while he hugged and absorbed Harold realised Hazel had a very good point. Higher maths might or might not be any good, Geography outside the UK had probably become almost useless and judging by the TV, French could soon be extinct.

"Maybe we should look at changing the curriculum. You could learn sewing and knitting and woodwork instead of some lessons." Harold felt Hazel's sobs change, dying down a bit as she listened. "Bricklaying or plumbing, or maybe you could be an electrician's apprentice?"

"What about skinning rabbits and archery?" That came out between sniffs but Hazel's interest seemed to be aroused.

"I suppose rabbit skinning comes under cooking now. You could learn how to set traps?" Harold frowned about the archery. "Daisy asked about bows and arrows. I told her she needed to learn geometry first."

"That won't work with me." The trace of humour in Hazel's voice fooled Harold for a moment, then she sobbed again. "If I could have used a bow I could have helped."

"No love, nobody could."

Harold wasn't quite sure how long he stood there while Hazel went from questions about possible new subjects to sobbing and back again, but eventually a bleary fourteen-year-old face looked up. "Sorry. Thank you Uncle-Harold." A wan smile appeared. "Are you going out with Holly?"

"Yes. Cripes, does everyone have a personal messenger pigeon or are you all psychic?"

"No silly." Hazel's smile became a little stronger. "You just walked her home and kissed her on the doorstep, which is kinda sweet. I could see you through the dining room window. I'm glad, because you having a girlfriend will stop some of the girl club saying things and I like Holly." Hazel let go. "I'll go and get cleaned up, and maybe go to bed."

"Daisy might still be awake."

"We can talk about school for a bit." This sniffle morphed into another try at a smile. "Or archery."

As Harold came off the bottom of the stairs Sharyn's eyes lit up but he got in first. "Don't even think about it. I've got a girlfriend, and not the first but at least give me chance to get used to the idea. Right now we've got to talk about school, curriculums, beads in hair, and the list of people who need to be primed before Daisy gets to them. Oh, and suitable archery classes for five and fourteen-year-olds."

"Cripes, I thought you were in charge up there at least."

"Fat chance."

*   *   *

Despite the discussions, Harold went out like a light and slept right through. That meant he got up late and had to race around seeing people about Daisy. Curtis agreed to help Daisy with peas and blackberries, providing she had a good report from school. The idea of a different curriculum for the fourteen and fifteen-year olds intrigued Hilda. Susan, Betty, Kerry and June all laughed at him over Daisy. They were taking on the school teaching between them and were definitely pleased of a reward to offer one child. Harold left them wondering how to encourage the others.

Holly opened the door of the girl club, and mornings meant a girlfriend kiss. She whispered in Harold's ear afterwards. "That's a level two girlfriend hello. Last night I learned about a lot of other kisses, but I think some of them are advanced." Looking at the grinning faces behind Holly, Harold didn't even try to imagine.

"I'll just have to wait and hope, though first I've got a request." Harold smiled. "A Daisy request and no, she appears to be the only person who doesn't know yet." Harold explained archery and geometry, and went to check on Pippa before heading home to breakfast.

He ignored the comments about getting lost on the way when the woodcutters set off, and spent another day nursing his rifle and watching for a bloke who never turned up. Though the occasional level two girlfriend hello, and a level three because Holly needed to practice, did brighten his day up. As far as the gunman was concerned, Harold wondered if he would ever come back.

Mid-afternoon the following day the radio called Harold back to Orchard Close. As he pulled up Harold could see a new refugee. Maybe a refugee because this one looked reasonably well dressed and brought a hand cart. Harold parked on the road and walked up behind him.

"Hello. I've been called back to talk with you." Harold put out his hand. "Harold."

"Leonard, usually called Lenny but I'll answer to Len. Is this Orchard Close because they won't even confirm that?" Lenny stood a couple of inches below Harold's six feet, medium built and looked fit rather than muscled. His washed-out blue eyes met Harold's without hesitation. Harold's first impression, especially with the neatly cut dark brown hair, had been that the man was military, but that wasn't right. Lenny looked controlled and confident but not disciplined, or at least not the Army way.

"We have unpleasant neighbours. Not only that, but you have a lot of luggage for a refugee." Harold looked pointedly at the hand cart.

"Gifts. These days I understand it is usual to buy into a community?"

"We have a different system. If you agree to the rules and we like you, that's good enough." Harold smiled. "Knowing what you expect and what you can provide in the way of skills is a good way of knowing if we'll like you. Where are you from?" Leonard puzzled Harold and he wondered if the man had run from the neighbours. That hand cart screamed an invitation to be robbed, so how had this man pushed it through at least one territory?

"St. Mary's Hospital."

Harold put his hand on his machete and moved out of the direct line from the guard houses. He wouldn't use the machete because if trouble started this bloke would have three or four shafts in him in a heartbeat. "No you aren't. That was attacked and burned."

A shadow crossed Lenny's eyes. "I know, I was there. I hid and I've been living on the catering supplies and vending machines. Some days I mingled with people nearby and that's where I get my ideas of how this new world works." Lenny gestured towards his cart. "I heard of your place, where there is some sort of civilisation, and came to look. I brought enough food so I could hide all day and walked all night."

"That's full of food?"

"No, that's whatever medical supplies were left here and there." Lenny smiled. "I knew where to look."

"What was your job?" Harold prayed for surgeon and knew that wouldn't happen.

"Paramedic, or I would have been in six months if I qualified." Harold felt pretty sure the man's sigh came from the heart. "Our ambulance was attacked while we were taking someone into A&E and then the attackers came through the doors."

"Would you know what to do for a woman with a smashed forearm, smashed by a bullet?" Harold held his hand up. "Not what a fully fitted hospital or ambulance did, what would you do now?"

First Lenny had his own question. "What facilities do you have, because if it's too bad her arm will need amputating. Depending on how long ago the shooting happened it might be too late, and she might lose more of her arm anyway from infection, gangrene."

"Can you do that? Amputate?"

"Christ no. Or maybe but you wouldn't want me to try." Lenny stared. "Who have you got as a medic?"

"If that hand cart checks out you'll know because she'll give you a job interview. Is there a firearm in view when you take off the cover?" Harold glanced up towards the Army.

"No chance! I'm a pacifist. That's why I ran and hid." Lenny sighed. "I'll patch people up but I won't injure them." He looked up towards the Army. "Have you asked them to take her?"

"She's married with a child so she'd rather stay. I think the interview is over." Harold gave a clear thumbs up to the guard houses and the car started up to move the middle of the barricade aside.

"Isn't moving that a pain?"

"We're working on it." Liz had made a temporary gate for when visitors came to shop, but that wasn't really strong enough as a permanent barrier. "It's got to be strong enough to stop a car."

Lenny looked down at the road and up at the narrow gap. "If your cars don't go through anyway why not put in some of those barriers, the posts that were used to stop cars going down cycle paths?"

"Good idea, you just bought your way in." Harold gestured. "Walk through and someone will search you. I'll bring the cart."

Thirty minutes later Patricia had a tear trickling down her cheek, pure relief because she finally had someone who'd actually dealt with wounds like these. As a paramedic on an inner-city ambulance Lenny had dealt with both knife and gunshot wounds, though only enough to keep people alive to the hospital. He also brought a good selection of dressings, drugs and a small sterilizer.

"Lenny says the vet's needles and supplies, the ones I used on people, are fine but he's brought some of the right ones as well." Patricia smiled happily despite the tear. "I've even done enough of the right things with Pippa's arm, and he's going to look at the other wounded. Apparently, if they're still alive, we were good enough." Her smile dimmed. "Can you go and see the Army please, Harold, and find out just what happens to wounded who go to them? Neither of us are up to amputation, or not one like that, and something has to be done soon."

*   *   *

"Hello Army!" Harold took off his coat and twirled to show he wasn't obviously armed.

"You know the drill. Come on up nice and slow." Harold did. Relations with the Army included occasional chips and beer and a few jokes when shopping, but the rifles were still pointed at him all the way up. The search had become cursory these days because the soldier ran a wand over him first, which was a relief when women needed searching.

"What can the Army do for you today, Soldier Boy?" Sarge's slight smile meant he was in a good mood. "Since you aren't carrying anything that has to be impounded."

"We've got a badly wounded woman down there. A gunshot wound to her arm and what we've got as doctors say it's got to come off." Harold shrugged, not so dangerous these days because this lot weren't into accidental shooting. "I want to know what will happen to her if we bring Pippa up here. I won't send her to a work camp. She's a baker for God's sake, not a criminal."

Sarge's face hardened. "They're all work camps now, but the criminals are kept separate from the rest. No orange suits, but definitely guards. How old is she?"

"Twenty-five. Why?"

"Don't send any young woman there." Sarge looked uncomfortable, embarrassed, which definitely wasn't like him and Harold realised they'd moved away from the soldiers. "I've heard rumours about conditions there. If she's got any chance of living, keep her and do your best." Sarge glanced back at the soldiers. "Now we'll talk about the real reason you're here because they don't need to know what the world is becoming."

"We will?"

Sarge raised his voice. "Not only did I hear a grenade, but then there's a bloke in his underpants with a young woman. I thought you were decent people down there."

Harold raised his voice a little. "Some yob made a pipe bomb to show off and frighten people so we explained he can't throw as far as a, a crossbow." Harold only just substituted crossbow for rifle in time, and saw a ghost of a smile from Sarge. "The bloke in his underpants is Casper, and he's gay so she was in no danger."

"She didn't look very willing."

"She thought she'd been sold. Casper was in his underpants because Umeko had been handed over starkers so he gave her some clothes." Harold knew he still sounded angry about that, because he was. "She's got the message now and lives with the other single women."

Sarge smiled. "Good enough." His voice dropped again. "Any chance she could walk up with some chips or beer one evening. The lads really are twitchy because there's a lot of rumours going round that aren't really rumours."

"I'll ask, because I won't force her and she's still nervous about blokes."

"Ah, right. Now tell me about the latest bloke so I can tell them and they won't suspect secrets. There's a bit of paranoia among the mushrooms these days."

"Easy." Harold laughed. "He's a paramedic, nearly trained thank all and any Gods, which makes him our second and now senior medic. Lenny even brought medical supplies."

"A paramedic could get a pass."

A shock ran through Harold and he thought hard. Part of him wanted to hang on the Lenny any way he could, because Harold could still see that tear on Patricia's cheek. He sighed. "I'll tell him."

"I thought you might." Sarge turned, looking out over the city, and the soldiers brought up their rifles. Harold tensed but remembered to stay still.

"Crap. Er. Can I go please Sarge, right now?"

"Why? What was that?"

"The arse with a 12 gauge shotgun just shot another solid slug at one of my people, or I'll bet on it anyway. They need me over there in case he hits another woman." They needed the big 303 to blow the bastard away. Harold cursed silently because he should have left the damn thing there.

"Go on then. Don't run, but I'll allow a quick march."

"Thanks Sarge." Harold marched as quickly as possible to the bottom of the ramp, relieved because he could hear Sarge telling the squaddies to point the bloody rifles at the gunshots, not the unarmed bloke.

*　　　*　　　*

"They knew, the bastards knew." Emmy shook her fist towards the Geek territory. "Whoever called you away was a fix, Harold. Let me at them with a knife and I'll find out."

"He's a paramedic so no, but that shooter knew I'd left. We've got a watcher, someone who knows me and possibly my truck." Harold looked over at the three people round Janine. "How bad is it?"

"Just clipped her leg, more like a cut. She can still walk on it thank all and any Gods." Emmy paced, too angry to stand still. "He didn't aim at her.

The bastard aimed at me again Harold, and Janine happened to be behind me. If we hadn't seen him again I'd be picking out a real Liz special for that Einstein." Harold realised that some of Emmy's anger had to be shock and maybe fear, a natural enough reaction to being hunted.

"Maybe you should work elsewhere for a while, until he's bored?"

"No, or in a year's time he'll be waiting again. Put your soldier head on and kill him, then send his head back to Einstein as a hint." Emmy's smile looked a lot more like a snarl. "I'll bag up what's left if that's where you hit him."

"Deal, but you've got to keep moving if you're in the open, and keep a bit further away. Usually sixty or seventy yards is tops with a shotgun unless he's got a rifled barrel and proper ammo, and if he had them?" Harold shrugged. "He'd have hit you."

"I can do that, keep moving at seventy yards from that fence. That might even tempt him over the fence."

"He'll never get back." Alfie waved the two-two. "At that range both me and Billy will nail him."

Harold opened his mouth to say he'd do it and realised, everyone expected him to stay away to tempt the shooter in. "It'll be easier with the 303, Alfie."

"Really? Oh boy, he is sooo screwed. That'll go clean through the fence." Alfie had been disappointed because the two-two didn't go through the thicker timber around the fence panels.

"In that case go and get it, and find a good place to lurk. It'll cost us three woodcutters, and your muscles will definitely be missed so get him first time." Harold turned towards Janine. "I'll take Janine back and hope he tries again, and misses."

"At least if we've got a paramedic he can sort Pippa's arm out." Emmy pushed him. "Go on. I'll remember, walk about a lot and stay back a bit." Emmy sounded almost eager now.

"Hey, girlfriend kiss." Holly whispered in his ear after the level two. "Keep it all normal, because that cheers the rest up." She grinned. "And I like the practice." Either might be right since several people smiled as Harold and Billy helped Janine into the pickup, maybe at the kiss, maybe anticipating someone nailing the shooter.

*　　　*　　　*

"It's not working. We've seen him twice, well back, but the bastard won't come closer. He's got a pair of binoculars and must know about the sentries."

The strain showed on Emmy. "I want to go over the border mob-handed and flush him out."

"Not allowed." Harold frowned because the continual tension wore away at everyone, that and the state of Pippa's arm. Though Janine limped around smiling because the wound had been quickly dressed and she knew there'd be no permanent aftereffects. "Maybe he sees the shooters setting up in the morning?"

"No, the three with rifles come in across the gardens and after the first day I thought about that. None of them even peek, just wait for him to shoot." Emmy paced, she did a lot of that the last few days. "Curtis wants me to stop." She smiled. "He's really sweet but I've explained. If its Einstein the swine will just wait."

"Maybe there's a watcher our side, deep inside the border. Someone who tells him when the rifles come up?" Alfie frowned. "He'd have to live there or come in really early, in the dark."

"We can do that, earlier than he can." A little smile broke on Harold's face. "If we catch the spotter, I'll bet Emmy can make him talk."

Alfie looked at Emmy's face. "Cripes, yes."

* * *

"I ought to come." Harold felt useless.

"Someone might be watching for you as well. If you disappear he'll get nervous." Emmy had come to see the party off

"But still." Harold gave it up. "Just be careful."

"Yes mummy." Alfie grinned and hefted the rifle. "You can come when this goes off." He let himself gently down over the wall at the opposite end of Orchard Close, in case someone was watching the gate. This bloke needed killing before the general paranoia grew any more. Harold, Emmy and Holly watched in silence as the three men disappeared into the dark. The trio would spend a cold night lurking in position, a lot nearer the border than expected, and even with taking a couple of hours to sneak up slowly they'd be in place by two a.m.

"I'm going home, though I might call by Curtis for a hug." Emmy's teeth showed briefly in the gloom. "I wouldn't want to be shocked by whatever you pair get up to on the doorstep."

"We'll walk you to Curtis's door first." Holly's smile showed. "So I'm sure you're safely occupied." From the welcome when she turned up at midnight, Emmy was definitely going to be occupied for a while. Harold turned down a half-hearted offer to come in for a cuppa, and walked Holly home.

"I'm worried about the others, Harold." Holly had been holding his hand tightly while they walked so Harold already knew that. "Not only that, but Valentine's is in two days."

"True, but you've been practicing your level four." Three times on the doorstep and once in the pickup, and the level four in the pickup had been just as tempting the second time.

"I'd better practice again, because that might help me to stop worrying." Harold recognised the pause while Holly wet her lips. That innocent licking stayed the same, but looked a lot sexier to Harold every time he saw it. Then all his concentration went into not turning the four into a seventeen. Having a girlfriend backed off the others, now Harold had to keep himself backed off.

Sharyn had waited up to report that Daisy had been good enough for her first lesson with Curtis. "Though Hazel isn't so keen on the new curriculum after skinning a rabbit. Well not actually skinning it, but watching seems to be gross enough for now."

"Holly has agreed to take Veronica and Hazel out to empty traps one morning, then she'll be faced with cats and rats as well." Harold went into the kitchen. "I'll just have a drink and work through some things."

"You'll go to bed and worry there, about Emmy and Alfie and Pippa's operation. I feel just as useless but Patricia and Lenny are certain they won't kill her." Sharyn pushed Harold towards the stairs. "I stayed up to make sure you didn't sit down here all night, worrying."

"But they're going right up to her elbow, just to be sure."

"They're trying to leave the joint, then Sandy and Liz will try to make a limb so Pippa can still give Robert a Berrying now and then." Sharyn pushed harder. "Go, before I get big-sister on you." Harold went. He stayed awake worrying quite a while but eventually went off to sleep.

*   *   *

"Go away." Hilda smiled, a tired smile. "I'm not disturbing Patricia and Lenny just to answer questions. Go and soldier." She relented a bit. "I've already told Sandy to joiner, Casper to mother, Finn to electric and Janine to limp. Oh look, more people to say no to."

Harold looked round and yes, half a dozen more were hanging about or drifting closer. He raised his voice. "I've been told to go away, really politely. Hilda will let the guards know once she does." Harold took out his radio and waved it. "I'm giving Hilda this, so most of you will find out before me."

Hilda looked at the little plastic gadget. "Really?"

"Yes and no. Press that and let us know the operation is over, then any other news to make us all feel better. Then use the phone and get Faith on the switchboard to tell everyone on the system. I'll be someplace near to the gate or Casper so I can hear their radio or phone." Harold went to find Casper and keep occupied, which turned out to mean knocking down some of the ruins and barrowing the bricks across the open ground to strengthen the wall. Harold soon found out why; pounding on things with a hammer helped with anger, worry and frustration.

*   *   *

"Crap."

Harold didn't answer, saving his breath for running across the open ground towards the pickup. Running and worrying because the 303 had fired all by itself followed by the pops of the 22s. No shotgun first so something had gone wrong. Neither spoke as Harold did his best street racer impression in the pickup until a frantically waving figure stopped him.

Bernie's huge grin spoke volumes. "Alfie nailed him before the bastard took a shot." He glanced over his shoulder. "Emmy reckons she knows where the lookout is so I'm here to watch along these gardens, just so Mr. Sneaky doesn't run off when Emmy comes to call."

"We'll stay and watch as well." Harold smiled. "Wouldn't want Mr. Sneaky to get away. How does Emmy know?" He took his two-two out of the cab and settled down to watch the long strip of open ground at the back of a row of houses.

"The woodcutters were all talking in the minibus, apparently, and decided that the watcher couldn't use a radio in case it was overheard." Harold nodded at that because he had the same problem. "As soon as the minibus arrived, three of them went into houses and ran upstairs into a back bedroom. Then they watched the houses they could see, back into our bit. He uses the curtains on a derelict house. Toyah saw them close when nobody with rifles came up."

"The gunman must watch for the curtains." Harold grinned. "The watcher would see there were no guards coming in secretly today."

"Yeah, and then the three in the bedrooms moved to the front and watched for the gunman. Sal wandered down and across the road where he couldn't see her, and into Alfie's house to give the exact position. Alfie pointed your big rifle in the right direction, then popped up and fired. The bastard went back and down and both Billy and I hit him as well."

"Dead then. Well done." Harold would have liked to question the bloke, but dead was definitely good.

"I reckon the first did it, or would have. Here we go." Harold could hear voices, then the crash of a door going in. Casper's radio crackled.

"I tried Harold's radio and got Hilda. Where are you?"

"Hi Emmy. With Harold, helping Bernie to watch the back door."

"Come along to the next side street, and turn down there. Someone will wave. He's alive." Even on the crackly radio, Emmy sounded really happy about that.

The unshaven scruffy man on his knees in the garden didn't seem happy. "Who sent you in here?" Harold resisted an impulse to smack him one just on principle.

"I've asked, and I think he's being truthful." One look at the man's face and Harold believed Emmy. "The scroat got caught on Geek territory, living rough. Someone who sounds like our gunman offered him a place in the gang for this one job. He's got food for another week in there and the water is working."

"I didn't know it was about shooting a woman."

Harold looked at the terrified face. He would have loved to shoot the man out of hand, and thought that right now Emmy and several others would do a lot worse. "There's a woman having an arm amputated right now because of you."

"Eye for an eye?" Emmy lifted her machete. "Someone pull his arm out straight."

"No Emmy. He'll bleed out so you might as well just kill him." Harold held up a hand to stop her reply. "I know you're good with that, but he's an unarmed man. Later you might not want to think about that, late at night."

"I want him to suffer." Emmy still hadn't given up on his arm, the way her machete kept going up and down a bit.

"Send him to Cadillac." Alfie curled a lip. "Send him unarmed in his underwear, you know what a nasty sod Cadillac is."

"Cadillac might sign him up and give him a gun." Holly frowned. "But he can't do that if this bloke is a runner, can he?" A big smile broke over her face. "Unarmed, in his underwear, and we send a message first saying he's a runner."

Emmy scowled at the man. "You'd better sneak all the way across the Hot Rod patch without being seen, because if Cadillac hands you back I'm taking that arm."

"But it's freezing. I'll die of cold or starvation." Emmy lifted her machete again. "All right. I'll do it!"

"There'll be curtains and maybe clothes and food in some of the houses." Alfie's smile wasn't pretty. "Though if you get caught scavenging the Hot Rods will kill you anyway. Their far border is only four or five miles south and maybe the next gang will be less trigger-happy?"

"To be fair, if we wound you badly enough the Army will take you for the work gangs?" Emmy hadn't quite given up on eye for an eye.

"I'll run." The man stood, very carefully, and started to strip.

"Don't ever come back."

The face looking back at Harold meant every word. "Not in this life, no chance."

As Casper and Bernie set off in the pickup to get rid of their prisoner, Harold sighed. "I'll give him a day before telling Cadillac or they'll hunt him down for fun. Now let's see this gunman."

When he saw the body Harold agreed that the first shot was enough, and at least one of the others would probably have been fatal in time. Billy inspected the ammunition. "At least we've got another shotgun. Why didn't you make all ours shoot these big bullets?"

"If you miss they're no more use than anything else, and shotguns aren't accurate. I've put nine smaller balls in ours which will spread but they're also big enough to hurt, really hurt." Harold looked along the border fence. "Leave the posts but take this thing down and we'll use it for pyres. His for starters. Do you still want to send Einstein his souvenir, Emmy?"

"Too true." She moved forward. "Who will deliver it?"

"Robert wants to. He promised not to go ape and start shooting but wants to see their faces." Robert, back in Orchard Close waiting to find out how well his wife came through losing half an arm, deserved that much. "Casper can go as well, with a white flag on the pickup. He can complain that the Geeks are letting assholes use their territory to shoot at the neighbours." Harold inspected the small binoculars with an inbuilt rangefinder. "I can't prove this or the coupons were given to him by the Geeks."

"At least we can get on with the trees now." Alfie flexed his shoulders. "I need to hit something."

Harold grinned. "Me too." He felt even better mid-afternoon, when the radio told them that Pippa's arm was off and the bleeding stopped. Despite the shooting, the woodcutters were in a terrific mood at the end of the day. Some of that showed in the banter about Valentine's, because anticipation was growing. Not least because the girl club were winding the men up with promises of something special.

Chapter 6:
Visitors and Visiting

Sharyn produced her very best older sister look. "Here, this disgusting exhibition is for you."

Harold took the sheaf of cards and envelopes that hadn't needed a postman to arrive through his door. He leafed through them and sniggered. "Not all for me. There's some for you." Harold lost the smile. "And Hazel."

"Ooh, your face!" Sharyn scowled. "Who sent me a card? I'm not interested in all that."

"You don't really expect me to look at my big sister's Valentine cards, do you?" Harold mimed being sick. "How about you open yours and I open mine?" He hesitated. "What about Hazel's?"

"You're going to open hers? She's fifteen in a few days, Harold, and don't tell me you never looked at the girls at school." Sharyn's eyes brightened. "Did you send anyone a Valentine?"

"Maybe?" Harold sighed. "Sorry, I came over all Uncle-Harold for a moment." He put Hazel's envelopes on the table. "I shouldn't be getting any cards now. Well one, hopefully."

"Hopefully? What happened to just a girlfriend to back off the rest?" Sharyn nudged him. "I'll close the curtains so you can walk her home."

"You'll be too busy with whoever your Valentine partner is." Harold sniggered. "Maybe that's the real reason for shutting curtains." He looked at Sharyn's stunned face and gave her a hug. "Hey, I'm joking. Everyone knows you aren't after a bloke. Why do you think your partner is always one that the girl club aren't interested in?"

"I know. But it's just not Valentine's without Freddy." A long hug later she sighed. "I'll put these up or that girl of yours will ask where they are, because I'm more or less certain the hussies over there sent them."

"But you can't be sure." Harold ducked the Berrying, and opened his cards. As expected none had a name, though he was fairly certain who sent the one with a big 'Level 5!' written in kisses. The one about wimps might have been from either Casper or Liz and had the original writing blacked out. Next year all Valentine's cards would be reused ones, or they'd be back to home-made because not very many had been scavenged. Sadly, there were no Birthday, Christmas or any other greeting cards in the mart.

Harold got out before Daisy started asking questions about cards with kisses, because answering that sort had to be a Mummy's job. Halfway up the path he realised that his Valentine's kiss might be the real reason he'd hurried, and Harold stopped dead in his tracks. Crap. Holly might not be up for that sort of fun if this got much more serious. Holly only had one boyfriend before the crash, one who never walked her home or kissed her properly. Worse, Harold didn't want someone more serious, he enjoyed the quiet talks walking Holly up to her door and his level two and three hellos.

Someone had watched the path, since the door opened after one knock and Harold's worries went out the window when Holly met him with a big smile. "Happy Valentine." Holly was already wetting her lips so conversation never happened. Then she hugged hard and whispered. "Are you ready to try five?" She giggled. "Since you are definitely walking me home."

"Hey, that wasn't fair, none of us got a kiss like that this morning." Sal had a huge grin.

Liz laughed. "Cripes, fair doesn't count in love and war. That was counting coup." She shook her head sadly. "I tried, oh how I tried to explain, but she's only an innocent. Totally taken in by the macho stuff when he's only a wimp."

"Personally I call it bribery." Suzie waved a card that Harold recognised. "A number fifty four and a number nine stapled together? We're supposed to draw numbers."

"Can we all do that? Staple a couple of numbers together and fix the draw?" Matti smirked. "I could send gramps home with Hilda." Hilda lived about as far from Celine's house as possible in Orchard Close. A chorus of comments rose from further inside. Behind Matti a shy smile from Umeko and a glimpse of a Stetson meant the girl club had gathered early. More faces looked to see who had arrived and smiled or waved, including a waving needle with wool attached that could only belong to Patty.

One usual face was missing. "Where's Emmy, or has she already set off to give Einstein's Valentine to Robert?"

"She's banned, or will be if she ever dares to show her face." Laughter made Patty's voice unclear until she tried again. "Delivering Valentine's a night early, all night? Anyway, Einstein's present is still in the rat-box."

"Where?"

Holly sniggered. "We decided Robert would rather be with Pippa until she's over the worst, so we put Einstein's present in with the dog and cat food, the frozen rats." Holly let go of Harold. "Let me get my coat and then you can tell me what we're doing today. After all, you don't have to stay away from the woodcutting now that oik is dead." A rousing cheer followed that.

"None of these cards is from a lumberjack, so woodcutters it is." Casper waved over the intervening crowd, his bald head covered in lipstick kisses. "If we attract one I'm hoping my designer hairstyle will make him jealous."

As the woodcutters gathered the rest of them, mainly men, were also a bit hyper, laughing at silly jokes and threatening to chase the women round the trees for a Valentine's kiss. The mood persisted all day, and Harold finally realised why. He'd spent three years in the Gulf where at least half the population wanted him dead, and had a sort of tolerance. These people hadn't, so living with the threat of one gunman had been eating away at them.

Though the increase in threats and promises as dusk approached had more to do with dancing, and walking home. The laughing crowd disembarked at the other end and climbed the wall, then fell silent. Three strange youths were stood inside the gate, backed against the wall with crossbows pointing at them. Another four gangsters were watching with interest but not interfering. The three vehicles parked on the road outside meant that the men would be visitors from the neighbours, but something had gone wrong.

"We knew you'd be coming soon so there was no point in calling. We didn't want to advertise on the radio." Sharyn passed Harold his stick. "Just to make this official."

"What happened?" As Harold looked around he realised why the men stood so still. As well as the crossbows, there were five firearms aimed at them from places the Army couldn't see. Bess grinned and waggled her pistol from number three, while beside her Matthew held a shotgun. Not to his shoulder because that hadn't healed properly yet, but the youths wouldn't know that.

"He happened." Lilian pointed her crossbow at one of the youths. "A bigmouth who thought that because you and Casper and Emmy were away, the rules didn't apply."

Harold headed for the youth in question, his face hard. "What did he do?"

"Nothing. Christ, I did nothing." The youth looked from side to side. "I never touched the bitch. Ask her. She hasn't even come to say so."

"No, because she's bloody terrified, and if you call her bitch one more time I'll pull the trigger." Lilian glanced at Harold. "He spotted Umeko and sort of cornered her. She kept shaking her head but he kept moving in, telling her she could be his Valentine. When I saw them she was backed against a wall and he might even have been touching."

"I wasn't, I swear I wasn't. She didn't say no." The youth was holding his hands low at the front and Harold remembered, touching without permission could mean gelding.

"Umeko says he didn't touch, but he sure as hell would have. That means he pays but what, little brother?"

Sharyn calling him little brother calmed Harold a bit. "No touching means he won't be gelded. What have the rest done?"

"Nothing, they just tried to back him up. These three are all Geeks." Harold really wanted to geld the little scroat now; no wonder Umeko was terrified.

"I'll pay the fine. Just call that lot off." Harold almost smiled because he knew who that lot would be. Emmy and Holly were already well known, as was Casper, and the woodcutters included some of the fittest and strongest of the residents. They were all armed because of being outside the walls, so there's be a wall of crossbows and machetes behind Harold.

"You two move away or you get the same punishment." There was the barest of hesitation before the pair left their comrade.

"You fucking pussies. Wait until…" His voice died away.

"Yes. Foul language is a fine. What did he bring in?" Harold looked at number two, the guard house.

"A machete, Harold. No other weapons or ammunition." Conn leant to the side and produced the weapon.

"That's the fine. Now there's the abuse." Harold turned to those following and yes, they would have frightened him. "What is the penalty, short of killing or crippling since he didn't touch?"

"Hey, I'll pay the fine. There's stuff in the car."

Harold glanced back. "You pay with what you've brought in. Now shut it before I lose my temper." As he turned back Harold saw that the four gangsters from the GOFS or Hot Rods were very interested in that as well as amused. "We need a punishment that none of these here will think is worth it." Harold saw several heads nod slightly as they understood why. Some gangsters wouldn't worry about a straight fine if they got their jollies.

Harold glanced at Sharyn. "Bring Umeko and every other woman you can. They can stay inside the houses but I want them all to see, for the pure embarrassment factor at least."

"Good thinking, little bro." Sharyn set off up the road, calling out names.

"You could smack him about with your stick, Harold? That would hurt. I'd do it but?" Casper waggled his machete and grinned because he'd given up on sticks or baseball bats to carry a blade.

"No, he'll have been hammered by Soldier Boy and might even brag about it." Holly glared at the culprit. "He should strip down to his boxers for starters, he won't want to brag about that."

"No. I'm not..." When Harold looked the youth had shut up because Lilian had raised her crossbow to her shoulder. She was a crap shot but at that range it didn't matter.

"Can I strip him? It's Valentines and I haven't had a boyfriend for ages?" Casper waggled his eyebrows and wiggled the fingers on his free hand. Some of the laughter came from the other gangsters, and then Holly pouted.

"Hard luck Casper, unless he's stripping because he's keen?"

"Now we just need a suitable way to hurt him." Patty curled her lip. "It should be a woman."

"All the women." Emmy grinned. "We should all hurt him, including Umeko."

"But without crippling or killing." Harold thought he'd better remind them, especially with the savage look on a few faces.

"I'm not using my hands on him." The sheer disgust in Doll's voice at that idea should have been embarrassing on its own.

Curtis laughed. He was in the other guardhouse with a pistol on the other gangsters in case they decided to interfere. "Garden canes. Has anyone here been caned?" A round of denials mixed with a couple of offers to try anything once came back. "My gran caught me at the back of the legs with a garden cane a couple of times and raised a welt through my jeans."

Harold could see the idea take hold among the group in front of him. "How many garden canes have you got, Curtis?"

"Hundreds, all bundled up in a shed near the greenhouses. Enough for every woman in Orchard Close to have ten."

"We'll have to line up or some of us might not get a turn." Harold turned back and the youth shook his head.

"No, not a chance."

"It's that or gelding?" If he hadn't been a Geek, and gone after Umeko,

Harold might have negotiated the actual amount of beating.

"They'll beat me to death anyway." He had a point. Once the likes of Emmy and Holly had him immobilised, they wouldn't let the youth get away.

"How fast can you run?" The youth looked back blankly. "A hundred yards? From that house there to the gate?" A jerky nod answered this time. "You run from there to the gate, and the women will line up and take a swipe at you with a garden cane as you run past. Stop outside the gate and wait for this lot to get a good look at the result, or we'll stick a crossbow bolt in you as well." Harold indicated the other gangsters, some of whom were starting to smile.

"Nice one little brother." Sharyn had finished her errand.

"I had help. Did Umeko come?"

"Yes, even Celine came."

"Good, now do your little brother a favour and persuade those two and any other woman who has a real problem with men to take a cane." Harold grinned. "Therapy."

"I'll get the canes." Bernie set off at a dead run.

Harold lifted his stick. "Take your shoes back off, and follow me." The stunned youth did as he was told, because the crossbows were still following every move.

Lilian and the other women handed off their crossbows to take a garden cane and Harold wasn't the only one to wince as they swished them a few times. He grinned at the Geek. "You run down this footpath, and the women will space themselves out each side between here and the gate. They'll all take a swipe as you run past. Don't swerve off the footpath or these blokes will put a crossbow bolt through your legs and you'll have to crawl the rest of the way."

"Ooh, please, swerve." Emmy swished her cane. Beyond her a woman in a hooded jacket took a cane from Holly and nodded at whatever Holly told her. Harold smiled because that looked a lot like Umeko.

"Emmy, Patty and Holly? You three take the first three swipes, all right?" All three smiled and nodded, then set themselves. Harold wanted those three first because they'd strike, and hard, and that should firm up the rest. Though Lilian and Bess already seemed keen enough as did a few others. Harold looked back at the youth. "Three, two, one, go." The spectators cheered as he set off.

The youth looked fairly confident as he started running, and then he stumbled and screamed because the first three all left a line of blood and broke their canes. After that he moved slower because he kept putting up his arms and crouching to stop the thin sticks. Not every woman turned out but twenty three did and every one hit him. Most of the strikes struck his forearms and back, and not all brought blood, and he kept on his feet long enough to stagger through the gate.

"Righto, the rest of you can collect your gear now and have a good look on the way out. We take our rules seriously." The other gangsters weren't laughing now, but were definitely impressed. Most had stopped laughing when the youth started screaming. Now, as the other men collected their weapons and walked out, some of them flinched at the thin red marks and lines of blood on his limbs and body. The whimpering and the tears streaming down the youth's face were gravy.

*   *   *

Harold half thought the beating would dampen Valentine's a bit. Judging by Sharyn's smile when she came downstairs dressed to dance the beatings might have had the opposite effect. "What happened to Womble?"

"That was a stupid idea. I'm a grown woman. The scavengers have been looking out for sensible frocks for the rest of us, and came up with this." Sharyn gave Harold a little twirl of her long, dark blue evening dress and smiled sadly. "Freddy could have taken me to a dance in this without scandalising anyone."

"I'm the black sheep in this family, sis, so scandal is down to me." Harold gave a twirl as well since he wore a cloak, or someone had been having fun with green velvet curtains. "I'm not sure if this is some sort of romantic thing or a vampire costume. Where did they find a green velvet jacket to go with it?"

"How would I know? The jacket would look better buttoned up."

"They'd pop if I breathe too hard." Harold laughed. "Vampire then, because they don't breathe."

"Does that mean you'll be dragging a poor maiden back to your crypt? Should I give her a chance to get out in the morning before Daisy and Hazel see her?"

"No! Holly isn't, well, we aren't." Harold gave up in the face of Sharyn's laughter.

Sharyn calmed down to a big grin. "I know, but you've actually blushed. That hasn't happened for a while little brother. Have you got it bad?"

"Typical." Harold raised his head to do the haughty bit like a vampire in an old film. "A man treats a woman with a modicum of respect, and his sister assumes ulterior motives." He grinned. "Maybe I like going out with a woman who has no designs on my body." Sharyn found that funny as well and still wore a big smile when they left Susan and Rob to babysit. That pair were in a good mood as well, and Susan asked where the canes were in case Rob misbehaved.

Harold stopped at the dance-house door to murmur in Sharyn's ear. "I detect a conspiracy. A vampire conspiracy. I also detect fast work with a needle."

"But only one has a matching cloak." Sharyn headed for the cloakroom but Harold kept his cloak as part of his costume.

Holly's cloak came from the same curtain or bedspread as Harold's, though shorter with some lace trimming, and hers had numbers nine and fifty-four pinned to it. Eight other women and six men wore varying lengths of cloak so the vampires were out in force tonight. Sal smiled and then bared a pair of plastic vampire fangs, and both Jon and Billy offered their necks and glared at each other. Harold put his arm around Holly as the music struck up. "May I have the pleasure?"

"Of course. But first?" Holly unfastened the fifty-four from her cloak and pinned it to Harold's. "In case there are any poachers."

"Doubtful now. Though there'll be a lot of disappointed blokes since you've covered up your legs." Holly wore a long green dress, almost down to the floor. She opened her cloak to show that the dress came right up to her neck. "That's lovely." Harold leant forward as they started to dance. "So are you." Holly looked much older than usual with her hair up and a velvet choker around her neck, and drop dead gorgeous.

"That's worth a two." Holly laughed after the kiss was delivered. "Maybe a level three later to work up to level five."

"Hey, slow up. Some of us have to warm a man up first." Doll swept past and Billy looked warmed up already.

Harold whispered in Holly's ear. "A vampire cowgirl?" Doll's wore a denim cloak with a fringe that didn't reach her shorts.

"All those lonely cowboys, out in the dark? Now we know why nobody could ever kill the hero." Holly sighed and cuddled a bit. "I suppose you'll find out because I'm not allowed to monopolise you."

"You needn't worry too much, everyone has covered up tonight." Apart from Doll, Matti and Suzie all the dresses were at least mid-shin and mostly full-length. Several of the men without cloaks wore suits with ruffs at the cuffs and on the shirt fronts or bow ties so the theme must be romantic-vampire.

"The scavengers have taken until now to get enough of the right clothes. Nearly enough because Suzie, Matti and Doll have some sort of competition going. Liz says it's who can get nearest to showing her knickers without doing so." Holly giggled. "I'm banned from wearing my tutu until they've stopped, because Patty says that actually is underwear and I might not like the prize if I win."

*　　　*　　　*

Harold danced with an undead cowgirl who moved a lot like a live Doll, and with several other vampires. Sal wore her red dress under her red cloak, but with white makeup instead of Jessica Rabbit lipstick. Sal's dancing wasn't chaste, but she didn't shimmy or insist on skin stroking, and Harold noticed she avoided dancing with Jon.

Though Lenny the paramedic looked startled when she descended on him. Sal had mentioned rewarding him for deciding to stay and the dance might have been her idea of a reward. Harold just felt grateful the man decided to stay. Lenny thought Orchard Close were decent people and needed a paramedic more than the people outside the cordon.

Two of Harold's dances were very chaste. The first with Umeko, as a thank you for her therapy she told him. Harold took his cue from her carefully placed fingertips on his shoulder and waist, and did the same. Umeko only danced a few times after that, in exactly the same formal style with Nigel, Barry and Finn.

"After that version of therapy, I thought a dance or two is the least I can do." Celine managed a hand on his shoulder, but held Harold's other hand.

"Always happy to help. Your dress really suits the themes this time." Celine's white gown looked perfect this time and she had even found some white fur for a choker, another theme tonight.

"Except for those three." Celine sighed. "I had a little green dress for Valentine's and other dances that would have matched Suzie's. It would have gone with your outfit, though not as well as Holly's does." Harold thought the dress probably went well with her red hair as well, and realised Celine must have been a lot more of a party girl than he'd thought. He'd never met her before the rape, so somehow he'd always thought of Celine as the quiet type. Celine hummed the tune for a couple of bars. "You have some strange ideas about therapy."

"But did it work?"

"It worked on that nasty little scroat. Oops, Liz language." Celine hummed a little bit more of the tune then looked up with just a hint of humour in her eyes. "The NHS might not think much to your methods, Harold, but I approve. I really do believe I will need my little dress again one day."

"Good. I'll keep an eye open for more therapy." Harold glanced over towards where the spectators were stood. "The same therapy seemed to work for Umeko."

"Possibly, and if nothing else I'll bet the Geeks daren't even look hard at her again." Celine smiled. "This is working; I forgot I was dancing with a man."

"Great. That does wonders for my ego."

"Your ego has a pretty blonde booster to keep it strong. I meant I was talking properly without tensing up."

Harold smiled. "Don't let Alicia know you're weakening, she'll be moving Barry in."

"Not yet, and she reckons Finn can shoot well enough to be reassuring so he might get the job. Alicia really does know that women guards are dangerous. Unfortunately we both have the same problem, logic can't persuade the bit in our heads that has bad dreams." Celine sighed. "There are a few of those about, bad dreams."

"Oh yes." Celine's look sharpened and Harold smiled. "Don't worry, I know my job. Liz told me."

"Alien killing machine parked at the end of the road for when it's needed." Celine nodded. "Those are handy, but what do you do with them when nobody needs killing?" She smiled as the music stopped. "Thank you kind sir."

"Thank you, fair maid."

Harold turned at a voice from behind him, "None of the fingertip stuff for this one, Soldier Boy."

"Hi there Suzie. Are you three having a competition?"

Suzie sniggered. "Sort of, but not the knicker one Liz reckons. Don't worry, you're off the prize list." She hugged a bit tighter. "Handy to practice on though."

*   *   *

"This cuts out a lot of wondering and waiting, and promising chocolate and treats to trade tickets," Holly smiled happily, "since you've already got the right number."

"What were you trading for? You always end up with one of the older ones and walk them home?" Harold started to slow dance as the music struck up

"Oh. Right. Um, I didn't mean me. Though I might trade in future to get a level three at the start of last dances." Harold started to wonder about random and Holly's walking home and then a prolonged level three while slow dancing wiped it from his mind.

"Another of those and I might start taking you home right now."

"I might say yes, since the place is empty." Holly blushed. "But I'm not Sal. Did I see you dancing with Celine?"

"Yes, and Umeko."

"Enough talk. Since this is the last dance, and I'm your girlfriend, we're supposed to snog a bit. It's one of the rules."

"I'm a great believer in rules." Though the level three at the end nearly meant Harold forgetting a rule or two. At least with no coats they weren't waiting at the end and were outside fairly quickly. Though not first. Doll and Matti were almost towing Liam and Jon up the road before gramps got clear of the cloakroom. Liam wasn't hanging back this time.

Harold didn't even ask when Holly went up Betty's path and round the back of the girl club to the orchard. There wasn't much moon but Holly did manage to find some buds where leaves were starting to form. "You should have captured Curtis if you like plants that much."

"Oh no. I decided that…Look, another one. I like seeing the buds, especially this year. It means that everything will grow again, clean and new. No matter what happened to the tree last year, when the leaves start like this it's all wiped out. Everything new." The sadness in Holly's voice prompted Harold to put an arm round her and they walked through the trees in silence, checking for new growth. Behind them Harold could hear some of the others being walked home, and others arriving later having seen the likes of Sandy to their door.

"We'd better go before Casper sends out the search party." He turned and they headed towards the back of the girl club, not far since they'd done a circuit of the small potential orchard.

"Cripes yes." Holly sniggered. "Cripes? Liz is getting to me."

"To everyone. Celine used scroat tonight."

"I like that one." Holly turned towards him. "Level five. Oh, no buttons."

"The cloaks are already unbuttoned."

"Yes, but." Holly parted Harold's cloak. "You've got buttons anyway, but they're undone."

Harold parted her cloak. "It's a good job there's no buttons on this. That might be advanced."

"Yes. Ooh, yes!" Holly giggled. "Right, arms round and…" Harold knew what the pause was and had sort of prepared himself for wet lips. Not for wet lips, no coat and Holly kept going for the full level three time.

"Cripes. In the nicest way."

"I thought. I said not advanced and Liz said this wasn't." Holly's laugh sounded bit shaky. "That felt sort of advanced."

"We can back down to level four if you like." Harold thought that would be safer because if Holly did that too many times he'd really kiss her back, and really hug, and Holly would run a mile.

"Yes. No." Holly blew out a long breath. "I don't know. But yes, I think just a four right now." Harold barely had time to realise Holly really did mean right now. "Whew, I forgot there were no buttons so that was level five again. I'd better go in now. Because of Casper?"

"Happy Valentine's Holly."

"Oh yes."

Harold spent the short walk home trying to work out what to do about these levels, and decided if Liz would stop pushing, everything would settle down.

*   *   *

"I need advice, or maybe you do."

Liz laughed. "I can barely remember now." She put down her hammer. "Ooh, serious face. Why? Considering the big grin Holly had you should be a really happy boy."

"The smile is because she survived the latest hurdle you shoved her through, but only just." Harold perched on the edge of a bench. "Maybe you could ease off?"

Liz grinned. "Exactly how? Just which bit of these hurdles is Holly having trouble with?" Harold sat trying to work out how the hell to say this without sounding crude. Liz's grin widened. "Is it you having trouble? Don't tell me you really are a wimp and can't even fight Holly off?"

"I'm trying to resist going something that means she has to fight me off. Or thinks she does and runs away!" Harold stopped. "Oh cripes, that sounds gross."

"That sounds like hormones." Liz sniggered. "She might not run."

"Holly's not old enough. No, she is because I could see that last night with her hair up. Maybe that was it? But she's innocent, so sort of young?"

Harold glared. "If you breathe a word to Sharyn or Holly or Casper I'll go alien killing machine."

Liz held up her hands in mock surrender. "All right, but exactly why is this my fault?"

"You keep telling Holly to lick her lips and move from one level to another. Then unbutton things." Harold sighed. "That really shook her. It bloody near ruined everything."

"What thing? No, hang on, buttons undone. Did you stick a hand up her dress?" Liz didn't look quite as happy.

"No!" Harold sighed. "But when she did the wet lip bit with hands under cloaks, I was bloody tempted. Just don't tell her any more levels, all right."

Liz sniggered. "If you're tempted to go up her skirt, I don't need to." Liz held her hands up again at Harold's glare. "I promise, all right. If you wanted some nookie why didn't you grab Sal or Doll or Suzie, or possibly Matti? Any of those might have liked a hand up their skirt in the right setting."

"I wanted a girlfriend, someone to hold hands and snog a bit and back off the rest, especially those four." Harold listened to himself and that didn't sound right.

"So you don't fancy Holly really?"

"Of course I do, idiot. She's bloody lovely, but doesn't need a randy soldier getting a bit hands on." Harold held his head in his hands. "It isn't like that. I'm just worried that Holly thinks she's got to, you know, keep moving up these bloody levels. She was talking about rites of passage because someone is filling her head with all sorts. Though at least Holly doesn't think she has to compete."

"No, but you're right in one way. She was definitely a bit worried about you expecting a bit too much to start with." Liz grinned. "To repeat myself. Holly looked happy after last night."

"Because I said we could go back down a level if it worried her. She wasn't expecting, er, whatever she felt. I don't think she was smiling about me." Harold sighed.

"I'm a slut so I don't see the problem. If Holly liked whatever, she'll do it again. If not, she won't." Liz laughed. "Cripes, you make it sound like a problem."

"It isn't put like that. Providing someone stops pushing and giving instructions and suggesting things." Harold glared again and couldn't keep it up so he smiled. "Why am I talking to you about this?"

"So I don't give your girl ideas. Perish the thought, that's your department. I promise." Liz grinned. "So do you like her Valentine's dress or the tutu most?"

"Cripes, if Holly wants a level five in that tutu, all bets are off. After all, there is no skirt." Harold smiled wider because Liz teasing him worked better than Liz coaching Holly.

"So which did you like most? Or was that the answer?"

"Oh no, not a chance. Anyway, because my thoughts are pure, I never looked below her neck." Harold stood up.

"But you hugged." Liz smirked. "With your sorts of hugs, you don't need to look. Maybe Holly could try for Jessica Rabbit next time if Sal will loan her the dress?"

"You promised to be good. Anyway," he says, in a desperate attempt to change the subject, "how are you for spare knives? After the demonstration at the gate, I reckon Umeko at least is a possible for spear wielder. She put some real venom into the caning."

"That was a lovely sight. Made me wish I could hit someone." Liz smiled happily. "Just what a few of the little scroats deserve, a proper spanking."

"So just in case Umeko wants to upgrade from spanking?"

"I've not taken the hafts off all the spare knives because someone might need one. Unless you want me to replace the early ones, the ones from the fire, I can make another dozen." Liz frowned. "I could make those up with lighter shafts so someone could throw them. That should slow some little scroat up a bit."

"Magic." His radio crackled. "Damn. I'll have to go outside because there's too much metal in here. We'll have to sort out a phone for you."

Harold's radio buzzed several more times before he could make sense of the message. "Everyone to the gate and bring everything. We've got GOFS, Hot Rods and Geeks and they aren't happy."

*　　*　　*

"They're not happy, but they're not shooting either." Harold inspected the line of cars and the men armed with crossbows and machetes. "They've put on the white flags and that's Cadillac, Gofannon and Hawkins so it's not too serious. They're all bosses," Harold explained to a baffled Billy. "The bosses wouldn't all expose themselves like this if they meant to fight." Harold didn't think so, but kept remembering the comment about rolling over Orchard Close and dividing the spoils.

Harold stepped up onto his box so they could all see him. "You! You said fines." Hawkins wasn't waiting for the polite parts.

"Are you here to talk or fight? If you want to fight come ahead. If you want to talk, say so and three of you come ahead."

"Talk, you idiot. You don't think we'd stand here like this for a fight, did you?" Gofannon waved a hand at the houses either side of the gate. "In range and in plain view?"

"No, but then Hawkins started shooting his mouth off."

"We want a meeting, about rules." Gofannon pointed at Hawkins. "He says you changed them and cut up one of his men."

"If you'll talk we will explain. We had a situation, and the man lived and kept his nuts. Now will you come in and discuss it in a civilised manner?" Harold thought the ensuing argument a close thing until Hawkins threw up his hands in disgust.

Cadillac stepped clear of the rest. "I for one find your rules fascinating, but we have a problem with hostages. Have you got three top people?"

"Yes, but if they come down there some idiot will open his big mouth and people will die. One hostage. After all, if I kill you then all three gangs will combine and wipe us out."

"Your logic is impeccable. Send him out." Cadillac understood who wouldn't start a bloodbath.

Casper had already passed his shotgun to Alfie and Jon started the car and moved the gate. Cadillac looked at the car as he came through and Harold sighed. "Still working on it. We've had interruptions." A quick search showed that all three only carried a machete and belt knife, and they were soon in number three with the fan heater blasting away.

Hawkins really was upset. "You cut up a man and he never even touched a girl."

"He threatened her, and she shook her head and he kept coming. Shaking a head is no. He's lucky he didn't touch her." Holly came in and smiled at Harold. "Holly, what happens if someone claims a girl without her permission?"

"Whoa, we all know that one. But he didn't touch?" Gofannon interest sharpened at that. "What if a bloke thinks he's got a yes, he puts his hand on an ass or whatever, and she says no and he backs off? A bloke can get the wrong idea."

"True and if that is clearly what happened we can work around it. But shaking her head and backing away until a wall stops her isn't giving out mixed messages." Harold gave Hawkins a long level look. "Especially when it's a Geek and Umeko." Harold glanced at Cadillac and Gofannon. "The girl he called chink."

"Oh, now that makes more sense." Cadillac smiled at Hawkins. "Doesn't it?"

"Cutting him up is still over the top. Not only that but you took down the fence and came over the border." Hawkins glared. "You killed someone our side."

Harold glared right back. "He was shooting at us from behind that fence. A woman lost an arm when she was hit."

Hawkins checked both Holly and Emmy for damage. "Who?"

"Our baker, so not a fighter. Are you missing anyone? Maybe you'll recognise the man?" Harold watched carefully as he spoke but Hawkins kept himself under control or wasn't involved.

"I thought he was dead?"

Emmy stood up. "I'll get it."

While Emmy went to get the 'it' Harold explained the border fence and the number of attempted shootings. By then Emmy arrived back with a frosted plastic bag and a garden cane. She gave Hawkins a beaming smile and rubbed away the frost on the outside.

"Bloody hell! Why did you keep his head?" Hawkins flinched at the next thought. "Where did you keep a frozen head?"

"Not with our burgers. We kept this in with the dog food as a present for Einstein." Emmy's curled lip spoke volumes about her opinion of Einstein. "We freeze rats and that seemed appropriate somehow."

"Why for Einstein?" Harold had hoped for Hawkins's reaction, but Cadillac just had to know.

"In case he had anything to do with it. The bloke shot at Emmy and had three tries." Harold smiled sunnily. "I wanted Einstein to know that if we were going to start deliberately targeting people, I was up for that."

Cadillac laughed. "Well Hawkins? Do you know him or do you let strangers set up on your patch and take potshots at neighbours?"

Hawkins hesitated because those options either made him look incompetent, or invited a sniping war. "Never seen him before. Fair enough, you were shot at but what about cutting my man up?"

Emmy held out the cane. "Here, we beat the little scroat with these. He should have run faster." Before Hawkins could answer Gofannon started laughing.

"Oh Christ I'd have paid to see that. I thought you'd got creative after the rest had left and took a knife to him, because the Geeks were dead certain you actually cut him." He shook his head and grinned at Cadillac, who had a big grin as well.

"May I see that, please?" Emmy passed the cane to Cadillac. "Educational as usual, Soldier Boy." Cadillac looked across at Hawkins. "He'll be scarred from what you say, but was your man crippled?"

"No." Hawkins sounded sullen but there was little he could do in the face of laughter from the other two. "I thought he'd been cut. There was blood everywhere."

"Scars, bleeding, pain and humiliation, but not crippled. Very informative." Harold flinched internally because Cadillac seemed to like that idea a bit too much. "Anything else we need to know, Soldier Boy?"

"Yes, you've got a runner on your patch. We caught him spotting for the man in the bag but he got away, though he's in his shorts so maybe he froze to death." Harold shrugged. "I was going to let you know but we were busy yesterday with it being Valentine's."

"I'll bet your lot didn't get a traditional Valentine reward, not the way your women are about men." Cadillac looked straight at Holly and she gave him a lovely smile.

"But we like men. We just like men who ask nicely. I found one." She reached out and took a firm hold of Harold's hand. "So I asked him to walk me home."

All three gang leaders opened their mouths to make a comment, looked at Holly's or Harold's weaponry, and shut their mouths. Gofannon did manage, "Lucky boy."

"Are we all square?" Harold wanted Hawkins out of there before Cadillac wound him up over something else.

"I'm done." Hawkins stood.

"Don't forget Einstein's doggie bag. He might recognise an old friend." Cadillac smiled and pointed at the bag. "Maybe Soldier Boy will sell you a cane to spank Einstein if he's been naughty?"

"That's a stranger. We'll keep a better eye on the borders in future. Are you lot coming?"

"I want to talk business, especially beer." Cadillac settled back in his chair.

"Me too, but I also need a plumber." Gofannon grinned. "I can trade hops and malted barley. I'd pay even more for either a decent brewer or some lessons?"

"We've got a brewer now, but note I am here to buy my personal supplies." Cadillac shrugged. "Perhaps you could visit to deal with the rest of the business? It's more firearms so you'll have to look anyway before we fix a price."

After Cadillac left with his beer Gofannon really did want to talk about plumbing as well as buy beer, because the GOFS had a serious problem. The increasingly restrictive laws about only using tradesmen for plumbing and electrical work had left most people incapable of even minor repairs, and the GOFS's problem wasn't minor.

*   *   *

The GOFS's plumbing problem turned out to be major enough for a visit by Rob which meant a GOFS hostage. Wayland grinned. "I volunteered because I want to talk to your smith about his artwork." The GOFS smith shook his head. "Though crossbow heads like that really are too time-consuming."

Harold smiled. "I'll ask but our smith is bashful." Liz definitely worried about others knowing who she was, and everyone called her the smith to outsiders. "You might have to find something else to amuse yourself until our plumber gets back." Outside the gates Rob and Bernie were getting into an SUV, one in a convoy of four. The GOFS weren't risking losing the Orchard Close plumber, not with their toilets all backed up. Harold grinned. "We've got a library?"

"Really?" Wayland looked genuinely interested. "Most of the books in our library were burned. We can swap for any that are doubled up, though a lot of ours are schoolbooks."

"I'll check with the teachers. Conn will keep you company, just so you don't get lost." They both laughed because the library was easy to find, but the wrong side of the 'No Entry' signs. Visitors were restricted to one road of Orchard Close, with notices to mark the edges. "I'll go and see if our smith is feeling chatty."

Harold smiled happily to himself as he walked to the garage near the girl club, the forge these days. "Hi there Liz. Someone wants to talk to our smith, one of the GOFS."

"Cripes no, Harold. I don't want any of that lot knowing who I am. That Cadillac would kidnap me because the Hot Rods reckon his smith is crap, worse than me." Liz shivered. "I really don't fancy that creep getting me. Mouse, remember."

"Oh well. It's a pity really. He was really taken with the artwork on the crossbow bolts." Harold shrugged. "Must be an ironwork thing, with him being a blacksmith."

Harold smiled happily as Liz's eyes widened. She lifted her hammer. "You, you, you, Wimp!" Then her face fell. "I can't tell him I'm the smith. Damn. Where is he? No, don't tell me. I don't want to be too easy. Sod it, where is he? Is he really a blacksmith?" Liz glared. "If he isn't, or he's gay, I'll kill you."

"His name is Wayland, and he's got those big muscles you go all weak-kneed about. He might be either educated or gay, because he's gone to the library instead of for a pint with the barmaids?" Harold shrugged. "Still, as you say, you can't let on in case Cadillac finds out."

"You rotten little creep. You could have just not told me. Is this supposed to be revenge for the Holly licky-lips thing? Well just let me tell you a few things." Liz paused. "No, just leave while I hit some metal and try and work out an approach that doesn't involve drooling over his anvil. Can you bar the other women from the library?"

"Hilda and Faith are the librarians." Harold had trouble talking through his laughter, which was mean. Hilarious but mean.

"You could close it for repairs, but not tell this Wayland?" Liz looked at Harold's grinning face and shook her head. "Leave, now. I refuse to provide further amusement, but there will be payback." Harold did leave, and winced as he heard hammer hitting metal with real feeling. He tried to work out how Liz could get Wayland on his own without losing her cover, but she'd go soppy about ironwork and blow it.

*　　　*　　　*

Though Liz had plenty of time to either work on methods or beat the hell out of metal, because Rob still wasn't back by dark. Harold didn't worry, because the GOFS were basing their offers to trade on the quality of their sharp steel so they wouldn't give up the smith. The current deal for Rob's plumbing included machetes, real weapons rather than the undergrowth clearing type looted from garden centres.

"This is your house for the night." Harold smiled. "Please don't sleep-walk. There are guards and they are twitchy about strangers, especially if you climb the back fence."

"Not a problem." Wayland waved a cowboy novel. "I like your library, and it was interesting meeting some of your people when they aren't aiming sharp things."

"We're quite civilised when we aren't under threat."

"As I'm finding out." Wayland smiled at Holly. "For a start you are quite charming, instead of a blood-stained maniac. That was a bit of a relief really."

"I've mellowed since people stopped threatening me." Holly had her arm hooked through Harold's. "Finding a man with manners helped."

"There aren't many left. All of us are forgetting, or the veneer is slipping." Wayland shrugged. "Your smith really is shy, but please let him know we aren't interested in kidnapping. I just wanted to talk metal with another iron beater."

"I'll pass on the message. We'll see you in the morning." As he walked Holly home, they both agreed that it was a pity Liz hadn't been able to suppress her sooty yearnings enough to talk to Wayland. The ringing of hammer on metal in the forge underlined how Liz felt.

Sooty yearning were forgotten as Harold came in the door to hear Sharyn repeating "cripes, cripes, cripes" in a voice that wanted to really swear.

Harold walked through to find glass all over the kitchen floor. "Blimey, is Daisy learning to juggle? You should start her on tennis balls."

"Don't. I'm not in the mood. Those jars had lids, proper screw ones for reusing, and now they're smashed." Sharyn gestured at an open cupboard. "I was stood on a box putting some more in there and slipped, and grabbed. The whole blasted shelf came with me. Why aren't they fastened in properly?"

"Pass. I'll ask Sandy." Harold jiggled another couple of shelves, gently. "None of them are, it's how they're made. I'll look out for more jars."

"They won't be any good because the lids will be rusted. Curtis reckoned we can make vinegar if the mart stuff is expensive and make pickles later." Sharyn took a broom from a cupboard and started on the mess. "We'll need even more jars for jam and I've ruined all this lot."

Harold bent to sort through the glass, carefully. "Save the lids. I'll get jars with rusted tops and then try to get a match for these." He frowned. "There should be pickles and jam at the marts. There had to be warehouses full when the crash happened."

"Yeah, and designer jeans, and corned beef, and real Coco Pops, and a thousand other things. Oddly enough none of them survived. Where do you suppose they ended up?"

"Market Rasen." Harold spoke to himself but Sharyn stopped brushing. "Where?"

"Someplace not inside a city where those smiling people on the mart adverts go to do their shopping? Sorry, just thinking aloud." Harold smiled. "To cheer you up, let me tell you about Liz."

* * *

"If I had a hammer, I'd hammer…. Cripes, you're up early." Liz looked around, almost shifty, but everyone else was still getting up or having breakfast.

"We wanted to check on Wayland, but I suppose he's smiling." Harold was, and Holly was starting to as she caught on.

"What makes you think that, or that I'd care?"

"From the ground up? Dinky boots I've never seen before, short leather skirt ditto, lovely lacy white blouse without a trace of soot, cream all over chin, and then there's that singing?" Harold sniggered. "Who stole our sooty, iron-beating butterfly?"

"I thought you were worried about him finding out you're the smith?" Holly had been giggling while Harold spoke but was serious now. "Or about him telling Cadillac?"

"I've told him I'll pass on his comments to the smith, but then I explained the smith doesn't put on those little spikes and twirls." Liz smirked. "I explained about how I used to make ornaments but I'm too fragile for the heavy work. We got onto how much I admired all those big muscly men, beating on iron." She sighed. "The rest is not for delicate ears but probably hit level thirty three. I've invited him for the Harvest Festival, so we'd better have one."

"I'll have a word with the boss." After the level two mouth to mouth word Holly smiled. "He says yes but I might have to make sure later." The two women hi-fived each other and Liz carried on up the road, singing happily. Both Harold and Holly laughed as Liz put out her arms and performed a couple of little dance steps before going round the corner towards the girl club.

Harold looked up and down the empty street. "Perhaps we should keep that quiet, and give Wayland a little while to recover?"

"Cripes yes. You once said you wanted to walk me around Orchard Close hand in hand? That should take long enough." Holly hugged Harold's arm with hers. "We could check on sentries to give you an excuse."

"How long do you reckon it will take for Wayland to stop smiling?" They went off to check on sentries still sniggering.

Liz was nowhere in sight when Rob came home and Wayland left, though Wayland was definitely smiling. Rob wasn't when he reported.

"Maybe the GOFS aren't trading women but women's rights have died, big style. I was offered a girl, or asked if I wanted one." Rob sighed. "Though to be honest maybe it wasn't the same offer Cadillac or the Geeks would make. Maybe a prostitute?" He frowned. "Maybe there is a brothel, a voluntary paid one?"

"Did they ask for pay then?"

"No, but the phrasing was did I want fixing up with a girl. They do seem more civilised round their women than the Geeks, or the bosses do. The rank and file are cruder. You'll know about Cadillac soon but we've heard and seen enough to know the Hot Rods' attitude to women. I'd like to think at least one neighbour doesn't act like that."

"So would I." Harold didn't want to have to tell Liz her sweaty fix kept an unwilling woman. "Maybe Bernie will know?"

"No, Bernie turned the offer down as well. He might have been worried about her not being willing, or spoiling his chances with one that is." They both smiled at that because Bernie had been walked home at least once by Sal without a dance first.

"Apart from that, the women, what do you make of the GOFS?" Harold wanted some idea about other gangs before he saw whatever Cadillac had come up with.

"The GOFS have a real stronghold, an old school with a central court-yard. There's a little community in there and at least some of the women, the ones I saw, seem to be voluntary or just paid help. There are cooks and cleaners and all the rest in the stronghold, not just gang girlfriends, and some non-gang men. I also fixed some leaks where pipes had frozen in the housing on one of their streets, and their people didn't seem terrified. Wary, but not outright frightened." Rob shrugged. "They've got the same system as the others though, the people in the houses pay protection."

"But they're not nasty bastards like the Hot Rods, or vicious little shits like the Geeks? We can trade with the GOFS without having to count our fillings and fingers afterwards?" Harold thought Cadillac would try for both by bargaining hard or threats, and the Geeks would try to steal both and preferably from a body.

"Probably, if we look strong enough." Rob smiled at Holly. "Now I'd like to go and get the same sort of greeting I bet you did this morning."

"Cripes yes. Sorry." Harold smiled. "I'm a bit worried."

So was Bernie, and not about the GOFS themselves. "If we get a woman visitor wearing a blonde wig, get a squad locked and loaded."

"Why, and how can we tell if it's a wig?"

"The wigs are a uniform, and the women could be any colour and probably covered in tattoos. They'll also be carrying a lot of weapons, chase men and women, and don't think much of rules." Bernie sniggered. "The ordinary soldiers, that's what the GOFS call them, are scared of being caught by them."

"Wayland and Gofannon never mentioned that."

"Did they mention Barbie Girls, because that's what they're called? They live in a shopping mall and nobody visits unless they're tied up and dragged there. They tortured one of Cadillac's men to death." Bernie frowned. "Though he might have asked for it."

"Are they at war with the GOFS? Why would they come here anyway?" Harold stopped and gave Bernie a chance to answer.

"Not a war but there's guards on the border, shooting guards." Bernie smiled. "The Barbies stole some beer and want to know where it came from. They've offered a truce in return for more beer, Berry Beer even if it had no labels." He stopped and looked alarmed. "They try to kidnap tradespeople as some sort of sport or hobby."

"Them, Cadillac, and possibly the Geeks. Right, watch out for dangerous blondes." Harold put his arm round Holly. "Oh look, there's one right here, help. Thanks Bernie, now go and see if you can find a blonde for yourself." Both Harold and Holly laughed at the speed Bernie went blonde-hunting.

*　　　*　　　*

Holly hugged. "I'm worried about you going to the Mansion."

"Don't worry; I'll say no." The Berrying was worth it to see Holly cheer up. Harold hugged her again and set off after a level three.

"Come on, put him down." Alfie smiled but a strained smile. He'd volunteered as Harold's escort and pointed out that he wouldn't be taking any offers either.

"Do I take over his duties?" Charger, the hostage, held up both hands when Holly glared. "Only asking, and only joking. I was told you'd mellowed."

"I have when I've got Harold's hand to hold. Fair warning, I might be a little bit short tempered until he's back." Holly stalked off.

"Sorry, that really was a joke. Can I ask for a beer without risking bloodshed?" Charger did look sorry, but the Hot Rods all seemed to be adopting insincere as a way of life.

"Beer isn't a problem, as long as you remember the other rules." Casper waved a hand up the street.

"Hell yes. Caddi, Cadillac, has adopted your little caning lesson and that is brutal. At least it is the way he does it." This Hot Rod was older than most although he also wore overalls and carried a machete.

Harold checked that nobody would be going out scavenging today. He worried that someone might be tempted to raid while he was gone even though Emmy, Casper and Holly were perfectly capable of organising resistance, as were several others. In the end Emmy shooed him away. "Go, before I start crying and Alfie gets corrupted by your escort." Harold's escort consisted of a pickup with four armed Hot Rods in the back.

Harold drove his pickup, because Alfie had never learned. He took note of the route and mileage, almost four miles from door to door, and also took a good look at the housing estate the two vehicles passed by. That had an SUV parked across the entrance with armed men inside, men with firearms. The entrance to the Mansion had been built to stand an assault, protected by a gate and brickwork breastworks at each side. Harold brought a pistol and his two-two but left them in the pickup along with Alfie, because Harold suspected inside Cadillac's home could be upsetting for anyone from Orchard Close.

"Rules, Soldier Boy. We all have them." Cadillac smiled as Mack quickly frisked Harold but allowed him to keep his sheath knife. "I told you my place was called the Mansion."

Harold looked around the walled estate of large detached houses, all probably qualifying as mansions. The Mansion, the one Cadillac pointed at, had to be the largest of course. Cadillac had claimed a huge house built of rustic brick, with timbering and stonework on the walls in some attempt to make it look rural. "Very cosy. Couldn't you find a big one?"

Cadillac laughed. "Come on, we'll get comfy. Would you like a blonde as a comfort fuck since you've not brought your own?"

"Some of us just like pleasant company, and prefer them voluntary. What are the rules in here?" Harold smiled as best he could, because Cadillac seemed to have decided to push him. "If someone gets too lippy and I slap him down, what's the fine?"

"Nothing, because they aren't allowed to do that to my visitors. We don't have many visitors so the language might bruise your delicate ears, though if you do let rip none of the women will object." Cadillac caught hold of a young woman. "What would you say if my friend here pushed you over the bench and said he was going to give you a good fucking?"

"I would explain that I'm not here for that, Mr Cadillac, not while I do my job." She glanced at Harold and lowered her eyes again. "Then I'd send your friend to the girl's house."

Harold wanted to hit Cadillac, but today Big Mack stood right behind his boss holding an aluminium baseball bat. "No thanks."

Cadillac let the woman go and she hurried towards one of the houses. "That's true, she's safe while her cooking is up to scratch. I liked your idea of all the girls in one house so I've done the same, though not for the same reason." Cadillac swaggered towards his own house. "Not for me of course. I like my comforts handy, but so do you."

Harold decided to just let it wash over him. Cadillac seemed intent on indulging in his usual winding up but here the raw edges, the real Cadillac, showed. Harold looked up at the bodyguard. "Have you been busy?"

"Cadillac keeps me busy, keepin' 'im safe."

"So how come we never see you when he visits these days?" That didn't add up to Harold.

"I keep an eye on this place while 'e's visiting."

Cadillac turned at that. "Only while I'm visiting the neighbours. After all, we wouldn't want one of this lot arranging accidents and assuming they'd live. Here we are. The study is through that door, it's what I use for business."

"Very civilised." The room gleamed with leather and polished wood, with a huge home entertainment system and a flatscreen on one wall.

"That's all stopped working. It's why I want your electrician, that and more mundane problems." Cadillac pointed a remote at the screen and nothing happened.

"Two electricians. Mundane to make the electricity go where you want, and the lights and showers and sockets work. Then one to look inside the likes of that to tell you if it's knackered." Harold took the seat Big Mack pushed into place by the expanse of gleaming dark wooden desk. The bodyguard put a thick cloth on top of the polished wood.

"Refreshments first. We wouldn't want to tempt the staff." Cadillac actually rang a little bell and a young woman came in, dressed in what must be Cadillac's idea of a maid's uniform. Harold thought the gang boss must have found someone's fancy dress, though the lass in fishnets and a short black dress and lacy apron didn't look happy about the result.

"Yes sir."

"Well, Soldier Boy? Beer, hot drink, redhead?"

Harold had trouble letting it all slide off him as Cadillac pushed harder. He looked at the red-haired woman and smiled, a small, non-threatening one. "White coffee with two sugars please." She gave him a little curtsy and left.

"That's the downstairs maid. I've got a blonde one for upstairs. What do you think of my setup?"

Harold though about how to answer that, very conscious of the big man two steps behind his chair. "Different folks, different rules. I prefer mine of course." Harold glanced round towards Big Mack. "Don't you get to sit down?"

"No he doesn't, not when people like you are this close to me. I've heard rumours about you, Soldier Boy, but now I don't think some are true. I've been told that you go apeshit at the drop of a hat, you're a maniac, but there's no sign of you losing it. What does wind you up?" Cadillac's urbane smile remained but his eyes sharpened.

"Maniac in a fight and well trained in a tight spot can look much the same to the uninitiated." Harold assumed some of the visitors had heard tales from residents. "You wind me up Cadillac, but you're smart enough to do it where I'm not going to react. Why don't you show how annoyed you get when visiting me?"

Cadillac laughed, and Harold thought this one might be genuine. "Yes I am winding you up, and yes it is a test. Most of my visitors so far would have failed. Not that test because they don't give a fuck about how I treat women." His eyes narrowed. "What is it with the swearing? Are you religious?"

"No, when I was in the Army I would eff and blind with the rest. Here we've found that stopping the foul language reminds everyone to treat the women decently. I doubt you could come up with profanity I haven't heard before." Harold smiled. "And if you did, in here, I couldn't care less."

"So if I threw that girl over the desk and pulled up her skirt?"

"I would consider that bad manners in a business meeting, and wouldn't watch because that's not my thing." Harold shrugged. "Since that sort of behaviour would be deliberate bad manners I wouldn't come here for business again." He sat and did his best to look unconcerned while Cadillac tried to see if Harold meant it. Harold tried very hard not to show his real reaction, because in truth he'd try to get Big Mack's baseball bat and brain Cadillac before going down.

Eventually Cadillac nodded, very slowly. "Maybe that's what it takes to be a real shooter, a sniper. No nerves and no conscience, you really can just turn it off just like the books say. I can kill a bloke but I couldn't do that, wait for hours to shoot a man in cold blood." Cadillac grinned. "I'd have to crow a bit and piss on the body."

"I've learned bladder control." The maid arriving with the coffees came as a relief to Harold as Cadillac stopped prying. Once Cadillac had patted her ass and told her she was a good girl, and she'd left, the gang boss became all business.

"Mack, let's see the goods."

"Mack? That's easier than Big Mack."

Cadillac waited until the big man had put four handguns and a rifle on the cloth laid over the desk. "The big is a sort of joke about how many burgers he can eat. He answers to Mack well enough, since that's his real gang name."

"Does he have a lorry to drive, since I'm told yours is really a Cadillac and Cooper has a Mini Cooper." While he spoke, Harold assessed the weapons on the desk and decided what he could offer to fix.

"I wish. That's one of those really annoying details. All the big lorries seem to have left the city before the rioting, apart from a couple that were broken down. Odd, isn't it?" Cadillac scowled. "Some people think I'm paranoid but sometimes paranoia is just common sense. Are you paranoid, Soldier Boy?"

"I'm alive, so I must be." Harold pointed to one of the hand weapons. "That's beyond repair but I might take it as spare parts."

"Really? What have you got spares for?"

"Not much, so I'm building stock. After all if you lot don't know how to treat weapons, you'll break them." Harold smiled. "Though that's a bit beyond rough usage."

"That was a hammer on the hand holding it, a big hammer. Two seconds thought and the twat with the hammer could have smashed the bloke's wrist and saved the gun." Cadillac's eyes lit up. "I tried out your idea with canes and everyone else will be more careful now."

"I'm not giving you much for it in that case. Most of what's in there will be knackered. What's supposed to be wrong with the rest of them?" Harold grinned. "Remember, if there's more you'll just wait longer to get them back, because I'll stop repairing until you've agreed."

"Yeah, yeah, smartarse. Though spares are worth more if you haven't got many?" Cadillac hunched forward and settled down to haggle. Harold sipped coffee and bargained, and didn't think he'd been stiffed too badly. Sat in the study, sipping coffee and discussing business, made it easy to forget just what a shit Cadillac was. Harold was reminded both by the sights as he was escorted to the gate, and Alfie's red, angry face.

"I really want to shoot someone Harold." Alfie looked mad as hell and ready to blow, and the gate guards were laughing.

"Keep yourself under control just a bit longer while I drive up the road. Then you can get out and hit a wall if it helps." Harold drove for a few minutes while Alfie stewed in silence, and then it came out.

"They offered me a woman like you said, and I told them no." Alfie shut up again but a glance showed Harold the lad still had his jaw and fists clenched.

"Sorry, maybe I should have brought someone else." Sometimes Harold forgot Alfie's age because of his size and build.

"No, it's just. They said since I'm young, maybe the first one was a bit old. They brought three more out." Alfie shut up again but gently pounded white-knuckled fists on his knees.

"I understand, Alfie. They paraded one for me. It's to try and get us to do something about it, so the bastards can kill us inside the rules." Harold tried to figure out who to take as bodyguard another time.

"But." Alfie took a breath. "They brought young ones and they were crying. Really young!"

Harold stopped the pickup. "Go over there and kick that wall down. Shoot the rifle at a few things. Throw bricks through windows or hack at the frames with your machete. They brought young ones just to get to you. If the girls were crying it's because that's not what they are there for." Please, all and any gods, make that true Harold thought. Even if it wasn't, Alfie needed to believe it right now. Harold sat for a while and tried to persuade himself while Alfie kicked and threw things. He also decided that he'd go alone to The Mansion in the future. After all, if Cadillac decided to sacrifice the hostage to get Harold, one bodyguard wouldn't make much difference.

Chapter 7:
Levelling Up
and Betrayal

At least Cadillac came to collect the weapons and buy more beer for his private use, which meant Harold didn't have to visit again just yet. Cadillac traded beer and hops at below the price TesdaMart now sold them for, which with the sacks from the GOFS topped up Nigel and Berry's stores nicely. He also brought a large quantity of screw top bottles, and bargained for beer. Harold told Cadillac to bring any bottle caps even if they were bent, he'd not get much each but they'd add up. That had become another shortage now.

The teams were working through Orchard Close's territory again, re-checking the houses already checked three times. Now the scavengers wanted glass jars even if the tops were rusted and the contents ruined. Many metal tops had been pierced to help open them but now several women thought even the lightly rusted ones could be used. The preservation squad would use a bit of plastic bag inside the lid to get a seal once they had jam or pickle to fill the jars with.

Orchard Close sent out larger groups now because of the occasional shots at them, singles or small volleys. The shooters would run while the scavengers took cover, which puzzled everyone. One bullet went clean through the minibus but whoever fired ran towards the GOFS and Ogou later reported they'd shot a trespasser from this direction. Visitors from all three other gangs claimed they'd exchanged shots with small groups of armed strangers moving through their territory.

Eventually the Hot Rods caught one and solved the mystery. The survivor of a small group trapped and wiped out claimed they were looking for some-place not claimed by anyone else. Elsewhere other gangs were also agreeing boundaries and squeezing all the loners and small independents out. A large area of the city to the south, badly damaged during the original riots when the Army sealed the city, was allegedly uninhabited. Cooper gleefully related how he'd stripped and caned the man, and sent the prat south towards the allegedly unclaimed areas.

The Geeks seemed to have let dead dogs lie, and traded two-way radios for gun repairs and cement for beer. Wellington came for that trade and despite the scars and his mouth being twisted up at one side, seemed genuinely grateful. With cement available the windows in the perimeter houses were finally bricked in properly, though the plywood remained as well. As the nearest ruins were slowly cleared the wall around Orchard Close thickened and grew taller.

Eventually the scavengers found the answer to the gate problem, four short thick steel girders. Two days of hard digging drove four deep holes into the approach road, and the girders were concreted in with about three feet protruding. At last the car could be retired, and a real, steel-faced pair of gates put in place. The visitors were impressed, but none of them thought the same method would work in their stronghold. The top men were too fond of their motors to leave them outside. The visitors were generally better behaved now despite a few joking requests for a spanking, one on one.

Several weeks of relative quiet were ended by prolonged gunfire, and this time the volume sent everyone in Orchard Close running for cover and weapons. The radio didn't make anyone feel any better. "Emmy. Come mob handed. Not a gang attack. B6." That covered the essentials including the location on their customised maps. Harold took the newly adapted minibus with fourteen passengers.

"If it's the usual lot heading south they'll run when we arrive. Just in case they aren't, everyone keep low, below the windows." He ignored the grumbles and mutters as the crowded fighters scrunched down lower because more firing had broken out ahead. Harold peered through a slit in the steel plate replacing the windscreen, the only window protected because of the sheer weight of steel plate.

Liz had worked long and hard on the minibus after the bullet went right through, and this wasn't artwork. "Down!" Harold slammed on the brakes as a hurricane of lead rattled and clanged off the minibus from dead ahead. He hoped the screams and cries from behind were shock and bruising, because the steel mesh on the windows wouldn't stop or deflect all the bullets.

Bullets rang and whined off the steel and there were more cries and then some talking back there. "Nothing serious back here." That meant some wounds but Bernie sounded relieved so not too bad.

Harold kept his head down as he called back. "As soon as they stop to reload, the first two by the doors stick a gun out and empty a clip. Aim at the two houses dead ahead on the junction. Spread them around to keep heads down. Everyone else run for the houses each side of the street."

Even as Harold finished the volume of incoming began to drop. "Ready Harold." He heard the side doors slide the first couple of inches and pause.

"Go." As the gunfire started from behind Harold moved back into the minibus. Holly blazed away on one side and Bess on the other, and the last four of the rest were pouring through the open doors and running. The gunfire from the houses ahead seemed to have stopped so Harold called Emmy on the radio.

"Emmy, where are this lot from?"

"Don't know. We bumped into them and they started shooting. What happened to you?"

"We bumped into more, or the rest, or their rear."

"Same group from how near the shots seem to be. We've got wounded and so have they and we're either side of a street. It's a stalemate here. They've got women and kids."

"Are the women shooting?"

"One or two are."

"Harold, do you want me to shoot again?" Holly had stopped shooting and put in a fresh clip, as had Bess.

"Wait a minute." Harold raised his voice. "You lot, give it up."

A man's voice sounded loud and clear. "Back off. We just want a clear run."

Harold actually considered that, but there were women and kids. "The next gang you meet won't back off. They'll shoot you and take the women. We'll cease fire while you decide."

During the silence that followed Harold checked again if any of the wounded, his or Emmy's, were serious. They were all flesh wounds and in Emmy's opinion the firing had been a reaction to seeing her scavengers, more blind covering fire than aimed attack, so he asked her to call for a cease fire. The occasional shooting further away stopped. Harold used the open side doors to gesture to those in the houses either side, and they began to move up the street using the houses or fences and hedges as cover. If they'd understood the signals everyone would stop in the houses on the corners of the T junction, just over fifty feet from the shooters.

The same voice finally spoke up. "We're heading south. There's still free space there so just let us through."

Harold thought about the numbers coming through in previous weeks, according to the other gangs. "There'll be no space left when you get there. All the enclaves are organising so join one or someone will wipe you out."

"You mean a gang? We don't want to join a gang."

Harold wasn't sure but thought he heard others speaking, so maybe that wasn't everyone's viewpoint. "We might not be what you consider a gang. How many want safe haven, and how many want to keep going and risk dying?"

"There is no safe haven. We can break through." An arm waving from a window of the end house, on the side only Harold could see, made that unlikely.

"No you can't and you don't have to. I'll let through anyone who really wants to risk it, but anyone who prefers sanctuary under our rules can stay."

"What rules?"

Harold used his radio. "Emmy, give them the rules. It'll be better coming from you." He put a hand on Holly's shoulder. "Shout out the rules please, luv."

"Really? All right."

Harold shouted up the street once Holly had finished. "Are you up there yet, Bernie?"

Bernie appeared from an upstairs window, where the shooters couldn't see him, and waved.

"Unwrap one as a demo. Do your best when I say." Bernie had become the Orchard Close bomb maker, under careful supervision from Barry. He had two pipe bombs with him, both wrapped in clingfilm holding screws and nails, washers and any other small scrap lying about.

Even without knowing about bombs, the shouting had worried the opposition and the man called out. "What are you shouting about? Who is Bernie? How do we know it's true, the rules thing? We're safer risking it."

"You're surrounded. Bernie is going to show you why it's smarter to talk, and then maybe some of you might decide to stay." Harold wasn't risking his own people, but Alfie had another couple of bombs so he'd waste one to avoid shooting at women. "If you break out a lot of you will die. Keep your heads down, right down." Harold paused then shouted again. "Bernie, now!" Bernie did well, throwing from an upstairs window, and the bomb bounced from the tarmac into the front garden opposite.

There were some shouts and a scream when the pipe bomb exploded, then the cloud of smoke drifted away in dead silence. The man didn't sound anything like as confident when he finally spoke up. "What the hell is that?"

"That's why you can't break through. How many will risk coming to talk to us? We've got people just across the road, and the next bomb has shrapnel in it."

Harold's radio crackled. "Just shoot the arses, Soldier Boy."

"Sod off." That had to be Hot Rods, Geeks or GOFS.

"Nasty. You can send them through if you like, especially if they've got women?" Harold ignored what now sounded like Hot Rods.

Instead he called out to the group ahead. "The neighbours listen to the radios. They are waiting and seem keen on the women."

"We heard." Harold sighed in relief at a different voice since that might mean a different attitude. "How can we trust you?"

"Someone will show themselves. If you shoot, even one bullet, you all die." Harold lowered his voice. "Holly? If you show yourself, quickly, we're too far for real accuracy using a handgun. Don't hang about."

"All right luv."

"All right luv." Even as Harold grappled with two answers and the re-alisation he had called Holly luv, she'd gone outside. Holly's arms went up in the air, she twirled, and dived back in. Bess did the same the other side, and grinned at Harold as she came inside. "To split their fire. Luv." Harold concentrated on the level two shading to three as Holly pulled him round.

"Stop it."

Holly smiled happily. "Yes luv." That threw Harold completely for a moment but the voice from ahead brought him back to here and now.

"Some of us want to come and talk." Harold sighed and relaxed, just a bit. With luck, nobody had to die today.

An hour later five women, seven men and three children agreed to obey the rules in Orchard Close. Seven men and two women opted to ask the GOFS, but would try to get five women to the far border first so they could approach the Barbie Girls. None opted for the Hot Rods ahead, having heard the radio message, or wanted to go back to the Geeks.

As he watched the drawn faces on those trudging past Harold wondered how many more out there were still homeless. This group were scavenging as they went because they couldn't sign on to get coupons. Intentionally or not, the government were forcing every resident to pick an enclave. Harold watched them go, then called Emmy to come and tow the minibus home.

Two days later Harold tried to get the minibus repaired. "Bloody hell, why bother? How come there's no blood in there?" Charger had come in response to a message sent to the Hot Rods.

"Nobody inside it when they opened fire." Harold didn't mention the steel plates inside the van at the time. Liz had muttered cripes more than once as she fitted the plates inside, where they couldn't be seen, and muttered even louder getting them back out. She muttered very loudly while removing the plates she'd laboriously fitted to protect the driver from the engine compartment. The half inch and three eights thick plates weighed just over a ton in all, but those who avoided getting shot willingly helped Liz.

"We can fix the tyres and the engine, make it a runner again, but why not find another?" Charger looked the minibus over. "The paint job is knackered." He waved a hand at the bullet holes along the sides, many were long tear marks where rounds ricocheted back out from the plates.

"They'll fix that and repaint the pictures. This minibus has sentimental value to the girl club, but only just so much value. Tell Cadillac if he tries to stiff me he's got a minibus wearing a paint job that none of your lot will be seen dead in." In truth Harold was willing to be cheated a bit to get the minibus back, because the survivors from the burned flats really did care about their wheels.

*   *   *

Despite the better weather Patty made her first knitting sales. Harold's new thick sweater, a dark blue Arran with a plain panel in the middle of the pattern on the front, had been designed as an advert. Patty had knitted the rest using every Arran stitch she knew. Then she knitted SB in what she called blackberry stitch on the plain panel, and every gang boss or top man who saw it wanted their own. Not identical of course.

"How much of the price do you want for Orchard Close, Harold?" Patty waved a wad of coupons as the GOFS car departed. "You took a share of what Rob and Finn charged."

"I didn't take it; that went to the Coven. That payment covers the bodyguard for them and guarding the hostage." Harold grinned. "I daren't ask what the Coven do with it."

"They make sure we've all got enough food and clothes until the crops grow." Patty frowned. "If you hadn't sneaked around stealing the wool, and if the guards didn't stand to every night and search the visitors in the day, I'd never be able to do business. We should all pay, everyone who sells anything to visitors. Call it a tax." She grinned. "ADP, Asshole Deterrent Payment."

"PMT would scare them more." Liz looked at the coupons. "Cripes, did you rob someone? I can give you an alibi for a cut."

"That's a good point, as Caddi said to Holly, if we tax the sellers we should pay Liz for making weaponry. Even if it's just artwork to her." Harold scowled. "I can feel a headache starting."

"What level?" Patty grinned at Harold's glare. "That's your fault. You said a level three cleared the last one." Harold smiled because it had. Level threes seemed to be more common and in public now, and the level five after the last walk home definitely inclined towards whatever a six might be.

"He doesn't care what level as long as he gets a lip-lock, and anyway he's totally wrong as usual. Artwork costs more than brute ironwork, philistine." Liz frowned. "The government pay me with a meagre issue of coupons, the scavengers bring in iron and trees, and the nearest sucker gets roped into charcoal making." She looked at Patty's coupons. "Though if I can get enough to buy a proper anvil?"

Harold pointed towards his house. "We need the head witch, and the Coven, and maybe a few others."

"I'd lay off the coven bit in there. I heard Daisy asking about covens at school, and two of the teachers are on the committee or whatever it's called." Patty sniggered. "Maybe Coven works."

"Oy, I'm on the whatever as well. Sometimes. Now explain PMT payments and coupons." Liz and Harold chewed over payments and taxes with Patty on the way up the street.

"Cripes, we've got to sort this out because there are things like that everywhere on Orchard Close. Kerry sews up anything that's needed, Hilda teaches the older kids and sees to the library, and there are our medics." Liz sighed. "Since we can't get enough free love going for a commune, it'll have to include some filthy lucre." She turned towards the girl club and raised her voice. "Holly, leave embroidering your underwear and get down here."

"Really? What's her embroidery like because mine isn't up to much and I'll trade." Patty caught Liz's grin and Harold's pink face. "So what is she doing?"

"Sharpening spear and arrow points, but that's a labour of love." Liz pointed up the path at Holly heading towards them, pulling on her coat. "If she'd had to sort out underwear that would have taken longer."

"Hi Harold." Holly delivered a level two hello. "What's up?"

"What level are you pair up to?" Liz grinned at Harold's warning look. Holly didn't even blush. "Five until Easter, why?"

"Because he's going to have a really bad headache after this meeting, unless you can really chill him out. How about you deliver a level five to take the edge off and stand by for a repeat afterwards?" Liz narrowed her eyes, watching, then smiled when Holly finally turned pink.

"What? A five, now?"

"No, she's winding you up Holly. We've no idea what the meeting will be about and the people aren't here yet." Harold took her hand. "Come on, you can join in to add some common sense."

"No, it's all right. I don't mind kissing because you always get a headache at meetings. It's just that, well, level five in public?" Holly's blush grew to become more red than pink.

"You can use the forge since I'll be in his house, organising people." Liz waved towards her garage blacksmith's shop, her smile becoming a grin. "Take your time."

"Stop embarrassing Holly. She said no." Harold put his arm round her and Liz grinned even wider, and Patty started to smile.

"I didn't say no and I'm not embarrassed, not if we go to the forge." Holly smiled happily. "It'll be warm in there." She flapped the edges of her coat, not yet buttoned, to remind Harold of one requirement for a five. "Come on." Harold went.

*   *   *

Though when they finally reached his house he made a beeline for Liz. "What was all that about?"

Liz patted him gently on the back. "Calm down. You were worried that Holly might be frightened by how far your goodnights had gone. From the way she dragged you off to someplace warm I'd say the last month has dealt with it." Her eyes narrowed. "What the hell is a level five anyway, and if it's a doorstep kiss why do you need someplace warm and private?" Harold gave it up because if Liz had decided to pretend ignorance a crowded room wasn't the place to argue.

Ten minutes later Harold wanted another level anything or just a quiet place. Fourteen people all had their own ideas how Orchard Close should be organised so anyone doing extra work could be rewarded. They were also trying to make sure everyone ended up fed, clothed and educated, and keep a reserve for emergencies. The phone call came as a blessed relief. "Sorry, I'm wanted at the gate."

"I'll come in case it's stressful." Holly stuck her tongue out at Liz and followed Harold out. "I needed to get out of there as well. I've already got two jobs, trigger puller and stress relief." She hooked an arm in Harold's. "Any idea what this is about?"

"A car and four men who have something to sell me." Harold shrugged. "That could be anything."

Five minutes later a man offered Harold a large preformed case labelled Pelican. He stood in the front room of one of the ruined houses along the neutral road while Alfie stood in one corner with a shotgun. A man with a revolver stood at the opposite corner, while the salesman stood in the middle with Harold. "We offered it to some gang called the Gods of Fire and Steel, and they said to come to you. It's only got four bullets and that one clip so they don't want it. We found it in a safe when a wall collapsed but there's no more ammunition, which is stupid right?"

Harold didn't point out the ammo would be kept separate because it took all his concentration to keep the sheer lust from his face. He had no idea what a Blaser R8 Professional Success hunting rifle meant in performance except that it looked like pure lethal perfection. The Pelican case obviously went with the weapon, neatly holding the clip, sights, and the broken down weapon. Harold had never used a setup like this, but already he itched to try that pistol grip set into the usual rifle stock.

"What else came with it?"

"I told you." The man with the pistol scowled. "They said he's a shooter so sell him the rest and don't fuck up the deal."

"There's a kit for cleaning. Then some oil and an empty pouch thing for extra bullets, and another sling." The man hesitated.

"And?"

""And this. It's a really flash knife and has to be worth something?" The knife came in a pouch rather than a sheath and had an extra saw-toothed blade. Harold pulled the clip out of the case and inspected the exposed round, trying to work out if he'd got any like that. He had boxes and jars full of empty brass now since everyone knew to collect them when scavenging.

"How much?"

"The blokes said you'd pay in coupons and guns, real guns not that bloody sixgun thing. We'll trade that in for a nine mill because we can't get ammo for it." The salesman sneered at the pistol. "It's only got six shots and you can't change clips."

"I might spare a gun, not guns, not if you want coupons." Harold tried to work out what crap weapon he could give these men, because even if there were no more rounds this rifle came as a godsend. Harold had no telescopic sights and daren't try to buy one. The mediocre riflemen out there with half-way decent rifles and scopes could all outshoot the 303 with iron sights. So far Cadillac and the Geeks in particular hadn't realised Harold didn't have better sights, but that couldn't last.

Alfie stirred and for a moment Harold thought he'd object to selling guns. "It's all right Alfie. I'll pay with my private gear because with only four rounds it's not much good, but it's a nice poser job." Harold hoped Alfie would back off. He glanced at the man in the opposite corner. "Let me see that pistol."

"Sod off. What, leave us unarmed?"

"You were told I'd deal fair. If I wanted to rob you I'd take a quick step back and Alfie would pull both triggers. My lot would shoot the shit out of your mates as soon as they heard the shot, and then we'd strip the bodies. Give." The two men exchanged glances and the man handed the heavy revolver over for Harold to inspect. "It's in crap condition. How much ammo is there?"

"Another dozen rounds. We'll want two guns if you take both? Nine mill because we've got that." That wasn't a surprise since everyone else had nine millimetre, a seemingly unlimited supply.

"I'll put this rifle together to make sure you didn't mess around and ruin it." Harold looked over at Alfie. "Take them into the next room." He didn't want these men to see what sort of pig's ear he made of this.

Not much of one, because the rifle went together quickly and smoothly. Harold brought the weapon up to his shoulder and instantly fell in love with that pistol grip. He laid the rifle on the case. "Come on back in." Harold gestured towards the weapon. "Two semi-automatic nines. No ammo, no clips." After some haggling he agreed to let them have an empty clip in each. "One of you comes out with me, the other stays with Alfie. I go in the gate and get the weapons, and we trade." Harold grinned. "I've got your guns anyway."

The bloke in the corner turned on his friend. "Stupid fucker."

"We have rules about foul language. Serious ones. Keep it clean or we'll fine you." The men glanced at Alfie, and then at Harold who nodded.

"Now keep your traps shut, we finish the deal and you leave. Then you don't come back because we shoot armed intruders." Harold tapped the rifle. "You'll never see me because there's only four of you." Harold picked two decidedly well-used weapons out of the spares in his gun room, and completed the trade. He strolled back after packing the rifle away again, nursing the wrapped case and trying to explain the difference to Alfie. Alfie still looked dubious as they came through the gate.

Holly tried to see what he'd got under the wrapping. "What was that all about?" Harold put the case down, then picked her up in a bear hug and delivered a definite three. "Wow. If I see that look again I'm gonna lick my lips." Holly smirked. "That's the first time without a walk home or a kiss being offered. Now I really do need to know."

Harold explained to her, then to the rest of the group in 'his' house and none of them got it. That shook him. They'd all had an unshakeable faith that Soldier Boy would outshoot any scroat armed with anything. Harold stopped trying since, and he smiled happily at that, he probably could now. Better still, The Coven had done all the hard work and hammered out a system to make Orchard Close work.

Harold felt even happier after the meeting, because Holly insisted they walked back via the forge because it would still be warm. Harold realised that not only wasn't Holly put off by how enthusiastic the level five became, she seemed very happy afterwards. Maybe Liz had a good point? Later he discovered that those meagre four rounds were 308 and Harold's happiness was complete, because he had a small plastic tub full of empty 308 brass picked up by scavengers.

Alfie, Emmy and Holly all put in a bid for the old 303 since Harold had a new toy. Harold held out until he was sure that his new toy really did what its appearance promised, even with his reloads. Alfie and Emmy agreed to share the 303. The big heavy beast had become easier to shoot accurately now Harold had upgraded with peep sights from a ruined rifle, one taken for spares. Holly settled for learning to shoot Harold's two-two "because I'll be right next to that new posh one, and I prefer pistol practice anyway."

Just how near Holly stayed became clear as various residents in Orchard Close started to refer to Harold as luv, with big smirks. Holly didn't smirk when Harold said it, and Harold found himself calling her luv more often. Just for the smile, he told himself. More sniggers and looks meant the girl club had some mischief planned for Easter, in a week's time. Harold would have worried, but Liz had been right and any level up to five seemed be fine with Holly. He just had to remember to keep at five.

*   *   *

When Harold arrived at the gate, the first words he heard worried him. "We heard you'll sell guns."

"That depends on what you've got to trade." Harold didn't sell guns and didn't want a reputation for doing so, but perhaps these men had something Orchard Close really needed?

"We'll have to do it where there's no witnesses." The car had four men in, again, and had pulled up tight against one of the ruined houses. "We can go in here?" The man pointed at the house.

"Two men and the goods." Harold knew the two watchers in the guard-houses, one with binoculars, would make damn sure no extra men went in. He didn't expect the hiss from the side window of the guardhouse.

Harold looked up and a very angry looking June looked back. "They took a woman in there. Bent right over so you couldn't see from here."

"An armed one?" That wasn't typical though a woman fighter wasn't un-known.

"We couldn't tell."

"Thanks." Harold smiled and turned. "Holly, you know I never ever took you on a proper date? This might be the best I can do."

Apparently a walk down the road to trade with a bunch of yobs counted as a date, and ticked off another rite of passage. Holly's dating jewellery tended towards sharp steel, but that seemed to be the current style.

As before Alfie stood in one corner with the shotgun, and a gangster stood in the opposite one with a pistol, a nine mill this time. This time four people stood in the middle of the room, two men and two women. Or rather one young woman and one definite girl, about eleven or twelve Harold thought. He kept his temper in check until he found out why they'd brought her because she wasn't obviously armed. The man opposite Harold gestured towards Holly. "We were told you didn't trade women, but since you brought one?"

Holly put her hand on her machete and the man's eyes widened. "If you actually make an offer she'll cut off your nuts. We don't trade women, and certainly don't buy them with guns." Harold didn't want a stream of men bringing women to sell.

"She's all we've got to trade. We tried swapping for someone older but we'll take weapons?" The salesman glanced nervously at Holly. "She's not been touched."

"Will you take her across to the wall luv, and see she's not armed, or harmed?" Holly flashed a brilliant smile for the luv but soon lost it when she looked at the apprehensive girl's face.

"Come with me and it'll be just fine, I promise." Holly held out her hand and the girl took it after a nervous glance at the salesman. "Over there to the wall, away from that pair." Holly took her over and they spoke quietly before Holly turned to Harold. "She's not been hurt Harold, just bruises and from the looks of her what she needs is food."

"We feed her." The man scowled. "What will you trade for her? She'll grow up in a year or two and be worth more, but we need more weapons or ammo right now." He glanced at Holly's set face and then Harold's. "This was a waste of time."

"No, we'll buy her." Harold glanced at Alfie. "Rifle trading style." The man looked baffled but Alfie straightened a little. Harold took a long step back and Alfie's shotgun came up. "Don't be stupid or you both die. Holly, cover the man in the corner." Holly's hand went under the back of her jacket and came out with a pistol.

"Robbery. We were told you lot are straight." The man sounded disgusted but resigned, and just robbing him did tempt Harold briefly.

"We are straight dealers so I'll buy the girl for food and beer. This is to make sure you understand that we are definitely buying her because we are straight, that we really dislike people who trade women, and we don't sell guns." Harold took out his own nine mill. "Weapons on the floor please. Your friend in the corner might beat the shotgun, or Holly, or me, but not all of us."

"Put it down, Skiff. We'll pass the word how they deal here."

"Please do. We do not trade in women, as you were told, but we don't rob people. Don't stop to tell the neighbours to the south or they really will shoot and rob you." Harold relaxed a bit as both men placed their weapons on the floor. "You get them back once we've come to an arrangement over beer and food. You'll need food because taking any from houses within at least five miles of here warrants a death sentence."

Harold gave the men enough to prove he hadn't robbed them, but certainly not enough to encourage a repeat. More to the point, he didn't pay enough to encourage any nasty little sod to kidnap women for profit. The men stood out in the open at the end of the trade with their guns in one pocket and the clip in the other, and Holly took Jilli, the girl, into Orchard Close. Holly sent out the food and beer, Harold and Alfie went inside the gates, and the men loaded up and left.

"Where is she?" Harold wanted to know how the hell a young girl like that ended up in that car.

"Jilli has been scooped up. The girl club will find a suitable mum for her and one day she'll appear again. Why didn't we kill them?" A hot spark of anger still showed in Holly's eyes, the same hot spark that had probably encouraged the man with the pistol to surrender.

"Because we don't want to frighten people away by getting a reputation like the Barbie Girls. The Geeks and Hot Rods kill on sight and the GOFS are a long way from angelic, so we must be the calm, civilised place where decent folk can find a refuge." Harold scowled. "If they'd touched her I'd have happily killed the lot."

"I can live with that." Holly hooked an arm into Harold's. "I've never really dated but I'm sure that was unusual at least. Where are we going on our next date?"

"Someplace without guns?"

"I'll settle for traditional. You can take me to meet your family, and we can cuddle on the settee and watch TV." Holly smiled and hugged his arm a bit tighter. "That's another rite of passage, honest."

*　　　*　　　*

Harold stared at the TV. "That settles one thing. We'll be digging and planting every square metre of land we can clear. At least there's more land available as we clear ruins."

Sharyn shook her head in mock despair. "Is that the next excuse you and Casper will use to get everyone carting bricks to build up the wall? That's a bit of a stretch, even for you."

"No stretch. Where do you think that lot will go next? They only have to get one of those big ships across the channel and bang goes another chunk of farmland." Harold scowled. "I might be paranoid but I can't see the Royal Navy ships keeping going for much longer. They need fuel as well. After all, where are the French warships?" Harold pointed at the TV.

Onscreen medieval walls shattered as the naval shells smashed into them. The view switched and a cruise ship staggered as if under an immense hammer-blow and then burst into flames. Behind it a shipyard disintegrated in fire and smoke.

"The ungrateful refugees, not satisfied with destroying the camps provided for them, are marching north through France. The ancient fortifications at Guerande have been overrun, the inhabitants slaughtered, and the shipyards of St-Nazaire captured. The Royal Navy has exacted retribution and destroyed any possibility of the refugees crossing the channel. Once again the British Government has acted swiftly and decisively to protect our citizens."

"Citizens, but not voters. I really fancied voting but we're already overdue." Holly lifted Harold's hand up and round her. "Sorry Sharyn but this is hugging stuff."

"I knew it was a mistake when I let you sit next to him. Don't worry, I'm too interested in the TV to notice. Especially after that little gem about Navy ships running out of fuel." Sharyn picked up her mug and glanced over. "In fact, now Hazel's gone upstairs and there's room on the settee I might want his other arm, especially if we get another food warning."

"British farmers have worked valiantly over the winter, but the late spring has defeated all their efforts. The amount of smoke thrown up by the rioting and burning here and in the rest of the world, aggravated by several small nuclear exchanges, has affected the amount of sunlight reaching our fields and crops. All citizens are advised to take any measures they can to conserve food. Vitamin pills are available at your local mart to alleviate any shortages caused by lack of fresh fruit and vegetables."

Sharyn sat next to Harold. "C'mon, give me that other arm because this is cobblers. Curtis reckons all the veg is coming up on time, near enough." Her face and voice were bleak. "Are the bastards going to starve us?"

"No, because there aren't enough soldiers on the bypass if all the gangs were desperate at the same time and tried to break out. I saw what that needs around London, though even there the people trying to escape didn't combine properly." Harold hugged both women hard because he needed it. "Though we've definitely got to grow more of what we need. All of what we need."

"Can we do that Harold?" Holly leaned over and then stopped, glancing at Sharyn.

"No snogging, I have standards." Sharyn pointed towards the curtains in the direction of the girl club. "Take him over there for all that nonsense."

"Fat chance. Can you imagine that lot if I dragged Harold inside to watch telly?" Holly stopped smiling and cuddled in closer. "That's a mart! Is it ours? What idiot is attacking a mart?"

"Despite the desperate circumstances, an armed mob has attacked their local mart. The mart that supplies food to the women and children in the surrounding area."

Onscreen the guards and an armoured car were shooting down swathes of shoppers, many of whom were breaking and running, desperate to escape.

Harold caught a glimpse of the background ruins and a wide motorway. "Not our mart. That one is near a major route, not a bypass."

As the crowds broke apart figures could be seen hurling missiles that exploded, either cutting down guards or bathing the armoured car in flames.

"The cowardly attackers used the innocent shoppers as cover and are throwing improvised explosives. This unprovoked attack has surprised both the mart guards and the Army personnel, who are fighting bravely to the last."

The camera pulled back to show an Army post on the nearby motorway being overrun by a crowd shooting pistols and wielding machetes.

"It's the same old crap. Where are the helicopters and tanks and the fire, the napalm? Where are those exploding cannon things or even machine guns?" Holly's other hand curled in a tight, white-knuckled fist.

"Waiting at the other side of that wide road if the attackers try to cross." Harold sighed. "That's the M25 round London because I've just seen the line of rubble along the other side. It'll be a lot better organised since I served there, but the bulldozers had already done some of that when I left the Army."

"With deep regret the Army has taken steps to prevent the attackers stealing weapons and looting the mart. These heartless savages cannot be allowed to profit from their cowardly acts. Despite the food shortages this will mean for the local population, the Royal Air Force has been sent in to prevent the looting."

Explosions marched across the captured Army post and then over the mart itself, smashing the sandbagged enclosure and then tearing the mart itself apart. The relatively innocuous puffs of smoke in the air above cut down scores of people either crouching in terror or running about in sheer panic. A few aimed weapons upwards. A helicopter, then another, swept over the scene and flame blossomed in the wreckage of the mart.

"That's written by the same, er, person that wrote the, the rubbish on-screen when the mayor died. Nobody is looting. They're dead, dying, badly wounded or running for their lives." Harold hugged hard with both arms.

"What about the locals, those who shop at that mart on the other days?" Sharyn glanced up to where the children were hopefully fast asleep. "How will they get food while the mart is rebuilt?"

"I hope none of our local lunatics are thinking of doing that, looting a mart." Holly's voice had become a whisper now. "They won't, will they Harold?"

"Not after seeing that. After all, the mob didn't get anything." Harold really, really hoped someone like Cadillac hadn't had the same idea. "There'll be more marts along the motorway, it'll just take the locals longer to get there. With luck there'll be enough food at those marts for the extra people."

None of them thought there would be, not after the warnings about shortages. The three sat watching as helicopters hunted anyone openly carrying firearms, using gunfire and then fire to kill them and destroy the weapons. Periodically the commentary hammered home how much food had been lost, and how terrible that was because of the winter.

"The foreign terrorists have brought their terror weapons with them and attacked the forces of law and order with no regard for the nearby innocents."

A view from far overhead showed smoke trails rising from buildings deep in a city and curving to fall in the general area of an Army post. Very general, the explosions that followed spread across both sides of the cordon and some rockets landed in an enclave. Jets screamed across the launch site and turned it into a sea of flame. Shortly afterwards helicopters arrived and hunted through the buildings in a wide circle, periodically firing or burning smaller areas.

"The RAF is even now hunting down any similar launch sites. The marts serving this area will not be selling any sugar until we can be sure the local terrorists will not be using it for rockets. With true regret the marts will be restricting the amount of sugar being sold elsewhere to protect the innocent citizens from danger."

Holly looked at her mug. "Oh well, I can always pretend I'm on a diet?" She grimaced. "That's one way of cutting down on coffee because most people prefer sugar in that."

"Luckily there's no way of turning tea and coffee into explosives, I don't think, or they'd stop them. After all, they must be imported somehow." Harold looked at his own mug. "I can manage without sugar, but mornings without coffee could be a real stretch. At least there'll be some sugar now and then."

Sharyn frowned. "Does brewing use sugar? If so Seth will have all the sugar in Orchard Close locked up by daybreak and Berry standing guard."

"Beer, or sugar in my coffee, that is a truly nasty choice to be forced to make." When Harold walked Holly home the kissing levels were subdued but the hugging was intense.

*　　　*　　　*

In the bunker the mood was sombre. Today Grace wore a dark grey suit, and for once an uncertain expression. "I'm still not certain. What if the other population centres react badly?" This time none of the well-dressed people sat around the polished table were watching the mart burn on the wallscreen.

"None of the others will be short of food. Well, a little bit short to keep them in line but there will be enough." Ivy, the redhead, smiled. "They'll behave once the consequences are pointed out."

"How long will that take?" Grace paused. "We don't want any incidents in the interim."

Joshua, the balding man in Army uniform, leant forward. "I'm really interested in Ivy's answer as well since we still haven't the fuel to move men and tanks all over the country. We'd be relying on air strikes and I doubt there's much fuel for them either."

"Enough, because we managed to take a lot of aviation fuel from the airports before the mobs got around to them." Faraz the RAF representative smirked. "Enough of them were outside population centres to be defensible."

"The Navy still have plenty because in addition to our reserves we have commandeered every cargo and passenger ship we can reach and drained most of them. Though the French reserves in Brest will still be handy if we can persuade the local authorities to hand them over. We now believe that most of the French captains and crew are willing to come over the channel, but we'd like all their supplies as well." The naval officer shrugged. "Otherwise Brest and Cherbourg will be another Mers-el-Kebir and a terrible waste of trained men and materials. Enough ships will come over so the Royal Navy can deal with the rest, but sinking allies will still leave a bad taste in the mouth."

"Can't Cherbourg and Brest hold out? Those ships can supply artillery support." The youngest member looked in a file. "There are some big guns on these ships."

"Sorry Gerard, but most Naval shells are for punching through steel. They won't be as effective against a screaming horde in open country who simply don't care about losses, and we simply can't afford to let that lot get any major warships." The naval officer, Victor, shrugged. "Don't rely on the base defences because Toulon didn't slow the mob up much, nor did Taranto or Venice though at least most ships scuttled in time. Now can we please concentrate on the UK?" He looked expectantly at Ivy, as did the rest.

Though first, the chairman, Owen, had a point to make. "I'd like to point out that holding those refugees in the barren areas to starve failed not only in France, but also in Italy and even Greece where the strength of the Army and the terrain should have stopped them. That happened because the armed forces facing them were indecisive, and because refugees and locals combined to swamp the soldiers. We must ensure that lesson is learned here, in the UK. No more miscalculations." Owen nodded at the woman dealing with marts. "Ivy?"

"I have consulted with the retailers. Tomorrow they will close all the marts around London and Joshua will send armour across the M25 to protect the facilities. They believe six days should be enough to empty all the marts though we've allowed nine. Anyone nearby will be told the lorries are bringing in extra supplies. Then we will tell everyone elsewhere in the country that London will not receive any more food supplies until their armed rebels are brought under control."

"The Londoners will go crazy." Gerard looked over at Joshua. "I hope your men and tanks are well dug in."

"They will be, and also around the Tower and one or two other places but there'll be no mass attack. We won't tell the Londoners. They'll find out the hard way and the news will spread slowly over the next fortnight. By then they'll be shooting each other for food." Joshua smiled. "They can use up their ammunition on each other."

Owen looked around the table. "The food we save by not feeding London will mean there is plenty for the rest, and London will be a good test before extending the method to other population centres. The reduction in sugar elsewhere will mean that land used for sugar beet can now grow food, and as a bonus our people calculate there'll be a drop in demand for coffee."

"Will that be enough? We're spinning out what there is but there were supposed to be more supplies arriving." Ivy frowned. "That attack on the mart was sparked by cutting off tea and coffee. I didn't believe the analysts when they said that would happen, but now I worry about shortages elsewhere."

"Not only because of the tea and coffee but they helped." Owen smiled. "If necessary the Royal Navy will escort a couple of ships to Brazil to bring nothing but coffee. We already have stockpiles of tea and you are mixing in other leaf to spin it out." He opened his file. "Now let's concentrate on providing enough food for the citizens outside the barricades, the ones we actually need." Heads bent over their files as the screen continued to show death and destruction, completely unheeded.

*   *   *

Because of all the work clearing rubble for gardens, Holly's handgun practice had to be postponed until evenings. "I hope that's not how you congratulate the others when they hit the target." Holly glanced upwards. "If it wasn't for the rain I might have been tempted to try a level six." Her finger went on Harold's lips. "Our own rules in our own time, I said I was tempted not that Liz told me."

Harold sighed, perhaps he had been a bit paranoid about all that. "Since it's raining, perhaps we ought to go home? I just wanted you to realise how badly the flash would mess up your night sight."

"Cripes yes! I was blind for a moment and now I've got funny spots in my eyes. How on earth do the Army fight at night?"

"Flash suppression, special propellants, glasses, and night sights." Harold chuckled. "If someone is attacking, there's either plenty of light from gun flashes or someone puts up a flare. Though I've never been in a real night attack." Harold cursed mentally, but Holly didn't seem to have noticed.

"So that's why you want us out here to practice in the dark? Not as an excuse to get me away from your sister and the girl club?"

"It's a plan, though it was you insisted on coming out here to practice tonight, in spite of the rain. Now come on or your coat will never dry out by tomorrow."

Holly laughed. "You're right, I just wanted to get you out here in the dark." She hugged. "Well not really just that, and anyway it's raining so there's no point." Holly picked up her empty brass and then arranged the string of little lights hung around her neck. "Fairy time."

"Casper loves this part." Harold wore lights as well. After a flesh wound when a scavenging party coming home at dusk met a nervous guard, everyone wore lights when outside Orchard Close. Anyone returning after dusk lit up their little string of battery powered glows before coming clear of the ruins. Harold knew they'd still be challenged, in fact they'd better be or he'd be giving lectures again.

"Come on in, fairies." Matthew greeted them with a big smile. "I think you're the last tonight." Harold paused and helped Matthew to put the iron bars across the door to stop the ungodly opening it from the outside. Matthew's shoulder had healed but still hadn't fully recovered.

As Holly came out through the front door of number six, the main guard house, she paused. "Someone's showing a light in the dance house."

"Why, the Easter Dance is still four days away?"

"Maybe they were getting the place ready?" Holly set off that way. "We'd best turn it off in case some oik takes a potshot." That had happened four times since Christmas so Harold followed.

Though as he opened the door warm air struck his skin. "It's warm in here, warmer than it should be?" Harold frowned and then his face cleared. "Is someone using the place?" Couples were occasionally finding somewhere to be private, because nobody lived alone.

Holly headed up the stairs. "If so I'll tell them about the light. They won't want a bullet through the window." Harold waited until Holly came back down, shaking her head. "Just a table lamp and the curtains not quite closed. Maybe someone had plans or perhaps they've already gone home." She looked around the dance room and smiled. "Since its warm you can have the last dance with me and walk me home."

"I'm walking you home anyway, idiot."

Holly pouted. "I prefer luv."

"I'm walking you home anyway, idiot luv."

"Yes, but walking home after a last dance is different. Maybe level six different if you dance properly. At least another practice five." Holly walked over to the CD player and looked through the selection and then in the player. "This one is definitely mood music for last dances. Some of the old stuff we've been finding is really smoochy."

Harold hung up his coat where it could drip a bit because Holly had already taken hers off. "I just want to take your time." Holly sang softly. "I'll bet an old bloke like you can remember this."

"Cheeky, I'm only three or four years older than you, depending on the time of year."

"So you are. In that case." A good while later Holly sighed. "We're supposed to undo buttons on a five, but if we do that without coats it'll be a six."

"A fifty six if you kiss me like that with any more buttons undone."

"OK, we'll stick to five and a half, but a lot of them." Four dances later Holly put her hand behind her and moved Harold's hand down a bit further. "Your hand keeps straying that way and is making me curious, so it's time for level six." Two dances later Holly pulled her head back and actually looked embarrassed. "I've got a confession, Harold, and this song has reminded me I have to do that first."

The current song was 'Love you a little bit more' by Dr. Hook which sounded intriguing at least. "What is it? You've forgotten what number we're up to?" Harold had, he thought he'd gone to level seven a couple of times.

"Mmm, about the numbers." Holly sighed. "They only go up to four. After that Liz said I was on my own."

"That was my fault."

"No, because the numbers were my idea to sort of slow me up, not you. I was frightened of getting carried away too soon." Holly giggled. "Four surprised me, because that really turned out different with wet lips, really different. I worried about level five."

"You can stop whenever you like." Harold knew there had to be a punch line of some sort coming. Hopefully an eight when he walked Holly home after dancing like this. Though dancing in private and all the five plusses meant he already didn't want to walk Holly home, or not to the girl club anyway.

"I didn't worry about you, well maybe in a way. I worried about knicker inspections. The five made me curious instead of frightened." Harold opened his mouth and Holly stopped him speaking in the nicest way. By the time she'd freed his mouth again Harold thought that might have been an eight, which made him wonder about level nine. "I put the heaters on in here before we left, to find something out." Holly giggled, then sobered. "Harold?"

Harold looked into a pair of very serious grey-blue eyes. "Yes Holly?"

Her eyes twinkled in humour and Holly giggled. "The answer is yes. The bed upstairs is warm, Harold. I really am curious about knicker inspections, and Mummy Casper isn't waiting."

"You told him?"

"No, Casper hasn't waited since level four. Nobody knows, which is what I want, just in case this doesn't work out." Holly kissed him, and Harold gave up on levels since he wasn't trying to hold back any more anyway.

Though his conscience insisted on one last try. "Are you sure, Holly?"

"I put the blanket on upstairs just in case, and after whatever level that is I really am sure." She paused and her smile died a little. "That is, if you're sure?"

Harold admitted what had finally become obvious even to him. "I've been hooked since four, possibly two?"

*   *   *

"Mmm, you are warm. Everyone wondered." Holly sighed. "Though I've found out one bit the films skip over. I'm bursting for the loo and it'll be freezing in there."

"I'll turn the heater on if you can wait?"

"Is that a real gentleman thing? Go on then, I won't even peek." Harold got out and put on his shirt because chilly didn't quite cover this morning. "Maybe." But Holly's voice still sounded muffled since she'd pulled the covers over her head.

Harold hurried back because his shirt wasn't warm enough. "Coming in, ready or not." Harold waited a few moment and opened the door, and Holly had hidden her head under the covers. "I'll turn on the blower in here as well." Harold got into bed and Holly squealed.

"You're freezing."

"You will be in a minute. Use my shirt, it's still warm."

"No peeking?"

"I promise." Harold wouldn't look because that wasn't a tease. Holly had insisted on lights out last night so he didn't see her in underwear. Harold hadn't realised just how shy she was, not after Holly had worn that tutu for dancing. A shy girl was a first, and so was a blonde. Holly giggled when Harold confessed she was his first blonde girlfriend, because he was her first anything. After that Harold had worried about Holly waking up tearful, but apparently his first blonde no regrets.

"Coming in, ready or not." Harold turned his head away and shut his eyes, and heard the door open. Moments later she slipped into bed. "Brr. Cold. Ooh, you've warmed up. Come on, share. My birthday present."

"Today?"

"Yes. That's why the girl club were all smirking and sneaking around. They'd got something planned for the dance, something for us." Holly sniggered. "Liz threatened to tie me to the bed in a nightie and set fire to the house so you had to carry me down a ladder, but I don't know the real plan. Speaking of fire and warmth, what about my present?" They shared until either Harold had cooled a bit or Holly had warmed up, since they were about the same.

"The bathroom will be warm enough for a shower now. We'd better get up soon or you'll be late for breakfast and the girl club will know." Harold smiled. "My sister will be waiting with her eyes agleam."

"Maybe I don't mind the girl club knowing? Do you mind Sharyn knowing?"

Harold laughed. "No, I don't mind who knows because after all, you're my girlfriend. Providing you can stand the teasing?"

"I was all tense and it was all sort of new and a bit sort of confused last night. I'm not sure if that was worth a lot of teasing." Holly paused. "I'm not tense now and a warm up wasn't much of a present? I should get a birthday kiss at least."

"We could try a level four birthday kiss? See how it goes?" Four without clothes turned into about eighty-four.

*   *   *

"Hi Sis. Am I too late for breakfast?"

"Nearly too late for lunch. Did it take that long to dry the poor girl's tears?" Sharyn had her hands on her hips and Harold could see exactly where Daisy got it from.

"No, because I'm not crying. Good morning Sharyn." Holly only blushed a little bit. "I was told there might be late breakfast here."

Harold savoured the moment as Sharyn went from berating him for abusing Holly to dealing with a smiling Holly here for breakfast. Eventually Sharyn got her head realigned. "I hope you're not going to start kissing and all that. There's children present and I've just eaten."

"I don't mind if Holly kisses Harold. I think it's sweet, and romantic. Hi Holly."

"Hi Hazel. Hi Daisy."

"Holly! Can you draw a ship, a pirate ship?" Harold left Holly to the tender mercies of Daisy and the drawing book, and followed Sharyn into the kitchen.

"Is Holly moving in?"

"Er, we haven't talked about that." She'd done it again. Sharyn had completed flummoxed him. Harold's head went around in circles. "What about undies in the bathroom and all the rest? Snogging after you've eaten and sitting on the settee?" That all sounded like a bloody good idea even as he said it.

"As long as you remember the kids live here, I'm OK with all that. There won't be underwear in the bathroom anyway since I suppose she'll use your en-suite shower room?" Sharyn laughed. "Cripes, you've blushed. You march in here the morning after, bold as brass with Holly in tow, and then blush about her underwear in the bathroom."

"She's shy." Harold kept his voice down. "I hadn't connected the dots, all right?" Harold paused. "You really don't mind?"

Sharyn hugged him. "No little brother. It's about time she reeled you in and the alternative is you moving out. You could move out if you wanted?"

Harold considered that but only until he registered Sharyn's voice on the last bit. "You'd rather we stayed? If Holly agrees to a 'we'?"

"Liz likes an alien killing machine parked at the end of the road. I like my little brother parked in the spare room, because life is unpredictable these days and Freddy isn't going to be here if I need him." This sister hug was for sister, not brother. "The toast is ready. You can cart it all through since she's your guest."

"Uncle Harold, Uncle Harold. Holly draws a fantabulous piggy, but piggy's ship has crashed and is sinking. He needs rescue." Daisy held out the pencil. Daisy's ships tended to crash or catch fire.

"Are you going to draw a helicopter or a lifeboat?" Holly looked at the selection on the table and curled her lip. "Margarine? I didn't think anyone actually ate it."

"We buy it for cooking and put jam or honey on toast but I didn't know if you used the stuff." Harold swept a hand across the jars. "Blackberry, marmalade or plum jam. We'll have to make a ton of jam next year because all the scavenged stuff will be gone. The honey is nearly solid."

"That's OK, I don't mind solid. Someone found strawberry jam last week but it only lasted a day over there. I suppose strawberry jam and honey are extinct now, and unless we find enough jars all jam might be." Holly took a plate and toast. "I'll get started and you send a helicopter for piggy."

"No helicopter, or lifeboat. Daisy explained that in cat and dog pirate land where the ships have sails there are no engines. That only an idiot would expect a helicopter to come and rescue a pirate cat." Hazel grinned. "The idiot found a solution."

Holly looked around and everyone else looked at Harold and smiled expectantly, so he shrugged and confessed. "The Red Cross Elephant."

"Hurray, the Red Cross Elephant is here." Daisy tugged at Harold's arm so he carried on drawing.

Hazel sniggered. "A cartoon elephant with huge ears so he can fly and rescue cats and dogs and piggies. The Red Crosses are on his ears." Harold let the laughter wash over him. Daisy liked the elephant idea and Holly was laughing and having breakfast with him and he felt incredibly mellow.

Holly finally went home mid-afternoon, after seven different people had called by for one reason or another. She greeted each one, blushed to varying degrees, and sniggered after they'd gone because Daisy stopped most of the intended comments. Though Holly blushed again as she left, because of Daisy's parting shot. "If you come for late breakfast tomorrow I'll be at school." Harold followed Holly out before the enquiring looks from Hazel and Sharyn turned into words, and they both went scavenging for a while.

The five days to Easter were a bit of a blur. Numbers were abandoned for just kissing, and Harold wandered through a daze of teasing and congratulations. He took Holly home for breakfast twice and waited for the right moment because Harold really did like the idea of her underwear in his shower room, as it were. The rest of Orchard Close were happy, sympathetic or having a wonderful time mercilessly teasing both of them.

*   *   *

Easter Day turned into a long party for the younger kids. They made chains with blossom and willow catkins and thread, hunted pebbles painted as eggs, and had a party with jelly and raspberry ripple ice cream that Hilda had saved for a special occasion. "What's that, Uncle-Harold?"

"A Maypole, or our version. You hold the ribbon and dance around, but go in and out. In the end the ribbons are all plaited together." Harold held out a ribbon, a ribbon knotted to a rope four feet up which led to a large knot in the middle of a thicker rope, strung from one chimney-stack to the one above the street.

"Where's the pole and why aren't the ribbons longer and how can dancing twizzle them together?"

"Imagine a pole, and we haven't got any longer ribbons." Harold looked round. "Casper? Dancing teacher needed."

Casper had a simple solution. The big idiot insisted that Alfie, Veronica and Hazel joined him to dance with the littler kids, and even Jilli and the three latest young refugees joined him eventually. Luckily a CD supplied the music rather than someone playing an instrument because most of the adults were breathless and almost hysterical with laughter by then, those not dragged in to join the dancing.

The Easter dance that evening went on too long, because Harold only danced with Holly and Holly wasn't embarrassed by public kissing any more. Various girl club members told Harold that he'd ruined Holly's birthday surprise, but birthday girl seemed happy enough. The girl club provided a cake, and presents, and Holly blushed when she opened some and wouldn't unwrap them. She wore a pair of clip-on earrings, green ones that Harold bought. Truly bought because all jewellery found by scavengers went into the Orchard Close emergency fund, so Harold had to pay with coupons.

None of the women even came for a dance with Harold, though they had plenty of other entertainment. The new refugees had never been to an Orchard Close dance and the three women and five men old enough and up for dancing were fresh blood. Harold paused at the raised voices while collecting his and Holly's coats, but those quickly quietened so he ignored them. Instead he helped Holly into her coat. "Mmm, walking a really kissable girl home, I wonder what level we'll get to this time?"

"Home?" Holly glanced upstairs, because that's where advanced kissing had already ended up two more times.

"Maybe the level depends on which home I walk you to." Harold whispered quietly in her ear. "Daisy is in bed, Sharyn claims she's as deaf as a post, and Hazel is staying with Betty tonight."

"But in the morning?"

"We might not be late for breakfast if you're already home?"

"Home?" That was barely a breath and Holly smiled happily before pulling Harold towards the street. "Will you walk me home please?"

Sharyn never even batted an eyelid in the morning. Holly relaxed and stopped blushing, and by evening had moved in properly. Harold did blush when he brought her bags across, as did Holly. The girl club lined the path with garden canes and baseball bats held out to make a tunnel of sorts. They threw handfuls of tiny bits of chopped up plastic because confetti had become extinct as well, then swept them up for next time. Hazel found the whole idea romantic, and Daisy loved having an Aunty-Holly storyteller and piggy-drawing assistant.

* * *

The TV seemed hell-bent on destroying any temporary happiness. "Christ, crap, they'll starve in there."

"Sit down Harold." Holly pulled on his arm and Harold sat on the settee and for once Holly wrapped her arms around him instead. "You fixed them up in that library, and said the playing fields behind meant plenty of land for crops. If they've survived this long, your friends will be as safe as anyone in London."

"More to the point, brutal as it sounds, you've got people here who need keeping alive. Concentrate on making sure that if that happens here, if they stop feeding us, we'll still eat." Sharyn returned Harold's stare. "How far do you trust the bastards if there's a bad harvest?"

Harold stayed awake talking quietly to Holly until the early hours, but then he slept without dreams. Holly had that effect, and Harold hadn't slept this peacefully since the first time he pulled a trigger in anger. In the morning the news about London meant that nobody objected to more digging and clearing more land, then or in the following days. Curtis took full advantage, expanding his gardening plans.

"Harold, Harold!" Harold fought himself up from sleep, a really deep sleep because he slept like that now. Or he had done for six straight nights.

"Hazel?"

"Liz is downstairs. Don't use the radios but be really quick." No radios, so gang or Army. Harold and Holly untangled and regardless of stereotypes she dressed as fast as Harold.

Liz started talking before Harold got to the bottom of the stairs. "Kill them Harold, they took Matti."

"Who took Matti, where?" Harold threw on his leather coat and unlocked the study to collect his rifle and a pocket full of ammo. Holly followed him and collected hers and a box of two-two ammo. A rattle of gunfire sounded towards the city. "What the hell is that?"

"That means Emmy and the rest were quick enough, I hope. They must've caught up but there's only eight gone in case it's a trick. Casper is walking the boundary. We're checking and so far we're missing Liam, Jon, and Willtoo and there was another and then there's Matti." Liz sighed. "Doll swears Matti can't have gone willing, and they killed Sandy and took guns."

"How did they get out with Matti?"

"We'll find out. Just get her back and we'll let you know if there's anyone else missing." Liz pushed at him but Harold had already started moving, quickly.

His radio crackled. "E3 medic." That sounded like Emmy.

More firing sounded out in the ruins so Harold called "Medic E3, quickly" over his shoulder and kept moving, running now. The distinctive boom of the 303 echoed in the night so Alfie or Emmy had taken it. Tim and Curtis were waiting at the wall, and Harold told them to escort Lenny the medic to whoever had been wounded. Conn and Lillian were joined by Finn, then Philip, one of the new refugees, and Harold clicked the radio. "Numbers please."

"F4 and there's five we think." A storm of gunfire broke out, and the 303 again. "Four."

"Coming." Harold looked round. "We are going fast and cutting the corner because they are curving towards the Hot Rods."

Lilian stopped. "I'm too slow. Take Tim and I'll guard Lenny and get the wounded."

"Done. Come on." Harold didn't wait to make big plans, just headed for where the escapees would hit the border if they kept going.

Twice a rattle of gunfire broke out and after the second the radio crackled again. "G5. Three left." Even as Harold closed in a prolonged burst of gunfire lit up the houses not far ahead. The radio spoke clearly, and Harold could hear the bitterness in Emmy's tones. "Two got away. The Hot Rods are shooting this way and we had to take cover."

"Anyone hit?"

"Cuts and bruises. How soon?"

"A couple of minutes." Harold headed for where the flashes had come from and he soon spotted a set of fairy glows. Someone had hung them from a wall so anyone coming from Orchard Close would see them. "I see fairies."

"Come ahead." As he came nearer Harold saw a waving arm. Emmy waited with Doll, an absolutely livid Doll.

"Shoot them. The Hot Rods. Kill them Harold. They let the bastard get away."

Harold ignored that for now to talk to Emmy. "Where's Matti?"

"Back there, safe but shaken up. Have they found Sal and Bernie yet?" Harold shook his head and Emmy sighed. "The bastards put a knife to Sal, and Bernie gave up how to make pipe bombs. One of those who escaped is Jon and the other one is a mystery. He must have met this lot outside the boundary wall." Emmy brandished the 303. "I reckon he's a Hot Rod and I want to kill them as well for shooting this way. We had to duck or I'd have nailed Jon at least. We've got two of ours with bullet wounds but those were from before we got here."

"You said cuts and bruises."

"I left Seth to guard Matti, and the two wounded went back there. That leaves me with only five people and possibly outnumbered so I kept my big mouth shut." Emmy sighed. "Sorry, that came out a bit sharp. This is planned I reckon because Lemmy ran towards the Hot Rods as we were coming up. He shouted 'it's me, Lemmy' but they opened up and killed him anyway. While we were ducking Jon got away, and our mystery man."

"Good enough. Now let's see what the Hot Rods say. Organise these four to cover wherever you want them." Harold raised his voice and shouted towards the border. "Who's in charge over there?"

"Cooper. Is that you Soldier Boy? We just shot a runner from your lot."

"Good. Now hand over the other two."

"Other two? One of our blokes had nipped over the border to see what the fuss was about and came running back. We didn't see anyone else. Who was it?"

"His name is Jon and either you hand him back or he gets a lead headache one day soon. Unless you are altering the rules and if so I can find all of you long before you get home." Harold used the little glasses from the Geek gunman and could see moving figures.

"Maybe not. You missed a few tonight."

The 303 had fired five times and Cooper thought that was Harold's gun. "Not me, I've passed that one to an apprentice. I've got a new one."

Harold listened to some muttering, too faint to understand, then Cooper shouted again. "Bullshit. It's a poser job and got no ammo."

"It's got really good sights and a hell of a range. Pick one of your blokes, just point to him. Be sure to tell Cadillac you gave me permission to shoot him so you could hear the difference. Left eye or right?" Behind him someone murmured 'macho bullshit' and sniggered.

"No, but I will tell Cadillac what you said. I'm sure he'll send any runners back." Someone over there muttered. "What about the one we shot? Do we get the body?"

"Yes, once we've stripped it." Harold turned back and the murmuring from behind him had been from Alfie. "Alfie, will you organise two people and strip that body naked. It's got something Cooper wants." He raised his voice again. "If anyone accidentally points a weapon this way while he's being stripped, I'll accidentally kill them."

"Yeah, yeah. Tell you what, to avoid accidents we'll pull back." There were raised voices in the buildings ahead and Harold saw moving figures. Soon afterwards engines started and vehicles drove away.

*   *   *

A grim group trudged back in the darkness, stripping the other two bodies on the way. Even a radio message confirming that everyone else had arrived home and Bernie and Sal were okay didn't cheer anyone up, nor the news that nobody else seemed to be missing. Betrayal cut deep, because Liam had been with the original escapees from the flats, and Jon had fought well to defend Orchard Close when the mob closed. Doll muttered and kept looking back and Harold moved closer. "We can't start a war Doll."

"But Jon got away and he's a bad one, maybe the worst. The bastard wanted me as well."

"What happened?"

"Willtoo called by and said Jon had a present for me, and Liam had one for Matti, and could we call round to get them. Usual stupid prank we thought but Matti said she'd go and see what the silly sods had got." Doll sighed. "It's our own fault really. This place is too nice, too safe, and we'd started the same games we played at home. Winding blokes up a bit. Though it was the old habits that saved Matti."

"What habits?"

"We used to go to dances and have fun and sometimes the blokes thought we were up for it. Then we'd stop snogging and point over the car park. Oh no, Dad's arrived." She sighed. "We relied on Dad being there, bless him." Doll stayed silent for a few steps but Harold waited. Talking seemed to calm Doll down a bit, taking the edge off her sheer rage. "It was the other habit saved Matti. If we met a nice fella and wanted to get a little bit more personal, we always told each other. You know, I'll be in the kitchen, give me five minutes or however long?"

"Five minutes?"

Harold could hear just a little humour in Doll's reply. "Well very occasionally a bit longer if we really liked a bloke but not if we'd just met. Five minutes is enough to get ruffled and breathless. Christ, are you a priest or what? I'm confessing!"

"Only once."

"Cripes, sorry. Heard about that." Doll sighed. "Anyway, Matti said she'd be fifteen minutes, more as a habit I think. By twenty I was out of the door because Jon had to be told no very firmly sometimes and that's why I didn't go. Matti thinks Liam is sweet because he's shy, which is why she did go. Thought. Was shy. Nobody answered the door so I bust a window." Doll sighed again, Harold preferred that to getting more angry. "I dithered a bit first, worrying about replacing the glass, but no-one had answered. Not even Matti telling me to sod off."

After a dozen silent paces Harold prompted her. "And?"

"Empty. When I got to Jon's room, well here, his note." Her hand pushed a piece of crumpled paper into Harold's. "A real piece of filth though I barely started reading because then I knew." Doll sobbed. "They'd taken Matti someplace. I started shouting and ran to get a gun." She sobbed again, Holly's arm came around her and Emmy spoke from Harold's other side.

"Doll went to get a gun from Sandy and found him dead and the gun store open. Since she screamed blue murder all the way anyone nearby got roused." Emmy's voice sounded tight with anger. "By then they were over the wall but only just going into the ruins and we set straight off. Matthew in the guard house had let them go when Jon called in to explain." Emmy took a few silent steps but Harold didn't interrupt. "We do that sometimes, use the wall to go and set traps or something similar rather than piss about with all the bars on the door. Jon told Matthew they were going for night-time pistol practice, and everyone knows we need to try that."

"That's always planned so we know what the shots are."

"There's no list up and Jon let Matthew know, so he thought you'd agreed. It's eating both him and Bess because he actually saw Matti going over the open ground in the group. It was dark so he wasn't sure who the woman was, and she had a scarf up over her mouth but its chilly early morning and so did two of the others." Emmy sighed. "Matthew and Bess pushed too far ahead and Matthew's been shot again. Bess nearly blew Willtoo to bits for that, put a whole clip into him."

"Bloody stupid name that."

"Not a problem now. Blame the girl club's fault for it. When your Wills met Will he said you're a Will too and someone thought it funny." Emmy shook her head angrily. "How did we miss it, Harold? I would have trusted any of them with my back. Hell, we all have now and then on guard or in a fight."

"Blame Cadillac. He found a weak link someplace. Jon got upset about Sal dumping him after New Year, and I heard some sort of ruckus after the Easter dance. Something little like that got blown up." Harold felt bloody sure this had been orchestrated by Cadillac because the fifth man, a Hot Rod, must have been waiting out here and Cooper didn't hang about at night on the border just for fun.

"The ruckus as you call it was Lemmy. He ended up walking Liz home and no kiss to teach him a lesson. He got a bit pushy and hands-on with Suzie after the previous dance so he drew a blank this time." Emmy sniggered. "Suzie says she doesn't mind a little bit of hands-on if the bloke is nice about it and works up slowly but he was an arse, so she traded for Billy."

"Even that could have been enough if he had already been got at, especially if Billy said something, wound him up when he got back." Harold looked around. "Did Bess go back with Matthew?"

"No, I needed guaranteed shooters. She's over there at the end beyond Billy, keeping her head down." Emmy pointed. "He's feeling guilty because he went to visit Gayle and Suzie."

"I'll go and tell her it's my fault if anyone's, for not making shooting practice more formal and Army-like. Then I'll tell Billy they would have just waited for another time or stuck a knife in him." Harold turned but Emmy put a hand on his arm.

"Billy is mad as hell and I thought he was going to charge the Hot Rods. But before that." Her voice dropped. "Can you really shoot out eyes in the dark with that new rifle?"

Harold chuckled, the first bit of humour since he woke up. "No, but I want Cadillac to get a message. With luck we'll get Jon back."

"Heh. I won't tell anyone. Liz always says she doesn't want to play cards with you and I don't, not now." Emmy waved him away. "Go on, give Bess her hug."

"My hugs are spoken for, but all the bedrest Matthew will need might do the trick for Bess."

"He's only hit in… Oh, yes." Harold did end up with his arm around Bess as she apologised several times before agreeing that anyone else would have done the same. Whether she'd ever believe that was anyone's guess.

*   *   *

When Harold arrived back in Orchard Close a distraught Matti couldn't or wouldn't wait. She wanted to explain and apologise at once, and didn't seem to know which. Either way Harold just let her get it said, so she could relax a bit. Though since the whole affair seemed to have started with Matti going to see Liam, maybe Harold could get the complete story and some hint of a why. Since Matti told him in public, with Doll and half a dozen others present, she also answered a lot of other peoples' questions about what the hell had really happened.

"I'm sorry Harold. It's my own stupid fault. I shouldn't have gone, or I should have shouted right at the start. They gagged me and Lemmy had a gun against me over the wall and as we walked away. I thought if I went along but slow, dragged my feet, they wouldn't kill me and I might escape or be rescued. At worst I'd survive, you know, what they did, until I got a chance to get away." Matti shuddered. "That stranger wanted to cut my throat before they left me. Liam said no, he stayed until last to make sure they didn't." Which was probably why Liam had been killed first but Matti didn't need that news just now.

"It's not your fault. You were set up from the sounds of it. Neither Sal nor Bernie shouted either." Harold tried for a good side. "They missed getting Doll as well or it might have been worse."

"Lemmy and Willtoo both wanted Doll because they couldn't get to Suzie. Jon wanted to take Sal but Bernie said no. He said if they tried to gag or tie him or Sal they'd both scream the place down." Matti shuddered again. "Jon really wanted Sal but the others wouldn't risk the noise. In the end Bernie gave up the bomb stuff as a deal for both to be locked in a wardrobe." The first ghost of a smile appeared. "It was the only way to shut them up without gags. Jon and Lemmy were heaping the bedroom furniture against the doors when a window broke. Then they just wanted to get away before any alarm was raised."

"You were there with them all the time? Did anyone say anything about a plan, whose idea it was?"

"No Harold, no names. Jon and Lemmy talked about a reward when Liam and the new youth, Willtoo, got a bit wobbly. A reward for the guns and another for the pipe bombs, how to make them. They all wrote the pipe bomb stuff down and carried it. If I hadn't been gagged I reckon there were a couple of moments I could have talked Liam out of it." Matti shivered and hugged Doll. "Maybe not after one of them killed Sandy. That was Jon or

Lemmy." She glared at Harold. "I want to see Jon die. If he gets handed back I'll pull the trigger, I swear. I'll pull one whenever you want now Harold, because never again. I want him, Harold."

"If I can, Matti." Harold left her with a mix of older women and the girl club, and visited the wounded, then Sal and Bernie. After that he tried to persuade various people apologies weren't necessary, or that he couldn't go over the border and shoot job lots of Hot Rods. He also persuaded Billy he couldn't go over himself and do it. As dawn broke Harold kissed Holly and went to sort out the last job.

"Hello the Army."

"Coat off and turn slowly."

"Can I put the coat back on?"

"No, leave it there and walk up very slowly. Do not make any sudden moves." Harold knew from the voice there'd been a change up here, and this one didn't sound very friendly. He walked up very, very slowly.

"Stand very still." Harold would because there were four rifles rock steady on his chest. A gaunt, hard-faced man with a little grey on his temples had replaced the usual sergeant. "We will use a wand and search you." A soldier came over and searched Harold thoroughly even after the wand. Harold wasn't offering chips and beer to this lot because the women wouldn't stand for that sort of search. "Right. What do you want?"

"We are having a funeral later today, a pyre. I came to ask permission to spread the ashes on the exclusion zone."

"No."

"May I explain?"

"You can try but it's an exclusion zone. I don't care where dead gangsters go, as long as it's not there."

"The dead man is a fifty-six year old arthritic who was stabbed in the night by a thief. The thief can rot for all I care but Sandy deserves better. I explained to the previous soldiers that we don't want the animals to piss on our dead. If you shoot someone so they bleed on the ashes, our dead might appreciate it."

"I'm still not convinced. The last sergeant said you are decent people but I lost two men to supposedly decent people. I really don't like the idea of someone inside the exclusion zone."

"May I point?" Harold wasn't making any sudden moves today. The sergeant nodded and he pointed to the row of tiny markers, fifteen feet inside the exclusion signs. "Each of those is for someone we lost. We are asking for one person to spread the ashes and put in a marker. We've got no priests down here, and we have to burn our friends on a pyre, so at least let us put the ashes in a safe place." Harold really didn't want the dead anywhere else but didn't know what else to say. Putting the ashes safe comforted some people.

"One woman. Tight jeans and tight top which won't be a hardship for your type, and she makes no threatening moves."

"Take a look at how our women dress before saying that about them, please. How about a woman who had an arm shot off by some scroat six weeks ago? Sandy tried to make her a new forearm so she'll do it. Give her a bit of time though because she's still not well." Harold stopped and took a breath because he'd nearly messed up then. These soldiers wouldn't like either bitterness or sarcasm.

"That won't be necessary. An unarmed woman in clothing that shows she isn't concealing a weapon will do it." At least the harsh edge had gone off the sergeant's voice. "I will check how your women dress and how you treat them, because I have very low expectations of anyone inside the city. Please walk down very slowly." Harold could recognise goodbye and did walk down very slowly. He also walked round the corner before giving a wall a damn good kicking. Men only on shopping trips until the soldiers changed again, because there'd be no weapons smuggled past this lot.

Though first another surprise awaited him. "Why is she here?" A vaguely familiar woman and young girl stood waiting inside the gate, with a suitcase and a rucksack.

Emmy looked uncomfortable. "She wants to talk to you. That's Elizabeth, Willtoo's mum, and that's his little sister Pricilla."

"Hello Elizabeth, Pricilla."

"I waited to apologise. Will wanted to go with the others to those GOFS but I didn't want Pricilla there. Not with what you said about women. The women who went there already had fellas." She gave a big shuddering sigh. "He was a wild one, Will, especially since the crash. I thought a decent place with rules might straighten him out. I thought it was working." A tear trickled down her cheek. "He was really chuffed when that little Asian girl, Suzie, let him walk her home. Then he started getting upset about that name, Willtoo. I told him, stop reacting and they'll quit." She glanced at the girl. "I'll go, but can Pricilla stay?"

"No mum. I'll come with you. Don't leave me on my own." The girl hugged her mum, tears streaming down her face and Harold looked from one to the other, baffled.

"Who said you had to go?"

"Nobody, but Will killed that old man and kidnapped that Matti." She sniffled. "Someone said he shot at you, and you killed him."

Harold opened his mouth to say he didn't kill the youth, but he'd make a better target for Elizabeth's anger than Bess. In any case, her Will wasn't the problem. "Will did those things, not you, and Will is dead. That's the end of it if you let it be. I don't mean not grieve, but will you hold a grudge?"

"Maybe, a bit. I understand why but it's hard. The others, they'll feel the same way about me because of that old man." Elizabeth turned to her daughter. "You have to stay Pricilla. There are bad men out there."

"You can both stay. I won't turn a woman out into that." Harold lowered his voice to speak to Emmy. "Will there be a lot of bad feeling?"

"Not if you kill that scroat Jon. Some might think she should have sorted her kid out but I remember mama trying to keep track of my brother." Emmy glanced at the pair. "You can't turn her out, not out there Harold."

"I won't and you explain the rest. I'll get the gate shut and you organise enough people to convince the pair of them to stay." Harold frowned. "Unless she really does hold a grudge and then sorry, but she has to go."

"Fair enough. I'll get Berry, Liz or Patty to sort out anyone with a real problem." Emmy waved Lilian and Susan nearer and the trio descended on Elizabeth and Pricilla. Harold got the gate closed and worried about if he'd just made another mistake.

For once the rain held off while several people said their piece, and Harold lit Sandy's pyre. Before that Casper and Alfie waited in the ruins while Elizabeth told her son's body that he'd been a fool, and wished him well. Then they collapsed the wall of a ruined house onto Will so the wild animals didn't get to him. Since that was all Elizabeth asked for, Harold couldn't bring himself to refuse. The following morning, early, Pippa and Matti scattered Sandy's ashes after the Army agreed that neither looked threatening.

*　　　*　　　*

Everyone near the gate looked threatening when the next Hot Rod arrived. Charger didn't look comfortable as Holly, Harold, Emmy, Billy and Casper glared at him. "I'm a messenger, all right? Cadillac sent me to bring the minibus and let you know. He can't find a runner, so maybe the bloke went to the GOFS or kept going right past our lot and went further south."

Harold bit back the first response, because he couldn't prove Cadillac did anything. The letter from Jon, handed over by Doll, didn't mention names. It did say some foul stuff about a lot of people living here and Jon was racist as well as resenting women in charge and being rejected for an older man. Jon had slandered every young woman he knew, and the older men were all perverts or forcing the women. Harold had burned the thing and said nothing to any of them.

"In that case, if I see him on Hot Rod territory he's hiding so I'll just shoot the little scroat. Or does Cadillac believe the rubbish Cooper was spouting, that I can't really shoot?" Harold was ready to deal with that one after Cooper's reaction.

"Well Cooper said your big gun missed a few, and the four men we shot up a while back said what they sold you was a poser job with only four bullets." Charger shrugged. "Just saying, OK?"

Harold raised his voice. "Alfie?" Alfie went through the door and returned with the Blaser rifle, assembled. Harold took it and smiled at Charger. "Does this look poser, Charger?" He slid the clip out. "These are big bullets for a poser job, and look, a lovely telescopic sight." Harold put his hand in his pocket and pulled out a fistful of loaded 308 rounds. "Lots of ammo. Let Cadillac know that if Jon gets in range he'll be a head shorter."

The Hot Rod nodded. "I'll tell him I've seen that rifle and the ammo, and I know sod all but it looks dangerous to me. The guy who said poser was dying anyway, so maybe someone heard wrong." Charger took a breath. "So now that's settled, can I get a beer because none of this is on me?" He smiled, a totally genuine one. "Your girl club owe me a beer for fixing their ride. Tell them to be more careful where they park in future."

"We will and it's worth a beer." From that Holly seemed to have taken Charger's personal innocence at face value, or be happy about the minibus being fixed. Almost fixed, the steel would be going back inside and the paint job needed a lot of TLC. Harold had asked, again, and the girl club were adamant. Steel on the outside would spoil the look, and wouldn't surprise some nasty little toerag if he ambushed them.

Smiling, Holly watched Charger being driven away and Sal bringing the minibus up and around the side of the enclave. Then she frowned. "You never mentioned getting our weapons back."

"Cadillac will plead innocence. He might even send one for repair eventually and I'll refuse because it's stolen property."

"They're all stolen."

"Not from me." All the corpses had been carrying stolen weapons, but Harold knew he hadn't got them all back. "I'll know them because most of the missing ones are the oddballs, mostly calibres I didn't have much brass for or single shot target pistols. That's why they weren't in the guardhouses. The three dead ones were carrying nine mills so we got six of the eight back. The rest of the nine mills are all in guard houses or personal weapons anyway. Though I would have traded guns for one life, because the lot weren't worth Sandy dying."

"Maybe they just killed Sandy because they were arses. Sal is certain if they'd got her and Bernie tied up, Jon would have killed Bernie and taken her." Holly hugged his arm. "Now people are worried how many more are like that, waiting their chance."

"None. Tell everyone all our bad apples took their chance and those of us left here are solid." Harold smiled as best he could. "We have to believe that or we'll fall apart, so be confident. Give them that flashing smile and make everyone believe."

"This smile might need topping up. You do know the best sort of re-charge?"

Harold did, and it was both a joy and a wonder to him. Holly really hadn't minded kisses getting more intense, and now he no longer had to beat himself up about pushing her limits. "Level four?"

"At least." Better still, kisses like this seemed to be keeping his nightmares away and might even stop Sandy coming to accuse him at nights.

Chapter 8:
Lucky Lucky

Billy pointed. "He wants to bring that inside, right inside and not give it up. Says he's got a sale for it." The young man dressed like a Geek boss carried a big metal crossbow with a winder on the side.

"I've unloaded it. She said I could have two of those jumpers like yours and four scarves with Geek Freek knitted into them." Though the man in the suit and smock looked a lot less certain now.

Harold smiled and turned to Holly. "Nip and get Patty please, luv. Tell her to bring the jumpers and scarves because her migraine cure has arrived." He turned back to the Geek. "You're a new one, top boss or whatever. Come into this house, here, and let me look at that thing. Patty doesn't know much beyond pointing one of those but I do, and it had better work." Harold reassessed the weapon. "Though it'll make a good club if all else fails."

"It will work. I'm one of the Geek Freek managers, Galileo, and helped Tell to make this and it's a beauty. Look, there's five thin plates here held together with these steel bands and they create a hell of a lot of tension. That's why we use wire instead of a bowstring." Galileo rabbited on as they went inside number three and Billy followed with a shotgun.

"How long before those plates are bent permanently?" Harold thought the rest of it looked solid enough, providing the weapon wound and released properly. Galileo was right about tension, those steel plates should throw a bolt with a lot of power. How much power would need testing. Harold smiled and clicked his radio. "A special crossbow bolt to number three please."

Galileo didn't sit, he was too busy explaining his pet project. "The plates will bend a bit eventually, but look at these two slots in the front. Undo those, reverse the front bit and you're bending the plates the other way. They'll last for ever. The slots will take the back of a machete. Oh." He'd put his hand to the empty sheath at his side.

"Here, let me." Harold assessed the setup as he unscrewed what were two bolts. The plates would slide a little against each other and need a bit of grease now and then, as would the winder. A simple catch and trigger to release did the rest of the job. No safety, no frills, but a real brute metal approach that worked.

"Where is it? Ooh, that's bloody huge. How heavy is it?" Patty tossed the bundle she carried onto an empty chair and held out her hands. "Gimmee, please."

"Hello Patty. This is Galileo and he seems to think you want that."

"I do. Look at the thing, Harold. I could brain the little scroat with it if I miss." Patty hefted the crossbow. "I'll have to beef up a bit. Maybe I can spend some time beating metal, making arrow heads?"

"First we'll find out if the thing works. Thanks Holly." Harold accepted a crossbow bolt, a real Liz special.

"I was told you wanted it." Holly eyed the crossbow. "Does that thing actually work?"

"Let's go and find out. What sort of damage do you reckon Patty can do with this?" Harold held up the bolt and Galileo's eyes widened and he smiled.

"I'd heard about those. I've no idea but it'll put an ordinary one through a house door clean as a whistle from across the street."

A few minutes later Harold hacked at a chunk of old roof beam while Patty finished her deal. As Galileo left with his payment Harold finally extracted the bolt head from the mangled timber. "We might be interested in more at that price." Harold pointed at the timber and sniggered. "The head would go clean through an actual leg so getting the bolts back will be easier, though he'd still lose the leg with all the artwork ripping through."

Patty glanced down and around, coloured a bit, and shuffled her feet. "I sort of paid more than that, Harold. I gave coupons, quite a lot." She sounded more defiant than apologetic now. "My coupons, not Orchard Close's." Her embarrassment or defiance vanished in a beaming smile. "But look at the thing. That'll stop any little bastard from…. well, you know." Patty's smile had gone again.

"Oh, it'll stop him. It'll probably stop his car if need be." Harold hesitated then conscience pushed him. "I don't want to rain on the parade but you'll have to practice, really practice. That won't shoot like any of the others and it'll be slow to reload so make sure of the first one." Harold grinned. "If you hit the scroat anywhere with the first you'll have all the time in the world to reload."

"Cripes, too true. It is heavy though." Holly eyed the weapon up. "Alfie still can't sort out that fancy bow but he'd handle one of those dead easy.

Maybe we could swap?" She patted Patty on the back. "Alfie can explain how to get muscles like his."

"Bloody hell no, Liz or Casper would be eyeing me up. Don't worry Harold, I'll practice until one is all I need. Is there any way to fix up a moving target?" Patty sniggered. "We could add it to the list of fines. Five minutes as a moving crossbow target?" She hefted the crossbow again. "Surely one like this would suit Casper?"

"He's useless with a crossbow, pistol or rifle which is why Casper uses a shotgun. He lets the spread correct his aim. It's got to be his eyes but we haven't found an optician yet so we just save any spectacles we scavenge and hope." That worried Harold since four residents wore specs full-time and if their eyes got worse there was nothing could be done.

"Hell yes, I treat my specs with tender loving care. They're supposed to be reading glasses but work just fine for knitting." Patty turned to go. "I'll go and pay my tithe to the coven and I don't regret a coupon, not one." Everyone paid a regular tithe now, in coupons and a few hours gardening or extra scavenging if they had no extra skills. That covered the bulk buying of food and items such as buying thread and growing the basics and entitled everyone to a share of the crops. Those with skills donated some time or goods free, but paid extra tithe on earnings from outsiders which paid for cement, putty, new machetes, or a bolt of cloth to make cheap clothes. Whatever coupons the residents had left could be spent as they pleased, though the lack of shops limited the choice. One particular skill didn't bring income but Harold wanted to exercise it as soon as possible, on Jon.

*　　　*　　　*

Harold knew he was being stubborn but he wasn't risking losing someone else. "I should go alone."

"You need someone to watch your back." Holly had a stubborn set to her jaw.

"I won't risk you."

"But you'll risk yourself."

"It's my job. Are we having our first argument?"

Holly smiled but still looked stubborn. "Yes, we need a councillor. Liz."

"Patty." Harold shrugged "Both, at least."

Which didn't take long, and Barry and Casper also joined them in the forge. "Why am I here?" Barry looked round the rest.

"Sanity check." Holly poked Harold in the chest. "He wants to sneak off on his own and shoot that scroat Jon."

"He needs shooting." Barry frowned. "What's the problem? It's been over a week so he's already had time to tell them anything he knew." Barry felt bitter over Cadillac getting information on pipe bombs even if Bernie only gave the traitors the Permanganate version, not the truly nasty stuff. Since Bernie had been a bit sparse on the health and safety part everyone hoped Jon lost a hand at least.

"Harold waited so the bastard thinks he's safe and shows his face." Holly pointed at Harold. "Him going on his own is the problem and my objection."

Holly barely finished before there were more objections and they settled into two sorts. Casper glowered. "You might be superman or the gay angel, but you haven't got eyes in the back of your head. What if you can't find him and have to sleep someplace? I'll come and watch your back."

"No, one of the women should see the little er, scroat die." Liz glared at Harold. "We'll believe you killed Jon but you won't give Sal and Matti and Doll the gory details. They need those. Hell, I do." She suddenly smirked. "As therapy. Just like caning therapy, unorthodox but effective."

"They won't want to see this." Harold knew that sometime he'd dream about Jon dying, and didn't want that in someone else's head. "Nor will they want to live rough, camping out and eating cold food for days because there'll be no fires." Harold looked around the disbelieving faces. "You surely don't expect me to just wander over there, shoot him and come back? I can't be sure of seeing the scroat, maybe for days."

"But the visitors say Jon is there. You get in sight of the place and use that rifle. Pow." Patty frowned. "No?"

"Some of the Hot Rod visitors talk about a new man named Jon-athon with a big pause in the middle and a smirk so he's there. Now I've got to find someplace I can see the gates, and wait for Jon to come out of them. Either that or hope he shows at a bedroom window inside." Harold looked at the puzzled faces and then understood. "None of you have been there, the Mansion has a six foot wall all the way round the houses." Realisation dawned on them all.

"So he's safe." Liz looked at her hammer, probably considering hitting something. "Those three women need closure Harold. Anyway, if you can't be sure of seeing him, why is it suddenly important to go now?"

"The weather forecast is good for three days, with light winds so I can shoot further and still hit him. If the winds pick up I'll come home and try again." Harold smiled without any humour. "The further away I shoot Jon from, the more of a wake-up it is for Cadillac. With luck he won't try any more cute tricks."

"Take a woman. No Holly, not you." Holly closed her mouth and Patty continued. "If anyone catches sight of you from a distance it's a man and woman wandering about or going into a building. Not Holly or she'd distract you. Holly, could you resist kissing this lump for three days?"

Holly grinned. "No."

"Which would definitely distract me. So who? Doll is too excitable. I need someone with a cool head, but a trigger puller in case it all goes pear-shaped." Harold chuckled. "Bess?"

"She'd shoot, but so will Matti." Barry put a hand on Harold's shoulder. "I'd be grateful because it's eating her. Matti reckons if she'd fought and screamed at first, then Sandy would be alive." Barry hesitated, then continued. "I would have lost her then because Jon at least would have knifed her, so I'm torn. Matti has sworn, with absolutely sincerity, that she'll shoot any man who tries to take her or anybody else again. She's got a gun under her jacket all the time and sleeps with it."

"I'm good with Matti." Liz looked around. "You shut up, wimp, because you don't want to take any woman at all. Any better ideas since hot-lips is disqualified?" The rest agreed while Holly wavered between indignant and smug at the hot-lips.

Harold definitely appreciated the hot-lips part when he returned three fruitless days later. He had no idea what Matti would do to work off her frustration at not seeing Jon after spending so long watching. From the way she stomped down the road, chewing iron bars and spitting nails might be on the cards.

*   *   *

"He never showed for three whole days last time. Why should we have better luck this time? It's been nearly three weeks and if he's still hiding, maybe we'll never see the bastard again and he'll get away with it." Matti put the rangefinder to her eyes and inspected the group coming out of the mansion. "He's not in that lot." Matti refused to use Jon's name.

"Cadillac told me once that he couldn't kill a man like this, wait and wait and then just shoot him from a long way away. He said that's what makes a sniper. I don't know if that's true, but I'm angry enough about Jon to take as long as necessary." Harold stretched out on the sleeping bag. "I'm also patient enough to make sure I'm alive and at the party to celebrate afterwards."

"Ah. Put like that, I can wait." Matti sighed. "Your turn to sleep so I'll stop complaining for a bit." Matti carefully crossed the roof space using the beams and looked out of a hole in the tiles at the back, and then where a brick had been removed at each end. Satisfied that nobody had approached unseen, she settled to watch the gate again.

Though despite all her patient watching Matti missed spotting the target when he finally showed up. "Matti." Harold nudged her dozing form with a foot. "This might be it."

Matti sat up, wide awake now. "Might? It's the bastard?"

"Yes. He's growing a beard but that's Jon." Harold offered the binoculars. "Here, double-check the back please." While Matti did, Harold carefully slid his rifle out and set it on the crude rest of old pillows and bedding, then laid behind it. As Matti came back to look out of the front through another broken tile he worked the bolt and slid a round home.

"Clear all round. Oh yes, that's him. Shoot him Harold, right through that filthy mouth." Matti hadn't told anyone exactly what Jon said to her but mentioned filthy mouths more than once. Now Matti watched eagerly as the group came clear of the gates.

"Maybe, if he's in the right spot. If not, then hopefully when he comes back. Patience, Matti, remember the party afterwards. Now calm down and remember your job." Harold settled in and let himself go off to the quiet place in his head, the shooting place. He aimed at the lamp post the range-finder said stood five hundred and fifty metres away, the one the sights were set for, and moved sideways to where the men would come. Harold reminded himself of the light crosswind, and he'd burned off enough practice rounds to allow for that now. He'd also practiced shooting downwards, only eighteen feet down this time. His breathing settled.

"He's walking away from the Mansion gate in a group. They're laughing and joking. He's in the group, just back from the man on our right." Harold could hear the excitement in her voice, the eagerness, but Matti remembered what she'd been told to do and reported.

"Got him." Jon moved into the view in Harold's scope, partly obscured by another man. Someone must have called from behind because the group stopped. Jon half-turned to answer or hear what someone else said, as good a target as he'd ever be. Harold had a clear view between two of the others, his finger tightened just enough, and the rifle pushed back into his shoulder.

"Go, go, now." Harold pushed the Blaser into its impromptu carrying case, slung it and started for the trapdoor. "Matti!"

"But you didn't…" Matti shook her head and snatched at the pack with their food and the sleeping bag. "Go, I'm behind you." The pair of them slid down the loft ladder and pounded down the stairs and Harold glanced out the back.

"Still clear." Matti pushed past with her cycle and Harold snatched his from just inside the door. They ran down the garden, lifted the cycles over the fence, and in moments were pedalling like lunatics along a rubble-strewn road straight away from the Mansion, hidden from view by the houses and fences. Twice the pair picked up the lightweight racing cycles and crossed gardens from one street to another to stay away from the open roads, the through roads. The cycles stuck to impassable routes, impassable to motor vehicles, swerving around burned cars and jinking around rubble faster than a man could run.

Seven or eight minutes later Harold called out. "Stop." Matti came to a halt and looked back, and both listened.

"Nothing. Cars that way but no motorbikes." She pointed towards the east, towards the bypass. "That's the road to our place."

"They'll stop at the border and probably spread out. No cars coming ahead so let's go." Another minute or two pedalling, and a run across a garden, and Matti cautiously looked around the corner of a house, up the short street.

"The curtains are closed so no Hot Rods." The curtain signal used against them by the Geek shooter worked just as well when helping. Both cycles raced up the short road and the pair dismounted to run between a pair of houses and over the back fence. As they came up the side of the next house and around to the front, a pair of arms seized Harold with a whoop.

He dropped the bike to deal with a blonde whirlwind saying hello in a way that didn't help Harold catch his breath. "Woo, let me breathe a moment. Any cars?"

"None, well not near here. There are cars that way towards the GOFS and some shouting." Holly's eyes were alight with pure excitement. "Did you get him?"

"I'm sure I hit him but didn't stop to check the result." Harold hoped any sort of body shot had been good enough, and getting away had been more important than gloating.

"What!"

"It's all right, he got the bastard. He's dead, Doll, he's dead." Matti hugged Doll then she looked round and lunged. When she turned away from Jeremy, one of the new men, he stared open-mouthed and wide-eyed until a big smile grew. Matti whirled. "Hey, Harold, why didn't you shoot him through the head?"

"What?" Doll stared at Harold as did several others now.

Matti sighed. "I'd focussed right in, waiting for that, the head splat. Then the arse sort of crumpled sideways like he'd been shoulder charged, and a spray of red flew out behind him. The bastard went over and down and when I brought the glasses down there was blood all over the road and he was sprawled in the middle of it." Matti grinned. "I wanted to see if he moved but someone yelled at me. So why not in the head like you always threaten?"

"Head shots are painless." Harold shrugged. "It might not have lasted long, like a really severe heart attack, but do you think he felt it Matti?"

"Christ yes. Holly, kiss him before I do." Harold enjoyed the kissing even if he'd told a little porky. He'd shot Jon through the chest because that had been an important shot. Harold daren't risk missing because then Cadillac would assume all the shooting business was bullshit. At a paper target on a range, with that rifle, Harold thought he could hit a head sized target most times and probably every time. Unfortunately he really hadn't enough experience with this sort of outdoor shooting. One little gust of wind and he'd have missed and this time the one shot kill really mattered.

Holly's radio lit up and Casper had a message. "I've got Cooper here all wound up about something. He wants to talk to Soldier Boy."

"Hang on and I'll see if he's got enough breath. Tell Cooper he's a spoilsport." Holly grinned and passed the radio over. "Casper is half a mile that way on our border where the main road to the Hot Rods crosses over."

"Hello Casper, what's got Cooper's knickers twisted?" Around Harold everyone hi-fived.

"You. He's thinks you've been up to something. Are you busy?"

"I was up to something but not now. We'll be with you soon."

*   *   *

Casper, Alfie and another ten from Orchard Close were standing off three cars and a dozen Hot Rods, but doing so from cover. Harold drove straight up and got out, and the other six spread across the road behind him. "Where have you been?"

"Hey, steady up Cooper. Why am I supposed to account to you what I do here, at home?" Harold grinned. "Did Cadillac put you in charge and not tell us?"

"You were in our territory. You can't just shoot people in here and walk away." The Hot Rod glared, literally quivering with suppressed violence.

Harold had been going to have a lot of fun, but now he realised that an enraged Cooper would lose it and start a fight. Then Caddi would be upset about ten dead Hot Rods. "Who's been shot and why is it me? Apart my alibi, scavenging with my girl here while whatever happened."

"You know who was shot. It was..." Kev touched Cooper's arm. He shook the youth off and turned back to Harold. "Let me see that rifle. I want to know if it's been fired."

"Sure Cooper. Providing your lot heap all your weapons in the road right there first." Harold pointed at the tarmac in front of him.

"We're not doing that!"

"So why should I hand over my rifle? Calm down Cooper. You wanted to see me and here I am, now is it a message from Cadillac or are you just here to annoy me?" Harold spread his hands to take in the people in the houses either side, Harold's people. "We're on our side of the border so I'm not going to take any crap, am I? What would Cadillac do if you spoke to him like that?"

Another nudge from Kev and a snarl from Cooper and the Hot Rod began to cool down at last, or to realise this was the wrong time and place. "You'll hear more about this. You'll answer if Cadillac asks."

"If he actually asks a question, politely, I'll answer. Remind him of that please. Politely." Harold shrugged. "If we're done? I was busy before you called."

"Harold has been hunting for rodents, dog meat." Holly hadn't been able to keep quiet.

Cooper hesitated for long moments, and Harold knew what still wound the gangster up. Every one of Harold's people he could see was grinning, but they were also pointing weapons. "You'll hear from us." Cooper spun on his heel and went to his car, and at least four Hot Rods heaved a sigh of relief. Harold stood in the road watching as the three cars left, and the rest had the decency to let them get out of sight before starting the celebration.

*   *   *

"That was a really good party, azshpe, eshpeshul, cos we relaxed the rules on alcohol." Liz hooked an arm through Harold's free one and waved a bottle. "All it needed was a blackshmith and a lummerjack."

"Greedy." Patty led the way, also waving a beer bottle and dancing to whatever music her head supplied.

Liz concentrated, brow wrinkled, and spoke carefully and clearly. "No, the lumberjack is for Casper." She sighed. "The next time you're gonna to shoot scroats, Harold, invite a GOFS." Liz wiggled her eyebrows. "A big sweaty sooty one."

"Don't do that with your eyes. I'm already dizzy." Gayle giggled, "And I haven't self-preshcribed anaestics. Anstethics. Stuff." She held on tighter to Phillip, one of the new arrivals. "Stop wobbling."

"I'm not." He smiled, "not as much as you."

"The woman is always right." Liz wagged a finger. "Ask any woman." A chorus of assent and dissent came from the girl club and their escorts since the women were being walked home en masse tonight. "If you don't agree, you can't come to the party."

"The party is over." Finn shut up when June whispered in his ear.

"It is? Oh no." Liz sang The Party's Over as everyone but Harold and Holly went in through the gates to the girl club.

Harold watched them with a big smile, because everyone went indoors so the party wasn't over. "Mummy Casper will need a club for that lot."

"Mummy Casper is walking Celine home and Barry is walking Alicia tonight." Holly sniggered. "June wouldn't trade Finn, because she's fed up of being walked home by geriatrics or pimply youths."

"Finn and June?"

"I don't think as a regular thing, but maybe June is in a really good mood and wants a goodnight kiss." Holly hugged. "That should liven up the rumour mill now Sal is fully booked. Being locked in a cupboard together seems to have settled any doubts there. Goodnight Nigel."

"Goodnight Harold, Holly." They both turned to watch the brewer hurry down the street.

"He's worried that Seth will be chasing Berry round the brewery, or that Berry has cornered Seth in the brewery." Harold smiled. "That's why he keeps getting drawn with Sharyn, to give that pair a bit of time to decide which." Harold smirked. "Sharyn doesn't mind because he's hell-bent on getting home, not saying goodnight."

"It's sweet really, he thinks Berry is still fourteen." Holly opened the door. "Cooee, are you decent?"

Sharyn replied from the kitchen. "Cheeky. Do you want a drink?"

"No thanks. I've just remembered something important. Come on Harold." Holly tugged his hand.

"Ah, young love and alcohol. Just shut the door first, and the bedroom one."

*　　　*　　　*

"All done." Harold came out of the en-suite. "That's a wicked smile. Why?"

"Just leave the light on, the little lamp." Just before she closed the door Holly giggled. "And brace yourself."

Harold laid and watched the end door of what looked like wardrobes. He'd slept in here three nights before finding the en-suite shower room. Brace yourself was intriguing combined with leaving the light on, given that he'd still not seen Holly in her underwear, or less. "Ready or not, here I come." Holly stood in the doorway with one hand up the doorpost and the other on her hip, waggling a leg at him. "I can't find the other stocking."

"That was your stocking?" Two more of Harold's brain cells sparked. "That's my, er the garter Emmy had."

"Your garter? Explaining that will be interesting." Holly giggled. "That's the girl club garter, donated by Emmy for each girl to use as she seals the deal. Liz is the official keeper until she scores a blacksmith." She smirked. "My deal is sealed so Sal wanted me to get a move on with the garter part so she can borrow it, and tonight I'm a bit squiffy so?" Holly stuck out a hip and giggled again. "Do you like me in lingerie? It's another first and maybe a rite." Holly waggled her hips a little. "These were a birthday present."

"I told you once that you'd be gorgeous in a set of thermals but those are even better, a lot better. Do you really want the other stocking?" Harold had put the Rambo stocking back in his memento box and didn't want to retrieve it with Holly watching.

"Oh yes. You've got to put it on me first to make up the set." Holly giggled again and her blush started, just a bit. "I've never had anyone else put a stocking on before."

"I've never put one on anyone." The memento box seemed less problematic, and maybe a good idea.

"I've never had stockings taken off either." Holly giggled again, definitely a bit squiffy and now decidedly pink-faced. "I think that might be extra advanced. Now where's the stocking?"

"Just hold that pose." Harold stopped worrying and headed for the wardrobe and his memento box.

*   *   *

"Bloody hell, it's all dancing, kissing and shooting these days." Holly claimed she didn't have a hangover, but she seemed a bit short-tempered. "I like the first two, but why does it always end like this?" She frowned. "Depending on who it is, I might shoot them just for spoiling my lie-in."

"We aren't going to shoot anyone, I hope. Cadillac is here to talk or we'd be hearing bangs and booms." Harold hugged her. "Maybe he wants to borrow that garter?"

"Then there'll be shooting. There's at least three lining up after Sal even if the bloke isn't sure yet." Holly looked up "Hey, Liz, something for Sal." She waved a bag with something small and light inside.

"About time. Wait up because I'm coming as well. Us mice need to know if we've got to run away." Liz disappeared from the window even as Patty came out of the door with her new toy.

"Cripes Patty, point that elsewhere." Harold mock-flinched.

"I cranked it ready but there's no bolt in there. Liz is right, you're a wimp." Patty reached over her shoulder to her quiver. "I brought my biggest knitting needle."

"Make it count, that one took ages to make." Liz hurried down the path. "Everyone else who'll pull a trigger, as you put it Harold, has already left. Except Umeko. She dithered a bit but now she's accessorising so just give her a minute."

It took a couple of minutes but then Umeko came out wearing a coat with the hood up to hide her face. She carried a child's crossbow with a Liz special, and a spear, and joined them in silence though they could hear plenty of shouting ahead. Harold smiled at a line of homemade bunting, a row of triangular bits of scrap cloth on a rope, still strung between two houses. Harold hadn't realised just how badly Jon's betrayal had affected Orchard Close, or rather how much they resented him getting away. Last night's party had been spectacular, noisy, and very, very happy.

Liz stayed two houses back in her 'mousehole' while the other three women went into a guardhouse. As soon as he stepped up onto his box Harold could see just how angry the shooting had made Cadillac, too angry for common sense. A show of strength made no sense against someone inside buildings armed with crossbows and firearms, especially since the Hot Rods had to keep firearms concealed from the Army. Unless Cadillac wanted everyone here at the gate? "Alfie?"

"Yes Harold." Alfie looked down from a window in his guardhouse.

"Where's Casper and Emmy?"

"Emmy is over there in the other guardhouse, Matthew has the side wall and Casper is at the far end in the corner house." Alfie grinned. "Just like you told us. Don't leave the back door open."

"Sorry, I'm not quite with it yet."

"You and a few others. I'm too young for booze so my conscience and head are clear." From his smile Alfie also seemed to be in a terrific mood.

"Ouch. Stand by, here we go." Out front Cadillac and four others wearing overalls had stood clear of the crowd. Harold cupped his hands. "Good morning Cadillac."

"Soldier Boy. I've come to get some answers."

"I told Cooper you should. Did he pass on all the message?"

Cooper stood on the right. "Yes I did you cheeky shit."

"Careful Cooper, that is a bit borderline and you aren't at the border. Cadillac, are you here to cause a problem or solve it? A loose mouth won't help either way." Harold watched Cadillac and Cooper speak to each other before Cooper glowered and turned away.

Cadillac turned back and shouted. "I told you, I want answers about yesterday."

"Then come in here and we'll do it civilised. I won't play question and answer like this." Harold didn't mind the question and answer part, but shouting in public like this Cadillac would grandstand. He had to be the big tough gang boss where his men could see and hear. "Bring up someone who can keep a civil tongue."

"Send the pouf down."

"Not today, not after calling Casper that. You can come and talk without a hostage, or we wait until all that lot go home and then do it the usual way." The pouf part was grandstanding, and if Cadillac kept it up someone in the guardhouses would get angry and start shooting. "If you are trying to wind me up, remember the discussion we had about that the first time I visited? Some of my people might have weak bladders."

Harold could actually see Cadillac bottling his anger, forcing it down. Cooper still stomped up and down on the far side of the seven cars and thirty plus men. "I'll bring Charger, but I will want answers. I keep my machete."

Harold understood a face-saver. "You can, but Charger turns his in. Come on up when you're ready." Harold watched as Cadillac talked to some men, shouted at some and punched one. Cooper came through the group and dragged that one away into the crowd. Kev wore overalls and helped to control everyone, but Porsche and Bugatti were missing today. Another muscular type in overalls smacked gangsters round the head when they argued.

Eventually most of the men got back in their vehicles and Cadillac started towards the gates with Charger. "Alfie? We'll need beer in number three please."

"And a shotgun I reckon. Do you want a second one so Emmy can stay here and keep watch? Doll could bring one?" Alfie laughed. "Sorry, it's the look on your face. I'll send someone sensible, not Doll." Alfie really seemed in a hell of a good mood. He called to someone inside and Hazel came out the door and ran up the street. By the time Cadillac and Charger reached the gate Seth had appeared in the doorway still hiding his sawn-off. Holly came from the other house and Harold smiled as Patty followed, lugging her crossbow.

"Seth, please search them and don't get too personal because neither will have a serious weapon. They aren't stupid, or won't be when they see that sawn-off. Just be careful where it's aimed." Harold turned to greet the others. "The same with that Patty."

Patty smirked. "No problem. I'm the sensible one." Both Cadillac and Charger heard that as they came through the gate and neither seemed convinced. They still didn't seem certain when both were sat in comfort in number three.

Alfie followed the rest in. "We should call this the embassy." He took off his coat and slid the shotgun strap off his shoulder. "These are my diplomatic credentials."

"Mine too." Seth had already opened his coat, then Holly took off her coat to show the two-two rifle and finally Harold took his coat off. Cadillac's eyes fastened on the rifle slung below Harold's shoulder.

"That's what I wanted to see. How far can it shoot?"

"Accurately? I don't know. A thousand yards maybe? This is a real classy bit of kit." Harold sat and moved the rifle so the light played on the stock inset. "I don't know exactly what a Blaser R8 Professional Success is, or who the hell Ivythorn Sporting are, but I bet I couldn't afford to buy one from the other."

"So you can't shoot it?"

"Of course I can because this is a superb bit of kit, and I'm genuine shooter not some half-trained scroat. I totally stitched the idiot I bought it from. I've trained someone else on the other big rifle now and Holly with my two-two, because I won't need either. We've got four people now who can probably shoot as well as your man, hit bodies at three hundred yards." Harold shrugged. "Just in case I suffer a mishap. All four would do even better using this."

Cadillac scowled. "But they couldn't kill a man stone dead with a single shot at six hundred paces. We paced it out."

"Cadillac, I have not shot any of your men lately. I only shoot people who ask for it. Who got shot?"

Cadillac hesitated. Harold could see how hard the gang boss had to struggle keeping his temper but he managed it. "A newcomer from somewhere else but I will not stand for people being killed on my doorstep. I have to take action."

"Because your men demand it? I saw them out there, Cadillac, they're in a hell of a mood. What's winding them up?" Harold saw the anger flare, then die back. Charger kept very quiet and watched Cadillac rather than the ones with guns.

"You are, you and your shooting! Half of them are shit scared. Who the hell else could it be?" Cadillac pointed. "There aren't many big rifles about and you've got two."

"I'll bet you have as well." Harold waited until Cadillac conceded that with a short nod. "It doesn't have to be ex-Army, and anybody who owned something like this would be a damn good shot." Harold shrugged. "I had to show off to back you lot down, but someone else might keep their shooter as a surprise. Tell me what happened."

"You know."

"Pretend I don't if you won't believe me. Humour me."

"You, he, did it from six hundred paces lying in the roof of a house. At least two men were there for a while according to the marks in the dust and the crap in the toilets. One shot that killed him stone dead and then they disappeared." Cadillac scowled again. "Now explain how that isn't a sniper, you."

Harold frowned to hide his smile. "One shot through the head at six hundred? That really might be ex-Army."

Cadillac sneered. "No, through the body. Even you can't head shoot at that range."

Harold smiled now. "I told Cooper once to remember what I said about placing the original test targets. Why didn't I use a scope?"

Cadillac couldn't remember but Charger spoke up. "Boss, Porsche was on about it. Soldier Boy said he didn't use a scope because there wasn't time to take the targets half a mile."

Harold held his smile, careful not to let it become a mocking grin. "I shot the furthest target through the head, not the nearest."

"That was…. bullshit." But Cadillac had paused. "Bugatti reckoned the bullet was right through the heart though I doubt anyone could be sure. Half his f… bloody chest came out his back on the other side."

"It would if someone used a hunting rifle like this." Harold grinned. "I know one thing about hunting from seeing the toffs hunt deer on the TV. They kill a deer the size of a bull when it's on the next hillside over, by shooting it through the heart and lungs." Harold leant forward. "That's a hunter's shot, to stop the whatever running off wounded." He pretended to think. "How high up, was it a house or a bungalow?"

"House, why?" Cadillac anger still flickered in his eyes, but now curiosity showed as well.

"If it had been an Army sniper he wouldn't have waited for the target to come outside your gates. From up there he'd see over that wall of yours and shoot whoever he wanted on their front doorstep, up to a thousand yards. I think the top kill to date is over a mile and a half but with a proper sniper rifle and ammo. That bloke killed two men with only two shots." Harold smiled. "But not through the head." He held both hands with the palms up. "See? Innocent m'lud. I wouldn't have pissed about for days in an attic."

Caddi frowned and sat quiet for long moments. "Run through that again, please." Curiosity had definitely dampened his anger now. Five minutes later, after going through the hunter versus sniper part again, Cadillac accepted the shooter might not be Soldier Boy. Or at least the gang boss claimed he accepted that and would explain to his men. Then maybe he'd cane a few or send them to patrol the border with the Barbie Girls so they really were frightened.

"Surely they'd like that? All those girls?"

"Fair warning Soldier Boy, if you see a woman in a blonde wig, shoot her." Cadillac's smile became more snarl. "Through the head. They got Porsche and that wasn't pretty."

"What about Bugatti?"

"He's cleaning his boxers after I suggested he came with us. Pussy. That's why I've got Chevy and E-Type out there to kick arses." Cadillac stood up. "I accept what you said, that you haven't shot any of mine on my territory. I hope we can avoid these sort of misunderstandings in future." The careful phrasing had to mean that Caddi still thought Harold did the shooting, but conceded the target wasn't a Hot Rod without openly saying so.

Cadillac's really had bottled his temper now and although not his usual urbane self, the gang boss had himself back under control. Harold shrugged. "I hope so as well. We've got enough troubles without. Do you want any beer?"

"One crate please. I'll go down to sort out my blokes and send some of them home, and Charger will wait here for the beer." Cadillac nodded to Holly and left followed by Alfie and Patty. Harold sat and chatted about how the stream of groups and loners had stopped now, and if there might actually be unclaimed areas down south, and the possible food shortages and London. Charger kept well clear of anything to do with shooting.

Alfie and Patty came back with the beer, and Seth followed the Hot Rod to the gate. "Most of the cars have already gone." Alfie chuckled. "They're not happy."

"But they'll be good now. Wait until I tell the rest." Patty also had a huge grin.

Harold frowned. "Tell them what? Cadillac is still as mad as hell, even if he hid it."

"He was crapping himself. Maybe not quite but you just frightened the nasty bastard." Alfie smiled happily. "All of a sudden he wants a nice peaceful solution, even if he has to beat it into a few of his men."

"No, he finally got his temper under control."

"Helped by the bucket of cold water." Patty sniggered. "What was it?" She looked up and held one hand out palm upwards. "See, innocent. I would have shot him on his doorstep." She sniggered again. "Cadillac realised just whose doorstep would be in view from that house, or a lot further away." Harold, and then Holly, began to smile because that was exactly when Cadillac had really started to calm down.

"Don't tell the others. One of our lot will say something to wind up a Hot Rod, it'll get back to Cadillac, and he'll have to kill some of us to save face." Harold nodded gently. "I mean it. Settle for the Hot Rods backing off a bit, if that happens." Harold grinned and hooked an arm round Holly. "Someone is fed up of the shooting after the dancing and kissing."

Patty took the bolt out of her crossbow and let the tension off. "Aren't we all, even if some of us ain't got to kissing yet." She smiled as Alfie blushed bright red.

Nobody crowed about Caddi backing down, but they did smile happily at the visiting Hot Rods, and a couple asked how Jon-athon was? That or mentioned Harold shooting stray dogs.

*　　　*　　　*

"That's odd. We've seen three stray dogs today and I haven't seen three dogs in one day for ages." Holly frowned. "Not since the council banned them."

"Yeah, it's bugged me on and off. All the films and books had packs of them roaming around hunting people." Harold laughed. "They're all heading for Orchard Close so Lucky will have company."

"Oh. Are they all dogs, boy dogs? Some of the girl club thought Lucky was acting strange and then, well, Sal took her to Patricia, and Lucky is in heat. She's wearing a sort of nappy thing while we find out what the times and procedure are, especially when we'll need a bucket of cold water for Rascal though Hilda says he's too old." A big smile broke over Holly's face. "Puppies, we could have puppies?"

"Maybe. This lot aren't exactly the tail wagging type of dog, and might eat the hand that tries to feed them or puts on a lead." Harold watched a big crossbreed as it ran between two houses. "Maybe the whole arm?"

"We'd better get back and warn Sal she's got gentleman callers."

Sal already knew. "Rascal tried to get rascally. Hilda is utterly mortified." From inside Bernie's house Lucky complained loudly about being locked in, while several Prince Charmings answered with promises of rescue from outside the wall. "How long does this go on?" Her face dropped. "How often does it happen? Is there a pill for dogs?"

"Not this time because we want the tippety tap of tiny claws. Tiny claws that will grow up tame and bite nasty scroats climbing walls." Holly smiled happily. "Little waggy tail puppies. Bagsy one because Daisy will want one so we can share."

"Cripes." Harold turned towards the outside wall. "We'd better work out how to audition for suitors." One look over the wall and Harold went to find experts, or people with a vague idea. Seth reckoned his Mum's dog had injections to stop her coming on heat, and Patricia thought she's seen something in the vet supplies Harold had scavenged. Hilda never had a bitch but set into searching the library for information helped by Veronica and Hazel.

"We need a trap." Casper rubbed his hands together. "We can use old roof timbers and the wire mesh we scavenged to keep birds off, and make two or three cages."

"Two, three? How many boyfriends do you think my girl should have?" Sal glowered. "She might not be that sort of girl." Everyone laughed. "All right she will be, but even so?"

"I thought we could catch more than one dog. After all, Lucky turned out well. I'll get..." Casper's face dropped. "Damn. I'll go and get Sandy's tools instead of getting Sandy. Zach was sort of training and so was Wade, and Stewart wields a mean saw. We'll manage." Casper looked out over the wall. "Throw some rat or cat to keep the ones we want interested." He smiled at the laughter. "All right, it'll make them less wary, they can't be more interested."

Lucky started whining and wanting a run on the wild side six days after seeing the first potential boyfriends lurking in the undergrowth. The library books and the dog's condition agreed, so real auditions could be started and candidates wouldn't be hard to find. Several had already been chased back over the wall where it was only five feet high.

By the time the cages were set out anyone even slightly interested had looked over the candidates, and the debate heated up. "The snipped ones won't be interested, will they?" Bernie leafed through one of the books, because after all Lucky had moving in permanently. All official now, complete with plastic confetti so Liz must have passed on the deal sealer.

"Yes they will." Seth sniggered. "Mum thought that and had to beat one off with a stick when a friend brought him round."

"I know how she felt." Seth winced and looked guilty as Nigel spoke, but Berry laughed.

"We need a dog about the same size as Lucky. Don't we?" Harold shrugged. "That made sense until I said it."

"A larger dog might mean the pups are too big." Veronica ducked her head as everyone turned. "It says so here." She waved a book then passed it to Seth. "Here, you read it."

"Why? Oh, right. According to this doggy love can take a while. We'll need someplace secure for Lucky and her boyfriends to stop interruptions." Seth frowned at the cages. "We'll have to adapt those."

The following day a very happy Lucky bounded out of the house on her lead. Ten minutes later an unhappy Lucky sat in her cage and complained. "I don't like taking a bit of wall down." Casper pulled at the loose bricks. "Though at least it's a crappy bit."

"A low thin part which we'll rebuild thicker with all the nice bricks in those buildings over there." Harold grinned. "If we get some big puppies we might end up with a dog trailer to pull them."

"The wall had better be built before the puppies get big enough for that." Seth frowned. "Why am I heaving bricks? I'm a brewer's apprentice."

"It's not the brewer or the brewing you're learning about. Mind your fingers." Holly let go of her rope and a heavy sheet of ply dropped across the front of the cage. "Gotcha, daddy dog." She set into pulling on the rope to bring the ply up again. "What if we get more than one?"

* * *

"They won't share or come in together was a bad answer." The two dogs in the large cage were fighting while outside the lowered ply the Doberman and several others really wanted to get in as well. At the back of the big cage a slightly smaller version held a very excited Lucky. "Is she egging them on?"

"No Holly, Lucky wouldn't do that. We should let them out." Sal took hold of the rope.

"You'll let more in." Harold didn't think the cage could stand many more dogs rolling about inside it.

"But then they can run away if they're losing." Bernie waved his book. "Dogs aren't supposed to get real serious about fights. Once one of them has had enough it'll run away. Open the gate." Harold and Casper heaved, and the pair of dogs shot outside and set into each other again, then one legged it for the ruins.

"That worked." Seven or eight minutes of growling and posing and snapping and the choice was down to the Retriever, the Doberman, a big cross-breed and what Hilda guessed was a Staffy cross. Those weren't backing off and rest of the dogs didn't fancy a serious scrap with those four. Sal frowned. "That Staffy cross thing has no nuts. How do we stop him interfering?"

"Shout bad dog? Buckets of cold water? Offer him a doggy biccy?" Harold hadn't a blind idea but had no intention of going over there to interfere.

"Pepper spray." Emmy waved it. "Temporary it says."

"You'll get them all. Go for a bucket of cold water because that's what Mum used when the stick didn't work." Seth looked beyond the contestants. "How come those two, the rest of the Doberman's pack, aren't interfering?"

"Who knows? Chivalry?" Even as Casper spoke the cross-breed lunged, the Doberman put a shoulder in and then followed up and the big cross-breed was running. The Staffy cross tried to go up and under each of the others but they both seemed to have met that before and he moved back a bit, looking for another chance. The Retriever lunged, the Dobermann put his neck alongside the other dog's and used that and his chest and his opponent reeled back. Before the Retriever recovered properly the Dobermann charged, and the Mastiff and cross-breed surged forward, snarling. The Retriever bolted for the ruins, and after a hesitation that was nearly a mistake so did the Staffy cross, and the fight was over.

"Okay, not chivalry but it worked. Let him get right inside, oh cripes." Everyone watched as the three big dogs shouldered their way into the pen. Sal backed away. "If they start fighting I'm running away, because the pen will be history."

"Good idea Sal, but they're not fighting. Let bad boy in to see Lucky, since he's so interested, and anyone of a nervous disposition turn away or leave." Casper grinned. "I'll shut the outside and be ready to open up again if this lot get fractious."

Sal debated but Bernie shrugged and pulled the sliding partition. "These three will chew through the mesh anyway." But three didn't go into the back pen.

"How about we slide that back across, then I can open the outside and let the other two out. Chuck Romeo some rat if he loses interest in Juliet." As soon as the Doberman was fastened in with Lucky, Casper raised the outside panel. He held it there for a while but neither dog showed any intention of leaving.

"Those tails aren't unhappy. Who fancies a Mastiff bitch and a big hairy bastard?"

"Crossbreed, wammel or mongrel please, since he's a doggy." Emmy smiled happily. "He's even my colour." She moved closer and the Doberman snarled and lunged at the mesh. "Christ, what did I say?"

"I don't know but it's only him. The other two might still love you, especially if you've got rat or cat." Casper frowned. "Stay back Emmy and we'll work on getting these two out of here and into the other cages."

"I want the little ones." Seth pointed over the wall. "That feisty little git has a girlfriend along." He paused, assessing. "They're small enough for ratters and we haven't got a permanent cat in the brewery store yet."

"We?" Berry clipped him gently at the back of the head. "Don't let Dad hear that."

"Yes dear." Seth checked that Nigel had left. "Would you like to start a family?" He ducked too slowly, then Berry looked over the wall where he was pointing.

"She's got a waggy tail. OK, but you train the kids and clean up after them." Berry also checked her Dad wasn't about and kissed Seth gently. "Now catch them."

*　　　*　　　*

"We wanted a dog to get some puppies, not three. Not only that but the bloody Doberman is nasty. He snarled and lunged at Robert and Suzie as well as Emmy." Harold scowled. "For now anyone with dark skin is keeping clear."

"He's been trained that way by some racist shit. I'll bet I can retrain him."

Casper shrugged. "I'm strong enough to handle him. You can't say the same about the girl club and that Mastiff."

"It's your arm if you try to stick a lead on when Lucky finally spurns his advances, though at least he's already got a collar. The other two took to collars all right and I'm baffled about that." Harold shook his head. "All hell will break loose when Daisy finds out there's three more dogs."

"Cripes."

"Exactly. I'm going to check on the girl club and then Emmy and Sooty. Sooty? I'm already cringing about whatever the others get named." Harold's dog experience was singular. The thought of three feral dogs rampaging through Orchard Close didn't do much for his peace of mind though Harold needn't have worried about the girl club.

"What do you think to the new doorbell?" Liz opened the door wider. "It's all right, her tail's wagging."

"The noise alone nearly gave me a heart attack. Are you sure she's not just pleased to see a snack?" Harold looked past Liz to check and yes, the dog had a really waggy tail, and a big yellow ribbon around her neck. "Is that her new name, 'doorbell'? Is it safe to have her wandering loose like that?"

"Calm down wimp. She's a softy though somebody taught her to woof at a doorbell or a knock on the door." Since Umeko and Patty were both making a fuss of the big dog Harold came inside. Liz sniggered. "I'll put doorbell in the hat for a name."

"I still don't understand why you aren't worried. She's a big feral dog." Harold looked around at the smiling faces. "How come none of you are worried about that?"

"She's not feral. She's a lost and lonely girl who was probably very well loved and probably spoiled. Then five or six months ago her world was turned upside down and she lost everyone she loved." June's voice became softer and all the smiles in the room had gone. "She found some friends to help her cope, and they brought her to a safe place, and now she's loved again." A tear tricked down June's cheek.

"Lucky dog." Umeko bent over the dog with her face hidden.

Patty looked at Umeko, grief etched on her face. "Amen to that."

There was a brief silence before Liz spoke up. "She belongs here anyway, because she's managed something none of us ever could." She nudged Harold in the ribs, gently. "Our new girl tempted Soldier Boy inside the girl club." A few little smiles re-appeared, then more.

"Clever girl. Obviously a natural." Gayle turned away to rub her face but was smiling as she turned back. "Though too late since he's been nobbled."

Patty sniggered. "Nobbled, hobbled, trussed and oven-ready."

Harold did his bit to lift the mood. "Don't tell me all the girl club like being slobbered over? Haven't any of you got any taste or class?"

"Depends who is slobbering."

"A bloke is talking about classy?"

"We're training her to fetch, preferably men."

Harold shook his head. "I'm getting out of here while my innocence is intact."

"It is? I'll speak to Holly." Liz walked back to the door with him. "Some aren't so keen on a big dog so we're re-shuffling a bit, and next door will be full of cat-lovers and cats."

"Cripes. The cats. There's half a dozen now and what about feeding three extra dogs?" Harold shook his head. "As usual it all seemed so simple."

"The cats have all survived the same six months out there with the dogs, and are in here for the same reason that the dog is so happy. They are survivors but remember living with people, and fuss, and warm houses. We sometimes forget its only six months since everything really went to hell, less for some." Liz sighed. "Now give me one of those hugs and I'll promise not to tell Holly."

Harold hugged her. "I'll confess anyway."

"Good, I was going to brag." Liz pushed him away. "Go and grovel to your wench, wimp, and stop worrying. There's half a freezer full of rat for feeding dogs left over from winter and those with dogs will put out extra traps. We aren't going to be short of rats any time soon."

"Cripes no." Harold wandered down to see Emmy and Curtis and found Sooty enthusiastically giving paws for bits of something.

Emmy waved a tiny morsel. "We keep calling them dog chews and look, they are."

"They're supposed to be food, person food." Harold knew he'd lost the argument when Curtis came in with another dried strip and scissors. Sooty whined and put a paw on Emmy's knee because she was still holding the treat.

"Our person food, which I'm sharing with a guest. Aren't I, Sooty? Paw, Sooty." Either the black hairy doormat had already worked out his new name or the treat didn't need any more explanation, since a big paw obediently landed in Emmy's outstretched hand and his tail thumped on the floor. "Patty might want to knit something with this." A wad of black fur sat next to a wire brush.

"Don't blame me if you get torn limb from limb at full moon, or he steals your dinner and muddies your bed. Just remember that Daisy is off-limits and you clean up after, oh god shoot me now, Sooty." Despite his words Harold couldn't help grinning by the end.

"Yes, Sir! We'll walk him outside the walls." Emmy scratched behind a furry ear. "We'll see if he can learn to bark at lurkers."

"Luck with that. More luck than we had with Lucky. Now I'm going to warn Sharyn and Hazel and we'll make Daisy plans."

"Cripes. Luck with that."

*   *   *

"They didn't leave." Seth looked defensive and Berry lurked in the background looking worried. "The other three didn't leave either?"

"No because the girl club and Emmy kidnapped two of them. Then Casper stuck a chain on Fury when he'd finished having his wicked way and would have cried if I said no." Harold looked at what was either a very fat or a pregnant Staffordshire Bull Terrier, and a mongrel with some of the same blood, and they looked hopefully back at him. "Exactly how did they end up not leaving and in here?"

"A good few of the dogs that turned up were either frightened or snarled at people, but not these two. The rest left once Lucky stopped being interesting, and this pair didn't." Seth gave an embarrassed shrug. "We could do with a couple of good ratters?"

"For the giant rats?" Harold could already see another losing battle since both dogs were wearing a piece of rope tied round their necks as a collar.

Berry hadn't been able to stay out of it, and came over to administer a gentle Berrying to Seth's head. "Will you be more careful with the 'we' stuff?" She grinned at Harold. "I'll cry if we can't keep them? That one is fixed, the boy, and Patricia says there are oodles of dog contraceptive injections anyway."

Harold looked at the two humans and the two dogs and shook his head. "The same rules as Casper; you feed them and keep them penned or on a lead until we see how they react to others. Now you explain to Nigel that you're starting a family." The looks on their faces kept the smile on Harold's face right up to his front door. "Daisy. Oh cripes."

Three days of sulks, tantrums and general mayhem later Daisy accepted that as a little girl she had to start with a puppy. Though even then it took an archery lesson with Aunty-Holly to seal the bargain. Once she was old enough, both Harold and Sharyn wanted Daisy negotiating any trades for Orchard Close.

*   *   *

The smirking at Hot Rods lasted almost three weeks. "She shot me!" The man sat on the floor with a bloody bandage round his thigh pointed at Patty. "She can't do that!"

"I didn't use a special so he'll keep his leg." Patty didn't sound the slightest bit repentant and had a special loaded to cover the man's two friends.

"Keep that tight or you'll bleed out." Lenny's voice sounded mild and neutral but the man looked down at his leg, startled, and twisted the knife and sheath to tighten his bandage.

"All right, what did he do?"

"Grabbed Gayle's ass and when she told him to quit, said it was worth the fine." Patty curled her lip in a sneer. "I told him to quit and he said else what. So I showed him." She shrugged. "I could have aimed higher?"

"He's got three layers of jeans on when I cut them open to plug the holes." Lenny shrugged. "Maybe he thought that would stop the canes." Lenny might be a pacifist but didn't seem exactly neutral.

Harold looked down at the man. "Surely you knew we'd strip you and cane you at least?"

One of the man's friends spoke up. "When you carved up the Geek, Cadillac said he would sort it out so we didn't get cut like that. You can't strip Hot Rods."

"Did Cadillac tell you the result of that talk?" Harold watched the realisation dawn on their faces. "Patty, round up anyone wanting to exercise their arm." He smiled. "On the bright side he won't be up to carting bricks for a few weeks." Cadillac had insisted even his fighters joined in tearing down every house within half a mile of the Mansion, and building the wall thicker and higher. His fighters complained bitterly while safely out of Cadillac's hearing.

"I want first cut." Gayle glared. "Oh, sorry, first caning because we can't cut."

"F... Jesus, you can't make run him on one leg. They'll kill him." That was the other friend and he put a hand on his knife.

Harold waved his stick. "Pull that and I'll spank you, with this. Cadillac definitely agreed with that." Cadillac really had agreed after one of his men came back with a broken wrist and no knife. In fact Cadillac pointed out he'd have killed the stupid prat. The Hot Rods had been pushing a bit since the shooting, but only a bit so Harold didn't think Cadillac had sanctioned the harassment. Still, the man had a point about his wounded friend, a hundred paces on one leg and he might collapse. Collapsing before the gate might be fatal because some women would try skinning him with the canes. "He's still got one leg so half the distance." Three mouths opened to argue, looked at how many unhappy people wielding weapons had now gathered, and kept quiet.

"Do I get to have a go, Harold?"

"Of course luv." Holly had brought her cane.

A man behind Harold managed to speak through his laughter. "Ooh, people used to pay for that, a blonde with a cane." Harold smiled quietly because the sheer enjoyment visitors from other gangs got from these canings made up a good part of the punishment. None of the three since the first caning had ended up as badly injured as the first. Someone from the GOFS had pointed out that if the first one had run instead of hopping about screaming he'd have been done quicker. The next three yelled but kept running. Harold smiled more as he saw how many women were coming with canes and who some of them were; the therapy was working. Elizabeth, the late Willtoo's mum, startled him. She gave a wry smile and gestured with her cane. "I worked out the Hot Rods cost me my boy, not anyone in here, so they owe me blood."

"Hey, Harold, did you give him the option?" Patty waved her crossbow. "Five minutes as a moving target so we can practice?"

"Not a chance." The wounded man started stripping to his boxers. "I don't have to be a target, do I?"

"No, and good choice." Patty practiced on rabbits and rats and would definitely have nailed a man in well under five minutes. "Come on, everyone's ready." His friends carried the man to the start line, saving his leg for the run. Harold checked everyone had a cane. "Go."

Walking back home with Holly after the man left in the back of his friend's car, Harold sniggered. "I was impressed. He moved at a hell of a speed on one and a bit legs."

"He got nearly the same number of strikes but only a few had room to really swing. How many more will it take, Harold?" Holly sighed. "We could move up to target practice?"

"You heard me. I told him that was the penalty for a second offence." Harold glanced at the cane Holly still carried. "I reckon this time should do it. The Geeks have quit harassing women and the GOFS never were as bad, and now the Hot Rods will get the message. If we didn't need the business I'd stop them all coming but the coupons mean we can buy extra food. On a lighter note, how are the expectant mothers doing?"

"Barley should be a few more weeks but that's a guess. Lucky will be brewing or cooking for another two months at least. Forget all that because tonight we have a treat. Real lettuces, not just baby leaves. Radishes, spinach and spring onions!" Holly punched the air. "Salad!"

"No meat? Anyway they're not real lettuce, more like a handful of dandelion leaves." Harold protested automatically since he had a reputation as a carnivore to protect.

"Curtis says we have to get used to leafy types because the old iceberg lettuce is extinct. He can't grow them, but on the plus side there will soon be new potatoes." Holly pulled a face. "We can't have many because we need big fat potatoes, and Curtis is prepared to defend his baby beets with his life and Sooty. Every tiny bite size beet now is a pot of soup size beet if we let it grow up, or so he says and Emmy is backing him up. Traitor. Traitoress."

"Potatoes? Seth will be happy."

"No chips yet, or only the frozen ones. Seth filled whole freezers with them and burgers, which turned out to be a good idea. Look on the bright side, you won't be eating rhubarb for a day or two." Rhubarb plants had shown up here and there after winter and were carefully transplanted and tended as a source of vitamins. Everyone ate rhubarb despite the shortage of sugar because 'rhubarb is good for you' and if adults said no, the children wouldn't eat theirs.

"I'm surprised we're eating any veg at all so soon, because Curtis has still got us planting his seedlings and seeds."

Holly turned towards Harold. "Stop sulking. Come on, I want to dance. Then you can walk me home."

"In broad daylight? I never realised lettuce had that effect." Harold grinned.

Holly laughed. "You haven't heard about rabbits? That's all lettuce powered."

"I'll be out at dawn, planting more." Harold collected his kiss for dancing her home and opened the door.

"Stinky water, stinky water."

"Stop her." Harold snagged Daisy as she made a break for it and then sniffed.

"Whew."

"Stinky water. Curtis says it makes things grow but mummy wants to wash it off." Daisy didn't sound even a little bit repentant.

A harassed looking Sharyn came through. "Good. I was putting Wills in the playpen so I could catch this tyke and dunk her. While you've got a good grip there's a tub full of hot water up there so dump her in, complete with her clothes to get the worst off."

"How did that happen?" Holly smiled but kept well clear.

"Curtis told her his barrels of compost water, the ones with all the rotten leaves and stuff in, made things grow. Next thing Daisy is holding the watering can over her head. She wants to be big enough for a crossbow." Sharyn started upstairs after Harold and Daisy. "Though he did leave a heap of salad stuff as compensation."

"Since I didn't get splashed, that's a bargain." Holly and Hazel hi-fived.

Chapter 9:

Ferdinand, Roast Casper's Fury

"Do you think that'll get past the check?" Harold frowned at the pack, his Bergen but shortened a little and with a metal frame inside.

"They'll need a spanner to work out what we've done, and even then you can plead it's only a frame. It's allegedly there to help the pack with all the rough treatment it's getting." Liz and Rob both watched anxiously as Harold inspected the supposed frame.

"They'll find a spanner if I carry one." Though Harold had to admit the frame looked innocent enough, just steel tube with pipe fittings holding it together.

"Watch and learn." Rob unscrewed the cap on one of the front tubes by hand and turned the pack upside down. Two pieces of metal held together loosely at one end by a bolt through them slid out. "Swivel the two bits round edge to edge and you've got a spanner. The back two side supports and this front one are solid rods, not tube, but screwed together tightly. That gives any shoppers three three-foot iron bars for self-defence."

"You need them and if this works we'll fit shorter ones in some of the other packs. You called the shopping off because of how many armed gangsters were there last time, and cut it short the time before. We need groceries, Harold." Liz sighed. "You only take big men but even so you're all unarmed and someone will get badly hurt sooner or later."

Harold swivelled the bits of metal round and yes, the oddly shaped ends turned into the jaws of a spanner. "I called the shopping off last time because there were new computer games on sale and every nutter in town brought a machete and a bad attitude. Though I will try this next time, thanks." He grinned. "Iron bars are actually better than a baseball bat and scarier as well."

"No, Jeremy will try it." Holly, Liz, Rob and Casper all agreed.

"I ought to do it. I can't risk someone else." Harold simply wouldn't order anyone to take that chance even if the idea looked sound.

"No need. Jeremy has been bringing flowers back from scavenging, for Matti, and he's volunteered." Patty clasped her hands and rolled her eyes upwards. "To show the fair maid what a big strong macho bloke he is. He's in lurve."

"His brain is still jelly since Matti kissed him after you killed Jon." Holly grinned. "Worse, Matti is encouraging him, but just a little bit."

"She didn't ask him, did she, because that's taking unfair advantage. Sort of like playing cards with a drunk."

"Oh no, but she's mentioned privately that she might reward him. Something to do with ruffled and breathless." Liz tried very hard not to burst out laughing and more or less made it.

"Cripes. Is Doll competing?"

"No Harold, or his brain really would be jelly. Doll said she had the stopwatch. From that grin you understand the code." Casper wagged a finger. "Give. I hate not knowing."

"My lips are sealed."

"No they aren't." Holly smirked. "I'll tell you all later."

*   *   *

Shopping with an iron bar definitely felt more restful. Harold headed for the spices and stopped in his tracks. "Tessa?" Harold really wasn't sure. Firstly because he hadn't seen Tessa in years except as a succession of photos in Stone's wallet. Her appearance confused him as well because Tessa had always dressed to kill, in the nicest way. Or at least dressed to stun a seventeen-year old Harold. Now Tessa wore no makeup, a shapeless jacket and a long loose skirt with trainers.

"Harry? It is! What are you doing in this shit-hole? I thought you were in the Army?" Tessa glanced nervously around. "Watch out, we've got a minder and we're not allowed to talk to others."

"What gang?"

"Hot Rods. Christ, Harry, are you in a gang? You must be." Tessa curled a lip as she took in the iron bar and two muscular men behind Harold with similar weapons.

"Orchard Close. We're a bit different."

"I've heard of them." Tessa smiled which made her look a lot more like Harold remembered. "I'm pleased, but why are you here at all and not the other side of the bypass with a bloody great rifle?"

"I came to get Sharyn out and we didn't make it." Harold glanced back.

"That lot loading up at the end are with me. These two ruffians are Casper and Alfie and one's too young and the other too gay to be the sort of gangster you normally deal with."

"Probably not too young going by some of the animals we see." Tessa smiled at Casper. "Are you really gay or is Harry winding me up?"

"We call him Harold now, and yes, I'm the Orchard Fairy. Do you have any lumberjacks where you live?"

"Sod off. You're as bad as him, though he's lost the pimples and blush now. Ooh look, no he hasn't." Tessa raised her voice just a bit. "Pete, bring Eddy will you?" She turned back to Harold. "You remember Pete, my little brother? Eddy is Edward, you know about him."

"Cripes yes, Stones only mentioned little Ed about fifty thousand times. How old is he now?" A sour-faced youth with a small boy in tow came around from the next aisle, carrying half a dozen carrier bags.

"Cripes?" Tessa sniggered. "Eddy is nearly four. Eddy, this is Uncle Harry, or would have been if you'd ever seen him."

"Oy you." Harold turned and the Hot Rod stopped. "Oh, it's you. I thought you were all fixed up with that blonde piece." He grinned. "I've seen your women so why are you trying to poach another?"

"I'm not. I'm supposed to be looking for spices so I asked this woman for advice." Harold nodded to Tessa. "Thanks." He took a half dozen packets and hoped someone would use them. Harold knew that Cadillac would love having a friend of Soldier Boy's under his thumb, and that it wouldn't be good for Tessa.

"Where's your fancy stick?" The Hot Rod eyed up the iron bars.

"That's for official spankings." Harold hefted the bar. "This is for smacking cheeky oiks." Harold moved away, looking at other shelves as if totally disinterested in the woman behind him.

"Fair enough, though I prefer a blade." The youth turned to Tessa and Pete. "Come on, haven't you done yet?"

Once around the end of the aisle Harold heaved a sigh of relief. Until the guard turned up he'd relaxed, not even thinking of the consequences for Tessa if Cadillac or even Cooper realised who she knew. "Who was that? She made you blush, just a little bit." Casper grinned. "Ooh, gossip. Wait until I tell Holly." Behind Casper, half a dozen men including Jeremy and Tim smiled and leaned forward to hear.

"You can tell Holly. Tessa is, was, the girlfriend of a mate of mine and I was an impressionable youth." Harold told the pair about knowing Stones and Tessa, and why he didn't want Cadillac realising. "Now we'd better get on with shopping."

"Cripes yes, because staggering home will take a while." Alfie looked at his list. "These veg will weigh a ton. Oh, er, can we go round by the ribbons and lace and stuff like that?"

Harold watched a pink tinge spread over Alfie's face. "Ribbons and lace?"

"A private request so you don't know so don't look, all right?"

Casper laughed. "She should have asked me. Harold wouldn't have been surprised if I bought lace." His lip curled. "Though the selection here is a bit vanilla, cheap scratchy nylon stuff that costs a fortune. It's a good job I'm butch."

"I would have thought the scavengers found enough frills to keep them going. Don't worry Alfie, I'm no longer interested in what other women are wearing under their jeans or skirts." Harold endured some good-natured ribbing from all the rest about being hen-pecked and how Holly might be keeping his interest fixed on only one woman.

Though there wasn't much teasing or even talking on the way back, because they all needed their breath for carrying the packs. Missing two trips meant this shopping list leaned heavily towards bulk goods such as potatoes and all nine men were heavily loaded. Once home Harold did tell Sharyn he'd met Tessa, and endured her teasing as she told Holly about seventeen-year old crushes while Harold denied any such thing. Holly pointed out later that since Tessa wasn't in Harold's memento box she wasn't worried, but there might be questions if Harold bumped into the garter woman.

*　　　*　　　*

"Cripes Cadillac. Have you raided an armoury?" Harold looked closer. "Or maybe a scrapyard. Some of those look really rough." Harold pointed to a small calibre rifle with a crushed barrel. "I can't mend that for starters."

"Now we're all informal you might as well call me Caddi." Cadillac pointed at Harold's machete. "I've spoken to the GOFS and Geeks, and that's agreed with bosses now." He curled a lip. "Senior manager if you're a Geek. They really are a bunch of twats, though nasty twats who make a really mean looking crossbow. My lot were impressed and I've bought a couple."

"I swapped that bow, the one with all the wires and pulleys, for another crossbow. That Tell reckons he can use it and none of mine can." Harold grinned. "Alfie loves the crossbow though." He glanced down at his machete. "Can I bring my stick in the future?"

"Instead of a machete? Yeah, why not. Now, you've been eyeing up this lot while we were nattering so what can you fix? I'll want credit for the buggered up rifle as spares." Caddi pointed at one of the revolvers. "We can't even get the cylinder out of that and the bloke used it as a club."

"I can tell. These really are a lot rougher than your usual offering and that rifle is worth sod all even as spares. It's not a common calibre."

"I get it, the repairs will be more expensive. Just to put your mind at rest we're having a little disagreement with the neighbours." Caddi bared his teeth. "We're adjusting the border a little bit and these were left behind by the Ferdinands after our first disagreement."

"Who?" Harold liked to get news about other gangs, if only as prior warning if any turned up.

"The Ferdinands. They're based in a sports stadium and wear those American football helmets and shoulder pads. I reckon they've watched too many Mad Max movies though they've got a hell of a lot of aluminium baseball bats." Caddi hunched himself forward. "Now stop dicking about. What can you fix and what will it cost in my hard-earned coupons and powder?" Caddi held up a hand. "I know, propellant."

"Not quite yet, because if you want a good deal I have to be in a good mood, not frustrated by half-answers. Mad Max? The desert thing with idiots racing about on motorbikes and in beach buggies?" Caddi nodded and Harold frowned. "How come we haven't seen that, motorbikes? They're in every disaster movie, like feral dog packs." Harold paused. "You've got a couple of motorbikes out there."

Caddi laughed. "The Ferdinands did that, came hammering in on dirt bikes, and there's two reasons we don't use the bloody things. First, with all the fucking regulations and the insurance, not so many city lads learned to ride one recently." Caddi waved a hand at the desk. "The second is what happens when something hits the bike or the rider and why we collected these. They part company and then the bloke hits the road, a wall, a car, and definitely not a soft sand dune. We use the bikes for fast messengers and patrolling the bits the cars can't get to, because we've got a couple of suicidal idiots to ride them. We started that when someone mentioned strangers on bicycles." Harold ignored Caddi's long look and he hunched forward again. "I could bring in the dancing girls if you're still frustrated? Or we could sort these out?"

"I can concentrate on these now, thanks." Because Caddi would bring real dancing girls.

On the way home Harold smiled quietly to himself because for half a mile around the Mansion there were barely two bricks on top of another. Just under half a mile away the blunt concrete silhouette of a fifteen story block of flats had finally defeated Caddi's paranoia. Part of the smile was relief, because if the Hot Rods were at war on their other frontier they'd be too busy for mischief elsewhere.

Harold glanced in the rear view mirror. Caddi had sent an escort to keep his nine firearms safe on the journey since, as he put it, Soldier Boy swanned about on his own and someone might be tempted. The SUV directly behind Harold, the first of three cars and three motorbikes, had the front grill off a Rolls Royce bolted to the front complete with the winged lady. The driver, introduced as Rolls Royce, seemed to be polite and urbane but Harold knew that if the bloke wore overalls he had to be a nasty sod. Chevy, the muscular man Harold had first seen slapping gangsters about, subscribed to the Cooper school of blatant nastiness.

*   *   *

"We've got puppies!" Holly hooked an arm in Harold's and swung him around. "Barley has had a crop. Five waggy tails."

"Five? How many will Lucky have?" Harold had visions of spending his life hunting rats to feed dogs.

"Up to eight." Holly's big smile faltered. "Cripes, that's nineteen dogs altogether. How did that happen?"

"This woman said she wanted a puppy and in a moment of weakness I said yes. Then her cohorts kidnapped job lots of dogs and threatened to cry if I let them go." Harold laughed. "Oh gods we've done it again. I hope you enjoy skinning rats."

"We could bring them up uncivilised? The five new adults don't insist on skinned." Holly tugged Harold's hand. "Come on grumpy. Come and see the wrigglies."

Harold found several people peeking through a door and looked as well. "Those aren't wriggling."

"They've been busy at the milk bar and now mummy needs rest and babies need to sleep. Shoo, everyone." Seth waved a threatening hand. "Or else. Oh, Harold. Who wants a puppy?"

"Not yet Seth. You're the babysitter until they're at least six weeks according to the books. How did the birth go?"

"Kinda gross. There again Barley and Malt eat raw rat so I guess maybe not that gross." Seth sighed. "Berry will need a little while because there were six and one just never made it. Can she burn the body and all that?"

"Spread the ashes? Probably best just on the edge because that sergeant up there won't allow us on the exclusion zone with puppy ashes. He damn near didn't let us spread Sandy's." Harold glanced through to where the pups were. "Are you OK with all this? You might lose more because we haven't got a vet or proper food."

"Yes thanks." Seth smiled, just a little one. "There are benefits."

"Just don't let Nigel find you playing happy families." Harold raised a finger as Seth started to protest. "With puppies. What on earth did you think I meant?" He grinned as Seth spluttered.

"Do I get a puppy, Harold?"

"Probably, Holly. You'd better decide if you want a Lucky sized one or a Barley sized one, though Barley size might be a bit of a lottery. These are all very different sizes and one is definitely fluffy." Harold grinned. "Decide now and prepare your arguments because Daisy will want one of each and then the fluffy version as well."

"Cripes yes. I'd like a bigger one, but can I fend off Daisy long enough? I need the doggy books."

"Why?"

Holly smirked. "To check dates because if Lucky will be producing before Barley's lot wean, then it'll be easier. Now we'd better go and see how Casper is settling in."

"Yes, he's really taken to Fury." Harold shook his head. "I never thought the daft lump would move out of the girl club."

"It's the only way to get Fury calmed down and properly socialised according to Casper. He, Fury I mean, needs a home environment which includes sleeping in a house." Holly scowled. "Fury can't do that in the girl club. He goes for anyone with a dark skin, even Umeko and hers is only sort of olive. That name doesn't fill me with confidence."

"Tyson Fury was a world heavyweight boxing champion."

"I know, you said, but when the dog sees Emmy or Suzie or, well, you know." Holly smiled and hugged Harold's arm. "But Thandia is a real love."

"That big slobbery lump is called Thandia? That's different." Very, Harold couldn't place the word at all.

"She's called that because of what June said, about finding a safe place. Umeko came up with the name because it means just that, though her version had more accents and a hesitation. We anglicised it." Holly giggled. "A name like that should be a relief after Sooty."

"Patty reckons she can get a scarf out of black hair if someone can work out how to spin the brushing debris into yarn. Cripes, that's a hell of a door-bell." Harold took a step back before the door opened.

"Come in Holly, and you, Harold. Fury was just saying hi." Casper grinned.

"He was threatening to pull off my head."

"Wimp. Look, he's wagging his stump." Casper pointed and yes, Fury's stump was going side to side though that might be for Casper.

"Cripes, who the hell will look at that end, especially with his tail cut off?" Harold relaxed because the Doberman really did like fair-skinned peo-ple, or at least tolerated them. "You should stand in the doorway with him when we have visitors."

"That's why I've moved here, into the back of number two. Since it's the guardhouse Fury can earn his keep. I can teach him about scroats who are pale, and nice people who are dark." Casper smirked. "You watch, I'll teach him the difference between locals and visitors in no time. Come through and look out the kitchen window." Fury took a look at the visitors, then followed Casper.

"If you ever get it finished it'll hold an elephant, let alone a dog." A line of posts made of old roof beams went up the garden and the nearest had mesh up to about nine feet.

"Better still, if someone nips over the wall behind the guardhouse they'll land right in Fury's pen. Breakfast in bed." Casper opened the kitchen door. "This will let him inside to keep me company." Since the dog laid on the settee next to Casper while the humans talked for a while, that part seemed already settled.

Ten minutes later Harold gave Fury a treat as instructed and left with Holly. "Can he do it, get rid of all that training?"

"Maybe." Harold looked back. "Even if he can't, Casper seems to have fi-nally found a friend. Maybe he can teach Fury to track lumberjacks." Harold smiled. "He's big enough for a dogcart to shift bricks."

*　　*　　*

Two days later the corpse could have pulled a dogcart even if it wasn't a dog. Harold inspected the victim. "Is that a giant rabbit or a really giant rabbit?"

"Stop it. That's a deer." Patty patted her crossbow. "Though I was practic-ing on rats when it ran out between those houses, stopped, and stared at me."

"Maybe it's a good job you were practicing. A Liz special would have only left the skin. Is it a baby one?"

"No, that's a full-grown Muntjac. I saw one in a wildlife park once and thought it was a baby." Patty looked over her prize. "Barbecue!"

"Not a chance, Liz will fight you over charcoal or gas. Maybe a roast but split eighty two ways it'll be a really small slice." Harold looked round. "Do they come in herds?"

"Just a moment." Patty looked around and shrugged. "Sorry, Bear Grylls isn't here at the moment and there aren't enough of us for a séance to talk to David Attenborough. Can I get back to you on that?"

"I'll get my people to talk to your people." Harold bent over the deer. "I suppose you'll expect me to cart this home?"

"If you want your main squeeze to get her slice, yes."

"My what?"

"Well she is a bit past girlfriend, but not married. Though Holly might qualify as a mistress with that cane." Patty smirked. "Emmy is whatevered so main squeeze is an improvement. Unless Holly fancies wench though half the women in the city get called that?" She looked Harold up and down. "You could be her trophy, hunk, prize sucker, lummock or main man?"

"I am not going to be stupid enough to make any comment. Not without some input from my main squeeze mistress whatever." Harold heaved up. "I hope all the weight is meat."

A little later Harold found himself the target of a half circle of determined men and women. "That is not going into stew. That's real meat. Have you any idea how long it is since we chowed down on a hunk of real meat?"

"I know exactly, Bernie. My carnivore soul keeps track." Harold shrugged. "I'm told there isn't enough for everyone to have roast, and that stew is the most efficient way to convert a deer into calories."

"Not a chance or I'll build a bonfire out there and spit roast the next one, then eat all the evidence." Patty tapped her crossbow. "There will be a next."

"Amen to that, sister, though next time can you find a full-grown one?" Liz backed away, hands raised as Patty rounded on her. "Hey, no violence or I'll stop supplying points."

"We can have a lottery?"

"If so, Fury doesn't get a ticket, Casper." Several people grinned as Matthew spoke up because Casper did share his stew.

"Neither does Sooty, or any other cat or dog." Harold smiled at Patty. "Patty gets a slice as the mighty hunter, we raffle the bits that can be sliced, and the rest goes in stew."

"We've got new potatoes to go with either." Curtis held up a hand against the hopeful stares. "Just once, because we need the veg to grow big."

"Roast venison and new potatoes." Patty looked skywards. "Take me now Lord, cos it won't get better than this." The group switched from arguing over the deer to working out who actually went in the draw because some were leaf-lovers, and the children wouldn't appreciate it properly. At one stage men were going to be banned as well since they had no taste and could make do with roast spam. By the time a final agreement had been reached on the size of slices, the deer was almost cooked.

*   *   *

"They're not the same without butter." Holly poked at her new potato. "This is all wrong. I've been dreaming of new potatoes and now there's no butter."

"I don't dream now." Harold saw Sharyn's sharp look and smiled. "I sleep peacefully, honest sis."

"Me too. An alien killing machine at the end of the road is reassuring. Actually in the bed is even better because I finally feel safe and there's side benefits. Ah, right, butter. No butter." Holly blushed and then poked her new potato into the gravy. "This is all wrong."

"You're the lucky one since you've got meat with yours. Considering who is in charge, that has to be a fix." Sharyn looked at the half slice of meat on Holly's plate. "Though to be fair you gave us all a small piece."

"No fix." Harold smiled. "We might get more soon since all the real meat fanatics are going to be scouring the place for another, or a big brother. Now eat your stew because it's good for you." Harold glanced meaningfully at an oblivious Daisy, happily stuffing herself with the potato and stew and a selection of salad, because she still wanted to grow faster for archery.

"Oh yes, stew. So meaty, so delicious, so nourishing. We should have it again soon especially now we have spinach." Hazel grinned and carefully coated her bit of new potato with stew. "Can't we make butter from milk?"

"No because the milk from the mart is, according to Liz, double-skimmed. That means all the goodness removed twice until it's basically white water, and is why the cream cheese experiment didn't work out very well." Harold gestured towards the kitchen. "There's cheese in there. That's just hard butter?"

"There are two sorts of cheese from the mart. Hard, as in rock hard, and rubbery. Neither have taste unless they are grated into something else or toasted on bread, and then I'm not sure the taste is how I remember cheese." Sharyn sighed. "So new potatoes with stew it is. Oh yummy, how good for me."

"Tomorrow you can have gooseberry in one of several ways instead of rhubarb."

Sharyn looked upwards. "My cup runneth over."

Holly sniggered. "The toilets might."

*   *   *

"Cripes Holly, are you sure?"

"Don't you like my knees showing? It's not exactly short, or a dance frock." Holly looked at her skirt and did a little twirl. "I wore it for you, Harold."

"Oh, definitely on the short side and I really appreciate the result but we're meeting gangsters. Are you sure?" Harold hesitated, torn because Holly looked lovely in a light blue pleated skirt and flowered blouse, and dead right for a summer day. Except that the visitors wouldn't think that way. "They'll think, well, you know."

"I'm your main squeeze Harold, and you're my toy soldier, so I can dress to set your clockwork running if I want to." Holly sniggered. "Though I won't actually say that to those philistines. The scroats won't say a word about my skirt because I'm taking my cane, just as a hint. Suzie and Doll have gone above-knee as well, because summer is here." Her face became very serious. "We talked about this, and we refuse to live in permanent fear of some nasty little toad getting out of hand. If they can't control themselves over a bit of knee, then its spanking time. They won't do it three times." That referred to all those being caned now also being told they were crossbow targets next time.

"What about Matti?"

"Any above knee there just might involve Jeremy and her needing a garter. Doll reckons she needs a calendar now instead of a stopwatch. Barry and Finn have moved in next door to Alicia, Louise and Celine, so both sisters moved into the girl club and it's open season on unsuspecting males." Holly hooked her arm through Harold's. "Come on, let's see who this is. GOFS isn't exactly precise."

Walking to the gate from his gunroom, where Holly had found him, Harold could see that a good few of the women were dressed in summer clothes. The bright colours, and the smiles that came with them, did lift his spirits and everyone seemed cheerful. Out in among the crops some of the men weeding or watering were wearing shorts and a couple had their shirts off. "No chance."

Holly pouted and stopped eyeing Harold's jeans. "Just across here. Snip,

snip?"

"Behave, we're nearly there. That's not a GOFS." Harold's attention fixed firmly on the gate now. "Not unless she's a missus GOFS?"

"That's a Barbie Girl from her wig. Caddi said you should shoot her through the head from a long way away." Holly sniggered. "You'd see her all right."

"Yeah, a blonde wig looks a bit incongruous though there was a black singer once who was blonde." Harold frowned. "That's Ogou with her, I thought the Barbie Girls didn't play nice with neighbours?"

"I wonder what she said to Alfie because I haven't seen him blush like that since, er, since the shooting party." Holly inspected the Barbie as they came closer. "You shouldn't worry about my hem length, lover-boy." The woman had turned and her almost knee-length dress had been laced together up the sides by criss-crossed ribbons, with a wide gap.

"That's different. Not a look Umeko or Suzie will be copying."

"Maybe Suzie if there's another competition. Is it supposed to be oriental?" Holly giggled. "That looks more like two silky curtains, one in front and one at the back, lashed together down the side."

"The woman looks Asian so maybe she's supposed to be from a film dressed like that, or a musical? Though for a musical that dress needs a dragon on the front and some Hollywood oriental music." Harold straightened his face and raised his voice. "Hi Ogou. Is this your new girlfriend?"

"I'm no man's anything." The woman looked Holly over, especially her legs. "I thought your lot treated women different?"

"Hey, back off. It took us ages to sort out the scroats so I could wear a short skirt again." Holly glanced down. "Bloody marvellous, the first time I show my knees and it's a woman who gives me a hard time."

"Harold, we've got a problem with the rules." Alfie still blushed furiously. "Chandra has some questions."

"Then we'd better go into the embassy building and talk. Did you, did anyone?" Harold floundered because visitors should be searched and the woman had a huge smile. She turned round the other way and lifted her arm to show lacing and skin up the other side. Harold shook his head. "Forget it."

Though Chandra lost her smile as they crossed the gap from the guardhouse. Both Ogou and her flinched away as Fury hit the mesh, snarling and barking. "Hey, Fury, what did I tell you?" Casper came up behind the dog and took hold of his collar, then stared. "Ah, that's going to be difficult. He shouldn't bark at skin colour but should at visitors." He shrugged. "I'll refine it later."

"Where the hell did that come from?" Ogou stared after Casper and Fury. "And what the hell did he mean?"

"When the beer arrives. It'll take a beer." It did, and then came the introductions.

Harold frowned. "You really are a Barbie Girl? I thought you and GOFS had some sort of strife?"

Ogou shrugged and looked embarrassed, and Chandra smiled. "We sorted something out. Sort of armed neutrality. As part of the deal we wanted an escort for someone to look at your place, and check out the beer, and I won the draw." She shrugged. "I'm a bit puzzled by the rules."

"In what way?" Holly frowned, and looked at the dress. "What rule were you thinking of?"

"I can handle not swearing, with enough concentration. The thing is, what's the penalty if I grab a guy's ass, friendly-like?" Everyone but Ogou stared at Chandra, speechless. She sniggered and carried on. "Though I'd rather grab your wench."

"She's not my wench. She's my…" Harold floundered for a moment. "Significant other? Lover?"

"All official, I had to ask permission from his sister." Holly's serious look cracked into a laugh. "Well maybe I was a bit late with that part but we do live with his sister and nephew and niece." Two spots of colour appeared on Holly's cheeks. "Did you mean the bit about which ass, because Casper out there would rather grab a lumberjack if you find one."

"Let's get back to rules, rather than grabbing." Harold reran the highlights mentally. "You want to know the penalty if you abuse a man or woman without their permission?"

Chandra frowned. "That used to be called abuse, didn't it? How quickly we forget. I wanted to know because he was on about stripping and caning, and I don't mind, but can it be private and can I have a cane as well?" Chandra grinned and waved towards Alfie who blushed bright scarlet again.

"It's a windup Harold. Chandra has no intention of abusing men or women here." Patty moved her crossbow a little. "Though if she did, I'll bet she wouldn't laugh afterwards." She nodded towards Holly. "That cane isn't for Soldier Boy, and it leaves a stripe of blood."

Chandra eyed the crossbow and then Holly's cane for a moment before answering. "Fair enough. It's just that one or two of our lot might drift over now and then. Unofficially because we aren't allowed to cross GOFS territory." Ogou rolled his eyes. "What happens if they want a bit of voluntary fun with either a man or woman? After all, your lot are all fresh blood and ours will be willing."

"If its voluntary there's a house for overnight stays that visitors use, but that's rarely as couples." Harold shrugged. "Involuntary means abuse so stripping and caning. A second offence costs five minutes dodging crossbow bolts so our lot can learn to hit moving targets."

"Does that apply to your own lot?" Chandra's voice sharpened, and Ogou's interest sharpened as well.

"We had four who abused a woman. We killed them." Holly gestured with her cane. "No first, second or third chance."

Chandra leant back and relaxed. "Some of our lot will love your place. Oh, is there a penalty for tattoos?"

"Some of ours have tattoos. Why would they be a problem?" Harold glanced at the rest but they seemed puzzled as well.

Chandra smiled. "If they read the tattoos out loud they'd break your rules, but if they don't?"

That took an exchange of enquiring glances until Patty spoke up. "As long as they're covered up if there's a child about. Which is unlikely, but if it happens?" Harold nodded because the children were kept clear of the area the gangsters visited.

"Good enough. What do you do for music?"

"We share whatever is left on our music players and we've scrounged CDs and DVDs here and there." Harold scowled. "Occasionally we check the BBC again."

"Try going up the channels a bit. Barbie Radio, because Rock will never die!" Chandra punched the air on the last bit and grinned, and Ogou burst out laughing.

"The signal is strong enough so I reckon it'll reach you, and they actually say that on the air. We keep sending requests for a smooch hour or some Country and Western but no chance." Ogou sniggered. "If the BBC play a tune, Barbie Radio bans it."

Half an hour later, after a walk up and down the road, Chandra and Ogou left. Chandra bought six crates of beer and promised someone would bring the bottles back, and that before then she'd pass on the rules. For men or women, the last included a wink at Holly. Both Chandra and Ogou were interested in puppies, from Fury if possible but they'd settle for a Staffy cross.

"Cripes, how much of that was windup?"

"Quite a lot I reckon, but she was serious about Holly. Not about grabbing, but she looked at Holly with a lot more appreciation than at you or Alfie." Patty sighed. "Or me."

"Really? Maybe we should invite her for an overnight so you can put on a shorter skirt?" Harold already knew that drawing Patty for the walk home was classed as a blank by the young men, because they didn't get a kiss. Now he wondered if Patty preferred a woman walking her home.

"That's very kind Harold, but no." Patty smiled, a sad smile. "I like men, or did, but right now I'm a bit ambivalent. Not enough to be tempted to the other camp but I'd like to think I would be in with a chance if the moment arrived."

"I'll lend you the cane and skirt."

"Good thinking. Maybe a bit of black leather and boots?" Harold tuned out the banter as he tried to fit a different version of the Barbies into his mental picture of the surrounding gangs.

Caddi always maintained the women in wigs were maniacs. Chandra had been deliberately dressed to provoke the usual gangster and her gang members sounded a rough bunch, but not maniacs. She had definitely been armed to the teeth including a pistol under a jacket she'd left in the guardhouse. Obscene tattoos might mean prison or just some sort on initiation in this strange new world, especially with the odd blonde wig thing. That hadn't been an attempt to look blonde because Chandra's long dark hair had been clearly visible.

Footsteps behind disturbed Harold's musings. "Sorry about Fury. Now I don't know if he's accepting that he shouldn't bark at skin colour but can at strangers, or just reverted." Casper sounded really worried.

"It's only a matter of weeks, Casper. He might have been trained for years." Harold grinned. "It all worked out because those two want to buy one of his pups."

"You're going to sell Fury's children?"

"Calm down Casper. It isn't white slavery, or any other sort. We can't afford to feed nineteen dogs which is what Holly thinks we might end up with." Harold nudged him. "We were after one litter of puppies and then some soft sods decided to kidnap dogs wholesale."

"It wasn't kidnapping. Fury likes me." Casper glanced back. "He really does. I'd better get back or he'll be worried."

"I hope you train him to like lumberjacks."

"Cripes, yes." Casper set off back to his new home.

"He's really hooked by that dog." Harold watched Casper striding back to the gatehouse.

"We all need a little love."

"What?"

Patty waved towards the departing Casper. "Casper really is Mummy-Casper to the girl club, but he can't show real affection because he's our resident fairy. Some people would think it was weird. He can't pat a bloke on the back or be friendly without jokes or someone thinking it's more than that." Patty shrugged. "Casper can be as daft as he likes with that dog, and the bloody animal really does like him."

"Maybe it'll be good for him. I once offered to take him to that gang of gays." Harold smiled. "To kidnap one if he couldn't charm one. I feel guilty about bringing him out here really." He scowled at Patty. "Are you a psychiatrist or something?"

"No, just a late-comer so I see you all a bit different. There's the originals from here and those flats, and they're a solid group, bonded. The refugees who stood off the mob with you belong, and the rest are mainly just grateful." Patty nudged Harold. "Now you've got me at it. I'm one of the grateful ones, if you ever need a crossbow and a big knitting needle."

"Get off, he's spoken for." Holly grinned. "Especially tonight because I'm not tempted by the other camp and there's real lettuce for tea. Bunny food."

"Cripes." Patty paused. "Why does everyone say that? Is it an infection?"

*   *   *

"Six puppies? Well that's better than the top figure." Harold smiled. "Don't mention slavery to Casper but we'll have bids for some of these. Definitely for the two black ones with ginger markings because they'll look fiercer. All the gangs want either a Staffy or a Dobermann but I'm not selling to the Geeks."

"You are not selling Lucky's babies to that creep Caddi." Sal moved in front of Harold. "Not a chance. You do know the sick bastard has adopted the target practice idea, but not always as a punishment?"

"I know, though the one he made run about when I visited had actually offended in some way." Harold considered. "You're right. We won't sell pups to Caddi because he'll probably train them up like Fury has been trained. The Geeks really want some of Barley's and I know exactly why. The nasty sods were talking about dog fights and wanted a bitch to breed from."

"It'll take them ages to do that, set up dog fighting from one dog. Thank all and any gods." Sal scowled. "Now look what you've done, that's your saying. Cripes, we'll be speaking another language in a generation."

"Worse, you're wrong. They are already trapping strays to set up fights with the next gang the other way. The Geeks want a Staffy because they think it'll win and make them a lot of coupons." Harold scowled. "They want a bitch to breed more and sell them."

"Are the GOFS and Barbie Girls any better?" Sal looked over her shoulder at Lucky and her puppies. "We've got six to eight weeks to decide because you're right, we can't keep this lot. At least the cats seem to be feeding themselves now except the kittens, and they've taken to minced rat and mummy is catching mice. But not birds, thank all and any gods."

"Maybe there's not enough meat on a bird if they're hunting to eat? I'm pleased to see all the birds, because they seemed to disappear over winter." Harold smiled. "Except Curtis's Robin."

"We've got a couple of people who used to feed the birds. They reckon the birds all went out to the countryside, to the deserted fields, because the bird tables were all empty." Sal shrugged. "Now they've come back to pick over all those abandoned, overgrown gardens full of caterpillars and bugs."

"They've been back since March, some of them, but Curtis reckons they're eating more bugs this last two months. I really did get fed up with inspecting plants and trying to decide if a bug is beneficial or not. Then squishing the little swine." Harold pointed. "There's a Sparrowhawk nesting over there, I am reliably informed." Harold jumped as a voice sounded just behind him.

"More interesting still, there are all those pigeons trying to scoff Curtis's greenery. Liz has made me some long thin points with tiny spines on because the other heads turned pigeons into feathers and goo." Patty smirked. "After trying to hit pigeons, hitting some oik running about will be a doddle." Behind Patty another four hopefuls had crossbows with odd looking bolts.

"Not in the air, Patty, or someone will be doing a King Harold." Harold mimed pulling something from his eye.

"Wimp, though with your name I can see why you're nervous." Patty turned to the rest. "We've got to sneak up and get them on the ground so don't miss with the first one." The five of them set off through crops interspersed with flowers.

"Do all those flowers actually stop bugs, or is Curtis being influenced by Emmy?"

"Yes to both. Now go and collect bugs, knock down walls, plant even more food, or other Soldier Boy things. Anything but eye up innocent puppies with larcenous intent." Sal pushed him.

"Holly will be round to kidnap one soon enough, and she won't even pay. Daisy will come to help her choose. You have been warned." Harold went to do Soldier Boy things, which was a shame. Today was much too nice to be cooped up fixing guns but that's what paid the rent. Though first he wanted to see Liz.

"Hi, mouse."

"Hey, it's the wimp. I thought you were all canoodled up with that blonde hussy these days." Liz grinned. "At least I don't have to knock before coming into the forge."

"Blacksmith off." Harold parked himself on the end of the bench. "Patty said something odd about Casper and that dog, and now he's a bit protective over the pups. Is Casper okay?"

"He's as happy as a dog with two tails. Casper's got a friend." Liz smiled. "There, now you can desert me again."

"He's got a lot of friends." Harold frowned. "He moved away from his friends."

"Cripes, what makes you think I know any more than Patty?"

"Drunken mutual confessions. You mentioned them once?" Harold tried not to smile as Liz glared.

"You said you'd forgotten, and I certainly have." She rolled her eyes. "Obliterated in one night of sooty bliss. So what did Patty say?" Harold explained. "She's sort of right, but too complicated. Casper was lonely."

"In the girl club?"

"Yes. If you say a word I'll gang up with your sister and that blonde hussy. You do not want three-girl trouble."

"I don't. My lips are sealed."

"Drunken confessions, or one anyway. Casper was brought up to think gay was wrong. He can't do the pink panty bit and never fitted the gay scene, and isn't comfortable with my method of one-night stands." Liz reached over and prodded Harold in the ribs. "You turned up and didn't give a shit if he was gay, everyone in the flats accepted him as a big bloke with a machete, and suddenly he belongs. That's why he makes the stupid jokes, he's sort of drunk on coming out. He'd have been beaten to death if he'd done that before the crash." Liz stopped, frowning. "Where have you been recently, during the gay backlash? In a black hole?"

"Sort of, it's called the Middle East. What gay backlash? The Army doesn't have any, or rather none of the squaddies admit to being gay. Before that I was a quiet kid who shot little paper rings for fun." Harold frowned. "Spitting Sid was a gay, him and Karl, down at the rifle club. They were okay, used to hug each other if they got a good score but that's it. He showed me a lot about setting up rifles and how to reload empty brass, stuff that's dead useful now." His frown turned to a smile. "Those lessons are how I ended up in the group messing with old rifles at the Army range, and learned about custom loading and setting up different weapons. Dead handy now."

"Spitting Sid?"

Harold laughed. "They called him Spitting Sid because he had a speech impediment, he sprayed a bit so he'd look to the side when talking. Sid told me he'd prefer Sid Snot, which I never understood until I looked it up. Then they stopped coming, just before I turned sixteen."

Liz didn't laugh. "Quick and nasty, the gay backlash. A chunk of Human Rights was rescinded after one particular election about nine years ago, when you'd be more interested in porno magazines or playing with rifles."

"I do remember that. I had to learn feet and inches and pounds and ounces at school after working in metres and kilos since I started school. Then it changed to learning both just before I took my exams. It was a bloody shambles."

Liz nodded. "That was the same election. Some nasty things came out of attics. Blacks, Asians, immigrants and gays went back about fifty years overnight and mostly ended up in communities. Then another election and Human Rights were back and even more loony, but the attitudes and the isolated communities stayed." Liz sniggered. "Now Casper's got a friend who doesn't care if he's gay or wears no panties at all. A friend he can hug and tell all his worries and nobody gives him odd looks, and that's all you're getting."

Harold grinned. "What was your confession? The one you swapped."

"Your ears are too young and tender. Now soldier off because I'm busy. My best efforts have been spurned, and those ungrateful gits want arrows with barely any artwork at all." She smirked. "Though I get the first pigeon pie."

*   *   *

"Come and watch this Harold. Would you recognise the library and playing fields in London from an overhead?" Holly patted the settee.

"Doubtful looking from the air. Blimey, definitely not if it's turned into a farm." Onscreen the cameras were showing wide swathes of land covered in neat rows of plants. "That lake is the Serpentine in Hyde Park. Or Hyde Park until someone dug most of it up." The view changed. "Hey, that must be one of the other parks and they've penned the deer. Those are cows. Oh crap."

Holly sighed. "It's another of those broadcasts, isn't it? One taken hours or days ago with a commentary added?" Onscreen running figures intercepted others who were trying to take the deer and cows. Gunfire and clashes between two groups ended in a scatter of bodies in the grass. Mainly human, but some of the deer were dead, and others had escaped when fences were broken. Two of the cows were down.

"As can be seen, the inhabitants of London have failed to cleanse the city of rebels and criminals. Under these circumstances the marts are unable to open again. Worse, these rebels have conspirators in Brighton. If such breakouts continue, the remaining population centres in the south of England will face severe shortages this winter."

A horde stormed over an Army post and out across fields full of crops, near Brighton the caption claimed. Soldiers, and then armour and helicopters, eventually stopped them and the few survivors finally retreated back inside the Army cordon. The cameras panned across trampled crops and burned swathes of countryside.

"At least that's down south and won't affect us."

"That is definitely a blessing, Hazel. Perhaps you should listen to music in case we get more of this type of news?"

"Yes Uncle Harold." Hazel grinned at Harold's look. "I'd rather go and play computer games with Veronica and Alfie. We're trying to get Pricilla and Jilli levelled up so we can play as teams."

"That'll probably be even better." Harold smiled after Hazel as she skipped happily out of the door. "I did go a bit Uncle Harold there. Hazel seems to be spending more time playing games now there's more players, and she's a lot happier."

Holly sniggered. "Especially since there's all that levelling up to do. Hellfire, what is that?"

Onscreen huge explosions tore apart dockyards and several warships. One of the ships fired its main armament until missile trails tore across the screen and explosions smashed the ship into wreckage. A tall column of thick black smoke rose from behind warehouses before more explosions tore through them. Close-ups showed running figures in among the offices and warehouses, engaged in a fierce gun battle. More pictures revealed the smoking ruins of another port, seething with ragged figures waving weapons.

"The government has received information suggesting that the weapons used in Brighton were smuggled across the channel. The Royal Navy have taken measures to cut off the supply, which came from the French naval bases at Brest and Cherbourg when they were overrun. Some warships were captured by rebels and had to be destroyed. The British government had hoped to salvage fuel from the bases but the attempt failed, and cost the lives of many brave sailors. This failure means that the present fuel shortages will continue in the foreseeable future."

A tanker heeled over ablaze from one end to the other. Men could be seen leaping into the water but fire spread across the water to engulf them.

"I might be the nasty suspicious type, but those rioting refugees and general scumbags seem to have managed to get a major warship under way and work out how to use the armament very quickly. Just saying." Holly turned and stared at Harold, then back at the screen.

"What part of the first news item caused your nasty suspicious self to send Hazel elsewhere?" Sharyn spoke softly but her gaze was intent.

"The part that wondered if the mushrooms down south saw a breakout from somewhere like Leeds, and were told only the north of England would be affected." Harold sighed. "Now do I tell everyone that to encourage thrift and more food production, or leave the mushrooms feeling relieved?"

"I'd rather you hadn't told me which might be a hint." Holly looked over at Sharyn. "Look away because I need some comforting, right now."

"Maybe that's the real reason he sent Hazel away? You've got while I go and make a cuppa, since I haven't got a comforter these days." Sharyn stood up. "If that's not long enough you may as well just drag him upstairs."

"Okay, but I'll try this first. Thanks Sharyn."

*   *   *

The bunker looked almost empty this time, though through the glass the uniformed personnel were running about and obviously in the middle of something major. There were only four people around the big table deep under the countryside, and two were in uniform. "What actually happened with that tanker?"

"Sorry about that, Owen. That was caused by a suicide boat. We had to stop the operation then but most of the fuel from Brest had already been removed. The whole operation had to be rushed because the base had hoped to hold out." Victor, the naval officer, spread his hands. "We agreed with their assessment until heavy weapons were used to break into Cherbourg. The delay in attacking either base had to have been while those weapons were brought north from Toulon."

"There would have to be a delay to train people to use them."

"No Gerard. There were armed forces personnel among the attackers and the assault, the last one, had all the hallmarks of a military operation. Worse, there were sympathisers inside both bases, Cherbourg in particular which is why that fell so quickly and without much warning. There were fewer in Brest but we still didn't get everything out." The naval officer tapped his file. "That film doesn't show how many ships and how much material we destroyed in Cherbourg. Luckily most of the warships left Brest carrying dependents just before the lines broke."

The older civilian, Owen, frowned. "More mouths to feed. How are the French sailors taking the attacks? Our ships sinking theirs I mean."

"Not too well, although most are relieved their families are out of there. We're keeping them separated from the European aircrew who evacuated when their airfields were overrun. We'll need another brothel." The naval man looked across to the other man in uniform. "How solid are our soldiers, Joshua? The last assault on Brest included artillery and heavy armour and men still in uniform."

Joshua came halfway out of his seat, face reddening. "The British Army is lot better disciplined than the French! Our men will do as we tell them."

"Calm down Joshua." The older man pointed to the screen, now showing details of the attack on Brest that would never be shown on TV. "Those forces were loyal and disciplined until the tanks and soldiers were sent into Marseille with orders to clear the city. If we ordered tanks into London now, your Army, the British Army, would come apart at the seams." He chuckled. "Don't frown because it's true. But another year or two of nutcases shooting at them, and brutalised women fleeing to the Army begging for help, and that will change."

"Will a year be enough?" The younger civilian looked at his figures. "Though all those parks and playing fields that have been planted up would be a big help towards food production. So would farming a bit nearer to the population centres."

"Not yet Gerard, for the same reason we can't use the armies on civilians. If the soldiers saw all the tractors and combine harvesters chugging across fields, questions would be asked. Since the men asking would all have rifles, I prefer to avoid that. The areas around the segregated cities and Army bases must remain deserted." The older man also perused figures. "After Brest, I expected the container ports further north to see sense. That is your job."

"It's happening slowly." Gerard looked over at the naval officer and nodded acknowledgement. "I've been promised naval units to cover a serious attempt to move bulk stores in the next week or two, and we've already fuelled up several container ships. From the responses, we'll get into Hamburg first. The Germans are a bit more pragmatic than the Dutch and Belgians, probably losing most of their country helped that along."

Owen shrugged. "The old German government were warned about the numbers of refugees and migrants they let in before closing their borders. Did all of our people get out?"

"Over half of them, though some are still in Hamburg. Europe really didn't go according to plan." Joshua, the Army man, shook his head morosely.

"That was always a possibility, and why we are based in Britain where the civilian population isn't armed." Owen opened a second file. "I suppose we'd better start on the details. Just what did we get out, and how does that affect the overall situation?"

* * *

"We've got a pair of Barbie Girls in Orchard Close." Emmy smiled. "They've got to be considering the ironmongery both left at the gate and how Alfie is blushing. Both of them made a big fuss of Sooty and are now sat on the path playing with puppies because Seth brought the whole litter outside. If Hilda is serious about the fluffy one she'd better get her bid in." She paused. "That's if we can afford to feed extra dogs?"

"I'd better nudge Hilda along. She apparently thinks getting another dog while Rascal is still alive is being unfaithful, or some such rubbish, but she's terrified of being left without a dog." Harold smiled, though a sad smile. "I've been told by at least six people that Hilda will go to pieces when Rascal finally dies and will need another dog, sharpish. Hazel bends my ear over breakfast now so it'll be a relief to get the whole thing settled. Patricia says she's not a vet, but Rascal is old and already on dog pain killers so we'll only end up with the same number anyway."

"Don't tell Hilda that!"

"I wasn't going to. I'll tell her we need one of the puppies trained up properly and Rascal can help with that." Harold's smile had definite humour this time. "If I can say that with a straight face. I just hope he doesn't teach the new one to hump my bloody leg."

Emmy sniggered. "Not just yours, and he's got worse since Lucky was on heat. Think yourself lucky Sooty has better manners." The doormat in question thumped his tail on the path.

"How's he doing as a guard dog?"

Emmy shrugged, then smiled happily. "Useless, but Sooty is brilliant with the kids. Thandia tolerates young children, but won't play with them.

Ask Daisy."

"Cripes yes. At least Daisy has accepted that if Sooty will play, Thandia and the rest can be left in peace." Harold squared his shoulders. "I'll see Hilda, and then these Barbie Girls. Just how did this pair dress for visiting us?"

"Like women in jeans, though it's best not to read the tattoos out loud. That Chandra wasn't joking, though Hilda would mark them down for the spelling on some." Emmy went off laughing and Harold headed for the library. Hilda made a few half-hearted protests, but her heart wasn't in it so Mischief would be moving in once the pup had weaned. Harold hoped the puppy's name was in homage to Rascal, not some sort of premonition.

Harold spent the walk from the library up the street to the group with puppies worrying, once again, about selling puppies. That had to be an improvement over worrying about being murdered by lunatics, but still a problem. Knowing what the Geeks planned didn't help, though he felt a little bit relieved to see the pair of women. They weren't wearing wigs or dressed in weird clothes, but they were wearing huge smiles and playing with the puppies.

"Why aren't you wearing wigs? No offence meant, but everyone keeps warning me about women in blonde wigs."

Both women started laughing, then the taller one with light brown hair and obscene tattoos answered. "Those are in charge, the real Barbie's. We're just fighters." She held up a white puppy with black here and there. "Will you really sell her?"

"Maybe. I'm a little bit worried about what you want them for." Harold looked over at Berry and Seth, who had been watching over the pups and might have a better read on the women. "Well?"

"They seem to be all right. They really do like the puppies so maybe they'll be treated okay."

"Maybe? You cheeky f...person." The shorter woman with darker hair had started to rise and put her hand to an empty machete sheath. "Er, sorry. It's just that..." She struggled silently for a few moments, finding words. "We came, us two, because we had dogs before it all f..., before all this and there are no dogs in Beth's. Well one but she's claimed. We were going to just take some from some, er, people, but they'll just pine if we do." She cuddled a brown puppy. "But a puppy won't. Now are they for sale or was it just a, a wind-up?" The woman scowled at those watching. "How the hell do you lot manage if you're pi... annoyed?"

"We say cripes." Berry sniggered. "Or go somewhere private. I can hear

Seth muttering sometimes but he never lets me actually hear any words." She looked over at Harold. "I reckon they really want dogs, not for fighting or breeding to sell."

"We will train them to be guard dogs as well. That's got to be OK because some dogs will do it anyway. How much for this one? How many will you sell because we've got another couple of women back there who want one." The tattooed woman held up the black and white pup. "I want Splash."

Harold made his mind up, at least partly because Splash didn't sound a particularly savage name. "Not the furry one because she's spoken for. Would you prefer a bigger one? We've got Labrador crosses?"

"Crossed with that manic crittur by the gate? Chandra said the thing tried to tear down the fence and eat her, though he only barked at us." The two women looked at each other. "We don't want something like that, but the other two might want a bigger dog if possible." The taller one chuckled. "Kara has a spayed retriever bitch who's put on ten pounds with all the spoiling since she turned up."

"What do you feed them?" Harold pointed to what was probably going to be Splash. "These are being brought up on rat."

"Rat isn't a problem though we usually sell it to the neighbours in burgers. We've got puppy food and all the good stuff as well, and some little furry critturs and a snake because Beth's includes a pet shop. We can trade some? Does anyone want a hamster?" The woman looked around hopefully. "Or pot? We grow wicked pot in our weed patch." The other woman grinned and mimed taking a long, slow drag on, presumably, a joint.

"Not pot or if so our medic will want to talk about purity, and I'll ask about hamsters. We might be interested in flea treatment and I'll ask about anything else we need." Harold frowned. "Beth's?"

"The Queen Elizabeth the Second Retail Centre. Beth's. Customers will be robbed and hung, unless they're really hung." Both women grinned at that. "We've even got soft loo rolls, though we won't be allowed to trade those."

"It'll be a few weeks before these are ready and longer for the others, so how about you let us know what you can trade. For now, have a look at the pups and come back with offers." Harold smiled. "Buy a beer and relax."

"We want more than a pint. We've brought bottles back but can only take what fits in the packs." The taller one sniggered. "After all, we aren't allowed across GOFS territory so we could hardly bring a motor." She looked round. "So where's the brewer?"

Berry opened her mouth and Harold got in first. "Oh no. You buy your beer from the barmaid here, or the barman. I'll leave you to it for now, and someone will come for a natter about prices." Harold could already hear some fierce bargaining as he left because Berry didn't give up her beer without real persuasion.

*   *   *

Holly took off her pack with a big smile. "That's what we needed. Retail therapy, even at a Mart, though a visit to Beth's would be better from what Berry was being offered."

"Not a chance. You can only go to the Mart because the new soldiers up on the bypass are a bit friendlier. That and because we didn't have to buy bulk food this time so I didn't have to take just muscly types. Not now Curtis has finally allowed us to pillage his potatoes." Harold grinned. "Can I help you unpack?"

"Not a chance. You might see some of what we bought, but there's a reason you men had to turn your backs. Most of what you're interested in seeing isn't for me anyway. Go! Play with your Soldier Boy toys." Holly sniggered. "I sometimes wonder what you get up to in that workshop of yours."

"You could come and help." Harold frowned. "There's no gun work anyway. That's all died away which is a shame because we were paid in propellant and ammo.

Holly opened her pack and peeked inside. "What's in here will cheer you up, now go and dig or reap. You could pick cherries?" Holly licked her lips. "Now that might tempt me into some of what's in this pack."

With an incentive like that Harold took a tub out into the ruins where a solitary tree had been spared out of a whole garden just because it was a cherry tree. "Hi Alfie. I thought you'd be waiting to see if any more Barbie Girls wanted searching." Alfie blushed scarlet.

"That wasn't his fault. He just happened to be on the gate both times. Alfie isn't like that!"

"Er, sorry? Blimey Hazel, I was only joking." Harold frowned. "How come you're out here?"

"Alfie helps me with my crossbow lessons. That's if it's any of your business." Hazel waved a crossbow. "Honestly, it's not as if you're my father." Hazel blushed scarlet. "Oh, I'm sorry Harold, I really am." She seized Alfie's arm. "Come on Alfie, you'd better take me to safety." Harold stood watching them head back to the enclave, completely baffled. Hazel had been doing well lately, but something must have touched a nerve. He shrugged and went to pick cherries.

A very subdued Hazel ate her tea, including four cherries, in silence, and nobody else at the table seemed to know why. Though Daisy made up for any lack of talk because her personal tomato plant had produced a ripe tomato which had to be admired, and then shared. Even afterwards when a tearful Hazel apologised about her behaviour, Harold couldn't work out what he'd actually said wrong. She finally cheered up again after the nightly computer game with the other young teenagers.

Apart from minor upsets like that, July passed in relative peace and Orchard Close began to believe the worst was over. The neighbours all seemed to be fighting among themselves or with other neighbours, or maybe busy planting or harvesting their own crops. In Orchard Close some fruit and vegetables were already being preserved for the winter though everyone knew that would never be enough. The shoppers topped up on pasta because that was light, relatively cheap and filling, and could be kept for winter.

*   *   *

"Harold, Harold!" That came as a shock because Harold hadn't heard Hazel shout like that for weeks.

"Yes Hazel. Over here." Harold stood up and stretched because he'd been weeding, again. Curtis still insisted on planting more as soon as any crop had been picked or dug up, and then the new baby veggies had to be kept weeded.

"Come quick. Its Casper and Fury." Hazel turned and raced back towards the door in the guardhouse. Harold followed, walking because whatever had happened he couldn't hear any ruckus now.

"What's happened Billy?"

Billy turned from the window where he kept watch over the gardens and the cleared area around Orchard Close. "No idea Harold. Fury set off snarling and barking, followed by some shouting, but everything is quiet now. Then Hazel came through here running like a whippet." He smiled. "She always runs like a whippet, but more so this time."

"Ta." Harold came out of the front door and could see Casper sat in road, up towards the far end of the street. Fury laid next to him and as Harold came nearer Casper was hugging the dog and pouring water over his head. Casper turned towards him and Harold stopped in shock. Tears were pouring down Casper's face. "What the hell happened, Casper?"

"He." Casper tried for a breath. "Fury, and Sukie." He waved a hand helplessly towards Suzie's house and then hugged Fury again. The dog whined and rubbed at his eye, and Casper poured more water.

"He got to Sukie!"

"No. He got away, my fault." Casper hugged the dog again. "Sukie is safe. It's not his fault." The big man scrubbed at his face with a sleeve. "I can't stop him, Harold."

"But Sukie is safe, so what happened?" Several people were watching from a distance, but nobody approached and Harold sat on the kerb near Casper. "Why are you sitting here?"

"He's strong, Harold. I wasn't quite ready when he pulled." Casper hugged Fury and took a moment before he could continue. "He went for Sukie, Harold, but Suzie pulled her back in the door. Even then she needed pepper spray." Since Emmy had mentioned pepper spray for the dogs, many women carried it. Not for the dogs, for any stroppy gangsters. Casper gave a great shuddering sigh. "He didn't get much spray, but enough to slow up and Suzie got the door shut. Then I caught up."

"So everyone is safe?" That was the main thing. "Come on, let's get you two home."

"It's no good Harold, Fury doesn't understand." Casper sighed again. "I can't risk it. What if he gets Sukie, or Joey, or any of the adults? He'll have to go."

"You could keep him in the pen?" Harold would have agreed about the dog going, but Casper and Fury really had taken to each other and Harold remembered what Liz said, about loneliness. Casper would be a mess if he lost the dog now, and Fury made a hell of a guard dog at the gate.

"I found a small hole where he'd chewed the mesh, Harold. That was after he was shut in there for a few hours. I've been keeping him with me because Fury howls if I leave him." Casper shook his head. "I'll have to put him down Harold." Tears flooded down the big man's face again. "It's not his fault!"

"No, and there's got to be another way. He could stay in a pen out with the perimeter guards?" There were two guards out in the edge of the ruins overnight as an early warning in case of vegetable rustlers, or possibly a deer. "Maybe you could just take him a few miles and let him go?"

"I told you. Fury won't stay in a pen and he'd howl all night." Casper shook his head. "He'd come back and hang about if I turned him out, then Tim or Emmy would come across him out there. He'd go for them."

"We could sell him. The GOFS or Barbie Girls might take him? They've both got dogs anyway, and are buying some from us." Harold looked around but nobody came near.

"The GOFS and Barbie Girls have both got Asians and blacks. They won't want him and I won't sell Fury to that bastard Caddi or the Freeks. He'd pine, then get really nasty and they'd encourage him." Casper hugged the Doberman again and Harold shook his head. He was at a loss, because the damn dog was a pussy-cat with Casper. He was sat here hugging the bloody thing, yet Fury barely allowed others to stroke him.

"There's got to be a way, Casper."

"We'll go for a walk while I figure something out, Harold." Casper and Harold got up and Fury came to his feet. "I might take a while, to give them time to get sorted out." Harold followed Casper's gaze and saw that a dozen people had now gathered. "They'll want to talk to you."

"Take what time you need. We'll sort it." Harold clapped Casper on the shoulder and Fury growled, just a low one but Harold froze.

"He's just wound up, Harold. He'll be better after a walk." Casper turned and headed for the guardhouse and the way out with Fury trotting eagerly alongside.

*   *   *

Just over fifteen minutes of tears, anger and recriminations later everyone fell silent as a gunshot rang out over the ruins. "Casper has solved your problem, now I'll go and make sure there isn't a second shot." Harold turned on his heel and headed for the way out. What he'd said wasn't really fair, and said in anger, prompted by fear that there really would be a second shot in a few seconds. That worried Harold enough for him to trot across the gardens waving off or ignoring the shouted questions from the gardeners.

The thickening plume of smoke rising out in the ruins brought some relief as well as confirmation. If Casper had built a fire he wouldn't eat a bullet, at least not until Fury's pyre burned out. Harold walked up slowly until he could see Casper sat on the remains of a wall, head in his hands and talking quietly. Harold waited until the big man stopped talking. "Fair thee well, Fury."

Casper stiffened, then relaxed again. "I already did that, and the poem. I didn't think…" His voice thickened and Casper rubbed his face. "I'm all right, honest."

"No you aren't, so I'll just sit here nice and quiet until you're ready to come back." Harold found some bricks that weren't too uncomfortable and settled.

"It really wasn't his fault you know."

"No Casper. It was whatever twisted asshole taught him all that stuff. You didn't have to do this." Harold took a deep breath. "I'd have done it for you if that was the answer."

"I know. But this is the right way. Fury never knew a thing Harold, because he trusted me." Casper drew a long sobbing breath. "I pointed at nothing and he looked there, and never saw the bullet coming." He scrubbed at his face and sniffed. "Mercy should come from a hand that cares. Another poem."

"The kindest way." They sat in silence as the sun crawled across the sky until the fire finally burned down. Only embers remained when Casper stirred.

"You aren't going to leave, are you?"

"Not without you."

"Hard-assed soldier bastard."

"We're handy sometimes."

"I'll come back in a bit."

"I'll walk with you." A long silence followed.

"No hugging, or I might come over all gay, and then you won't respect me in the morning." There was a quaver in Casper's voice, but he was trying so Harold did.

"I'd be tempted but then Holly would beat me up."

"Wimp."

"Fairy."

Casper sighed, climbed to his feet and rooted about in the broken sheds until he found an old crockery plantpot. "Have you got any water? I used mine on Fury's eyes." He was trying very hard to keep his voice under control, but Harold could hear how near Casper was to losing it again.

"Here you go." Most people carried water while working in the gardens, to save going back in, so Harold had a couple of plastic bottles with him.

"Put it by the pyre, please." Harold did while Casper put soil in the pot to seal the bottom.

"Do you want a hand?"

"I'm good, thanks." Harold sat and watched as Casper pulled charred timber from the pyre and scooped up the rest with a piece of battered plywood. He sprinkled water in the pot until it stopped hissing, and tested the temperature of the outside. "Might be a little while?"

"Got nothing better to do." Harold had already waved away Holly and Alfie so nobody would be disturbing Casper until he was ready.

Casper sat by the pot, talking quietly to it and periodically testing the outside. "That'll do it." He picked up the pot and set off for Orchard Close, but not to the door in the guardhouse. Harold soon realised where the big man was going.

"Give me time to talk to the Army, Casper. Don't get shot over this. Please."

Casper hesitated. "You already dealt with that. It's not a problem now, Harold. I won't go over the line." He set off across the front of the gatehouses, ignoring the questions from two of the windows. Harold followed because he really wasn't quite certain Casper didn't intend doing something drastic. He was even more uncertain when Casper kept going towards the exclusion zone.

"Casper?" The big man ignored him and walked forward, carrying the pot and remaining water, until his toes were almost over the line. Harold winced as Casper plunged his hand into the pot. He did it again and again, scattering the ashes over the line until there were none left. The remaining water washed out the pot, and then sluiced Casper's scorched hand before he dropped the pot and turned.

Tears were streaming again and Harold wasn't sure Casper even saw him as he came past. Harold turned to follow and stopped after climbing the wall. At least a score of people were waiting and many spoke or put out a hand, while others avoided Casper's eyes. Harold didn't think it mattered, because he doubted Casper noticed any of them. The big man went straight to his home in the back of the guardhouse, and the crowd started towards Harold. Eventually he'd explained enough times and they let him go home, or maybe Holly just told them to go away and took him there.

In the following days the edge had gone off the happiness of summer. The gardens still produced, and still more crops were planted, but smiles were few and far between. Casper stayed in his rooms and wouldn't talk to anyone, and everyone missed him. They'd all become used to the big smiling man who made silly jokes and always turned up wherever a bit of extra muscle had been needed.

*   *   *

Harold opened his door to a deputation, and didn't have to guess what it was about. "We have to do something about Casper."

"Good luck with that, Emmy. Sorry, that was sharp. I've been and tried to talk to Casper every day, and he won't open the door." Harold shrugged. "I have considered breaking the damn thing down."

"We've all tried talking but someone finally came up with a solution."

Harold frowned. "Who?"

"Umeko and Suzie. They both feel responsible for letting Sukie run out. I blame the piece of shit that had Fury before Casper." Harold could hear the anger in Emmy's voice.

"Casper won't talk to those two either." Casper wasn't angry at any of them, he just wouldn't answer. If he hadn't seen Casper's unshaven face at the window Harold really would have broken the door down. "It's been a week and so far there's no sign of him opening up, except the night he came out and tore down the pen."

"What do you think he's eating?"

"The stupid sod is starving?" Harold started forward because the damn door was going in, but Holly put a hand on his shoulder.

"Listen to Emmy."

"Casper will open the door but not to adults. He'll open up for kids but won't let them in, so they take him food." Emmy's faint smile was a very sad one. "He can't bring himself to turn them away or refuse the presents they bring."

"Can the kids talk him out of it?" Harold frowned. "Do the kids understand enough to do that?"

"They know Casper is very sad because Fury died and they take him presents to make him feel better. The kids aren't stupid but they're going along with food as presents and they really do worry about him and understand he needs food." Emmy sighed. "It's mean but we can use them to get him out of this rut. To jerk him back into the world."

Daisy knew that Fury had died. Harold sat with Daisy and helped to draw a special place for Fury because Uncle-Casper loved him. Daisy had even gone down to ask Uncle-Casper why he wouldn't read stories, only to be told Uncle-Casper felt too sad just now. Harold couldn't see what else might work. "How?"

Emmy moved aside and Umeko presented a little bundle of fur. "She's marked like Fury, but she's a girl and brown." Umeko looked behind her for a moment. "Suzie is coming as well, and Sukie is going to hand the pup over. We're going to lie, and tell Sukie the puppy has been rejected and needs nursing, lots of nursing."

Ten minutes later all the adults involved were watching Casper's door, all except two from windows and doorways. They were too far away to hear as Casper opened the door, listened to Sukie, looked at the two women nearby and accepted the little furry bundle. Casper glared at Suzie and Umeko, and then towards the hidden watchers before stepping backwards and closing the door. "He knows."

"But he still took the puppy, Harold."

Harold, among others, waited. Two hours later the door opened and a scruffy, unshaven Casper headed towards the garage containing the rat freezers. He had a little wriggly something wrapped in a shirt and held gently against his chest. "Sukie told him the puppy needed her feed of minced rat every three hours." Holly tugged Harold's arm. "Come on. It might take time but Casper will be all right now." Harold wasn't so sure but he settled for being hopeful.

Chapter 10:
Nightfall

While Casper tried to get his head back together, Harold found himself with a bit of a problem because Casper made a superb bodyguard. Especially when meeting nasty sods like the Geeks. "Remember what I said, Bernie, Jeremy? Ignore the comments because they'll try to wind you up. Are you all right with this, Finn?" The four men sat in a pickup at the edge of an old car park. At the opposite side a wrecked Burger King outlet had been left standing in solitary splendour. Beyond that a wide swathe of ground had been cleared of ruins and rubble, right back to a chain link fence.

"The Geeks will pay well and we need putty and cement. I'll keep my trap shut, fix their electrics and be out of there long before dark." Finn glowered. "I won't stay overnight, not here."

"No problem. That's all agreed and we'll hold the hostage just over the border until you call." Nobody in Orchard Close wanted to go and visit the Geek Freeks after Umeko arrived. Harold handed Finn a small radio. "They've got radios but this way nobody plays silly sods. We know this one reaches far enough."

"Yeah, these things should reach more than a couple of miles, Trev reckons it's because of the jamming on all the other wavelengths." Finn grinned. "Except Barbie Radio. They must have one hell of a transmitter." He lost the smile. "Here they come." Four people came from the compound, crossing the open ground towards the wrecked Burger King, and Harold's group went to meet them.

Both groups went inside and sat at tables well apart, except Harold and Galileo who sat at the same table. At least the plastic tables and seating didn't deteriorate even when the rain or snow blew in. "Cheeseburger and fries please." Harold smiled as he spoke because this time Galileo had come to deal, and he wasn't quite as Geek Freeky as some of the other managers. The two armed men with the Geek managers smiled as well.

"In your dreams, Soldier Boy. Fair warning, there's rumours that some of the burgers for sale have rat in them." Galileo frowned. "The ones we had were in the right packets, but they'd been opened. At least if there was rat, it tasted okay. We've been tempted to try some out, though not personally of course." He hooked a thumb at the two guards. "On those two when they've had some of the weed those Barbies are selling to the GOFS." The guards still smiled.

"We're happy with bunny and occasionally deer. You know Finn, our electrician, but which one of you pair is the hostage?"

"You know which one, Tell because you aren't sure the rest won't trade me for an electrician. Before that, we reckon that house is six hundred yards from our gate." Galileo pointed.

Harold weighed it up. "About."

The Geek held up a pair of binoculars. "Almost exactly according to these. Don't get excited but watch the front wall." Galileo nodded to one of his guards who went outside and waved. A deep thrumming and clang rang out, followed by a crash as a hole appeared through the house wall.

"Impressive, but a slow way to knock the house down."

"Ha, ha. That's our new sniper deterrent. Tell and I upgraded the cross-bow and made a giant version. The hole was made by a six foot length of steel bar." Galileo looked straight in Harold's eyes. "Caddi passed on your concerns about mystery shooters with hunting rifles."

Harold kept his face straight. "That should do it. Is that why you've cleared the buildings back to there?"

"If Caddi reckons he needs half a mile, we thought this should do it. After all, we haven't annoyed anyone as much as Caddi does." Galileo sat back and relaxed. "Does Finn want a hand with his gear?"

"No thanks. He might want to take a few electrical bits from your store in part payment. We'll sort out the difference those make to the cement and putty once he's looked at what you've got." Harold turned and waved Finn over. "I've mentioned electrical bits. Don't talk price, okay?"

"No problem Harold." Finn held up his toolbox and smiled. "Let's get on with it." Tell stood up and came over for the exchange.

*   *   *

Finn had lost his smile when he eventually returned. "Jesus Christ Harold. Can you stop so I can get out and swear, please. If I say what I want to the women will cane the skin off me."

"We're barely out of sight Finn. Can you hold out to the border?" Finn could let rip now and probably wouldn't offend the men in the cab, but not swearing had become a point of principle among the residents of Orchard Close.

"If you drive fast."

Harold turned up the pickup radio and then smiled. "We might hear the odd expletive anyway." The Barbies didn't actually swear on the radio very often, but they did enjoy making up gossip about the neighbours. Caddi's exploits with various animals had become a favourite. Even so many radios in Orchard Close tuned in to Barbie radio, because they did play almost continuous rock music with an occasional protest song. Just across the border Harold pulled up and turned the radio up even louder. "Number of the Beast, we'll not hear a word over Iron Maiden."

After five minutes of stomping up and down and waving his arms about, and throwing a couple of bricks, Finn came back. "That's better. Now I can tell you with the expletives deleted. Though there won't be much left then. The Geeks are getting worse."

"Tell didn't seem different, though he talked about the weather and the marts and anything but what happens in there."

"I suppose the Geeks might be the same as always and some are a bit better than others. There were some cracks about Wellington coming to join us because he's got used to a woman bossing him about. The others are either worse or now its blatant and Einstein just glared when he saw me. Darwin is another bad one, and he brought me an assistant." Finn pulled a face. "He brought in a lass wearing sod all and told her to hold or pull anything I asked. The guards thought that was funny. I told her to stand in the corner and keep out of the way." Finn sighed. "The bastards insisted on bringing her along to every job."

"Was that it? We've all been offered women even if not as blatantly."

"Not just that Harold, it's the general attitude. The managers and even the fighters aren't pretending now. The men and women who aren't in charge are unarmed and treated, well not like slaves. More like..." Finn thought a few moments. "Maybe what a serf would be treated like? All orders and no manners, and the servants, serfs, run about obeying because they're frightened."

"The Hot Rods aren't that bad all the time, or weren't, or Caddi was but as a windup. I'll know better next week because Caddi has either been fighting again or his lot have ruined some weapons." Harold thought about it, but there was nothing Orchard Close could do. "Did you see that weapon, the bar thrower?"

"Just a shape under a tarpaulin that did resemble a huge crossbow on wheels." Finn smiled. "Even Patty wouldn't want that, though she might want the latest handheld version. They look lighter."

"I'll tell her. There's already enquiries about knitting and winter is coming."

Bernie sniggered. "Patty won't want it if there's any loss of power."

"If she does, I'd like the old one." Jeremy shrugged. "Matti said she'd like to learn to use a crossbow like that, because she won't have to hide it like she does a pistol." The last half mile home was spent teasing Jeremy about types of practice with Matti, which seemed to cheer Finn up a bit.

*　　　*　　　*

The Coven and girl club descended on the pickup on arrival back at Orchard Close to see what Harold had brought. "There's enough putty here to fix up Cherry Tree House." Susan smiled. "Rob reckons the plumbing isn't too bad and that would be ten flats if more of the girl club want to leave home." Between numbers four and six along the border wall of the enclave a long building had, according to Betty, been converted from a nursing home into the block of single bedsits called Cherry Tree House. Many windows were broken, and since the frames were odd sizes any repairs required glass, not complete replacements from houses.

"Hazel might want to go straight there where I can't see what she's up to when she moves out. We'd have to make sure the floors are all right but then if a few couples move in we might persuade Casper out of the guardhouse. Living in there with memories isn't helping him." Harold smiled. "Though he did have a shave this morning."

Patty grinned. "Amber is working her puppy charm. She'll be called porky if someone doesn't tell him that rat every three hours is a bit much. We need a bit more room in the girl club anyway, for when Hazel and Veronica move in because we're full again. If any more single women turn up on the doorstep they'll have to sleep on the floor."

Liz smirked. "I might take one so I can stay out all night and nobody will notice."

Harold looked her over. "I can't see either soot or cream?" He frowned. "It's not Harvest Festival."

"Some of us wash occasionally." Liz preened. "Some practice our fertility nights, oops, rites, on different days to you lot."

"Hmm, privacy could be handy someday." Patty looked out towards the crops. "I might take one of those flats, because they overlook the gardens. I could relax in an evening with my crossbow by the open window. Then when some pigeon, bunny or hopefully deer raids the salad, pow, cold cuts."

"Better still, if you're bored you could take potshots the other way at the visitors." Sal scowled. "Especially any Geeks."

"It's a plan. Between that and your main squeeze wandering about with her cane, it'll keep them all honest." The women all laughed.

"Will you lot stop calling her that." Harold looked at the four smiling faces. "I mean it. That sounds like I've got several squeezes, girls."

"So what do you call her? In private." Sal opened her eyes really wide. "What does she call you?" Harold retreated because he wasn't answering those sorts of questions. Though he did smile when his only anything turned up with her cane.

"Real Cauliflower tonight and Sharyn swears she can create a cheese sauce. No wonder you call her the head witch, because that cauldron of hers is magical. It must be magic because the cheese isn't real cheese, and the milk sure ain't milk. Better yet, Curtis has unleashed loads of good stuff." Holly gave a little twirl and laughed. "Cripes, I'm excited about fresh cucumber, peas and peppers." She hugged Harold's arm. "And carrots. Fresh crunchy carrots. Maybe it's all the rabbit we eat?"

"Could be. Though the rabbits don't seem to spend as much time as we do weeding and slugging." Harold had been on slug and bug duty again and wasn't impressed. "I thought all the flowers were supposed to stop the pests?"

"Stop grumping or I'll set Liz on you, I've only got to shout loudly."

"Not a chance. She'll beat on me instead of the iron."

"In that case, you can help me pick peas, a perfect job for a wimp I'm told. Better yet, you can pick flowers because that encourages more to grow, honest." Harold laughed and went to join the other pickers while the weather held. The mood had improved all round now as the bulk crops came in, and at least partly because Casper seemed better.

Though by evening something else had brought smiles to several faces, and a huge grin from Holly. "Real honey!"

"Calm down. Jeremy just said he followed the bees home. I think he has ulterior motives." Harold laughed. "I thought veggies floated your boat?"

"But fresh honey. Slurpy, drippy, yummy, sticky sweet crunchy-comb honey." Holly's lip licking became a real Sal special. "Jeremy said hundreds of bees, thousands, in and out of a pile of bricks. Some of us are going to have a proper look tomorrow. We won't destroy the hive, just steal some of their goodies."

"Does anyone know enough to make a beehive and capture them?" Harold fancied fresh honey as well, sweet was endangered because of the price of sugar in the mart. "They'll have to be careful, I distinctly remember the fuss about someone crossing African Killer Bees into ours to stop disease."

"Yes but only crosses which made them feisty, not real killers. I'll bet Jeremy won't care if Matti offers to kiss the stings better." Holly sniggered. "He'll take off his shirt."

"Cripes, there'll be a lot of volunteers for bee-knapping if that sort of first aid is on offer." Harold laughed. "That garter could get a serious workout afterwards. Though I'll be over at the Mansion arguing with Caddi and trying to resist punching that little smile of his."

"I'll have to work on compensation. After all, we have plenty of lettuce?" Holly frowned. "Lettuce and honey? Maybe not."

*   *   *

Harold looked up at the low clouds, squinting his eyes against the steady drizzle, and hugged Holly tighter. "Sorry about your honey, but this weather means I'll be here for the raid on the hive tomorrow or whenever the rain eases off. It'll probably be late before I get back since Charger turned up so late." Harold curled a lip in distaste. "Even if it's dark I'll come home. I am not stopping in that place."

"Good. I like my alien killing machine right where I can find him at night." Holly pursed her lips and debated on what sort of goodbye Harold should get. "Just a four now, to keep you eager to come home." Harold drove off up the road still smiling about that, despite the rain.

Harold's smile had long gone by the time he headed for home. Caddi had been a complete arse, haggling over every tiny thing. Worse, the Hot Rod boss been called away for an emergency and left Harold kicking his heels for over two hours. Now, at nine o'clock, Harold had to drive home in the dark, real darkness only an hour after sunset because today had been a cloudy, drizzly miserable day. The beams cutting through the inky blackness only emphasised how little of the city still had lighting at night.

An inky blackness suddenly split by the flickering of gun-flashes! The Army, it had to be. The shooting stopped but Harold drove faster, worrying in case some soldier had spotted a carelessly hidden firearm and shot someone in Orchard Close. He raced down the road and turned up the access road, driving quickly round to the side wall. As he scrambled over the wall the group coming to meet him seemed to be confirmation.

"Who?"

He couldn't see who was in the group but Harold's worry grew as nobody answered, then as they reached him a voice said "Holly."

Emmy's arms wrapped around Harold, tight, as he swung towards the bypass and the Army. "Not them Harold, they didn't do it. Don't go crazy Harold. The bastard is dead. He's dead." Emmy spoke quietly and hugged fiercely and now more arms wrapped around him.

"Holly?" She couldn't be dead, just like that, when she'd waved him goodbye with that big smile. "Holly!"

"She's gone Harold. Holly's gone." For once Liz had lost all her banter, the grief stark in her voice. "We've got her safe, but she's dead Harold."

"Where?" Harold turned back towards home, and the arms let him. "Where's Holly?"

"Safe. You don't want to see her just now. Soon, Harold." Liz sobbed as she spoke but held tight, and now others were sobbing as well.

"Why? I want to see Holly."

"We'll make her pretty. Soon, Harold." Emmy sniffed. "We won't let you, Harold." Emmy started to cry again and both women's arms tightened around him.

"I brought her home Harold. Your Sharyn's got her." Barry's voice was bleak. "Just wait a little bit, Harold. It really is best." Even above the sounds of grief, Barry's great racking sigh came through clearly. "Better to wait. I know Harold, please believe me."

The sheer certainty in Barry's voice got through, but didn't help as Harold tried to work out why he shouldn't see her. "But why? What happened? Why Holly? Who did it? Who's dead?" Because now Harold wondered what mistake he'd made, what sign he'd missed, which traitor he'd let in to kill her.

"Spike, Harold. Spike Pierce. The Minuteman." Bess sounded in shock, stunned. "It's my fault Harold, he came back."

Harold struggled to work that out even as voices rose, telling Bess it wasn't her fault. Then he remembered. The Minutemen, the armed men who brought Bess and Conn and the rest of the refugees from the Armstrong Estate, a million years ago. That was the mistake. That was how Harold had killed Holly. "I should have killed him. It's my fault." Sheer black despair swept in and Harold never really pieced the next bit together. He never really tried.

Sometime later Harold sat weeping and holding Holly's hand as people squeezed his shoulder and murmured something, and then they were alone. Barry or someone had laid Holly on a door, on trestles. Emmy had been right, and by the time Harold saw her Holly was pretty. But she'd been pretty when he left her, laughing about what level his welcome kiss would be. Not even a level one now.

Holly wore her vampire dress, the long green one down to her feet and up to her throat, with a wide green choker. Someone had put her hair up, as it had been for the vampire dance, but now her pale skin and cold hand mocked Harold. They'd made her up, more makeup than Holly ever wore, and had even put a little dusting of green on her closed eyelids to match her dress. Harold asked her about that, why she'd never worn eye makeup? He asked about the bees and talked about the amount of veg that had ripened. Harold started with those, and a lot of other bits about the pair of them, and ended up with how worried he'd been about kissing levels. About how happy he'd been to find that Holly wanted to kiss, had wanted advanced, had wanted to be his main squeeze. Harold talked until his throat was sore and he simply didn't have any more words so he sat there and held her hand.

Liz spoke quietly but Harold jumped anyway. "It's time."

Harold tried twice and croaked "What?"

"Three o'clock, the low time and you've stopped talking. Time for me to tell you. So you know." Liz sighed. "But first for you to have a drink. Otherwise you won't be able to speak." A mug pushed against Harold's hand. "Drink it all. There's more."

Harold drank, the whole mug of juice. "Fruit juice?"

"If you drink anything stronger, you'll keep going and never climb out of the bottle. Now I'm going to tell you, and then you hear Holly's goodbye."

"What!"

"Keep calm, Harold. Listen to me and then to her. It won't take long if you sit quiet." Liz paused for a while, and then started in a quiet, level voice. "You weren't home by dark, but nobody worried because you set off late. Holly left it an hour and then decided someone had to check the sentries. You always did that at full dark Harold, you did it together."

"But."

"Shush now. But nothing. At the gate Holly told the guards she was doing it to save you a job. That after your hello kiss you wouldn't want to go out again." Liz sighed. "I'd skip bits but too many people know and it will come out." Liz fell silent for a few moments. "They came across the gardens, and came slow enough for the watchers to miss them in the dark. We're all a bit casual about that side because of the two guards out watching for deer and rabbits." Liz sighed again. "They're both dead Harold, the guards. Three crossbow bolts in each one. The three of them had those things on headbands and could see in the dark."

"Three?"

"All dead Harold. Drink your juice and I'll get to the rest." Harold drank in some sort of a daze and Liz topped it up. "They grabbed Holly and stopped her shouting, but she got a hand to her pistol. That poser Glock thing you gave her for under her jacket. One must have stopped her aiming so she fired anyway." Liz reached out a hand and gently touched Holly's dress. "Under there is a big burn and a bullet track down the outside of her leg." Liz stopped and her grip on Harold's shoulder tightened. "I'm sorry Harold. I don't carry a gun. I came out of Celine's place and all I could do was scream. I couldn't help."

"I understand."

"I know you do." Liz got her voice almost level again. "The dogs started and others came out but the men dragged her over the wall, kicking and struggling and screaming. She didn't give up Harold."

"She wouldn't."

"They'd got handcuffs on her by then, and carried her, but we got lights on them halfway across the gardens. A dozen people called for them to stop or else, and they did." Liz paused. "They stopped to get behind Holly so we couldn't shoot and the leader, Pierce, put a big knife under Holly's chin. Said if anyone fired she died." Liz fell silent and Harold waited, because he knew what had to be coming. Not the detail, the ending.

"Bess offered to swap herself. Crap Harold I don't want to tell you this but half Orchard Close heard, maybe more." Liz paused again and Harold heard a catch in her breath. "He said no, that Bess is a bit used up but this one had plenty of mileage. Said she'd bring a decent price when they'd done. That she'd be trained and if Soldier Boy wanted her back to put in a bid." Liz stopped and Harold heard her take a drink. "All just to keep us listening instead of shooting because all the time the three of them moved back a bit at a time, getting further away. He put a hand on her leg, said he'd leave you a souvenir and Holly said something. He let her talk."

Liz leant forward and put a hand recorder on the door next to Holly. "Holly asked someone to record. Half of us carry these in case we think of something, to save paper."

"I know."

"You would. It's your idea. Now listen." Liz pressed play. Holly's voice came from a long way off, even though she was shouting.

"Hello Harold. Please listen to me. Don't follow them, or they'll ambush you in the dark. They'll kill you and then the animals will get us all, everyone in Orchard Close. Keep everyone safe. Find another girl, take her to level eighty-four, and have lots of babies. I won't let them touch me Harold, I'm yours." Voices were raised nearer, exclaiming, and then a brief storm of gunshots rang out. The recorder stopped.

"Holly brought up her hands and grabbed the knife blade, caught him by surprise. Then she dropped so her throat ran across the knife, Harold. No! Don't!" Harold had automatically reached for that wide choker Holly wore, much too wide and thick, but Liz's voice stopped him. "Everyone pointing a weapon pulled the trigger and all three dropped." Sheer savagery showed briefly as Liz spoke on. "All the shooters wished they hadn't, afterwards. We wished they'd aimed at legs to get them alive."

"Bad road to go down." Right now Harold wanted to go down that road, bloody-handed and with no remorse.

"You always said so." Liz's hand tightened briefly again. "Holly was really happy you know."

"Don't. Not now."

"Now is the right time. Holly thought it was funny how you worried. How you fretted that she still had to get over Brodie." Liz chuckled but without much humour. "She never needed to."

"But."

"Shush. Holly found out she wasn't angry about Brodie when Gabriela died. Holly was angry about everyone who died. So when a bloke kissed her at Halloween and she liked it, there was nothing to stop her."

That broke through enough for surprise. "Halloween?"

"Oh yes." Liz paused. "You frightened the life out of her because Holly suddenly wanted to kiss you again. Holly was terrified."

"Of me?"

"No, you big daft lump. Frightened of being too easy, or of you finding someone else, or that you didn't like her. Cripes, she went to the dance wearing a tutu and a halo so you'd notice her and then worried you'd think she was a tart."

Harold smiled, a sad one. "I never thought that."

"No you didn't. All the girl club laughed about Holly trading her numbers to get Sandy, or Barry, someone like that. Then they caught on, but too late. Casper nearly wet himself." Liz stopped. "Ah, Casper."

"Where is he?" For one awful moment Harold wondered if Casper had died as well, because he hadn't been waiting, or come round to see Holly.

"Alive. He insists if he'd pulled his fairy head out of his fairy ass he would have been with Holly, walking round the sentries. He won't talk to you yet."

"Idiot."

"So are you. I heard you. It's your fault because you didn't shoot a man in cold blood nine months ago." Liz drank and nudged Harold, so he drained the mug and accepted a refill. "Anyway, wetting himself, or myself. I nearly did when you came in all stern and ticked me off." Liz actually sniggered. "Level four rocked Holly's world and shook her rigid. She fancied level fourteen right then, but was still frightened."

"She rocked my world, Liz." Harold blinked slowly, then forced his eyes wide open.

"We all got that part, probably because of the big stupid grin. Grieve Harold, you have to, but remember Holly smiling and be happy for her. She's been happier this last nine months than most people in this stinking city will be in their whole lives." Liz paused. "That's enough. Why don't you sleep now? Holly won't mind."

"I can't sleep." Even as he said it Harold's eyelids drooped again and he fought them open. "Later, lots of time later."

"Now, so you can be washed and shaved when she needs you to be."

"I can't." Exhaustion crashed in and Harold swayed. "Wha...?"

"Sleep now, Soldier Boy." Harold didn't feel Liz catch him and hold him up in his chair. "Come on you lot, he weighs a ton."

"Let me check. Patricia, check him. Was it too much?" Gayle fussed as Patricia and Lenny checked and smiled.

Patricia patted Gayle's shoulder. "Sleeping like a baby. If I need a good solid night I know who to see, you and Lenny." Meanwhile Barry, Alfie and Bernie brought in a camp bed and put it up next to Holly. The men laid Harold out in recovery position, then almost everyone left. Liz settled down in an armchair just in case he woke up, but Gayle had got the dosage right.

* * *

Harold stumbled and caught himself when he saw the pyres, because he knew exactly which one had been built for Holly. He was still in some sort of daze but Sharyn had shaken him awake and poured coffee into him. She'd chivvied him into a shave and shower and clean clothes, in the main bathroom because Harold couldn't go back in there, into his bedroom. She'd said the pyre was ready, but not what they'd done. Some stupid part of Harold said the bugs would have a field day because flowers from the gardens and even from the ruins smothered one stack of timber. Someone even made a posy for Holly, and a Daisy chain to crown her.

Harold stood on the step and looked at Holly and couldn't say a word. No last words, they wouldn't come. Instead people came past and murmured this and that. Eventually he stood there alone, and Sharyn pulled him gently backwards. Someone took the step away and Harold never saw Holly again because experience and books had taught them to build pyres higher, shaped to concentrate the heat. "Here, Harold." He took the first torch and then the second, and bid Muhammad and Luke fare thee well. Liz lit the third, then Harold stood there with the torch burning until Sharyn gave him a push.

It took Harold three tries. "Fair thee well, Holly." The torch went in and Harold stepped back and turned towards the rest. He took a deep breath.

"Atoms reborn into grass." His sight blurred and Harold pulled in another breath.

"Fire and passion...." He couldn't say it, say the next word, and tears blinded him.

"Stilled at last." That might have been Liz, but then more voices joined. Harold's legs went and he sat down as the chant grew, and grew, until the voices of children joined the last two lines.

"Clouds, of happy what might be's
Scattered showers of grief and tears
Fading memories, not quite true,
One day, my friend, this will be you."

The final words rolled out across the pyres and Harold, and out over the ruins, and Harold buried his head in his hands.

*   *   *

Harold raised his head as he heard the centre of the pyre collapse, pulling some of the other timbers in as well. Dusk, but a large figure wrapped in a big blanket still sat about twenty feet away. "I'm all right."

"I know. Amber wants to watch." The blanket opened and a small head peeked out, then retreated.

"I mean it. I'm not going to throw myself on there."

"Not now." Casper made no move to get up.

"Is this payback?"

"More like an apology." Casper looked up and Harold could make out his face in the light from the flames. He looked shocking.

"You look bloody awful."

"Yeah. You too." Casper sighed. "Yes I'm staying, no I won't go, and yes it would have been different if I'd walked the sentries because you weren't back instead of being busy feeling sorry for myself."

"It would have been different if I'd told Caddi to stop fucking about and come home earlier, or shot that fucker back in November."

"Not that Harold. Holly hated the swearing."

"Sorry luv, except she can't hear me. That's the only problem with being a godless heathen. No happy lies." Harold sighed. "But you're right about swearing." Harold turned towards the pyre and looked up at the tower of flame and smoke. "It'll be a while yet."

"You know the answer."

"Yeah. Payback."

*   *   *

As dawn struggled through the clouds Harold stood up. It took a bit because he was stiff, almost set in place. The bottles of water people brought in the night had meant him leaving the pyre briefly, but otherwise he'd watched it burn. He'd watched the ashes glow and hiss in the light rain sometime after midnight, and then probably slept. Casper stayed where he sat, watching. "The urn is there. There's two shovels?"

"No offence, but no."

"None taken." Casper climbed slowly to his feet. "Amber needs her breakfast." Though he only went to a pair of dishes someone had brought out in the darkness. Casper watched as Harold did exactly as he had, pulling out charred timber and shovelling ashes, and then heaving the cooking pot up by its handles. "Sharyn said she'd go up to see the Army at first light. You should wait for the reply."

"Won't make any difference."

"Be polite."

Harold didn't answer and set off towards the exclusion zone. He'd gone somewhere far away in his head, a place where none of this was real. Almost as peaceful as when he went shooting, except in the back of his head something wanted to go completely apeshit crazy with a sword and a rifle and kill as many of the bastards as he could. Hot Rods, GOFS, Geeks, he didn't care because they were all the same, all Spike Pierce's waiting for some lass in the dark.

"The sergeant said stop and show them you're not armed, Harold." Harold walked past Sharyn and kept going despite the voices behind him. This would be quicker and cleaner, providing they'd got a squaddie who could shoot. Harold walked onto the exclusion zone towards the line of markers and someone had put another one ready to be hammered in. He heard more shouting as he knelt and began to spread the ashes, nice and even in the brick rubble. With luck he'd get them spread before Sarge stopped warning and started shooting. The voices stopped but still nobody fired and Harold kept tipping, then picked up the marker and a brick, and hammered it home.

When he finally turned to leave, Harold found out why the Army hadn't fired. A solid mass of women and kids stood right behind him, right where a high bullet or ricochet from the bypass would have gone. They parted and Harold walked home and sat down. He was lost, because he really hadn't expected to get this far, and now what? The study, he could work on the guns. Harold went in and stopped. There were no guns, no bullets, no brass. Just a camp bed. "I didn't think you'd want to go upstairs yet. Now try to sleep properly." The door closed behind him.

*   *   *

Harold remembered bits after that. Days smashing down ruins and barrowing bricks to build the walls higher and thicker. Too high for anyone to climb over, with a firing step inside so he could shoot the next to try, if he could find a rifle. Days when he was given a shotgun to watch over blackberry pickers, when he saw Emmy with the Blaser and Alfie with the 303 doing the same.

More days spent digging up potatoes and beets and turning over the ground for even more planting. Nights walking round and round the perimeter with a machete and an iron bar because his stick went missing. Harold found where the guns were, but didn't trust himself enough to break the padlocks. There were weapons in people's belts and the guard houses, but sitting alone in a room full might be too much.

Some nights Harold staggered home and slept on the camp bed and put on the clean clothes always waiting, others he slept in the nearest derelict house. If the shower worked he used it, and he shaved when Daisy complained too much. Harold's nightmares were back and there were new ones. Time and again he tried to shoot past Holly, to kill Spike Pierce. Time and again the bullet hit Holly. Other nights he shot Caddi, and Cooper, and Einstein and Gofannon and all the others, and they popped back up like fairground targets. Because it wasn't losing Holly that ate him. It was failing to protect her, and Cynthia, and Gabriela, and Toby, and the list went on. And now Muhammad and Luke, the two night guards, had joined the list.

Through all the nightmares and the blank days, no matter how scruffy or unshaven or tired he was, Harold felt a little hand pulling him out into the world again and again. Daisy insisted on dragging him off to practice archery or plait hair, to admire her latest ripe tomato or tie up her sunflower because he was tall, to make a daisy chain or draw. Though drawing the special place for Holly nearly broke Harold again, especially when Daisy insisted on angel wings.

Chapter 11:
Comeback Spankfest

"Get your bloody Soldier Boy head on and get down there or they'll kill the guards." Harold stared at Sharyn and his stick, and the pistol in her other hand. "Go. Stop it before we all die."

"Emmy's got it covered. Emmy and Alfie."

"Emmy and Alfie have done their best for nearly a bloody month now but it's not enough. Those animals won't respect a woman, a sixteen-year-old boy, or a gay even if Casper pulled his head out of his arse far enough to help. Now one of them has decided he can get away with rape."

Harold came to his feet. "What! Who? No, where?" His head spun. Rape? His fault, again.

"At the gate Harold, he tried to rape Celine and now he's going to tell Caddi I'm the blacksmith. He says he'll ask for the job of taming me." Liz looked pale and much too mouse-like just now. Her face crumpled. "Christ, what good is a killing machine if it's broken? The bastard may as well go back to Celine and finish the job." Liz turned and Harold started forward.

"Wait. Where is he? No, tell me on the way. Jacket." Harold could feel it now, like an old friend coming back or a light burning through the murk inside his head. The anger, the edges all going blurry with the centre sharp and the darkness, the smothering muddled mess, swept away by rage. He threw on the jacket Sharyn held out and headed across the living room to the door, taking his stick and shoving the gun in the back of his belt. "Tell Casper I want his ugly face and that meat cleaver now." He didn't see the half-apprehensive, half-relieved smile on Sharyn's face as Hazel flew past and down the street to deliver the message.

Harold set off down the street at a quick march. "What happened?"

"My music stopped and before I started another playlist I heard voices outside the forge. A man, a strange voice, so I went out." Liz sounded furious now, which had to be better than terrified or maybe she was both. "He'd got a knife to Celine and a hand up her skirt. I said stop." Liz stumbled and Harold realised that furious or not Liz was half blind with tears. "It happened again, Harold. I couldn't hit him. I screamed stop and he sneered and asked why." Her voice dropped. "The bastard said you were done, finished. Then he saw my apron and hammer and said they thought Jon had been bullshitting, about me being the smith. He left Celine to go and tell Caddi, because Caddi would pay him and he could come back for her or me." Liz's voice ended in a wail. "He'll tell everyone."

"No he bloody won't, he won't live long enough." Harold came out of his street onto the main road and could see a crowd of gangsters, though they all had their backs to him. Everyone's eyes were on someone or something just inside the closed gates, and voices were raised. He picked up the pace. "Find yourself a mousehole, Liz."

"Not a bloody chance this time, not if you really are going killing machine. I've seriously considered human sacrifice to get you back." Something had definitely cheered Liz up though her tone didn't sound like happiness, more like fierce anticipation. Despite sniffing and rubbing at her eyes she'd certainly stopped crying.

A man's voice rose above the rest. "You bitches can't stop us leaving, that's not in your stupid rules. Though now we know that fucker really is screwed up, I might stay."

"That's cost you a fine." Emmy didn't sound her usual confident self.

"Fuck off. We'll take her spear first and then sort you out. The bitch is nearly ready to drop it anyway and you've only got one bolt in that fucking toy." There were only two people in the windows of the guardhouses but one was Alfie with his shotgun aimed at the crowd.

Billy, the other, saw Harold and raised his crossbow to aim down towards the voice. "Touch her and you'll die."

The stranger's voice rose again, dismissive. "Then the rest of this lot come up there and throw you out of the window. You and the other twats who think they can fight." Harold thought that might not work out well because Alfie would definitely shoot.

Harold was only a few steps from the crowd now and had heard enough so he lunged forward and bellowed. "You! Move!"

Several men's heads came round and one said "fuck off" even as he turned. The jar as his stick caught the gangster on the temple felt like sweet release to Harold, and adrenaline surged.

"Fined. Anyone else?" He straight-armed the man in the way, put his shoulder into another and shoved between the next pair. By the time the startled crowd realised what had happened, Harold burst out the front and came up behind four young men, two slightly ahead of the other pair. Men who had all drawn knives. Facing them were Emmy, Patty and a definitely shaky Umeko holding a spear and a child's crossbow.

Emmy's bright smile swept away her frown and she raised her child's crossbow to centre on one man. "I said fined." She pointed with her machete. "You get caned as well for the repeat."

Umeko straightened as well and a savage grin grew on Patty's face. "All of you already owe one fine so be real careful what you say. You want this one Soldier Boy." Her crossbow centred on another man. The other two turned and one cursed and then screamed as his wrist broke under Harold's stick. He might not have been going to use the knife but Harold wasn't taking chances. Something in Harold warned him not to enjoy himself too much, but another part thought he should have done this a long time ago, beaten a few of them shitless. The second man dropped his knife and backed away a few steps, then stopped when Umeko prodded him with her spear.

The one Patty had aimed at spun and cursed, then grinned. "You touch me and I'll tell them all what I know."

Harold didn't speak because this one had to be the attempted rapist so he had to be shut up. Instead he jabbed towards the man's gut with his stick and kicked at the knife hand and the gangster bent at the waist and moved back to avoid the blows. Harold didn't have to do any more because Patty took a long step forward to ram her crossbow against the bloke's kidneys. "I reckon I can get the flights to go right through now. Drop it." She jabbed again. "Bet I can do it before you get two words out so be really quiet." The knife dropped, the last man turned, and his knife clattered on the road. Harold took the few steps to walk past them and join Emmy, then turned to face all the gangsters.

"Hi there Emmy."

"Welcome back, Soldier Boy." Emmy's huge grin almost split her face. "Are we really going to fine them all?"

"At least." Harold waved his free hand over the nearest men. "You three get him with the broken wrist over against the wall. If any of you say another word I'll kill you because you all pulled a knife." Harold really wanted one of them to argue, but none did. "Patty, watch them." Her crossbow followed as they moved. Harold looked over the score of gangsters watching and pointed. "Him on the floor at the back owes a fine, and you and you from when I came through. Any others Emmy?"

Before she could answer a Geek in a smock and suit spoke up. "You can't make that stick, not just for swearing. You might be SAS but there's too many of us."

"I've had to let it ride if it's not directed at one of us. Sorry Harold, but..."

"Not your fault Emmy." Harold fixed the Geek with his stare. "You're a manager so you should know the rules. I didn't alter them and Hawkins agreed." He took a deep breath and let the big smile come, the one born when he hit the first asshole. "I might not get you all, but who'll bet their lives on it?" Harold held the stick just below the boss with one hand and slid his other hand down below the decorated band, as if holding a club or axe. He'd be rusty but the training would still be there, his smile widened, when he turned into what Liz called the alien killing machine.

"This is buckshot not birdshot so he doesn't need to get you all." Alfie sounded actually cheerful. Other voices chipped in from the guardhouses and another two men appeared at the doors with machetes.

"Welcome back Harold. I came as fast as I could. Keep it to the left Alfie, and I'll get the ones this side." Seth's voice sounded from number three and from the muttering and movement among the men that side, he'd brought his sawn-off shotgun.

The Geek manager sneered. "You still can't change rules just like that. We've been allowed to swear." Two men on the end looked over, startled, and dived aside as someone charged out from behind the guardhouse. The apparition, wearing a blanket and underpants, seized the Geek and hurled him against the brickwork. Casper's manic grin appeared from under the blanket as the Geek slid down the house wall, stunned. The big machete flashed in the weak sunlight as Casper waved it in greeting.

"Sorry Harold. I was asleep." Casper looked, if anything, worse than the last time Harold could remember seeing him. Except for the smile, so maybe hitting someone worked for Casper as well? "Are there enough to go round?"

"I think you're in time." Harold glared at the crowd. "Anybody else fancy their chances?" Nobody looked keen to volunteer, so Harold turned to the four youths against the wall. "You four, inside that house. Can you handle them for a minute Jeremy?"

Jeremy waggled his machete and he looked happier as well. "Matti can't come to a window because of the Army, but she'd love to shoot at least one in private." He glanced backwards, then towards Harold again. "She says go gettem Soldier Boy." Jeremy looked at the four men nearby. "Come on, chop chop." He accompanied the last two words with the machete, everyone seemed a bit over the top just now.

Emmy spoke quietly. "I didn't get details but Patty said to stop anyone leaving until something got sorted. She didn't say why."

Harold answered just as quietly. "The one she threatened is probably a dead man once the legalities are sorted." Harold saw her look. "Because he deserves it, not just because I want to kill him."

Emmy shrugged. "Just wondered. What about this lot?"

"If they back off, are you and Alfie happy to keep them covered for a few minutes? I won't be long." Harold glanced at the guardhouse, where the last man had just gone inside. "I won't go far."

"Back them off a bit first to give us some room. Then with Seth as well, we've got it." She smiled happily. "I just saw Doll, Bernie and Finn at the upstairs windows of number three with guns and Bernie has a shotgun. We were short of gate guards because a lot of us shooters stay home to guard our families. Don't go away again, Harold."

"I won't, not now. Casper!" Harold beckoned. "We need a chat in there." Harold pointed to the guardhouse. He turned to the rest of the gangsters. "If you pulled this stunt on anyone else's patch they'd just shoot you, but we're civilised. You all get one chance to put your knives on the road and go back ten paces. Anyone still here or wearing a knife when I come back out runs the gauntlet, and I'll give this lot baseball bats instead of canes."

"Yee-ha, Soldier Boy." "I'm up for that." "Too bloody true." Startled heads looked up at the windows either side. The residents held crossbows or machetes where the Army could see, but the rest had firearms. Despite the quiet non-swearing complaints, knives started to clatter on the road.

Harold shouted as loud as he could. "Mouse? Get Celine and anyone else who has a complaint." He heard Liz reply and followed Casper inside. "Jeremy, if he speaks, cut out his tongue."

Jeremy moved his machete near the indicated man. "Er, okay Harold."

Casper stared at the prisoners and turned with a question starting. "Through there first Casper." The pair of them went past a Matti pointing her handgun steadily at the Hot Rods and wearing a huge grin.

Casper turned as soon as Harold came through the doorway. "Look Harold, I'm sorry. It was my fault and I should have been there."

"Why did you come here just now?"

"Hazel said you were in trouble." Casper grinned. "You needed my ugly face and meat cleaver."

"If you'd known Holly was in trouble, you'd have been there as well. If I'd known, I'd have shot Pierce months ago or told Caddi to piss off and come home earlier." Harold sighed. "How do you feel?"

Casper frowned. "Better? It won't last."

"No, and I'll feel like crap in a bit, but right now I think I know how to cope. If I beat some of these shits up now and then, maybe shoot the occasional one, I can manage. What about you?"

"Maybe." Casper frowned and then shrugged. "It's got to be better."

"Good. Now that little shit through there held a knife to Celine and stuck his hand up her dress. Then he told Liz he'd let Caddi know she was Orchard Close's smith. Wait up." Casper had started towards the other room, machete at the ready. "First we gag him, then try him all legal."

"Then execute him. I like the plan." Casper looked down at himself. "I forgot to bring a gag."

"Or clothes." Harold found a hankie in his pocket. "This is a start."

* * *

Harold held the brief trial in public. The four Hot Rods stood against the inside of the gate and Celine pointed "Him." She shuddered. "It was the knife, Harold. I fumbled the pepper spray, he put the knife to me and I was suddenly back there. You know, before."

Harold nodded. "Yes, I do know. That's the trial done with and the verdict is guilty. There's only one penalty for attempted rape, death, and the woman has the option of gelding the bastard first." The man's eyes bugged out but his gag held. Harold turned to the watching gangsters and raised his voice because they were still back up the road. "Anyone want to open their big mouth to object?" Nobody did so he turned back to Celine. "Do you want first shot with a crossbow, or a knife?"

"Crossbow please. I'm not up to cutting someone, but I can do that." Celine tried for a smile. "The therapy is working."

"More therapy first, to get you in the mood. Get a cane but don't tire your arm out." Harold grinned at the bound man. "He'll wait."

Celine didn't tire herself too much. Though the eight men covered in angry red or bleeding stripes from the canes were concentrating on getting dressed and not cursing, rather than if the line of women had been pacing themselves. One of the GOFS soldiers, one without cane marks, approached Harold cautiously. "Why him, Marconi? He didn't actually swear."

"What would Gofannon do if a Geek argued about GOFS rules? What would Caddi do if you stood in the Mansion and told him what he could and couldn't do?"

"Kill me, probably. Fair enough. It's just that Gofannon will want to know. He keeps track of what you do, rules and punishments." He looked over where a GOFS had just finished getting dressed. "Can we have our weapons back and go now? Do we get our knives back?"

"You all get your knives, and those who weren't fined get their weapons back, but there's another lesson first. Some of those we spanked should have been dodging crossbow bolts. The reason they weren't is that the women are getting their practice anyway." Harold smiled. "You all get your gear back after watching us execute a Hot Rod."

"F... Christ, you really meant that? Caddi will go crazy."

"No he won't. This is for attempted rape, and everyone knows the penalty for that. Just to be clear, the rules haven't been altered and if a bunch of blokes turn up waving sharp stuff like last time I will not be as polite." Harold pointed at the rest of the gangsters. "Hawkins and Caddi will get the same message. I'm done with playing nice."

Everyone got the message. Harold and Casper tied the Hot Rod to a pair of timbers nailed across an empty doorway and since they used a derelict house on the neutral road, everyone had a good view. A dozen men stood where the Army wouldn't see them, and pointed firearms at the crowd of gangsters. A line of women came out of Orchard Close with wound crossbows and lined up, with a few having to wait for a weapon. Harold called out the charge, and the sentence. "Okay Celine. Blimey Patty. Aren't you having a go?" Patty stood nearby holding her crossbow out for Celine.

"Too true I am." Patty sneered at the target. "But first I'm loaning Celine my crossbow, and helping her aim. She's got a particular target in mind but isn't very accurate. I'll get rewound by the time the rest have a go."

Celine waved a real Liz special and loaded it. "Therapy, Harold." Harold did wonder if he could avoid watching, because he knew just where that would end up. After Celine's shot and the muffled scream that followed several of the gangsters weren't watching, and others definitely looked ill. A pale-faced Celine came past Harold with a hand over her mouth and Liz took her inside. Patty waited for every other woman who felt up to it to stick a bolt in the man before taking her own turn. Harold didn't think Patty's bolt made any difference to the dead or unconscious gangster by the time her bolt crunched into his skull, but that sort of accuracy carried a message to the others.

Harold made sure the three surviving Hot Rods who'd pulled knives had a close look at Patti's bolt. "You were almost target practice for her. Let Caddi know we'll only leave him up a day because we don't want to attract more vermin, so if anyone wants the body come and get it before then. We'll chop out the bolts first." All three needed lifts home from their friends because all three ran the gauntlet and the women didn't hold back for these. They'd also lost their weapons, all their weapons, so Caddi would no doubt be less than happy.

*   *   *

Caddi visited briefly the following day, to check out the corpse and buy beer. He inspected the bolt in the man's head, and paced out the distance to where Patty had stood. Someone had given him that part of the message, how Patty stood at the other side of the road for her shot. "We thought you might have lost it, Soldier Boy."

Luckily Harold still felt better after yesterday so the little smile didn't annoy him too much. "No, it made me nastier. I'm a lot more likely to just kill someone now." Harold wasn't, he didn't think, but the neighbours would be looking for any sign of weakness. He'd thought about how to back them off. "I kept my head down because the alternative would have upset the survivors."

"I'll buy it. Survivors?"

"My first reaction would have involved seeing how many gang bosses I could shoot before one of their men got me. I reckon I'd have got a round dozen at least if I'd kept switching gangs." Harold held Caddi's eyes even as he saw the anger flare. "That's not a threat, Caddi, just how I felt. I'm past that but now you understand why I stayed home so nobody annoyed me even more, because the survivors would have attacked Orchard Close."

"Yeah." Caddi nodded slowly. "Never thought of that. If a man who can keep cool and shoots like you gets mad enough, he won't run about shouting." He frowned. "I was told you might be dead and your lot had lost their bottle, but the state of my blokes is convincing." He held up a hand. "I know, that was instead of dodging crossbow bolts. Considering where your lot aim, that was a really good option. Are you repairing guns again?"

The sudden switch of subject told Harold the real reason Caddi had come. Harold had stopped repairing weapons for a month. The ones Harold had agreed to repair before Holly died were turned away so Caddi still had those and possibly more now. "Have you been squabbling with neighbours again?"

"That and we're having to use reloads now. Those mess up the guns really fast, as you'll know, even if we try to clean them a bit." He scowled. "We can't afford to get too ambitious with cleaning in case it doesn't work because you'll charge double. Can you cast proper buckshot?" Caddi shrugged at Harold's quizzical look. "Someone mentioned buckshot and our version is a bit rough and ready. I've been told the proper stuff goes further."

"Sorry, I've just got a few shells that came with the weapon." Harold had no intention of improving Caddi's buckshot. Harold's own version took time because he also thought smooth shot might carry further. As a bonus, carefully filing off the casting marks to get the little lead balls nice and smooth seemed to distract him from his darker thoughts. "I'm repairing guns again, but sticking close to home for a while because Hawkins might get upset about Marconi."

"Nah, the Geeks will suck it up because I have, and they daren't go it alone." Caddi smiled. "I'd have sent his head, frozen." The gang boss smiled wider. "Their general, Wellington, is supposed to have gone soft on a woman and he likes your lot so maybe he won't agree anyway. Did you inject something when he had his tooth fixed?"

"Manners, maybe?" Harold vaguely remembered Finn saying something.

"Ouch." Caddi rubbed his hands. "If I'm bringing the weapons I'll expect something off, for the petrol?"

"Not a chance. You'd send an escort anyway in case I'm robbed. That might be a real mistake now especially if I'm killed, because quite a few more men and women are learning to shoot. They'd prefer real practice and I've still got people who can use a big rifle. Those have been practicing with the Blaser while I've been out of it." Harold frowned. "Anyway, you've got lots of petrol so why are you bothered?"

"Maybe not. Are you having any trouble with petrol? Some of the petrol cars are running rough and we found all sorts of crap in an engine when it was stripped down." Caddi seemed dead serious for once. "And yes, we filter the fuel."

"I usually drive the diesel pickup. I'll ask the girl club how that minibus is running." Harold frowned. "Why would it be the petrol?"

"Charger remembered an old urban legend thing, from before the crash. Something about petrol degrading if it's stored too long. Did you ever hear it?" Caddi looked genuinely worried, which worried Harold.

"No. How long is it supposed to take? It's been nearly two years since the refineries were first hit. How long after that did the tankers stop coming to the local petrol station?" Harold shrugged at Caddi's look. "I was in Kuwait with the Army."

"Ah, right. They stopped within weeks, to the public ones anyway. The coppers, firemen and ambulances got fresh supplies but nowhere else." Caddi's frown deepened. "I don't think any of our diesels have had trouble either. We're draining all the petrol stations, what bit there is left." Caddi smiled. "You haven't got a petrol station, have you?"

"Not really. Does it save better in cans then?"

The gang boss suddenly remembered where he was. "Bloody hell, why would I tell you? I'll sell you the information for gun repairs?" He held up his beer bottle and peered at it. "Have you been mixing some of that Barbie weed into your beer?"

Harold laughed. "No, because we drink that beer as well. A petrol shortage won't really bother us anyway. After all, we can walk to our borders in fifteen minutes, more or less, so it doesn't matter if the cars conk out."

"Smartarse. I'll bring the guns." Caddi grinned. "Carrying gear about to save petrol can go onto the punishment list." Though later the guns were delivered by car as usual, with guards and four motorbike outriders.

*   *   *

The discussion about petrol worried Harold enough to call an immediate meeting. A curious Seth followed Emmy into the room. "Take a bow, Seth."

"Okay. Why?" A grinning Seth did so.

"Remember a little conversation when we'd just survived the big attack, about petrol?"

Seth frowned. "No Harold. All I can remember is we survived, and Berry getting that crossbow bolt out and patching me up."

Emmy nudged him. "All you remember is Berry kissed you better and held your hand."

A big smile broke over Seth's face. "Guilty. So what did I forget?"

"You asked about moving the petrol into the enclave, and I said that was too dangerous, and might all go boom." Harold sighed. "Then afterwards I thought about it, and how having it all in one spot wasn't a good idea anyway. That's why we filled as many petrol cans, those plastic things, as we could find. Caddi has just started doing the same because there's a problem. Anyone, how is the minibus running?"

"Not so good. We need a better filter for the crap when we get petrol." Patty frowned. "Though we're pouring it through layers of old curtains now so we'll not get much finer."

"It might not be the filters." Harold explained. "Anyone heard of that?" Nobody answered.

"One of the survivalist types might have, but I don't know anyone who kept petrol for long before the crash. A can in the car for emergencies or one in the garage for the mower, maybe?" Casper grinned. "We could all ride lawnmowers, they wouldn't use as much." Thumping a Geek had definitely cheered Casper up.

Emmy glared at him. "Motorbikes wouldn't either and we can steer them. How much petrol did we stash in that cellar, Harold?"

"No idea, Emmy, and about half of it is diesel which might not have the same trouble. If you top up the minibus with two or three gallons of the canned stuff, then try it, we'll know. Then if the stored petrol is better, we'll save it and use up all the other first." Harold frowned. "Maybe we should drain the big vans since they drink most."

"Don't drain them completely, Harold. My Grandad did that with an old Beetle he wanted to renovate. When he filled it up again, every gasket and joint had dried out and cracked." Finn snapped his fingers. "There's got to be petrol, bits at least, in the cars inside garages out there or inside Orchard Close. The garages are probably leaking after the shrapnel and the cars might be seized up, but the tanks should be sound."

"Yeuk. I'm not syphoning diesel." Liz screwed up her mouth in disgust. "I did that once and got a gob full, and even spam won't wash that taste out."

"How did you syphon diesel, Liz, since you might be the expert? Better still, why were you syphoning diesel?" Emmy grinned. "Is this part of that dark past you keep quiet about?"

"With a rubber tube. Apart from that my lips are sealed, especially around diesel."

"We can do better than that. Rob and I were paid in fuel sometimes after the crash, and occasionally had to take it from car tanks." Finn shrugged. "Blocked toilets or no electric were more important than their motor working so we both have something a bit more advanced than tube."

"Good." Harold looked around his friends and advisors, what in another gang would be the lieutenants, senior members or managers with weird names. "I reckon we take what we can from anywhere we can find it, but compare what we get from each tank. Maybe we can spot the difference in the bad stuff?"

By the following evening they had answers, and glum faces. Casper pointed at four tumblers. "That's the good stuff at this end. That brown stuff at the other end is the worst of the rest though you were right, diesel does seem to look all right. These are all petrol. A lot of what we found needs filtering and those two little pumps had to be cleaned out several times."

"We mark what we got today and any other from the ruins to keep it separate and save the dark coloured petrol for starting fires. We'll also take what's left from the tanks under the garage across the car park, and really filter it and mark that up. Sal reckons the petrol from the cellar of number thirteen made a big difference to the minibus so we save that for a bit yet." Harold sighed. "I'll use the petrol pickup until the petrol is used up or spoils, then go back to diesel."

"A sigh? Has it got sentimental value, the diesel pickup?" Finn frowned. "You arrived with that one."

"Sort of a talisman, it's the only motor I ever stole." Harold grinned at the looks. "Ask Sharyn. Now let's sieve or curtain the take, and try them all in a petrol engine we don't care about." He looked round. "We've got four motorbikes. Who fancies learning to ride one?"

Everyone winced. There were still crash helmets, but they weren't exactly pristine anymore. Patty put her hand up. "Can I ride a pushbike?" Pushbikes went up the list of priorities because although many hadn't ridden one since childhood, allegedly nobody ever forgot.

*　　　*　　　*

Harold passed the same message about how many bosses might have died, and the extra weapon training for residents, to various gang members. Part was true because right at the beginning he'd considered doing that, going out with a rifle and a pocket full of bullets. Both Emmy and Alfie took long shots with the 303 while there were visitors about, to drive home that others could shoot even if someone took out Harold.

In addition more people, especially women, really did want to learn how to be adequate with a weapon, any weapon, at close quarters. Harold tried to train them, or get them started at least, and hoped a few would actually shoot or stab if necessary. Lengths of wood were sufficient for practicing machete work. In addition those learning to use a crossbow had plenty of bolts since those could be replaced as long as the flight and point were retrieved. The ammunition expended in firearms practice wasn't so easily replaced, but a flurry of weapons repairs brought propellant and those learning could fire a few live rounds.

Cleaning the guns afterwards confirmed that the new propellant definitely left more residue than Harold's original rounds, or the propellant he'd taken from gun clubs. Harold could repair again since Sharyn gave Harold the keys to get his rifle, ammunition, and all the gun repair gear. Emmy and Alfie already had keys, for emergencies. Harold set up a workshop there instead of bringing everything home, and over the next week often slept slumped over his bench. Harold worked until he slept, or staggered home to collapse on the camp bed, because that way he dreamed less. All his clothes were now in the study, and Harold used the washroom downstairs or the shower in the gun room house. Sharyn never mentioned where he slept or why he didn't go upstairs for any reason except to read a Daisy or Wills bedtime story.

Wills-story had been an attempt by Sharyn to get Harold out of his black hole, and since Daisy insisted he'd gone with it. Daisy insisted because she came to help with Wills-story and ended up with a bonus. Casper came round and took up both Wills-story and Daisy-story, and began to wear more clothes and shave. His visits included a rapidly growing Amber who now had a playmate.

Harold shook his head. "I can't do it. Hazel can help Daisy."

Sharyn cuddled the golden furred pup. "All right, Hazel will help Daisy feed and train her. But you've got to take Daisy on dog-walks because Angel will be too strong for Daisy within months, and for Hazel eventually if she ends up anything like as strong as Fury." As usual Harold winced over the puppy's name. He never asked why Daisy chose this one, because Harold just knew it was her blonde fur. Not the same blonde, thank all the gods, but Lucky's Labrador blood had produced one almost traditional coloured pup.

"All right, I'll take turns with Casper if he ever allows Amber to walk." Amber did both walk and run, but Casper still had a habit of carrying her about. "I'm trying, Sharyn, but it'll take time."

"I know, little brother." Sharyn sat on the edge of the camp bed. "Though if you aren't going to come and sit with us now and then, I'm moving a chair in here." She sighed. "At least you're sleeping here most nights."

"Yeah, the killing machine is parked downstairs now but still handy."

Sharyn's face crumpled. "It's not that! Well it is, but not just. One of your gods might know where Dad got to, Mum could be anyplace but probably in a bottle or an early grave, and Freddy's gone." A first tear trickled down Sharyn's face. "You're it, little brother, my family. I sat here and waited for Emmy, or Liz, or Patty, to come and tell me you'd done something stupid. Killed yourself or set off with a bloody rifle." She stood. "So yes, I'm really, really pleased you're parked in here at night." With that Sharyn whirled round and stormed out, slamming the door.

Harold sat and cursed himself, again. He sat while it grew dark, and then until voices from outside roused him. Harold stood and looked out of the window because he hadn't closed the curtains, and smiled at Alfie escorting Hazel home after their computer game. The pair stopped at the gate and spoke, and then Hazel leaned forward up and kissed Alfie! Harold turned and opened the door, to go outside and…. what? Hazel had turned fifteen and that had been a friendly peck, not a… His mind skittered away from levels of kissing. Harold had just decided he was better off saying nothing when Hazel came through from the hallway and found him standing partway out of the study.

Her eyes went to the dark study, lit only by moonlight, and she scowled. "You were spying! What did you think we were doing? Alfie brought me home to keep me safe, that's all." The next bit came out more of an embarrassed mutter. "It wasn't a real kiss." Then indignant won again. "Alfie isn't like that, he walks us home ever since, ever since…" Hazel stormed over to the stairs and up, her parting shot being "now he's going to walk Veronica home so you'd better run or you'll miss it."

Harold sat on his bed, and decided he should start talking to the people in the same house, at least.

*　　　*　　　*

The radio switched from BBC to Barbie Radio which meant Daisy had left for school, and Harold braced himself. He'd no idea what sort of reception he'd get, or even if Sharyn would talk to him after yesterday. The tune changed, and Harold smiled and stood up. He opened the door. "Hey, did I ever tell you I met her, Morgana? Oh." Oh because a startled Hazel stood alone in the living room.

"Um, good morning Harold." Hazel blushed and ducked her head. "About last night?" Her head came up. "You know her, Morgana?" Hazel glanced at the radio. "But she's in the charts, was, you know, she's young?"

"Not quite know her. We met though, out in Iraq when she toured with Dragonspawn. I've even got a souvenir, a signed one." Harold smiled. "I'm really quite modern and all that despite my long grey beard."

Hazel smiled as well. "You act old so I forget." Her smile wavered just a bit. "Alfie just keeps us safe, and I am fifteen. That wasn't even a level one and Holly told me to never go to level three or even two unless I'm sixteen and really, really, like him, the boy. Oh, sorry, we're not supposed to say Holly." Hazel almost whispered the last bit.

"It's all right Hazel." It wasn't but the whole world couldn't stop saying a name just for him. "I'm pleased Alfie has been watching out for you, and after all a kiss is supposed to be the reward and a rite of passage."

Hazel sniggered. "You are weird. Rite of passage?" She frowned and glanced at the radio. "So you didn't really meet Morgana, just got a signature."

Harold sat down. "I met her twice but the same day. Once because the officers brought me to meet her because of the medal, then later I met Morgana in the mess when she had a drink with the squaddies. She recognised me so I got to sit with her and the rest, and that's when I got the souvenir."

"Wow. Wait until I tell the rest. All because of a medal." Hazel glanced towards the kitchen. "Sharyn told me your medal was for being really stupid and surviving. Berry says you're some sort of deadly maniac and Liz says…"

"Whoa. Sharyn is right, sort of. I know what Liz says."

"Well you were reassuring. You are again, but Alfie is as well, at the other end of the street." Hazel giggled. "He'll have heart failure when I tell him you were watching."

"Well go and do that because I've found work for my lazy brother now he's got up." Two mugs of tea preceded Sharyn out of the kitchen and she put one on the coffee table near Harold. "Now scat because no school today means rat trap duty."

"Yeuk, yes." Hazel pulled a face. "That's worse now we've gone non-lethal though that's better than another one of our cats being snared. I had a lot of trouble killing the trapped rats at first."

Sharyn sat and sipped tea, not speaking until Hazel left. "She's already had a long talk or two about boys but not to me. Holly was near enough her age for Hazel to get over being embarrassed, and be inquisitive." Sharyn gave Harold a critical once-over. "Welcome back." At Harold's quizzical look she pointed. "Today is the first time you've cleaned your boots properly, and you're talking as well. Our soldier is finally ready for duty so you'd best get started."

"Cripes, let me finish my tea."

"Okay, and while we do, just how well did you know this Morgana? Is she the woman in the photo with the garter?"

"What? No! Have you been in my box?"

"Of course I have and Liz looked as well." Sharyn sighed. "I remembered about Freddy's clothes, about sorting them out and how I couldn't. Liz and I cleared your room, but we wanted to make sure you had something, for memory." Sharyn sighed again. "Liz said the stocking would do it."

"Is everything else gone? Who took them?" Now Harold worried he'd see Holly's clothes out there in the street, because nice clothes were too valuable to throw away.

"We dressed her up properly, in her prettiest things, and yes the rest have been shared out. You might think something looks familiar but it won't be quite the same. Do you want to move back in there?"

"No thanks, sis. I'll stay down here."

"I thought so. What about Hazel? She's a bit old to have Daisy as a roomy. Would you mind?"

Harold sat and thought about that and no he didn't mind, because he wasn't going back in there. "No, I'm okay with that. Tell her she can move in."

"You tell her. Hazel hasn't asked so she might need a bit of persuading and will need to know you agree, really agree. She needs a room of her own for practice anyway, before she moves out."

"What! Moves out? Why?" Harold stared, then dropped his eyes. "Me and my foul moods I suppose."

"No, or maybe a bit. Hazel will be sixteen next year and she'll move into the girl club because we really aren't her parents, which makes staying here wrong. Some of her friends, from her block of flats, are in there." Sharyn frowned. "Hazel needs this, Harold. First because yes, you and your moods aren't helping her get over Holly. Holly was her friend as well, and before you met either of them. On top of that Hazel needs time to be a young woman who doesn't have the dreaded Soldier Boy lurking behind her."

"What!" Harold managed a little smile. "I need a better vocabulary. Cripes? Dreaded Soldier Boy?"

"You are a bit intimidating for any boy wanting to walk her home." Sharyn smirked. "Those yobs walk round me as if I'm radioactive just because I'm your sister. That fell off for a bit but now they scamper out of the way. A few are scampering away from Patty now, as well as Emmy and Casper. You did good, little brother." She shrugged. "Even if I know it was because you finally lost your temper."

Harold wanted to object but if intimidating worked on the gangsters, he'd do intimidating. "All right, I'll park my Uncle-Harold persona and smile at Hazel. Now what's this work?"

"Not yet. What did you get from Morgana? We didn't look properly and now I'm intrigued about what souvenir you got from a woman who sings 'Dark and dirty, under cover, come and be my Dragon lover' and dresses like that."

"She doesn't dress like that. Well she does, and when I met her with the officers Morgana was all lycra and heels and attitude. In the mess she'd got rid of the make-up, the scales, cut about five inches off her heels and put on a dress. A rock singer dress but not like the stage stuff." Harold laughed. "I did meet them all and got a beermat. Dragonspawn are really quite ordinary and a lot shorter in normal shoes."

"Typical, a beermat. Who got the garter that time?"

"Just so you know, the beermat has all of Dragonspawn's signatures on one side, and Morgana's and a lipstick kiss on the other. That would have been worth a fortune in my dotage." Harold stopped smiling. "Crap. The BBC have banned all that music so I don't suppose she was on the happy list."

"Happy list?"

"The ones who are happy because a bus or a message came for them, and they are now sat with their feet up laughing at us." Harold shrugged. "You know I think this was at least partly planned. It had to be but what worries me is I can't see where it's going. We're penned up, but now what?"

"Maybe gradual starvation because while you were having a timeout the TV kept banging on about shortages. Creeping lurgy hits this, waffle-bugs of some sort eat that, the rain comes the wrong day. Curtis has been going crazy, running around looking for signs of the latest infestation. He's getting just a bit disillusioned since our plants don't have the same problems." Sharyn waved a hand to include all the gardens outside the walls. "Curtis has warned us that despite all the digging and planting, those crops might not be enough. We've stopped selling rabbit burgers which is a pity, ours fetch premium price because there's some suspicion about rat and cat in others. We let the customers see our kitchen."

Harold finished his tea. "What do I do first, since I'll bet the Coven have a solution to something with my name on it?"

"For starters go out there and talk to people, our people. Wander about and let them see the gangsters go shifty-eyed and move aside. Stop and have a natter with the gardeners, throw sticks for the dogs." Sharyn's voice hardened. "Then go on the next shopping trip and deal with the harassment, before staggering back with your pack stuffed full. That's in three days' time. Go mob-handed and take Alfie and Emmy so they can point out the stroppy ones at the mart and you can deal with the little scroats." Sharyn relaxed again, a bit. "Bring lots of those chews, spam and tubes of paste and plenty of fruit, potatoes and pasta, Harold, so we can save them for winter. It'll be a long one."

*   *   *

A sharp rap on the table cut across the babble in the bunker, and the meeting came to order. "What went wrong this time? We are supposed to have the acreage to feed the current population, or should have with what Gerard brought from Europe before the last ports closed. That surplus should last long enough for us to solve the problem of London at least and then we can cut down consumption elsewhere. Grace, Henry, why aren't we producing enough food?" Owen leant back in his seat as the two named people looked at each other. Beyond them, for once, the screen showed gentle rolling countryside instead of violence.

Henry, a portly man with thick black hair and a thick beard to match held up his files. "The farms with farmers and machinery are producing well enough. Where we are using work camps because the work is manual, or where we don't want mechanical methods seen, there's a problem."

Grace brandished her file, her thin face wearing a sneer. "My work camps have supplied the numbers. It's up to your people to give them the right jobs."

Henry waved her protest aside. "But the people are useless. They can't do the simplest jobs, even picking fruit that really is ripe and leaving the rest to ripen."

"Shoot a few to encourage the rest. That lot are scum anyway." A murmur of agreement went around the table.

"We shot a few. They're trying, but most of them are from cities." Henry looked around the table. "Which of you knows what is ready to harvest and what isn't? The workers from the camps are city bred and think food grows in bags in supermarkets." He glared across the gleaming expanse of wood. "Unfortunately someone decided that immigrant agricultural workers were a disposable minority."

"Let's not get personal, because we all signed off on the plan." Owen shrugged. "And in that plan we gave B level passes to horticultural specialists and farmers. Why aren't there enough?"

"Firstly, wastage because those people are from lower echelons and have their own ideas about who runs the world. A large number ended up in Grace's work camps or were sent to Vanna's facilities because they knew too much by then. What's left are capable of sorting out when to plant or reap, what to sow where, and the time and type for treating with fertilisers and pesticides. There aren't enough to actually supervise the work."

"If they had the pesticides organised, what about these losses?" A woman jabbed a finger at her file.

"Let me finish, please. That was what showed us the real problem. Our experts say administer this, here, and the local supervisor gives the job to a work gang. Unfortunately the scum would rather sniff the damn stuff than put it on the plants, that or they use too much, or too little. We need a lower level of supervision on some jobs." Henry sat back and spread his hands. "I'm open to suggestions."

"We can't issue B passes to everybody who had a greenhouse or allotment. There are too many Bs already."

"Too many old people were given passes of some sort, and they aren't productive in any way."

"Easy to see your parents are dead."

"Why can't the whole crop be lifted at once, using the machines? That's how it was done before."

"We need the rest to ripen, not be wasted."

"Back then the farmers also ploughed fields under because a ship full of cheap cauliflowers or whatever had just landed. Now we need every bit of food."

"We can't use machines for these jobs anyway, Henry said so."

"Trustees."

Owen, the chairman, had been sat back letting everyone talk but now he rapped the table with his small gavel. "Trustees? Explain please."

The tall middle-aged Asian woman, Vanna, smiled. "The Germans used trustees, put some prisoners in charge of others to make sure they worked properly."

"We aren't Nazis!"

"Calm down Henry. We aren't Nazis, though we have killed more people than the Third Reich ever managed." Owen smiled and turned back to Vanna. "I'm sure many others used this type of system, our own prisons for instance. Go on Vanna."

"Some versions are more proactive. Put someone in charge of a small group and treat them a little better. Give them some authority and back that up ruthlessly, but if the group doesn't produce the trustee is punished." Vanna nodded towards Grace. "Find the gardeners, those who know when a cauliflower or an apple is ripe, and give them a dozen scum. The first of the scum to object becomes fertiliser."

"That might work. That's exactly the level of supervision needed, and will be cheap. Then, when we can finally go mechanised, all the workforce are still disposable. After all, this is only short-term until the population centres are dealt with." Henry turned to Grace. "Can you do it?"

"Maybe. We tend to get the scum, as has been noted, so not too many will be gardeners. Perhaps the soldiers around the cities could keep their eyes open and find a few? Arrest them for something, anything, and send them to me." Grace smiled. "We will find them an incentive or a control."

"Excellent. If we are too late to rescue enough of the harvest this year, we'll stop the food to another city. I'm sure there's enough soldiers for that?" Owen looked enquiringly at Joshua, the Army man.

"Just about. When we discussed personnel levels, nobody factored in starving any cities this early. There are too many people and too much ammunition still in there."

"Fair enough. Now onto your other problem, Joshua. Newcastle. Your reports state that one gang leader has subdued a third of the city and has a small army. How small?" Owen leant forward. "Or more to the point, is it too large?"

"Too large, numerically they could break out easily enough and might get to Middlesbrough and break the cordon there. Once we brought in air and armour they'd break but then scatter all over the Yorkshire Dales or the Scottish Borders. That is all broken country so they'd be difficult to hunt down." Joshua clicked a controller and the screen showed a map of Newcastle with about a third highlighted. "At the moment the river and sea confine him better than we do, but our intelligence states that he will take over the rest of the city first. That's the extent of his ambition, but he will succeed within six months at the present rate and then?" Joshua shrugged and many of those present nodded slowly. They knew all about ambition.

"Can you stop him? Give guns to the other gangs or use artillery to help them?" The youngest man, Gerard, frowned. "Why not use air power now?"

"Economy. We still have to be careful with refined fuel. That's why helicopters are used instead of jets and they drop crude oil with only enough napalm to ignite the rest. Joshua can't openly use the artillery or hand out weapons because we are not involved." A ripple of laughter ran round the table at Owen's words. "Unless there is no other way. Joshua?"

Joshua hesitated. "I'd like to use the Army, but not openly. To be honest I'd rather use the private groups that Vanna and others utilise, the private security contractors, but they aren't up to it." He took a breath. "I want to use Special Forces."

"SAS, that sort of thing? Do we want them seeing what's happening in there?" Ivy, the redhead, looked worried. "Surely we are trying to keep the troops from seeing too much, to avoid fostering any sympathy."

"Special Forces are highly trained, and not prone to getting weepy over the plight of the scenery. They also tend to keep clear of the rest of the soldiers and aren't loose-lipped. Best of all they'll go in there, kill this man and all his top people, blow the hell out of the place with something improvised and won't leave Army boot-prints." Joshua shrugged. "If the worst comes to worst we can send the team on a secret mission they don't return from."

Owen looked around the table. "Any real dissention? No? In that case Joshua, we'll leave you to it."

"There is another problem, Owen." Joshua hesitated much longer this time. "A severe shortage of eligible young women. The British Army were late integrating women into active service and the A list, and many of the B list, don't want a soldier dating their daughters. Especially since, to be delicate, the soldiers won't be intending marriage."

"Not more brothels!"

"You have another solution, Nate? Are you volunteering your daughters to date a soldier?" Owen looked steadily at the glowering black man until he subsided. "If the women are already prostitutes, perhaps brothels are acceptable? After all we've had to accommodate the European personnel who expect such facilities. Grace, can you find volunteers?"

"Some of the women in the camps will probably prefer soldiers to their current options, especially if their conditions are improved?"

"Of course. We wouldn't want the staff unhappy. Joshua, add young women of an accommodating nature to gardeners on your memo to the Army posts." Owen glanced around. "Any more policy issues, or are we down to specifics? Good, then first we'll want the current fuel stocks please?"

As the room finally emptied, Owen waited and indicated for Grace, Gerard and Vanna to do the same. "A quiet word please. If we have to bring in brothels, or rather when, we may have a problem within our own ranks. One of you ladies may be required to find a solution either among your special facilities personnel, Vanna, or in your camps, Grace. Gerard can arrange discreet transportation, and will have the travel plans of any target. All of you, please think about this but only think. No records." The three murmured agreement and left quickly enough for the delay not to be noticed.

*   *   *

Back in the ruined city, Harold braced himself and set off up the access road. Another hurdle, another task to do on his own. Not truly on his own, but in those few short months all these trips and tasks had also included

Holly. He stood while the wand passed over him, and handed over his pass. "Soldier Boy. A word please, just while the rest come through." The sergeant beckoned a corporal to take over on the document scanner.

Harold followed the sergeant a half dozen paces away from the gap in the sandbags and the rifles covering it. "A problem Sarge?"

"Maybe. You are a very lucky young man, lucky to be alive." The sergeant scowled at Harold. "Exclusion means keep out. I was sorely tempted."

Harold kept his voice steady. "At the time I hoped you would be."

"Those women disagreed."

The barest trace of a smile flitted across Harold's face. "The old question. Who is smarter, the male or the female?"

"Ask a married man. Now I have a more pressing question. Did something snap in your head when we didn't shoot you? We understand the occasional thrashing because your young ladies explained." The sergeant glared. "Mass beatings and public executions is another thing entirely, and may lead us to reassess your threat level."

"I lost the plot Sarge. Not then, earlier because I'd survived so I hid in a dark place inside here." Harold tapped his head. "The visiting gangsters took advantage." Harold sighed. "We executed a man who tried to rape one of the women, publicly and yes, brutally, to stop any repeats. After all, the local forces of law and order were noticeable by their absence when three gangsters abducted and murdered a young woman."

"We daren't fire." The sergeant's shoulders sagged, and he lost his military bearing for a few moments. "We aren't allowed to shoot anyway if they don't show firearms. Though if there'd been a clear shot maybe someone would have tried." He shrugged. "At that distance, downhill in the dark? We'd have probably killed her anyway because we don't have snipers or even sharpshooters at every guard post." He straightened. "The mass beatings?"

"Every single one of those men had said something obscene to a woman at least twice. I used to stamp on that quickly, but this time it had all got out of hand." Harold really smiled this time. "We use stripping and canes and women for the humiliation. Just a beating wouldn't work, and our food is too precious to waste on prisoners."

"Obscenity?"

"Effing and blinding Sarge. If we stop them there it goes no further, and the women call it spanking to rub the lesson in." Harold watched the soldiers passing the rest of his group through, smiling and even making a couple of small jokes. "If they aren't stopped, hard, the likes of those gangsters don't stop. Do you lot have any idea what happens to ordinary people in the other enclaves?"

"Rumours, very nasty rumours which I don't want confirmed. Some things aren't rumours, such as women luring squaddies into the dark and lunatics shooting at soldiers for the hell of it." Sarge looked out over the city. "There is a growing habit of referring to everyone in there as the animals. I'm pleased you still seem to be civilised even if the term is stretched a bit."

"We call them animals as well Sarge, but only the ones in charge. Try to remember that; it's the ones in charge and the rest are just folk. Surely you see that on Mart days?" Harold looked along the road both ways but saw nobody. "Where is everyone?"

"The soldiers are no longer needed because very few people use this road to get to a mart. Something about having no weapons at the other end. Now you see our problem Mr. Miller, we don't see any of these ordinary folk you talk about." Sarge glanced at the crowd now gathered on the road. "Your little tribe is ready Soldier Boy. I will remind the men to be polite. Wouldn't want any of them spanked." He smiled, nodded, and went back to the soldiers.

"What was all that about?"

"I'll tell you on the way, Emmy. Just in case I forget to mention it, let the chips and beer brigade know they are doing a fantastic job. Ask them to keep smiling to remind the squaddies we're human, because the rest are now the animals." Harold frowned. "We really don't want the men with machine guns thinking of us as animals."

"Cripes no." Emmy sighed, shuffled her pack a bit and settled into a steady walk. "I really hope we find a couple of those scroats there today. I know you're all chivalrous and that, Harold, but could you do me a favour?" She grinned. "On account of my stunning looks, and the effect I have on all you bad boys."

"Maybe." Harold couldn't help smiling. "Though the effect is blunted by having your fella along."

Emmy scowled. "That's why if I point to a bloke and say lamp him, I want you to flatten the little scroat. Curtis isn't a fighter, Harold. He'll do it if he has to, like for Gabriela, but he's not like you or even me. A couple of the bastards said things, tried to wind me up." Emmy didn't speak for a few moments, then she continued but quieter, slightly embarrassed. "They did, but I'm not that much of a fighter either without a crossbow. None of us are except you and Casper and so we had to swallow it and that really eats at Curtis. If I point, break the little shit's arm for me, yeah?"

Harold thought, but not for long. "I owe you that at least. Would you like me and Casper to hold him so you can do it?"

Emmy giggled, a welcome sound. "I'd love that but a crowd would gather and there'd be a full-scale riot. Just smack him good and hard and do that macho bullshit thing."

"OK. I'll wander across and have words with Casper in case he's nearer."

*   *   *

They'd barely started shopping before a hand pointed. "Hit that one Harold." It wasn't Emmy who spoke, because by the time they'd arrived at the mart and distributed the iron bars another six people had mentioned someone needing a good smack. A few questions and they all meant one of two possible targets and Harold really did want to hit someone, so now he didn't hesitate.

"Fucking hell, why did you do that?" The man stared at his friend, curled up on the floor moaning and nursing his arm.

"Language, ladies present." As the speaker looked round Casper caught him with a full-blooded slap to the side of his head. Casper was bloody angry as well, and his victim ricocheted off the steel shelving and folded up in a heap on the floor. The other six with machetes and aluminium baseball bats backed away, brandishing weapons.

"Fair warning. Just because I'm not along when this lot come shopping, don't get mouthy." Harold glared at them. "That little scroat thought he could act tough if I wasn't here. Don't make the same mistake." Harold fought down a smile as something crossed his mind. "Just because I don't come a couple of times, don't get ambitious because?"

Emmy, Bernie, Sal and Jeremy got it and chorused "I'll be back."

"Cripes, missed that one. Hit another, Soldier Boy." Patty sounded disgusted with herself.

Harold picked up one of the two machetes on the floor and held it out behind him. "Here, hit your own."

"Hey, that's…" The man looked over the group facing him and changed his mind. "What are you going to do to him?"

"Nothing. By the time that heals he should have found some manners. Let him know when we've gone, will you? He's not really listening right now." Harold smiled happily as the gang retreated round the end of the aisle. Hitting a scroat really did make him feel better.

Casper picked up the other machete. "We could strip and spank them as well." He eyed the two men. "No, not my type. Patty?"

"We'll fine, them their weapons, those fancy shoulder pad thingies, and coupons because they'll have stolen the coupons anyway." Emmy bent over the man cradling his arm. "Remember me? I'm going to rob you. Do you want to make some smartarse comment?" The injured man actually shook his head and Emmy laughed. "Hey, Harold, I wanted him to give me an excuse. Does that make me a bad person?"

"I'm really bad as well in that case." Curtis grinned down at the man.

"Nope, just a bad girl's main man. Come on, give me a hand." Minutes later a laughing group headed off to get the rest of the shopping.

Ten minutes later Casper frowned and looked at the empty aisle. A couple of shoppers were leaving the other end. "I'm getting twitchy."

"Me too. Either someone is going to ambush us and doesn't want witnesses, or word about our manners is spreading." Harold looked both ways. "I really hope the marts are still banning missile weapons. A couple of crossbows would really ruin my day. Did we get carried away?"

"A bit, but you know it felt wonderful and the little scroat deserved everything he got. Mine was just high spirits." Casper smiled. "Spam."

"Wash your mouth out with soap. Oh, no, that would taste like spam anyway."

"Not as a swear word, idiot, as a missile weapon. You said missile and there it is in front of me. After all this is the meat aisle, loosely speaking." Casper reached out and then tossed a can up and down in his hand. "Bet I could chuck this right across the mart."

"Not just you. Emmy? Gather the faithful because Casper has an idea." The faithful looked at the cans, listened to Casper, and stocked up.

"I really hope someone else will eat all this." Emmy curled her lip and looked at a can before putting it in her pocket where it was handy. Any novelty associated with spam had worn off. "I'm lousy at darts, or those things at the fair, the coconut shy."

"Don't worry, we'll need volume of fire. Someone will dodge Casper's and you'll brain him."

"Spam for brains. Is that worse than crap for brains?" Patty looked at her can critically. "This could do with work. Liz could add a couple of big spikes and a dozen small ones, artistically arranged." The group carried on shopping in high spirits, chortling about the scroat-smacking and cracking more daft jokes. There were shoppers in other aisles here and there, but no ambush, and eventually Harold's group gathered by the checkout aisles.

"They're waiting outside then, but still can't use missile weapons." Casper frowned. "Or are they allowed crossbows outside now?"

"Not in the yard or those delicate guards might get scratched." Harold put the cans of spam in his pack. "We have to split up because only one shopper goes through at once. Has anyone been through the exit for non-shoppers? People not paying for anything?"

"No. We'll not be able to take the spam, but weapons should be all right." Patty seemed dubious.

"We'd better ask someone before most of us go through there in a group and get arrested. Who looks the most innocent and helpless? No Emmy, no, Patty. Actually, Patty, if you can keep that look then gormless might do it?"

Patty moved on to indignant and then laughed. A quick assessment and they had a candidate. "Me?" Matti giggled. "Innocent? I'm flattered." She looked around. "Wait one minute, here." Jeremy accepted her iron bar. Matti wandered far enough to not be in the group and waited.

"Excuse me but I've been separated from my group. Will I be safe going out through there?" Matti pointed at the big exit sign with the list of warnings. "Will people take knives and things in there?" Matti certainly managed to look naïve, or possibly stupid.

The youth looked suspicious, then smiled. "Yes, it's dangerous. I'll take you through if you like because look, I can protect you." He showed Matti a big sheath knife. "I'll take you to meet my group and we'll look after you."

"No ta, I've just seen my lot." Matti headed back to the rest sharpish. "He's going through with a big knife, so iron bars and machetes should be good." She looked at the packs. "Cripes, who's expected to lug that lot through the checkout?"

*　　　*　　　*

By the time Harold dragged the last pack into the second, smaller room after paying, and opened the outside door, loud cheering told him the result. Casper looked in and grinned. "I told you they'd be fine. They had to do this without you Harold." He looked at the heap of packs. "D'you want a hand?"

"Cripes no. If someone comes in from out there it might lock and send us off to a bloody work camp. Just drag them out as I put them near the door." Outside Harold could hear laughter and jeering and some cries of pain. By the time he brought the last bag out, a bedraggled group were limping or being supported out through the gates. "What happened?"

"We came out and seven of them were waiting though they didn't look so keen when we turned up in a group. Our lot didn't give them the chance to decide if they wanted a fight." Casper laughed. "Alfie yelled 'get the bastards' and the rest followed him, and three of those silly sods tried to run. By the time I caught up this lot had trampled the ones who stayed and run the rest down. The one you hit must have felt poorly because he'd stayed back there by the gate, and he got away."

"Hey, how many machetes do you want, Harold?" Emmy grinned and waved one in each hand. "It's a pity we can't take them home. We can't, can we?"

"Sorry Emmy." Harold smirked. "We could sell them to the mart guards." He looked at the shoulder pads. "You captured some of that lot?"

"Oh yes. We fined them all their coupons and weapons, then spanked three for potty-mouth." Matti beamed. "We told the guards on the roof what we were doing, and the one over there volunteered to come down for a spanking." The laughing guard waved back at her.

"With an iron bar?"

"No, we used the flats of the machetes." Patty sighed dramatically. "This is when I miss the internet. YouTube would have loved, it a zillion hits worth."

"We can't carry those full packs as well as ours." Harold didn't feel really comfortable with daylight robbery, but the robbery had already been accomplished. He settled for minimising the profit so as not to encourage his people down that road in the future.

"We can take the good stuff and just scatter the rest of the groceries about for the other lucky shoppers? Who were that lot anyway? They weren't any better at fighting than we are." Emmy looked thoughtful. "They weren't Hot Rods or GOFS and the Geeks reckon they go the other way to a mart."

"Those were Ferdinands and they're supposed to wear American football gear. The shoulder pads are right, but they didn't have any helmets." Harold frowned. "Caddi is fighting with them and told me the fighters wear helmets."

"Maybe the helmets are all used up, because one of them wore this and it's knackered now." Jeremy offered what looked like an American football helmet, but the two depressions and a deep thin dent across the crown had probably ruined any protective capabilities. "I hit it with an iron bar and he went wobbly-legged so Matti kicked him."

"I hurt my foot. He was wearing something under his jeans." Matti smiled happily. "So I bashed his arm and he dropped the baseball bat." She batted her eyelashes. "Can I keep it, pretty-please?"

"No, or one of those up on the bypass will come over all rough soldier. Now let's see if these guards want souvenirs." After a quick conversation with the laughing guards the weapons and shoulder pads were all thrown along the floor towards the armoured car. The guards promised to collect them later, and threw down cigarettes in exchange. The cigarettes would be traded, since everyone in Orchard Close had quit because of the price.

Eventually a dozen happy shoppers gathered behind a ruined shed and ostensibly moved items from pack to pack to spread the load. While that happened the iron bars were screwed back into place. By the time Harold led his group up onto the bypass there were people picking over the groceries scattered in the yard and loading up. The soldiers all had little smiles, but were meticulous with the wands to make sure no machetes were being smuggled. The whole trip back the group were still laughing and joking, and eventually Harold decided his conscience could live with the robbery part.

*   *   *

"Open up or I'll huff and I'll puff." Harold had turned the handle and then nearly hit his face on the door when it didn't open. A bar scraped inside and Liz opened the door. "Cripes Liz, when did you start locking yourself in?"

"After that scroat got to Celine. I never heard a thing, Harold." Liz did look worried. "Between my music and bashing on iron he could have been stood right behind me." She pointed. "So now I stick that bar across."

"You'll hear someone breaking that." Harold reassessed the flat iron bar. "I'll hear it, fast asleep at home."

"Good. I'd fooled myself that the first time, after Gabriela, was because it was the first time. If it was really life and death, I thought I'd manage to do something. Then I just froze again." Liz sighed. "Now you've done it, I need a wimp-hug." Harold hesitated. "Don't be silly. That wench of yours knew hugging me meant sod all, now come on."

Harold hugged. "I'm sorry but my brain doesn't really function too well these days."

"Nor mine apparently, when facing scroats. Luckily yours works fine then, so we're a team." Liz sniggered. "The shoppers seemed happy enough with you. Now what did you come for?"

Harold perched on the bench and that brought a little smile. "The shoppers. They're a bit hyper still and might do something silly."

"No they won't, because Emmy reckons they all agreed afterwards. The Ferdinands weren't real gangsters, and were crapping themselves that you'd come up behind them. The local variety of scroat is a tougher proposition. It did perk everyone up nicely though." Liz picked up a spear head and inspected it. "I've had another go at tempering steel but I'm running out of charcoal again. Every time I have to leave it, I have to spend time, sweat and charcoal getting back up to speed before making any more progress. I'll get it in the end, but even then I could do with some real gear. A proper anvil and a decent forge, so I can make a machete."

"You do good work Liz. Those bolts go in pretty well."

"Those are just case hardened. That's just the outside which is all right to punch through, but not for a blade." Liz knocked the spear head against her hammer. "See? That should sing like this." She repeated it with a knife taken from a gangster, and even Harold could tell they sounded different.

Though one thing struck him. "Case harden means hard for punching through? How small can you case harden, what metals, and does the metal deform after punching through something?"

"Very small, iron usually, and probably if I didn't case harden it all. Why?"

"I'm not sure. That depends on what you can actually do, and if I can use it. What can I draw on?" Harold looked around.

"No paper in here because sparks and paper like each other too much. Here, slate and a bit of chalk?" Liz passed them across. "I usually get the idea without a diagram, but I'm always willing to learn especially when I'm sweaty."

"Sooty slut."

"Wimpy wuss."

Chapter 12:
Recruitment Drive

Daisy stuck her hands on her hips in a definitely familiar pose. "That's not a pumpkin!"

"It is, you saw them grow." Curtis sounded indignant but the rest of the adults were trying not to laugh. "You grew one."

"But pumpkins are this big. Hooooge" Daisy spread her arms wide, and looked again at the selection. "Which one is mine?"

"You grew this one." Curtis pointed.

"Can I trade?"

Curtis glared at Patty. "This is your fault, letting her listen while you sell knitting."

"It keeps the customers polite. Works for me as well when I get tempted to chew one out." Patty smirked. "Come on, let's see you trade with a five-year-old."

"Not a chance. I haven't got enough shirts to risk losing one. Which one Daisy? Just one, because the rest are entitled as well." Behind Daisy the other children under ten waited impatiently. "You only get first pick because you helped to grow them." From the way little eyes lit up in the queue, Harold thought Curtis would get a lot of help with pumpkins next year.

"That one please, because it isn't as wrinkly. Uncle-Harold and Uncle-Casper can make gnashy teeth in that smooth bit." Daisy picked up her prize and turned to Casper. "I'll need two candles this year please, because this is smaller than tin monster last year, and needs scarier eyes." Casper led her away, gently shaking his head and hanging onto two adolescent dogs on leads.

"Just remember, Harold. Save all the innards because we need them for pumpkin pie, pumpkin soup, pumpkin chips, pumpkin ice-cream, pumpkin..."

"Stop it Patty. Though I will expect the seeds back or there'll be no pumpkins next year and then you lot can face the wrath of this lot." Curtis waved at the other children picking out pumpkins. He frowned. "Maybe not all of the seeds; I think roast pumpkinseeds are good for you."

"I'm forever surprised by the number of things that seem to be good for me." Patty glared. "Setting into a salad is bad enough, but finding that the flowers grown with it are also good for me is a bit borderline."

"There's no need to get bitter, just because you can't find any more deer." Emmy ducked away from a half-hearted swipe. Harold managed a real smile because the rest were definitely cheering up since he'd come over all Soldier Boy, as Liz called it. Then he frowned, because that wasn't a big pumpkin and Daisy would want the full set of carved ears, eyes, nose and lots of teeth.

*　　　*　　　*

"Are you sure there's no way to turn the skin, rind, shell or whatever from a pumpkin into food?" Harold poked at his portion. "Are you sure pumpkin pie should be like this?"

"That's a pumpkin pie according to the only recipe we found, except for a bit of artistic license. Quite a lot really since there's only egg powder instead of eggs, no cream, no nutmeg and only white sugar." Sharyn cut a piece of hers. "Eat up or I'll set Curtis on you, because pumpkin pie is?" She raised her fork like a baton to conduct the next words. "Good for you."

"Maybe that's the answer?" Hazel pointed at Wills and Daisy, both of whom had buried their pie in chopped up greens.

"I hope the soup is an improvement." Harold brightened. "We could send our soup up to the soldiers?"

"No chance." Hazel giggled. "They might think it's an attack. I'm going for the extra greens option and don't you dare mention cooking the rinds to Curtis." She glared at Harold. "He might actually try it."

"That one outside is already cooked, or will be by the time those candles have burned out. You can check as you go out." Harold smiled innocently. "Once you've sorted out a trick or treat costume?"

Hazel blushed. "Stop it! I'm too young and anyway, if I did, it would be weird showing you." She concentrated on dealing with the mound of green now hiding her pie.

"He won't see what you wear next year, when you are old enough. Here Wills, let me help. Maybe there's too many greens on there? You'll grow soon enough." Sharyn glared at Harold and he mouthed a silent 'sorry' and shrugged. She concentrated on persuading Wills that he couldn't catch up with Daisy by eating more greens than she did. Despite never knowing his dad, Wills had been very subdued since Freddy died and had only now started to really engage with the world.

*   *   *

Sharyn stuck her hands on her hips. "If you're staying home, why do I have to go?"

"Because one of the family has to be there and I can't do it. Not this year. You already managed to go to dances." Harold tried hard to smile. "You'll be safe coming home because the dreaded Soldier Boy is lurking."

"I'm safe coming home because Nigel can't run away fast enough, just in case Seth catches Berry." Sharyn snickered. "Too late I reckon, Berry already caught Seth."

"So invite Nigel in for a nightcap."

"No! What's got into you?"

"I didn't mean that sort of nightcap. I meant to talk to your brother to cheer him up, as a sort of gift for Berry and Seth. They won't get up to much because they'll be expecting Nigel home, but they'll get up to it longer." Harold did manage a smile this time. "Don't tell Nigel the second part."

"Cripes no." Sharyn sighed. "What about Rob and Susan? They usually babysit and canoodle."

"They can go to a dance for once, then walk each other home. They can canoodle on the doorstep as long as they like." Harold shrugged. "Then go inside and canoodle some more." Harold wasn't going to the dance and had already told Rob to take Susan dancing, since Rob had healed well past being an invalid.

"Will you be all right?" Sharyn sighed. "On your own?"

"Fat chance. As soon as you leave there'll be a voice coming down the stairs pointing out tonight's story was too short, or Wills can't sleep, or Angel needs a cuddle. I'll have to cart Daisy back upstairs fast asleep before I get any peace." Harold hoped so anyway. Despite Sharyn's attempt to keep him occupied, the total lack of any angels or devils on Harold's doorstep at Halloween marked the first of many bad nights the winter would bring. Sharyn had turned the TV up after the sounds of laughter were heard at the bottom of the street.

Tonight, Guy Fawkes, would be the second milestone. Harold had already helped to herd Daisy at the bonfire, and bobbed for real apples from Orchard Close trees, and this time he'd also had to herd Wills. Now Wills-Womble and the Firework Fairy were both theoretically fast asleep. The latter consisted of a dress made of multi-coloured scraps and was the only firework since there were no real ones. Barry might have made some, but bangs and flashes near nervous soldiers had been decreed a really bad idea.

"All right, I'll go." Sharyn picked up a broom made from real twigs and her witch's hat, and waved the broom at Harold. "That joke of yours about the coven is fast becoming less than funny. I've been offered a black kitten."

"Oh no, don't curse me." Harold cowered away, then straightened. "If I ever find thirteen of you around a cauldron, then I'll worry. Now go on, you'll miss the judging." Harold sat back and sighed in relief when she left, then turned on the TV. The noise drowned out the music and laughter down the street where a big bonfire had been built on some of the cleared garden.

Unfortunately the Firework Fairy stayed fast asleep, so Harold only had the TV. TV that was rapidly becoming farcical in some ways, as more reasons were given for shortages.

"Without any people out in the countryside grey squirrels have increased in numbers to epidemic proportions. Whole plantations have been ravaged, and nearby crops raided. These trees were intended for charcoal, so there will be less for sale until the pests are eradicated and the plantations have recovered. All citizens are urged to conserve supplies."

Onscreen a small plantation of firs seethed with small grey shapes, eating bark and twigs. The cameras zoomed in on trees with little of either left, bare skeletons. As the camera pulled back again a line of men in orange suits moved forward and Harold stared in disbelief. They were using catapults, nets and clubs, while further back guards with shotguns threatened the men, not the pests. The cordon of men tightened and yes, many squirrels died but the plantation of young trees was wrecked.

"The amount of ammunition necessary to clear the squirrels with firearms cannot be replaced, so we are using criminals to deal with the problem. Criminals because tests show these pests are infected with rabies and even more timber will have to be sacrificed to burn the bodies."

"Mushrooms, we're just mushrooms" Harold murmured, gripping his mug tighter as the next item started, because there were no squirrels around Orchard Close. One had appeared, investigating a scarecrow. After an argument when Curtis wanted it shot to stop the squirrel raiding the gardens, and several people wanted to catch and adopt it, Sooty scared the squirrel away.

The next news item showed a series of explosions and fierce fighting in, according to the caption, Newcastle. The soundtrack claimed the violence demonstrated how criminals and rebels were incapable of living anywhere without trying to kill each other. A tower block burned, with people throwing themselves from the top as the flames closed in. Below, the gangs looting the lower floors made no attempt to help, rushing to strip what they could before the rest burned.

The local news showed the usual scenes of shoplifters taken away in lorries, though this time in large groups. There were two instances of criminals shooting at the Army from the ruins. In one, the soldiers shot the lone gunman, in the other a helicopter arrived to burn out the attackers. Then something new, the Army taking in battered, ragged, desperate women. Instead of a lorry a minibus came to get them, with nurses in crisp white uniforms.

"The authorities are taking action to relieve the plight of some unfortunate women inside the population centres. These young women have been badly abused by criminals and perverts, and any other victims should try to make their way to the nearest Army post. These unfortunates will be taken to prepared facilities where they can be properly rehabilitated and become productive citizens."

The picture of a smiling young woman sat on a park bench holding hands with a soldier made a stark contrast to the ruined city, and Harold could see the attraction. That nasty suspicious bit wondered why the government suddenly wanted a lot of badly used young women.

*   *   *

The five people in the bunker watching the wall-screen knew exactly why the women were needed. "Do they really believe that rubbish?" Joshua, the Army man, waved at the screen. "Squirrels?"

"They have to." Nate smirked. "There's nothing anywhere to dispute our version." He frowned. "Though catching, penning and starving that many squirrels turned out to be a real pain."

"Surely there's some alternative news by now?"

"It's Guy Fawkes so half of the animals are dancing round bonfires getting drunk or stoned and won't actually see that, but will get the news about charcoal. There are some local independent stations with a strong enough signal to cover at most a small part of any city but they don't have any real alternative information." Nate waved a casual hand, dismissing them as irrelevant. "Perhaps a few local details, but nothing national, and we do want to cut down on the amount of charcoal sold."

"Definitely cut the charcoal, because some of the metal-working is much better than predicted. There is some really good steel being produced here and there, and we don't want some bright spark to get ambitious." Grace frowned. "So far it's swords but with home-made explosives, steel could be used to manufacture real weapons in time."

"They are not producing steel, though some are taking the scrap and shaping and tempering pieces into truly impressive edged weapons. Charcoal won't allow anyone to build a battle tank or an anti-aircraft missile." The Army man, Joshua, smiled. "Thank God."

"No, but why waste resources on making charcoal that will be used to make more such weapons of any sort? Our soldiers have to go in there sometime, and get near enough to be hurt. I'm more interested in Newcastle." Owen pointed at the screen. "That looks like success."

Joshua scowled. "Sort of. The team did a perfect job in one way, but they brought fifty-three women and children out as well. Women and children with some very harrowing tales to tell."

"So get rid of them." Gerard frowned. "I thought these Special Forces were, I believe the quote was, 'not prone to getting weepy over the plight of the scenery' and yet they rescued the women and kids?"

"Yes. Worse, the officer in charge didn't try to stop them." Joshua sighed. "He probably ordered them to do it but that's all a bit hazy because the only casualty allegedly made all those decisions. For disciplined forces that ten minutes or so is noticeable for a lack of clear reporting, and ends with the refugees being herded towards safety." He scowled again. "Worse still, the strike team are really interested in what happens to the refugees, so I can't send the whole lot off to Vanna. Special Forces personnel have to be intelligent and capable of working independently and that means they are also resistant to bullshit."

"Let us have the details. We may have to revert to a mission that fails."

"Be quick, because they might be close-mouthed to other units but not among themselves. The last people we should upset are the Special Forces." Joshua pushed a sheet of paper to each of the others. "This is the problem, and isn't in the official report." He gave a wry smile. "Not now."

"They were in a brothel or breeding centre?" Gerard frowned. "Maybe we can put them straight into one of our own brothels?"

"Not more brothels. I thought those were only a possibility yet?" Nate glared round the table. "I never signed off on that sort of thing. Brothels in Britain as an established part of society? I can't agree with that."

"They were in an involuntary brothel, but a collection of prostitutes is just a voluntary establishment not a brothel, Nate. Some of these might consider joining a voluntary version but others won't and we now have a classic situation. Damsels and heroes." Joshua shrugged. "Bringing the refugees slowed up the extraction. The team spent nine days getting out of there without being spotted, because all hell broke loose. Some of them definitely struck up friendships."

Gerard sneered. "Not very professional."

"Very professional unless you have a different definition of friend." Joshua sneered right back. "We must be careful how this is handled, unless you want some very talented and inquisitive types wondering why their new friend stopped writing back?"

"Calm down you pair. We may be better off keeping the entire group in the barracks." Owen tapped the single sheet of paper. "These women will probably end up absorbed as Army wives or girlfriends at least since alternatives are few and far between. The real problem is that we have more major warlords springing up." Owen used the control to change the view to a map of the UK, with five cities highlighted.

"Five? I thought we cut the heads off all the crime organisations?" Gerard looked closer. "Liverpool? We need the docks working when ships start coming from the Falklands and Argentina, at least minimally, so we'll have to quash whatever problem that is."

"But quash them without collecting another couple of hundred refugees." Owen sighed and indicated the screen. "These people are nothing to do with the old gangs; these are enterprising newcomers. Who would have thought the cities were full of potential gang bosses just waiting their chance?" The chairman chuckled. "It turns out the situation is closer to what the BBC has been saying than expected. The ruins are indeed still full of vicious criminals and a few are competent."

"You've seen that." Joshua pointed at the report. "Any men I send in will see a similar situation because the teams must infiltrate and observe to set the operation up."

"What if you had a time and place where the problem person is conveniently vulnerable. Could you remove them?"

"An air strike? No doubt, but we can do that by hitting their house or strongpoint." Joshua frowned. "You said no to air strikes before."

"Something more subtle because we have information on the ground now, people in place. How many snipers are there at the moment in the British Army?" Owen folded his hands together and sat back. Smiles slowly grew on the other faces.

Joshua nodded. "That's better. If our intel is that good a sniper team can go in, kill our man, and leave. Whoever takes over may also be capable?"

"So then you send a sniper to kill him as well, and the gangs just think a rival has a man who is good with a rifle. Is the intel that good?" Gerard looked at the map and rubbed his hands together.

"Yes. It's taken time but our shadowy friend has completed his preparations and claims to have a source in every enclave. Tell me when you can have the snipers in place, and how many days' notice you need, and he will forward times and places." Owen picked up the single pieces of paper in front of everyone and took them to a shredder. "We will save the Special Forces for less sensitive work."

The five members discussed the detail, how many sniper teams should be distributed to ensure that a sudden problem could be shot. Nate confirmed that the intelligence would be accurate, but due to the methods of contacting the deep cover agents there might be delays in getting the information to the sniper teams. The meeting broke up with agreement that the method would be reviewed once these first targets had been neutralised.

*   *   *

Meanwhile in Orchard Close Harold knew he had lost his fight, but still objected. "I said I wouldn't be a priest again." He shook his head angrily.

"This is different. Abigail doesn't want a christening but she wants a naming. Just remember to call the little girl Violet and bid her welcome." Sharyn fussed around Harold, making sure his medal was dead right even if it wasn't on a uniform.

"Bid her welcome?"

"Literally, fare thee well in reverse. Say something like 'Welcome to Orchard Close, Violet' or whatever comes to mind. Cripes Harold, you knew a week ago." Sharyn poked him in the chest. "I thought you'd spoken to Liz or Casper?"

"About what? You said we were all welcoming the new baby because she had no dad and her mum was worried about the kid being accepted." Harold batted Sharyn's hands away. "I'm not going on parade."

"Yes you are. This is important as you well know. Abigail escaped from a very nasty little group before turning up here. She had no choice about getting pregnant because the animals used her little lad to keep her compliant. Now she thinks we'll hold it against Violet, her dad being a nameless gangster." Sharyn sighed. "Some might, but not after that nasty Solder Boy type welcomes her by name. At least none of the other refugees has turned out to be pregnant, and that's got to be a miracle. Now smile or I'll hit you with this." Sharyn waved Harold's stick and handed it over.

"All right. Cripes, is anyone else pregnant?"

"No, calm down. I just told you."

Harold sighed in relief. "No you didn't, you said no more refugees."

"We're all refugees, dope." Sharyn pushed. "Go." She turned and called upstairs. "OK Hazel, bring the kids down. He's respectable now."

As Harold walked down the street he felt a strange reverse déjà vu. Sharyn had her arm hooked in Harold's one side with Wills on her other side, while Daisy held his other hand with Hazel holding onto Daisy. Only one short year ago they'd walked up here full of hope, because they'd survived. Harold didn't have long to think as doors opened and more people came out, until a solid crowd walked down to the gates. The Coven had organised everything, and the gates were allegedly symbolic. Harold had started wondering about a real cauldron.

"Perfect. I think we got everyone." Harold looked back and Sharyn might be right. "Remember. Welcome to Orchard Close, Violet, since you didn't sort out something else."

Harold opened his mouth to ask where Violet had got to when a motor started up, along the neutral road to the traffic island. He smiled as the girl club minibus drove down to the junction with the access road, and turned up towards Orchard Close. The vehicle came in peace, because the renewed paintwork said so. "That explains why you wanted the scroats banned today." Harold had done as asked, and all the neighbours had been told to stay clear.

He smiled again as Casper got out of the minibus and opened the rear door. Abigail came out and looked towards the gates, at first nervously and then in shock. Casper said something, put out a hand and Rory, Abigail's son, took it then Casper picked him up. Harold watched the four coming up to the gates with a certain amount of trepidation, since Casper wore a huge grin. "We have a new applicant to join Orchard Close. Will you give her sanctuary, Soldier Boy?"

Harold wanted to swear or call Casper a rotten bastard, because he'd been set up. Worse, he was stuck with it. Sharyn's elbow hit his ribs so Harold did his bit. "Welcome to Orchard Close, Violet." Then he jumped because the idiots behind started cheering! Abigail's face broke into a smile; she took the last two steps to the gates, and held the baby out. Harold froze.

"Hang on Abigail, he's better with rifles." Sharyn bent Harold's unresisting arm up across his chest, and Violet was neatly deposited. "Turn round, idiot." Sharyn murmured quietly but Abigail heard and giggled, and Harold turned very slowly and carefully. The cheering redoubled, and an aisle opened in the crowd. "To the dance house. Don't worry, she's been fed so

Violet is happy right now."

Harold walked slowly and carefully up the road to the dance house, then Abigail reclaimed her daughter and he could relax. "Bl... Cripes Sharyn, I'm better with pipe bombs than babies, let alone a tiny little thing like that. What..."

"Not now Harold. Now we have a party. Not a long one because its cold, but long enough so Abigail knows her baby is welcome. Everyone else gets the message and lets off a bit of steam. Next time you'll have had practice." Sharyn swept off to see to something or other before Harold could ask about next times. Instead he smiled and said hello to a lot of people, didn't drink everything he was offered, and watched as a few of the younger men and women held an impromptu dance in the road. In the road because the warm house had been commandeered for the old folk according to Doll, and as a warmup for Christmas Eve.

As promised the party didn't last long and an hour later Harold had his chance. "What did you mean practice? Nobody is pregnant."

"No, but in future we'll have a proper way to welcome children, and any more refugees." Sharyn grinned. "You asked us to sort everything out, so we did. You just do your bashing the bad boys bit, as advertised." Harold didn't really have an answer.

Though later he found he'd now got an answer to something else. He could consider his temper, and occasionally beating or shooting a scroat, as a way of providing a sanctuary for as many as possible. Harold could get angry if he wanted to, now and again, without beating himself up over it.

*　　　*　　　*

It took a while, but oddly enough Harold's head finally accepted that. All the scroats and lunatics he'd shot or stabbed or beaten faded from Harold's dreams. Now all that disturbed his sleep were those he hadn't protected, the Gabrielas, Hollys and Sandys, and they were entitled. Harold still had troubled nights, but he slept better overall.

After thinking through his options, and remembering what Emmy said about the Ferdinands and their fighting, Harold came up with another way to protect everyone just a bit better. He called together a dozen people who seemed keen enough to hit someone but lacked the skills. "If you really want to stick a scroat, properly, you'll need a better technique with a machete.

"But the idea is to charge in and hack and bash, isn't it? That doesn't take much technique." Emmy looked at the piece of wood shaped roughly like a machete. "Though some of them have those shields now, stop signs or whatever."

"Yes they do." Harold ducked nothing, dodged nothing, blocked nothing and slashed at an imaginary kneecap. "Think how confused they'll be if you do that?"

"I'll cut my own leg off." Billy made a half-hearted attempt to copy. "I think you've got an extra joint in your arm."

Harold grinned. "No, but you'll need lots of sympathy for your aches and pains while you learn."

"Pains? I thought the idea is to dish it out?" Emmy scowled. "What brought this on?"

"You. Remember a comment about the Ferdinands being no better at fighting than you are, and the scroats round here being a tougher proposition? This will even up a bit." Harold mentally reran what bits of his training could be applied to a machete. "If you thrust towards a face, they'll flinch or duck, then you slice the blade over the bastard's hand. When he swings down to chop you, move and deflect and choose your target. His machete will still heading downwards when you hack the back of his knee and cripple the scroat."

A few little smiles appeared, then more, and they grew. Though by the end of the first practice nobody smiled. "Cripes Harold, if someone starts now I can't lift the machete, let alone defend myself." Bernie rubbed at his elbow.

"Get Sal to rub you better, then practice the moves again and again." Harold smirked. "I'll bet Patty and Emmy don't feel as bad because they exercise with the girl club."

"Hey, does that mean I can join the girl club?" Billy raised his hands in defence as Emmy and Patty glared. "Just for the exercises."

"You could get Gayle to help you to exercise, or is it Suzie you have wicked designs on? Bernie laughed. "Every time anyone wants to find you, you're round there."

"Well Barry and Finn aren't exactly my sort of company on an evening. I can't even go round with them to keep Alicia company because of Celine." Billy looked at his practice machete. "Hey, if I learn this I'll be more reassuring."

"More dangerous." Jeremy pointed to his leg which Billy had clouted by mistake. "I'm going to see if Matti will kiss this better."

"Just remember, all of you, do the exercises. Then when you've got the muscles working we'll move onto the skills. Don't let the scroats realise though. On the plus side, the worst of the aches might be over in a couple of weeks so you'll all be demon dancers come New Year." Harold watched them going up the street, laughing and mock-fighting, with a small satisfied smile. If they built up the muscles and flexibility he could definitely make some of them more dangerous. Now he would talk to Casper and Alfie because they already had the muscle.

Teaching the potential fighters in small groups proved to be the perfect way for Harold to fill in any spare time, and kept his mind off Christmas and dances. On Christmas Day Harold managed to be civil, but spent much of the time polishing lead balls for buckshot he hadn't the propellant to make up, and similar pointless tasks. Indoor tasks since the rain persisted, dampening everyone's clothes as well as spirits. Harold even persuaded the keenest potential macheteers to practice between Christmas and New Year, another night spent by the TV muttering 'mushrooms' to himself. Especially on the nights when the TV showed the rising floods in some cities, and the state of the victims.

*   *   *

As usual, the trip to The Mansion early in January gave Harold something else to think about. "What would you charge to shoot a man?" Caddy smiled and held up a hand. "Don't worry, he's a truly nasty fucker, sorry, bad person, so your delicate conscience won't get bruised."

"Be careful Caddi. If I'm supposed to be shooting anyone who is a truly nasty person, the target list will be extensive." Harold wasn't in the mood for another windup from Caddi. The rain kept coming, interspersed with fog or dank, cold days, without any sign of the snow last year.

"Yeah, yeah, but we've got a treaty. It's just that a rumour came my way, from across the city. Some very ambitious gang boss died from a lead migraine. A single shot from anything between half a mile and three miles away according to the version being told. I've got a more realistic idea of the possibilities than some, but that low figure made me wonder." Caddi grinned. "Tell you what, send your shoppers over instead because he's a Ferdinand and they spanked one lot already." He sniggered. "You should have let me know about the weapons and I'd have bought them. So what will a bullet cost me?"

Harold grinned. "You, Caddi, can have a freebie, personally delivered any time you ask. I will not solve your gang war problems for you."

"Pity, but I didn't expect a yes. Worth a try though." Caddi rang his little bell. "Tea, coffee, beer, redhead? Oh no, redhead is off the menu. It spoiled." The dark-haired young woman who arrived wore the short black dress and fishnets but no apron.

Harold ordered coffee and she left. Caddy gestured to Mack. "Get the weapons Mack. Harold's only got that stick of his and he's the honourable type." Mack left and Caddi smiled. "See, I trust you."

Harold smiled back. "No you don't. There's a bloke with a shotgun or rifle pointed at me right now, peeking through a spyhole."

Caddi turned to look at a bookshelf. "You can see?" Then he turned back, wagging a finger. "Naughty, but smart as usual. I haven't tried it with anyone else but I will, if it's someone I want an excuse to kill." He chuckled. "The types who'll have a go if I tweak them a bit without Mack in here and I'll make sure there's witnesses so it isn't my fault." Caddi paused and then chuckled. "Samuel will be disappointed. Your bullet hit his knuckle and fucked up half his hand, so he'd really, really like to shoot you."

"Still a lot better than his eye. He should blame Bugatti and maybe shoot him."

The woman brought coffee and Caddi grinned. "Are you open for business again over there, Soldier Boy?"

"Yup, I told your lot we were only closed from two days before Christmas until the third of January."

"So you lot can have peace and quiet for your parties. We're really curious about them since you never send out invites. Your lot aren't very inviting at all." Caddi put out a hand and stopped the woman from leaving and she froze. "If our lads stop overnight, they're lonely. Maybe they could bring someone like this to keep them company?"

"Maybe one of our lot would make her an offer she wouldn't refuse, and she wouldn't come back." Harold managed to keep a little smile. If one of the Hot Rods brought an unwilling woman to the overnight house, all hell would break loose.

Caddi's eyes sharpened. "You aren't allowed to accept runners."

"If she's escorted through our gates by one of your lot, she isn't running. After all, if any of our women want to join you they can." Harold shrugged. "Come and ask them."

Caddi released the woman. "Maybe I will." As the woman left Mack came in with the weapons for repair and Caddi started haggling as if nothing else had been discussed. Harold heaved a silent sigh of relief because the gang boss did this every time, found something to try and get under Harold's skin. Though Caddi avoided the one subject that would have worked well enough for Harold to check out the view from that concrete tower block half a mile away. Harold looked over the cleared ground to the tower and smiled as he left the Mansion, because the building would be near enough if the day came to deal with Caddi.

The shot as he came up to the island near Orchard Close nearly stopped Harold's heart and he floored the accelerator. He raced down the road but as he came clear of the surviving housing there didn't seem to be an emergency, and a group crossing the empty gardens didn't seem to be in a hurry. Harold jumped out and called up to the guardhouse. "What was the shot?"

"Hi Harold. You'll wear out tyres like that. Emmy just shot a mangy dog and they're going to burn it." Jeremy sounded puzzled. "Are you all right?" He suddenly looked alarmed. "Are that lot chasing you?"

Harold felt the tension drain away. There'd been three mangy dogs now and the preferred solution, shooting as far away as possible, kept any infection out of the resident dogs so far. "No, they're my escort." Harold turned to the three cars spilling out alarmed Hot Rods. "Calm down you lot. No panic." He calmed them down without admitting the reason he'd raced off and left them. Sooner or later, Harold knew, he had to stop assuming every shot meant someone he knew had been killed.

The Hot Rods left after the guns went inside the gate and Harold stowed them in his gun room. When he finally turned the corner to home Harold frowned because the deputation outside his house were the Coven, or half of them. "I surrender."

"Wimp. We've got a solution that needs your glower." Liz sniggered. "Some people are still impressed."

"As I recollect, you needed a glower over shooting the sick dogs."

"I wanted to catch a really nasty stray for in the forge." Liz frowned. "Though after seeing the first sick one I'm convinced. Yeuk." She scowled and thumped him on the chest. "Hey, stop that, we're bullying you not the other way round. Orchard Close needs a canteen."

"I vote for a pub."

"Not a chance little brother. Do you know how many people cook their own meals? Or more to the point how many attempt to without convenience and part-prepared ingredients?" Sharyn rolled her eyes. "We're having to teach the teenagers in the school to make basic pastry, for cripes sake."

"Pass. I can make chips and burn toast?" Harold stopped smiling because nobody smiled back. "We have a problem?"

"Yes. Some people are perfectly happy looking at a bag of flour, a dead rabbit and a raw spud and saying ooh, yummy, rabbit pie. Some are learning but even more aren't." Faith waved a hand towards the rest of the city. "Blame the supermarkets, or schools, or sheer laziness. Worse, there's no takeaway, no TV chef and no celebrity chef book that doesn't need a fully stocked collection of spices and herbs and meat already neatly sliced or diced."

"But everyone has been eating. They must have." Harold racked his brains but no, everyone looked fed. Leaner, but fed.

"But now the last of the scavenged freezer food is more or less gone. Half our people at least are nipping round to share someone else's and handing over their coupons, the ones for food, and the people they visit sometimes aren't all that good at cooking. Now we want to make an official arrangement to fix that." Liz pointed over to the girl club. "We already do it in there."

"What, exactly? I do mean about cooking." Harold got the second bit in as Patty's, Liz's and June's eyes lit up.

"They pool all the food and cook one lot, then either eat in the dining room or collect their share and take it off to eat in private. Now everyone is eating home-grown and trapped we should extend that. The house next to the dance house would be a great canteen." A big smile spread over Pippa's face. "Finn and Trev have been working on fixing and repairing the kitchen because it's a real, de-luxe, to-die-for setup. They've replaced what couldn't be rescued and it'll feed everyone in shifts."

"I used to work in a restaurant, in the kitchens so I can help. I'll be better at that than gardening." Elizabeth shrugged. "I won't poison you, honest. I'm over all that." Elizabeth had gone from blaming the Hot Rods for Will dying to Harold for a little while, but was now firmly back to hating Hot Rods. Except occasionally, when she blamed herself.

"If that's all sorted, why do you want me?" Harold frowned, puzzled.

"To look like that, only more grim and determined than puzzled, when some people object. They can take their food ration home and cook it if they want, and buy extra bits with coupons, but the daily food ration for us all will come from one place." Faith scowled. "It'll stop the rumours."

"What rumours? Harold looked back at the small huddle of houses that comprised Orchard Close. "We're big enough for rumours?"

"There's nearly a hundred residents now which is plenty for rumours. Some, the worrying suggestions, are because recent arrivals expect nothing else. Rumours keep cropping up about the fighters and Soldier Boy eating better than others." Liz shrugged. "Bad experiences rather than nastiness but that sort of things needs stopping, and this will do it and also be more efficient."

"Especially since those TV pictures of flooded fields weren't the usual mushroom food. Those fields were really flooded and that means there'll be more food shortages." Patty grimaced. "Pooling the food means conserving food, though actually running the damn thing will be a bloody shambles."

"Not really. At least this way everyone will eat enough spam to give them the fat intake to compensate for rabbit." That had been a shock, finding an article stating that rabbit meat didn't supply enough fat if that was the only meat. "We just have to work out the calories and portions, and shifts to prepare and eat. I sort of know the theory, and we've got books." Elizabeth smiled. "We'll be putting tater peeling on the chores list."

"Right, Soldier Boy stuff, very urgent."

"The forge beckons."

"I hear the click of knitting needles."

"There's some books need cataloguing."

"I've got dough proving."

"Cripes, what did I say?" Elizabeth looked at all the retreating backs. "We're in this for the long run now, we've got to plan these things."

This ends Book Two of

The Fall of the Cities.

Find out what happens next!
Book 3 will be available soon!

CHARACTERS IN
PUTTING DOWN ROOTS

Harold (Harry) Miller – 21 – Corporal pay clerk with CGC Conspicuous Gallantry Cross. Civilian marksman even at sixteen but not comfortable with shooting live targets so won't take sniper training, or qualify as a marksman.

The flats: (27 remaining)

Alicia - 22 - Small dumpy woman who retreats into herself.
Billy - 17 - Newly arrived resident.
Casper - 21 - Big well-muscled gay man who becomes Harry's friend.
Celine - 26 - Slight skinny redheaded typist. Rape victim.
Daisy - 5 - Harold's niece.
Emmy - 21 - Jamaican - tall, well-built woman who lost a boyfriend.
Faith - 36 - Short stout woman - light brown hair. Probably a widow - son Toby killed.
Finn - 49 – Electrician.
Hazel - 15 year old orphan - parents were killed by looters.
Holly - 18 - Tall, slim after fanatical exercise. Blonde with pale blue-grey eyes.
Isiah - 35 - Reclusive - ex-telephone engineer - redundant.
Kerry - 33 - Shy -Isiah's wife and sold embroidered patches on the internet.
Liam - 28 - Reclusive ex-office worker from the flats.
Liz - 22 - Tall strong wiry woman who works in iron and bronze. Incapable of violence.
Louise - 30 - Quiet - small time graphic designer on internet.
Patricia Elliot - 27 - Trainee nurse. First refugee from looters.
Rob - 37 - Divorced - Plumber.
Sharyn - 26 - Harold's sister - Army widow.
Stewart - Mr. Baumber - 57 - ex-caretaker for flats.
Susan - 32 - Divorcee.
Veronica - 14 - Quiet - daughter of Isiah and Kerry.
Wills - 3 - Harold's nephew.

Original Orchard Close residents: (12 remaining)
Alfie - 16 - Probable orphan living with Betty. Absolutely hero-worships Harold.
Bernie - 27 - Slim and now fit. Wants to work out with girl club.
Betty - 60 - Older woman on the 'committee'.
Curtis - 25 - Short and stout, amateur gardener.
Hilda - 42 - Ex-clerical worker. Loves collating lists.
Matthew - 25 - Red haired ex Traffic Warden.
Sal - 27 - Blonde woman who tones up in the girl club.
Seth - 23 - Likes chips, beer.

Brewers: (2)
Nigel - 41 - Brewer, widower.
Berry - 17 - Daughter of Nigel. Taller, stronger, and also a brewer.

New Refugees pre-Armageddon: (23 remaining)
Bess - 20 - Ex-girlfriend of gangster.
Conn - 23 - Short slim man, prematurely bald.
Gayle - 19 - Dental trainee.
Georgina - 8 - Zach and Olive's daughter.
Janine - 35 - Laundry assistant.
Joey - 7 - Pippa and Robert's son.
Jon - 18 - Single youth.
Lillian - 20 - Tall overweight woman who moves in with Conn.
Olive - 30 - Part-time cleaner - Zach's wife, Georgina's Mum.
Pippa - 26 - Genius baker.
Robert - 27 - Pippa's husband.
Sandy - 57 - Carpenter but retired with bad arthritis.
Sukie - 5 - Suzie's daughter.
Suzie - 22 - Sukie's single Mum - Suzie's sister died in fighting.
Tim - 23 - Refugee with fiancée, Toyah.
Toyah - 20 - Refugee with Tim.
Zach - 33 - Ex-office manager.

After Armageddon: (39)
Abigail - 23 - Pregnant - young son Rory.
Barry - 62 - Ex-firefighter - refugee from Geeks.
Doll - Dolly - 20 - Barry's eldest granddaughter.

Elise - 13 - Turns up half crazed and starving.
Elizabeth - 36 - Mum to Willtoo and Pricilla - running from north.
Jeremy - 19 - Running from north.
Jilli - 13 - Jilli taken in trade, for food instead of guns.
John's Pat - 37 - Philip's mum - running from north.
June - 38 - Looks early twenties - trophy wife - runs from Hot Rods.
Lemmy - 17 - Loner running from a gang deep in the city.
Lenny - 26 - Nearly qualified paramedic.
Luke - 34 - Refugee from deep in city.
Matti - Matracia - 18 - Barry's granddaughter - almost raped.
Mohammad - 21 - Running from city.
Pat's John - 31 - Running from north.
Patty - 25 - Demon knitter who wants to have a crossbow.
Philip - 18 - Running from north.
Pricilla - 13 - Elizabeth's daughter - running from north.
Rory - 2 - Abigail's son.
Umeko - 17 - Asian girl rescued from Geeks brothel.
Violet - Abigail's baby girl.
Willtoo - 17 - Running from north.
TOTAL - 101- Less 7 dead

Hot Rods - Gang to the south:
Cadillac - Gang boss.
Big Mac - 7 foot bodyguard - named after trucks.
Bugatti - Full gang member.
Charger - Full gang member.
Chevy - Full gang member.
Cooper - Short for Mini Cooper - second in command.
E-Type -Kev - youth trying to get a gang (car) name.
Samuel - Man with shotgun loses a finger.

GOFS - Gods of Fire and Steel - Gang to the west:
Gofannon - Gang boss.
Ogou - Kabir - Gang member.
Vulcan - Full gang member.
Wayland - Gang blacksmith.
Geek Freeks - Gang to the north.
Hawkins - Gang boss - senior manager.

Darwin - Manager (senior gang member).
Einstein - Manager.
Galileo - Manager.
Marconi - Manager.
Tell - aka William Tell - Gang bowyer and archer.

Barbie Girls - Based in Shopping Centre beyond GOFS.
Chandra - a senior Barbie (blonde wig).

The Bunker
Gerard - Youngest of the dozen cabal leaders - transport incl. distribution of food.
Grace - Tall spare grey-haired woman dealing with work camps.
Henry - Portly man with thick black hair and beard in charge of farms.
Ivy - Stout middle-aged redhead in charge of food storage and supplying marts.
Joshua - Army commander.
Maurice - Bland, unassuming, mousy-haired and medium size and build. Spymaster.
Nate - Large black man in charge of propaganda.
Owen - Chairman.
Vanna - Tall Asian woman dealing with special facilities and private military contractors.

VANCE HUXLEY

Vance Huxley lives out in the countryside in Lincolnshire, England. He has spent a busy life working in many different fields – including the building and rail industries, as a workshop manager, trouble-shooter for an engineering firm, accountancy, cafe proprietor, and graphic artist. He also spent time in other jobs, and is proud of never being dismissed, and only once made redundant.

Eventually he found his Noeline, but unfortunately she died much too young. To help with the aftermath, Vance tried writing though without any real structure. As an editor and beta readers explained the difference between words and books, he tried again.

Now he tries to type as often as possible in spite of the assistance of his cats, since his legs no longer work well enough to allow anything more strenuous. An avid reader of sci-fi, fantasy and adventure novels, his writing tends towards those genres.